PRAISE FOR BILL YENNE

Bill Yenne writes "with cinematic vividness."

ROGER MCGRATH, *THE WALL STREET JOURNAL*

I can guarantee that you will be engaged by [Bill Yenne's] master storytelling from his opening words to the very last page.

COLONEL WALTER BOYNE, SMITHSONIAN NATIONAL AIR & SPACE MUSEUM

Bill Yenne is a perfect example what happens when a child reads too many books and doesn't watch enough television. He ended up with an imagination.

JOHN SMITHERS OF MONTANA'S *MISSOULIAN*

THE NEXT TO LAST MOONRAKER INTO BROUILLECOURT PARISH

THE NEXT TO LAST MOONRAKER INTO BROUILLECOURT PARISH

JIM HAMMER
BOOK 2

BILL YENNE

ROUGH
EDGES
PRESS

Rough Edges Press
An Imprint of Wolfpack Publishing
1707 E. Diana Street
Tampa, FL 33610

roughedgespress.com

Paperback ISBN 978-1-68549-638-8
Ebook ISBN 978-1-68549-637-1

THE NEXT TO LAST MOONRAKER INTO BROUILLECOURT PARISH

INTRODUCTION

So many people, from cruel Taliban warlords to duplicitous Pentagon bureaucrats, have learned the hard way that it is a fool's errand to find yourself on the bad side of Jim Hammer when he sets his mind to righting a wrong.

After twenty years in the US Army, he left the service, imagining he would be taking time off from all those wars.

He was mistaken. There was more work to do.

This is one of his war stories.

PROLOGUE

AFGHANISTAN, AROUND A DECADE OR SO AGO

THE COLD, dry snowflakes drifting lazily and randomly through the October air might have reminded US Army Captain Jim Hammer of his home back in Logan County, Montana. The Leupold rifle scope through which he was squinting might have reminded him of hunting season in Montana, but his head was not there. He was here in the mountains of Kandahar Province, and his mind was on the blood-stained hands of a Taliban warlord known as Akhtar Mohammad Dadullah.

Hammer had put in two twelve-month tours in Afghanistan—officially. After the United States pulled out—officially—things changed. The abrupt withdrawal left a lot of unfinished business. The American troops all flew out, and so did hundreds of Afghan civilians who feared their new Taliban masters. Not so lucky were hundreds more Afghans, including a lot of interpreters and Afghan army personnel who had aided American forces for two decades, but who were left behind as the Americans raced for the exits.

The State Department handed out a lot of so-called Special Immigrant Visas to civilians they had employed and put together Priority 2 refugee status for others. Unfortunately, "P2" came with a Catch-22. You had to get yourself and your family *out* of Afghanistan before you could even apply.

Hammer and his team had hoped never to see Afghanistan again. They were running an op down in Cartagena when they learned that the US Army was organizing an unofficial operation to send Special Forces veterans back into Afghanistan to extract the people who'd been left behind.

The poster child for the team's unanimous decision to volunteer to go back had been a young man named Rahim Faizullah. They first met him as a Kabul University language department grad student eager to sign on as their interpreter. Over time, he had become a de facto member of the team, working tirelessly at any task assigned to him. When they learned he was among those who were on the Taliban hit list, they were on the first covert flight back to Tajikistan.

Having infiltrated across the porous border from this former Soviet republic, they reached Kabul and found Rahim fairly quickly. He had been living with a cousin in a suburban basement, stuck in a room watching social media videos of people being beheaded by the Taliban, people just like him, and hoping he would not be caught.

Then he dropped a bombshell. Rahim Faizullah *did not* want to be extracted.

As he told his American friends, he wasn't ready to leave. There was work left to be done.

After commenting on the alarm which shown in the American expressions, he reminded them of Akhtar

Mohammad Dadullah. They all knew the name of this wily warlord of the mountains of Kandahar who had eluded them on several operations over the years. They knew his reputation, his pathological obsession with unspeakable torture, and his role in Afghanistan's opium trade.

They needed no reminder of the drug trade. Everyone knew that nine out of ten grams of the greasy black stuff that circulated in the entire world came from the poppy fields of Afghanistan, and that most of it bore the oily fingerprints of the Taliban. The Taliban were the most fundamental of Muslim fundamentalists, and as an intoxicant, opium was *haram*, or forbidden, by the *Quran*. However, for Dadullah, and for more Taliban chieftains than not, when it came to opium, money talked and the *Quran* walked.

As someone started to reply, Faizullah interrupted to say he knew what was about to be said. He knew that these Americans had not come to Afghanistan to be the world's drug police.

What Faizullah proceeded to tell them next changed that equation.

He laid out a surprising tale of intrigue that was believable only from the cynical point of view that greed trumps all other principles of behavior. In a land where tribal alliances are paramount elements of social order, Dadullah's cartel had made strange bedfellows of two of the most influential tribes that were in Afghanistan at that time, these being the international aid community, and America's Pentagon bureaucracy.

Faizullah had stumbled on this impossible scheme and claimed to have verified it.

His unfinished business and that which made him refuse to leave a land in which he was a wanted man, was to take down the cartel and its improbable allies.

Hammer proceeded to sit Faizullah down with Tim Tommis, the communications genius on the team, a man who could hack and conjure data and intel out of the ether in ways that seemed like black magic to even the most brilliant nerds.

A day and a half and an all-nighter later, when Hammer approached the antique carved table at which the two men had sequestered themselves, Tommis looked up and said simply, "We followed the money."

Tommis said he had verified a convoluted and intricate scheme that had been going on for years, and continued, under complicit Taliban protection, even after the American pullout. The unholy alliance brought the Dadullah Cartel together with senior members of both the Geneva-based Vision for Humanitarian Empowerment and the DOD's own Security Infrastructure Finance Organization.

Few things make a soldier angrier than to know that his own side is consorting with the enemy—and making a lot of money doing it.

———

The snowflakes drifting through the air on that high plateau in Kandahar did not remind Johnny Arnaud his own hunting trips down in Brouillecourt Parish, Louisiana. The bayou country was not so steep, not so dry, and Arnaud had never seen a snowflake down there. The hunting itself was similar, though. Long waits in a duck blind were a lot like today's long wait at his perch on the slope above the sawdust-colored hovel where Akhtar Mohammad Dadullah was supposedly waiting for his Western cronies to arrive for a powwow.

Down there, Arnaud counted just shy of a dozen Taliban fighters milling around the building, which was about the size of a two-car detached garage. Occasionally one or two of them came or went through the single doorway.

The rest of the team was scattered around on strategic positions overlooking the target. Arnaud could see Tyler Roullier about fifty yards east of his position. They called Johnny and Tyler the "two Cajuns" for obvious reasons, and everybody always remarked about the long odds of there being two of their persuasion on the same eight-man team.

Rahim Faizullah, who was about twenty feet from Arnaud's position, studying the target with binoculars, had deduced that today would be a big day in the nefarious affairs of the Dadullah Cartel. The associates who were expected arrive for the meeting included bigwigs from both VHE and SIFO.

This tour in Afghanistan was very unlike either of the team's earlier deployments. This time, there was no elaborate logistic and support infrastructure to back them up. There were no MQ-9 Reaper drones to call for air support, no MH-60 Blackhawks to call for a ride back to a forward operating base. There were no bases to go back to. The Taliban owned the whole country now. The biggest change was conceptual. The Americans were no longer fighting an insurgency; they *were* the insurgency.

Despite what he knew about the VHE and SIFO malefactors who would be coming into his crosshairs today, Arnaud still felt strange about targeting Westerners and fellow Americans. But this was war, and these clowns had sided with the enemy. That made *them* the enemy. Of their own free will, and for personal enrichment, they had aligned themselves with terrorists to bring misery to millions. It doesn't get more "enemy" than that.

For about a month now, the team had been picking at the Dadullah Cartel, with repeated smaller raids, and now they were here. Captain Jim Hammer was up on higher ground with his Barrett M107 "light fifty," his .50 caliber semi-automatic sniper rifle. His would be the first shot fired, and it would be aimed at Dadullah, when he showed himself.

This would be the cue for the rest of the team to leave no bad guys standing. They were not here to take prisoners.

Hammer had always said that "taking out foot soldiers never leads to the root of any problem. That's a tactical solution to a strategic problem. You've got to work your way to the top."

Today, if all went well, they would slice off that top.

———

It was shortly after noon, and the snow had stopped falling, when they glimpsed vehicles approaching from the valley below. It was a convoy of three pickups and three Humvees. According to the DOD Inspector General for Afghan Reconstruction, the Taliban had inherited exactly 22,174 American Humvees after the pullout. Three of that number were right here and purring like always.

At last, the vehicles pulled up near the meeting site and men started climbing out. There was a casual air to their manner. The apprehension that they might at any moment be targeted by a drone-fired AGM-114 Hellfire air-to-ground precision-guided missile had long since evaporated.

Among them were a half dozen Westerners, two of whom carried a pair of obviously heavy Halliburton metal suitcases. They all disappeared into the building, while most of the Afghans remained outside, talking and smoking. Finally, two of the Westerners emerged.

Through their binoculars, the team members watched them blink as their eyes became accustomed to the brightness of the snow-covered landscape. They both appeared to be in their forties, with recent, executive-style haircuts. One of them had a narrow goatee and wore distinctive, round tortoise-shell-framed glasses. The other man, who was overweight and balding, slipped on a pair of aviator sunglasses and led the way as they walked to one of the pickups. They conferred briefly with two older Taliban, then climbed into the vehicle and drove away.

Johnny Arnaud looked up toward Jim Hammer's perch. He could see the frustration on his face. He would have clearly liked to open fire on these retreating criminals, but the first .50-caliber round had been promised to Akhtar Mohammad Dadullah.

They did not have long to wait.

About five minutes later, the meeting broke up and all of the participants spilled out into the bright but overcast day. Dadullah was front and center, surrounded by his Afghan sycophants and Western facilitators.

Jim Hammer took a deep breath and closed his finger around the trigger of his rifle.

"Good night, Dadullah," he whispered. "See you in hell."

CHAPTER
ONE

BROUILLECOURT PARISH, LOUISIANA; PRESENT DAY

"WHEN ARE y'all gonna ask her out?" Tyler Roullier asked, teasing his business partner.

"It isn't like that," Johnny Arnaud replied. "All I said was that I liked the way she smiles and you go making this into something a lot bigger than it is."

"That's not exactly the way I heard you telling about it, and here you go with wantin' to go in there to Fredieuville to see her for a *third time* in just the past two weeks."

"Let me remind you that it was you...not me, but *you*...who had been sayin' that we need to get an accountant. Then you put it on me to get us one, and now you're complainin' about it."

"Who goes to see their accountant *three times* in just two weeks?" Roullier said, laughing.

Arnaud just shook his head and climbed into his Ford F-150.

Business is good, that's why we needed an accountant,

Arnaud thought to himself as he drove. *That, and the fact that neither of us is any good at bookkeeping.*

When they left Afghanistan for the last time, most of the team left the service. The two Cajuns went back to Louisiana, Arnaud to Brouillecourt Parish and Roullier back to New Orleans. Arnaud invited his friend to come down and go fishing, and within a year, Roullier had given up on city life and had moved to the bayous. A year later, the two men had started a machine shop on Bayou Langlois, specializing in small marine engines, for which there was a huge demand among the thousands of small boats that ply the waterways of the Mississippi River Delta.

As with a lot of small businessmen, they loved the hands-on work but were buried by paperwork. This led Arnaud on his search to find help. The guys at the big hardware store in town were happy with the accountant they used, so Johnny Arnaud gave her a call.

Nicole Kirbye had arrived in town a couple of years ago, having come down from Kentucky to spend time with a cousin. Like Arnaud and Roullier, she had decided to stay on and hang up a small business shingle. She worked out of a small strip mall just off Fredieuville's Main Street. Her place was sandwiched between an insurance broker and a pediatric dentist.

Roullier was right. Johnny Arnaud liked her, and not just for the way she had been able to untangle the finances of Bayou Langlois Motors. Nicole was a friendly woman in her thirties, who was especially studious-looking when she was wearing her reading glasses. She had dark, shoulder-length hair, which she usually tied back in a ponytail, and she had the kind of infectious smile that made you want to smile when you were around her.

Roullier was also right that Arnaud should ask her

out. He was bashful about that sort of thing, but intuitive enough to sense that there was a mutual attraction. *If you don't, you'll wish you had*, he told himself.

After the better part of an hour of depreciation schedules and quarterly tax filings in her office that day, she stood to retrieve something from a file cabinet, and his eyes, tired of looking at Excel spreadsheets, followed her. He allowed himself a moment to admire the contours of her slender, but nicely-shaped body and to notice she was wearing a rather short skirt. She usually wore jeans.

When she noticed he was looking, she smiled.

All of this came and went in seconds and just as quickly, they back in the arms of Excel.

A while later, as they were wrapping up, he decided that it was the now-or-never moment.

"Y'know, Nicole, I was wondering…" he said, trying not to stammer.

She looked up.

"I was wondering if you'd like to go out for lunch sometime?"

"Normally, I…yes, sure, I'd like that. Tax season is over, so I have some breathing space. So what about the day after tomorrow?"

————

They agreed to meet on Wednesday at the Main Street Grill, a block and a half from Nicole's office. It was a warm spring day, and the humidity wasn't too bad. He wore a fairly new clean, short-sleeved shirt, and she was wearing a dress. She ordered a Cobb salad, and he had a burger and fries.

The conversation began with a quick work-related question but turned quickly to her interest in what it had been like to grow up in Brouillecourt Parish, and his questions about Lexington. They discovered a mutual interest in horses, though neither had ever owned one. They were a little bit past the midpoint of their lunch when she commented on the small eagle tattoo on his left arm.

"I never noticed it before," she said. "You usually wear long sleeves. It looks nice."

"Um, thanks. I got it when I was in the Army."

"Where did you serve?"

"All over. Did two tours in Afghanistan."

"Mmm," she said thoughtfully. "I was there for a year."

"Army? Air Force?" Arnaud asked. He was startled and asked the usual follow up question he asked when he met somebody who'd served. Picturing Nicole in Afghanistan was the last thing that would have crossed his mind.

"Neither," she said. "I was a civilian, a DOD employee. I spent all my time crunching numbers, of course."

"Wow, I never would have thought."

"I guess you guys would call us 'fobbits.'" Nicole laughed, referencing the military slang for "hobbits" who never set foot outside a FOB, a Forward Operation Base. "We almost never went outside the wire at Bagram Air Base. Never even got as far as Forward Operation Base. As far as I got was to go into Kabul for meetings at the embassy or with NGOs. Where were you?"

"Mostly...well pretty much *entirely* outside the wire," he said, not wanting to get into detail. "A lot of time in Kandahar. I only went to Bagram to take a shower."

She laughed.

"Whose numbers did you crunch?" Arnaud asked.

"I was with a group called the Security Infrastructure Finance Organization," she said innocently. "SIFO was on the roster of groups that were alongside the Afghanistan Security Forces Fund, you know, ASFF, in the org chart of the Defense Security Cooperation Agency. DSCA was our parent organization. You know, the DOD agency that does overseas material and technical assistance."

Fortunately, he didn't have a mouth full of burger when she used the acronym "SIFO." He would have gagged. He took a long drink of Diet Pepsi as years-old images of SIFO criminal misbehavior spun through his head.

"Hmmm...SIFO," he said weakly.

"You've heard of it?" Nicole asked. "There must have been three dozen DOD agencies over there. I figured that you guys outside the wire never hear of most of them."

"I believe I *did* hear about SIFO," he said, gathering his composure.

"Well, we were involved in things like accounting solutions, and handling charges on separate program-wide support cases. We also handled case-funding for program management, especially financial management. We worked with Implementing Agencies and the ABO, that's the Army Budget Office, to set up funds distribution for administrative program support costs and MIPRs. That's Military Interdepartmental Purchase Requests. The last thing I did was to work jointly with ASFF on the CSTC, the Combined Security Transition Command."

"Wow, all that must have kept you real busy."

"I admit it," she said. "I've always loved numbers."

"With all that funds distribution and those interdepartmental purchases, did you ever have any contact with NGOs over there?"

"Sometimes," she said thoughtfully. She was a little bit excited to hear him taking an interest in her work. She would not have guessed why. "There were more than a thousand registered NGOs over there, from the World Food Program to CARE International, and so many that you've never heard of. Our mandate was infrastructure, so if an NGO was into that, we probably worked with them at some point."

"Did you ever hear of an outfit called Vision for Humanitarian Empowerment. They were out of Europe, Geneva, I think."

"That rings a bell," Nicole said. "How do you know them?"

"Oh, I met a couple of guys who worked for them." Arnaud didn't mention that this meeting involved a deadly knife fight, which he won. "Did SIFO work directly with them?"

"I believe so, but I think it was in a different department with a higher security classification," she replied.

Nicole was now aware that the tone of the conversation had changed. For the first half hour or so, everything was relaxed a friendly, and a few jokes had even passed between them, but now, Johnny Arnaud had become more serious and even a bit glum. This had happened all of a sudden, and she hadn't caught it right away. Was it her mention of her working for SIFO, or something about the NGOs? What was it that was troubling him?

He grew quiet for a moment, then shook it off, changed the subject, and made a lighthearted comment about an elaborate dessert that was being served to the neighboring table. His smile returned, but something had definitely dampened his mood.

———

"How was your date?" Tyler Roullier asked his friend as the wrestled a 200-pound Beta Marine 20hp inline engine onto blocks inside their shop on Bayou Langlois.

"It wasn't a *date*," Johnny Arnaud replied emphatically. "It was just lunch."

"Whatever," Roullier said with a smirk.

"She told me she was in Afghanistan."

"*What*? Where? Who was she with?"

"She was civilian DOD, part of that big hive of civilian bureaucrats out Bagram. She was there for about a year. Left before the final pullout. Like she said, her group never got outside the wire except for meetings at the embassy."

"What unit was she with?"

"Here's the wildly weird thing," Arnaud said, still processing the astonishment. "She was with SIFO. Remember SIFO?"

"That bunch of drug-dealing, double-dealing assholes? Sure, I remember SIFO. What was she doing for them?"

"Crunching numbers, she said. She went on about accounting and stuff like funds distributions and interdepartmental purchases, y'know, the kinds of things that go in one ear and out the other. She said she liked it because she likes numbers."

"Do you suppose she knew what was going on?"

"I would like to think she did not," Arnaud admitted. "I assume that SIFO *did* originate as a legitimate bureaucracy. I think, at least I hope, she was on *that* side of SIFO."

"Did you ask her anything about it?"

"You mean did I ask her what life was like inside an international opium cartel? *No*, I did not. I did ask her about whether they worked with NGOs. I got specific about VHE."

"What did she say?"

"She acted innocent enough. Said she remembered hearing about it. That was all. That's when things started getting awkward. I just couldn't stop thinking about when we took VHE and the Dadullah Cartel down. She picked up on my irritation. I think she was a little bit freaked. I changed the subject, but she was still a little bit defensive."

"What do you think?"

"I think she knows that she hit a nerve," Johnny said, noticeably unhappy that this had dampened what might have been a nice lunch. "It's just that I hadn't thought about SIFO in forever, and this just hit me all of a sudden. I wish that I hadn't reacted like I did, but I did, and that's that."

"I suppose there won't be a second date any time soon," Roullier said.

"I won't see her again until I bring her the end-of-month figures, so I guess I'll just pretend to forget this happened."

"Good luck with *that*."

———

Nicole Kirbye had enjoyed her lunch—the *first half* of it anyway. She enjoyed working with Johnny Arnaud, and she was starting to enjoy *him*. She liked the way he laughed and the easy-going way with which he seemed to approach life. She leaped at the chance to spend some time with him away from work and was starting to feel very relaxed around him. All of this made his abrupt turn to the taciturn doubly troubling.

What was wrong? What was it about SIFO and the NGOs that had jumped out and thrown his disposition into a one-eighty about face?

That evening, she poured herself a glass of Pinot Grigio and sat down to rack her brain and try to figure out what it might be. It had been so long, so many years since she had even thought about SIFO. She had come back to Lexington and had gotten a job at a major accounting firm, and her years with the included all of her most recent professional and personal recollections. SIFO was almost as obscure as her undergraduate years. Those were memories of the distant past. Mostly forgotten.

Finally, she decided to phone a friend.

Ashley Grahen, who lived up in McAlester, Oklahoma, was the only person from the SIFO days with whom she was still in contact, but this contact was confined mainly to Christmas cards and comments on one another's Facebook pages.

"Hi Ashley, this is Nicole Kirbye, I just thought I'd give you a call. Is this a bad time?"

"No, not at all. The kids are winding down and I was just sitting here watching a reality show about Hollywood real estate," Ashley said cheerfully. Nicole recalled that Ash was a mother of two, albeit a single mother, while all Nicole had to show for her domestic life was a three-year quasi-engagement that had faded to nothing a few years ago.

"What's up?" Ashley asked. "What are you doing now? I have been watching your posts. Louisiana, is it? And you have your own accounting business? How is that working out for you?"

"It's good. I have some pretty solid clients. Mainly small businesses. All different. All interesting. I've got a craft brewery and a three-store chain of homemade ice cream shops, among other things. How's the kids, Ash?"

"They're six and four and a real handful. To what do I owe the pleasure of your call?"

"Well, I wanted to pick your brain about something."

"Okay?"

"Remember SIFO."

"Oh yeah, you bet. How can I forget our year in fun city?"

"Well, I *had* almost forgotten about it myself...until today."

"What happened?"

"I was having lunch with this guy..."

"*A guy*? I'm all ears."

"It's not like that...exactly. He's a client, so it was *that* kind of lunch, but he's awfully cute and I love his Cajun drawl."

"You go, girl."

"Well, I guess that *is* in the back of my mind. Anyway, we were talking...the conversation had moved away from work, and it came up that he's an Afghanistan vet. I think he was in some real serious combat. He didn't say much about it. You know, the ones who actually *were* in combat, are the ones who don't talk about it."

"Especially on a first date."

"It wasn't a *date*, Ash, just lunch."

"Whatever you say."

"So anyway, I told him that I'd been there too, and he was really interested until I mentioned SIFO. It was like a dark cloud dropped over the table. He started asking about NGOs that we worked with, but I had mainly forgotten about those."

"I remember that we did work with them," Ashley said. "They were always coming and going."

"He asked about one in particular," Nicole said, reaching for some notes she had written down after the lunch. "Do you remember a Swiss NGO called Vision for Humanitarian Empowerment?"

"Oh yeah, I do," Ashley said. "Don't you remember, we were on the second floor doing Sustainment and Infrastructure, and there was that other SIFO group up on three that did Equipment and Operations. They had

VHE coming in a lot, especially toward the end of our time over there. They were always going out to Kandahar and places like that, and arranging flights and stuff. The head honcho was that guy who wore those round tortoise-shell glasses. I can't remember his name."

"Yeah, I know who you're talking about. He had that narrow goatee. His name was Wally or something."

"That's it," Ashley said. "His name was actually *Wallace* Gusche. Everybody called him 'Wally' behind his back, but he really hated it."

"It's *Wallace*," Nicole mimicked in a deep mocking voice. "*Never* call me by that other name!"

"That was him," Ashley confirmed. "I also remember that there was some kind of big scandal that broke just after we left, but they hushed it up. Something about smugglers and a lot of money disappearing."

"I think that my new friend knows more about all of this than he wants to talk about," Nicole said soberly. "He got really gloomy and distant when the subject came up."

"Something to talk about, or *not* to talk about, on your second date," Ashley said, trying to be cheerful.

"I wish," Nicole said cautiously. "I think I blew it by bringing up SIFO at all. At least I've got the columns of figures that will bring him back."

CHAPTER
TWO

BROUILLECOURT PARISH, LOUISIANA

TYLER ROULLIER WAVED to his partner as he climbed out of his pickup in the gravel lot next to Bayou Langlois Motors on a warm Tuesday morning. He would have shouted a cheerful "good morning," but their two part-time employees were in the midst of doing a test run on a 35-hp inboard engine that they had finished rebuilding the day before. There was no chance of being heard over that roar.

By the time that Roullier had hung his jacket on a peg and tossed his bag lunch into their minifridge, the engine had been shut down.

"This one's ready to go out," Johnny Arnaud said with satisfaction, nodding at the engine. "They'll be in about ten to pick her up."

"Great," Roullier replied. "That Yanmar 6CHE3 ought to be ready to go out Friday. I just have to check the valves one last time before we test run it. Now, by the way, remember last week when we were talking about SIFO?"

"Hmmm...how could I forget?"

"Have you talked to Nicole since?"

"Nope. Haven't had a reason to call."

"Well, I'm not one to give advice in this stuff, but maybe you oughta? You need to make up an excuse for why you got freaked out and go on and talk to her again. You and I both know that she's probably *not* a drug dealer, but I think we both know she thinks you're giving her the brush-off. I don't think you want to leave it like that for very long."

"Message received and understood, Sergeant," Arnaud said with a half-smile.

"Anyway, that's not the reason that I brought up SIFO," Roullier said, changing the subject slightly. "I've got something for you. Here, take a look in this issue of *Army Times* from about a year ago."

"You still subscribe to *Army Times*?"

"Never got around to canceling, but anyway, some-times they got something interesting. Anyway, last night I was bagging a bunch of old copies to put out with the recycling and this line on the cover about DOD orgs in Afghanistan caught my eye."

"What did it say?"

"Well, I didn't realize it, but y'know SIFO *still exists*."

"Who would have thought?"

"The Pentagon closed down most of those outfits because they didn't have anything to do anymore."

"Which makes too much sense for the *government* to do, right?" Arnaud replied cynically.

"But for some reason, they kept SIFO going. Or maybe the SIFO people just kept their heads down and didn't get noticed in all that chaos that was going around."

"What happened to them? Are they in the Pentagon?"

"No, they're one of those outfits, and there's a lot of

them, that landed at some random unrelated base elsewhere," Roullier said. "They're orphan agencies that became homeless when their base closed. There is a lot of that in the military since all the base closings.

"Like my cousin who lost his job and ended up crashing on my couch."

"*Exactly* like that," Roullier replied, obviously liking the analogy. "So that's how SIFO ended up at Keesler over by Biloxi."

"That was an *Air Force* base last I heard!" Arnaud exclaimed.

"It still is, but now they also got all sorts of other things, it says here, like they even got Marines and Space Command over there."

"What does SIFO do without an Afghanistan to do it to?"

"It doesn't say," Roullier said, scanning the article. "It just says they're there. I had no idea about that until I read this."

"That's only about two hundred miles away. Last I heard of them, they were eight *thousand* miles away."

"I don't think we have to worry that they're following us." Roullier laughed.

———

"Nicole, this is Johnny from Langlois Motors," Arnaud said, deciding to keep it formal. He had stared at the phone for almost a minute—it seemed a lot longer—before he dialed.

"Good morning, Johnny from Langlois," she said cheerfully. He had expected an icy reception after the way he thought he'd treated her. "What can I do for you?"

"Well, um, I think I owe you an apology for how I got

so downbeat when we were talking about Afghanistan at out lunch last week. I know that my negativity probably really put you off…"

"No, you don't need to apologize. I wasn't mad at you. I figured it was something that I might have said. I should have been more understanding of your feelings. You were outside the wire taking incoming and seeing things that we never saw in our cocoon at Bagram. I cannot begin to imagine…"

"No, it's not *you* misunderstanding," he said. "It's just *me* processing some bad memories of situations over there, y'know."

"I know, um, I used the wrong word…I think I understand. I hope you understand that I'm trying to understand, you know."

"It's cool. Thanks for indulging me in this."

"Of course."

"You know, actually the other reason I called is I meant to call earlier, but we've got engines stacked up all over the place and I haven't had a chance to call," he said, feeling awkward. "But I was thinking that maybe we ought to hit the Main Street Grill again one of these days?"

"That would be nice," she said. "How about Friday?"

"We've got an engine going out, but they'll probably be coming in the morning, so that should work. I'll get back to you when I know exactly."

"It's a date," she said happily.

Poor choice of words, she thought. The last thing she wanted was to appear overly eager. But, *wow*, she was glad that he'd called.

Nicole dove back into the spreadsheet for a tax filing she needed to finish by the end of the day and was so engrossed that she jumped a little when the phone rang again about an hour later.

"Nicole Kirbye, may I help you?"

"Nic, this is Ash. How are you?"

"Oh, Ash, I was in the middle of something and I didn't even look at the caller ID. How are you?"

"I'm good, except it's been raining off and on for a week. How is it down there?"

"Sunny today. What's up?"

"Remember when we talked last week, and we were talking about SIFO, and that scandal I remembered about money going missing?"

"Yeah?"

"Well, I just got off the phone with a guy I knew, remember Steve Ambel from Request Oversight Auditing?"

"Vaguely, wasn't he the one who always wore a pocket-protector?"

"Cleanest pockets in the building."

"Where is he *now*."

"He manages a carpet cleaning franchise in Terre Haute. But anyway, he was up on the third floor and his cubicle was down near where Wally Gusche and the Equipment and Operations bunch were at. Steve remembers the scandal, which was after our time."

"Oh yeah?"

"Apparently a lot of SIFO funds went into something that VHE was doing with the Afghan locals in Kandahar. SIFO was supposedly arranging flights that VHE was running back through Uzbekistan to Europe. Steve says that these flights were supposedly carrying drugs for a cartel that was run by...get this...the *Taliban*!"

"*No way!*"

"Yes, way. "

"Was Wally involved in that?"

"Steve seems to think so, but I guess we'll never know for sure. The DOD was all set to send auditors out, but then the drawdown started, and nothing ever happened."

"What happened with VHE?"

"They were one of the NGOs that stayed on after the pullout, and the Taliban took over the country again."

"I guess that makes sense that VHE stayed around if they were helping the Taliban push drugs."

"But that's only the part that leads up to the good part," Ashley said in a conspiratorial tone.

"Oh…"

"So the bigwig running this cartel was Akhtar Mohammad Dadullah, apparently one of the most notorious of the Kandahar warlords."

"I remember hearing that name bandied about," Nicole said. "They said he was awful. I remember them saying he was really into torture for torture's sake. Horrible man. Everybody was scared of him. I do remember that the coalition tried for years to catch him and never did. Just like they chased Osama bin Laden for years, they chased this guy for ten years or so."

"Dadullah was also one of the biggest players in the opium trade, on top of everything else."

"That's not surprising by the sound of him," Nicole said judgmentally.

"Here's the good part. Some months or so while after the pullout, some rival gang, nobody knows exactly *who*, caught up with him at a safe house up in the mountains of Kandahar. Steve saw the DOD report that included some in-house VHE docs about what happened. "

"What *did* happen?"

"Dadullah had his brains blown out. There was barely enough left of his face for an ID. And a whole field of his gangsters, all dead. Mostly it was headshots, so you know that they were up against some pretty skilled marksmen."

"*Wow,*" Nicole said. "*They finally got him.* Where did Steve see this report?"

"A friend of a friend, so he says, has it on a website. Somebody who officially wasn't supposed to have it. "

"Oh dear, that's sinister," Nicole said, shaking her head. "Like a spy movie. But what was VHE doing writing reports about this?"

"Because VHE was in bed with the Taliban in this opium deal, and there were several VHE people up there too. They also got shot. There were a couple of suitcases that looked like they'd been full of US currency. Only a couple of random twenties were left. All of this goes toward proving that the Taliban and VHE were in it together. Then *somebody* came along and took them *all* out in one big hit."

"And nobody knows who?"

"Nope, but here's the good part," Ashley said eagerly.

"You said that *that* was the good part," Nicole reminded her friend. "It *was* a pretty good part if you don't care for opium cartels."

"Okay then, this will be a *weird* part. SIFO names are all through this report. Most are redacted, but there's one that is not."

"Don't tell me," Nicole said. "Wally Gusche."

"Yup, Wally Gusche."

"I'm not surprised," Nicole said. "Was SIFO involved in the drug trafficking too?"

"It would seem *so,*" Ashley said. "And Wally Gusche was a drug pusher."

"I wonder what ever happened to him."

"Long gone, I would imagine," Ashley surmised. "Probably on an island in the Caribbean. Isn't that where drug lords end up?"

"Well, anyway, I am glad that *somebody* finally got Dadullah," Nicole said triumphantly. "At least there's *some* good news in there. Wish I'd have known about it earlier. Not that it really matters."

"On a happier topic...I *hope* happier...what's happening with that cute Cajun of yours?"

"Well," Nicole said. "I hadn't heard from him for over a week, but he called this morning and we're having lunch again on Friday."

"Good for you, Nic. I hope it goes well,"

"Me too," Nicole said. "At least I know what *not* to talk about. I'm certainly *not* going to bring up SIFO drug scandals or Dadullah getting his brains blown out."

CHAPTER
THREE

BROUILLECOURT PARISH, LOUISIANA

"SORRY I HAD to push our lunch back an hour," Johnny Arnaud said as he greeted Nicole Kirbye at the Main Street Grill early Friday afternoon.

"That's okay," she said. "We beat the noon rush this way."

"Thanks for your patience anyway," he said, returning her smile. Her smile told him it probably really *was* okay, so he relaxed a little bit.

"Did you get your engine delivered?"

"Yes ma'am. It was a Yanmar 6CHE3, a pretty high-end, 130-horsepower Japanese inboard diesel. We were doing a midlife overhaul."

Nicole feigned interest in inboard diesels, but her expression told him she was genuinely happy to have him share his interests with her.

They exchanged small talk and placed their orders, Johnny a burger and Nicole a BLT. They were on their sweet tea refills when Nicole asked him, "Besides inboard diesels, what's new in your world?"

"Well, there's an old saying about there being nothing new down on the bayou, but those guys who picked up the engine had an interesting story...or excuse, I guess... about why they were late."

"Oh, what was that?" Nicole asked. She was in the mood for a story that did not include bad memories of Afghanistan.

"Well, those guys with the engine, the Fortier brothers, Dex and Beau, they have a commercial fishing operation down on Bayou Gadreau. 'Redfish for restaurants,' they like to say, but they do a lot of other things too. So they were just heading out to come see us this morning and they ran into a couple of guys with badges looking around about a mile or so up the bayou from their dock."

"Badges?"

"Yeah. Well, we do see a game warden from time to time down there, but not often because we're too far out in the boonies for sport fishermen, and there are no ocean charter operations on Bayou Gadreau. They're not far from the Gulf, but far enough. That's why the fishing is great for their business."

"If not wardens..." Nicole prompted.

"It was our old employer, the US Army."

"What were the MPs doing down there?"

"They weren't MPs. They were Army civilian police, you know the DASP."

"Not even Army CID?" Nicole asked, referencing the Army service analogous to the Navy's NCIS, the outfit that everyone knows from the TV show.

"No, just the DASP, the Department of the Army Special Police. They're a step down from the CID, *but* they do carry badges. They said they were just doing a recon for some routine maneuver or something that's going to be happening down that way in a week or so. They didn't know much. It was 'above-their-pay-grade' stuff or so they said. They said it was routine. Mainly, they just talked about good places to fish from shore down on Bayou Gadreau and the side channels."

"Maybe it's a Corps of Engineers project," Nicole suggested. "They are always doing this or that in the canals and levees all over the Delta."

"That's what I was thinking," Arnaud said. "That makes complete sense. Speaking of the US Army, my partner, Tyler Roullier, found out something about your old outfit."

"SIFO?" Nicole asked, started. She remembered how anxious he became when she had brought up Afghanistan at their last lunch. She decided to tread lightly and let him do the talking.

"Did you know it still exists?"

"SIFO? No. I assumed it was shut down. I thought all those things were closed up and put out of business when they had no reason to continue."

"We all did, I guess. Tyler read about it in *Army Times*. He still has a subscription. He figured that whoever was in charge at SIFO kept their head down and the Pentagon wasn't paying close enough attention to notice that they were in need of shutting down."

"Are they back at the Pentagon?"

"Nope," Arnaud said. "That's what I thought too, but here's the funny part. They're over in Biloxi."

"*Biloxi?*"

"Yep. They're part of a jumble of random DOD agencies that ended up at Keesler."

"That's an Air Force base."

"That's exactly what I said, but apparently they even have Marines over there, too."

"That's the Pentagon for you," Nicole said, laughing at her former bureaucracy. "I'm glad to be in the private sector."

"Me too," Arnaud said emphatically, taking a sip of his tea. He was also happy with her in the private sector.

―――――

TERRE HAUTE, INDIANA

It was after eight o'clock on Friday evening when Steve Ambel finally got back to his apartment from a busy day at his Biz-Zee-Kleen carpet shampooing franchise. It had been a day of nightmares. One of his guys had a leaky carpet cleaning machine yesterday, so today Ambel had to meet a flooring estimator to work out a schedule for getting a wood floor replaced, and then the new guy got lost while on a call and his truck broke down.

Ambel could almost taste the gin and tonic he was planning to pour when he learned that the nightmares were not over.

"*Who are you?*" Ambel demanded of the man standing in his living room. "Who let you in?"

"We didn't expect anybody," the man said in surprise.

"*Obviously,*" Ambel said, trying to appear angrily indignant while worrying about the word "we."

The man was young, but not too young, and reasonably well dressed. Aside from the tattoo on his neck, he did not have the appearance that one would expect of a druggie who broke in looking for cash and laptops. The tattoo had the appearance of something that was supposed to look like a snake, but it had come out looking like a worm.

"You need to get out of here *right this minute!*"

"I'm afraid we can't do that."

Ambel was so keyed up that he almost leaped out of his skin at the sound of another voice behind him. Somebody else had been in his spare bedroom.

"*What do you want*?" Ambel demanded, accepting that he was surrounded.

"You've been getting your hands dirty with some classified documents," the voice behind him said.

"What classified documents?" he asked, turning to face the second man. He was older than the first, with a flushed, sunburned complexion, and he was also dressed fairly well. He realized that both of them were wearing gloves. No fingerprints. They were pros of some kind or other.

"Don't waste our time," the man said impatiently. "You know damned well what we're talking about. VHE? SIFO? Flying opium out of Afghanistan?"

"Who cares? That was years ago?"

"I think it's obvious that *we* care," the sunburned man said.

"It's open source stuff. It's all over the internet."

"If it was 'all over' the internet, we wouldn't be here now."

"What do you care?"

"That's irrelevant. Just know that we do care. Now show me *where* it is 'all over' the internet."

"Okay, my laptop is on the table," Ambel said, trying now to cooperate. "I see that your friend has already found it."

"If you'd be so kind as to tell me your password," the first man said.

"I'll type it in," Ambel said, now becoming irritated. "You can watch me."

The first man took notes as they both watched Ambel's fingers skittering across the keyboard.

At last, he arrived at a site with the header "DEEP-STATEWATCH" rendered in red against a black background and scrolled down to a sub-tab labeled "SIFO-

VHE Conspiracy." He clicked on it and a new page of tabs popped up.

"How did you know about this?"

"I was just browsing. I used to work at SIFO at Bagram," he said, not wanting to name the name of the friend who turned him on to "DEEPSTATEWATCH."

"What did you do at SIFO?

"I was in Request Oversight Auditing."

"Did you know about VHE and the opium while you were there?"

"No. You must know that everything at SIFO was stovepiped. Nobody even knew what was going on in the next cubicle."

"We both know that's not true," the sunburned man said derisively.

"How would you know?" Ambel said. "Were *you* there?"

"Don't insult me, Steve. You were a damned auditor, not a covert action hero. SIFO was full of accountants doing mundane shit. Everybody gossiped."

"Well, yeah. But I never heard anything over there about VHE helping the Taliban move dope."

"Who else knows about this? Who have you told?"

"*Nobody!*" Ambel said emphatically, thinking about having told the whole story to Ashley Grahen. "I'm thinking about starting a blog. Maybe I'll use it in my blog."

"I really hope you *don't* use it in a blog," the sunburned man said.

"I really don't think he'll use it *anywhere*," the first man interjected as he pulled a bag of cable ties out of his pocket. "I think he's got a lot to say, but he's not going to be saying it in any kind of blog."

CHAPTER
FOUR

BROUILLECOURT PARISH, LOUISIANA

"BRENT, DO YOU KNOW WHAT A 'MOONRAKER' is?" Wallace Gusche asked.

"It's a waterfront bar in nearly every seacoast town that I've been to from the Carolinas to California," Brent Lynse replied.

Gusche and his longtime aide were in Gusche's silver, late-model Chevrolet Malibu on Interstate 10, headed west out of Baton Rouge.

"Yeah, bar names." Gusche laughed. "There is that for sure. The explanations that I like, though, go back for centuries."

"Okay…"

"They have to do with the rumrunners who brought contraband liquor into England from France three hundred years ago or so."

"And the booze was called 'moonshine' I suppose," Lynse said.

"Distilled by the light of the moon, some say, or at least shipped that way. In some tellings, the booze was dumped in ponds and the locals used rakes to retrieve the kegs. They'd tell the customs men that they were trying to rake up the reflection of the moon."

"And they bought that story?"

"They already thought the locals were yokels, so it fit."

"For real?"

"It's a mythical tale, Brent. But my favorite legend is the moonrakers were the smugglers who 'raked the moon' with the sails of their ships as they brought the stuff across."

"And you're comparing these mythical characters to the people we're going to be working with?"

"Precisely," Gusche said.

Gusche had landed on his feet after the Afghanistan pullout, and he brought Lynse with him. A lot of civilians on the DOD payroll whose agencies had existed only because of the American presence in that conflict were left to scramble for new jobs.

Gusche not only kept the Security Infrastructure Finance Organization alive, but he had managed to keep doing his side hustle in Afghanistan even after SIFO officially pulled out of Bagram Air Base. He flew in and out on the American taxpayer's dime, via charter flights through Uzbekistan, and using SIFO's ongoing relationship with Vision for Humanitarian Empowerment as an official cover story while they all ran drugs.

The Taliban had closed down most of the NGOs, especially those with the discomforting taint of empowering or educating women, but since VHE was empowering the Taliban's own access to European opium buyers, they got a pass and flourished under the new Afghan theocracy.

That is, until the day that Akhtar Mohammad Dadullah and all his cartel chieftains were massacred on that hill in Kandahar. There were VHE bodies in the mix, and the Taliban could not be sure that there had been no double cross, so they gave VHE the boot.

Gusche had been there himself that day and still counted his lucky stars that he had driven away just before the shooting started. He had escaped by so narrow a margin that he had even heard the gunfire in the distance.

After that close call, the bureaucratic chopping block in Washington was nowhere nearly as terrifying.

The Defense Security Cooperation Agency, which oversaw most of those DOD agencies in Afghanistan, closed them as soon as they could file their final reports, but SIFO survived, thanks to the pivotal presentation that Gusche made to the Pentagon bean counters. Because all of the SIFO upper management had moved on, when the DSCA decided to keep SIFO, they found it expeditious to simply put Gusche in charge.

When it came to finding a home in the States, the new SIFO director got creative. He wanted to be as far as possible from the Pentagon, so he looked around. Keesler AFB in Biloxi had been an Air Training Command base, and they still did that. They had also become the landlord for a host of unrelated entities. There were contracting squadrons, logistics squadrons, a cyberspace engineering installation group, and a school of applied aerospace sciences. As Tyler Roullier had read in *Army Times*, there were also minor Marine Corps and Space Command units here.

Gusche had lucked out. Not had he survived the Pentagon chopping block, but the Taliban had called him again, this time in the form of a man named Abed Qalandar. A slippery dealmaker, he was involved in all sorts of shady deals, many of them involving the Afghan government, and some involving the Taliban. He had established himself in the United States with big plans to big plans and product to move.

Now, he wanted to do business with Wallace Gusche, who just happened to be operating out of a seaport on the Gulf Coast with a long history of nefarious characters willing and able to move illicit contraband.

Brent Lynse had joined SIFO a couple of years later. Gusche recruited the ambitious young man partly because he recognized him as a hand-worker and a good team-player, but mainly because he saw him as someone who would have no trouble stepping outside the lines to readily accept a role as Gusche's lieutenant in the reprise of the lucrative side business that Gusche had been running since SIFO's days in Afghanistan.

Gusche parked the silver Malibu on the leafy main street of Fredieuville and headed into the large, inviting café. Inside, they were met by two special agents of the Department of the Army Special Police, Len Ivermin and Jorge Sentyl They had been scouting bayous for the use of Gusche's moonrakers.

"It's a place called Bayou Gadreau," Ivermin said, pointing it to a large topographical map of the area. "It has everything you said you were looking for...a waterway that leads to the Gulf, a paved access road, but almost nothing else. Literally, it's in the middle of nowhere."

Nicole Kirbye had just walked into her bungalow from her usual Saturday afternoon visit to Rouses Market when her landline began ringing. Without caller ID, she had no way of knowing it would not be a time-wasting telemarketer, but on impulse, she answered it.

"Hello?"

"Nic, this is Ash…"

"*Ash*! What's wrong? You sound like you've been crying!"

"It's Steve Ambel…he's dead."

"*Dead*! *Oh no*! How? Where?"

"In his own apartment. He was murdered."

"*Murdered*? When?"

"Last night, apparently. I tried to call him. He uses only a landline, or so he says. He's into all of the conspiracy stuff and doesn't like to have a cell phone that can be traced. When I tried to look online for another number and typed in his name, the online version of the *Tribune-Star* newspaper there in Terre Haute popped up with the article."

"Oh no, Ash. That's terrible. Was it a burglary?"

"The police say he was tortured. They tied him to a chair and, well, they didn't say exactly *how* he was tortured. They trashed the place like they were looking for something. Some valuable stuff was left behind, but his laptop was missing. They found the laptop charger."

"Oh no. I'm sorry."

"Nic, I'm scared. I just had to talk with you about this. I'm scared it's about that SIFO stuff and that DOD stuff he got his hands on that he wasn't supposed to have. Mainly, I'm scared that they're gonna come after me now."

"Why?" Nicole asked. "How could they even know about you?"

"Because Steve sent me the link to this thing and I got curious and I clicked on it. There was all this that started to bubble up about 'cookies' and stuff, you know, you see it all the time. But then it said that they were using cookies or something to access my 'location data,' and suddenly my home address popped up."

"*Oh no!*" Nicole gasped. "You're afraid that they might...come after you?"

"*Yes*! They know where I am. I'm a single mom with kids...*small children*."

"You could call the police?"

"I thought about that, but how is it going to sound? How can I tell them that I'm afraid for my life because of a conspiracy that I can't explain, and because someone I barely knew a long time ago was murdered six hundred miles away across two state lines? They'll take me for a nut case! I don't know what to do."

"I have an idea," Nicole said. "Why don't you come down here and crash with me for a while. Tax season is over and I got time to show you around...my friends could take your kids fishing in the bayou. My house is too big for one person anyway. Please come visit."

"*Thank you*, that's actually not a bad idea," Ashley Grahen said, her voice turning cheerful. "I'll ask for time off work, and head south. I could dive down next week. Maybe I'll get to meet that cute Cajun of yours."

"Just maybe," Nicole replied happily.

"Does he have any friends?"

"Well, as a matter of fact..."

———

When they had finished their conversation, Nicole had convinced her friend it was impossible, at least unlikely, that she had anything to fear. Yet, she found her own hand trembling as she set down the receiver.

If Ash feared being targeted for what she had learned in a phone call from Steve, why in the world would Nicole *not* be targeted for what she had learned in a phone call from Ash? *OMG.*

As she unpacked her grocery bags and put her frozen stuff in the freezer compartment, Nicole tried to talk herself out of the same fear she had tried to lighten in Ashley.

Frozen peas. They will track me down and kill me.

Single-serving pizza. They will never find me.

Ready-to-microwave lasagna. They will track me down and kill me.

Rum raisin ice cream. They will never find me.

On it went on as she put the Honey Nut Cheerios and the creamy peanut butter into the cupboard. Finally, it ended with Nicole having "scientifically" confirmed that they would never find her. She breathed a forced sigh of relief.

To take her mind off it all, she decided she would pop over to her office and finish up several things she had left undone yesterday because she had allowed her lunch with Johnny Arnaud at the Main Street Café to go on for nearly two hours. She climbed into her blue Ford EcoSport and headed down Main Street.

She was in the midst of allowing her mind to drift to happy places, and to allow her eyes to drift toward the Main Street Grill and the good memories of yesterday when she received a jolt that sent her reeling.

There, in front of the café and getting ready to climb into a silver car, was a man with a narrow goatee and round tortoise-shell-framed glasses.

Wally Gusche!

When she reached the parking area of the strip mall where her office was located, her head was spinning.

SIFO. Conspiracy to export opium. Dead people. *Gusche.*

That was all behind her, many years and eight thousand miles away.

SIFO. Conspiracies of the past brought to life. Army

agents mysteriously sniffing around on Bayou Gadreau. Dead people and the sum of Ash's fears.

All this was here and now, and Gusche was back in her field of view, *right here* in Fredieuville.

———

Nicole Kirbye locked the door to her office, which was something she *never* did when she was in. It was not that she expected Wallace Gusche to follow her and kill her. It would be virtually impossible for him to have murdered Steve Ambel nine hundred miles away last night and be in Fredieuville now.

On top of that, he hadn't seen her drive by, and he had no probable way to know where she lived—if he even cared. Still, locking the door made her feel a tiny bit safer.

She stared at the stack of papers she meant to dive into and did nothing.

She stared at her phone, thought of calling Johnny Arnaud, and did nothing.

Finally, she decided that if she didn't, she would lie awake all night wishing she had. She really needed to talk to somebody who understood how all that evil in Afghanistan cast a shadow over your life.

"Johnny, hi, this is Nicole. I hope I'm not catching you at a bad time. I hate to interrupt your Saturday night plans. It's just that...I'd like to pick your brain about a few things."

"It's all that about SIFO, right?"

"How'd you know?"

"Listen, Tyler and I, we're just on our way into town. We were planning to get a pizza and a pitcher at the Quarter Moon. Why don't you join us? We'll be there in about forty minutes."

"Well, I'd hate to get in the way..."

"You're *not* in the way." Arnaud laughed. "It'll be fun. You like pizza, right?"

"Even with pineapple," she admitted.

"See you soon."

———

Nicole Kirbye arrived first but remained in her car across the street until she saw Johnny Arnaud's truck pull in and the two men climb out. She was not in the mood to be sitting alone in a bar on a Saturday afternoon.

The Quarter Moon Bar & Grill was an old-fashioned place, more grill than bar, a place without the throbbing techno music that defines the ambience in so many big-city watering holes. It had several flat-screen television sets, but not enough to make it a sports bar. It had pizza. You could take your kids.

When she spotted Johnny and Tyler, she waved and both men stood as she walked over. She had met Tyler a couple of times, but Johnny had been the one who brought her the paperwork every month, and more recently, more often than just once a month.

Tyler went to place their pizza order, while Johnny ordered a pitcher of Bayou Ghost Amber. It was brewed locally and it tasted a lot better than mass-market yellow beer. Johnny also knew that the craft brewery that made it was one of Nicole's clients.

"Okay," Johnny said with a smile, looking at Nicole. "What's this about SIFO that you wanted to talk about? You were sounding awfully uneasy. I guess we were all surprised to know that they still exist and that they're now less than two hundred miles from here."

"I'm sorry," she said. "I didn't mean to sound conspiratorial for the sake of some kind of far-fetched rumor. I don't believe in that stuff. I'm an accountant. Numbers are precise and invariable. The square root of…, say two-hundred-eighty-nine…is seventeen. It will always be seventeen. It will never *not* be seventeen."

The two men nodded. They had no idea about the square root of two-hundred-eighty-nine, but they had no doubt that Nicole *did*.

"I know that the real world can be messy, but in most cases, it runs in an orderly way, but I know that sometimes it doesn't. I'd be the last one to say it, but it looks like something's going off the rails here and I wanted to get your take on it."

"Okay," Tyler said. "What's happening?"

"I'll start at the beginning," she said, proceeding to run through the course of her recent discussions with Ashley about their time with SIFO at Bagram, about the VHE people coming and going, and about the rumors of mischief and corruption within the SIFO group on the third floor.

Their pizza arrived, and as Johnny took charge of plating the slices and parceling them out, the conversation turned briefly to how everyone liked the prosciutto.

When everyone had finished their first slice and had come up for air, Nicole resumed her story, going into what Ashley had learned from Steve Ambel. She explained that Ambel, their mutual friend from the SIFO days had gotten access to a long-buried DOD report about an investigation into SIFO corruption, which linked SIFO to VHE, and which explained that VHE was in turn working with the Taliban to smuggle drugs out of Afghanistan.

"Where did your friend get these documents?" Tyler asked.

"Ash just said that Steve told her about 'a friend of a friend' or something like that," Nicole replied. "It was somebody with a website, but we'll never know exactly where it came from."

"Why?"

"Because Steve was *murdered...last night*. This is part of why I needed to talk to *somebody*. That's why I phoned you, Johnny."

He put his arm on her shoulder and she squeezed his hand.

"What exactly happened?" Johnny asked sympathetically.

"Okay," she said, taking a long sip of her beer. "Here's what Ash said. He was killed in his apartment in Terre Haute. Ash said she tried to call him on his landline and there was no answer. She was trying to look up another number for him in Terre Haute and the Terre Haute newspaper website popped up. The story said he was zip-tied to a chair and tortured. The paper didn't say how exactly. Is this too much?"

"No, go ahead."

"Okay, so it said that the killer or killers ransacked the place looking for something. They took his computer."

"Oh shit," Tyler said, shaking his head.

"And now, Ash is scared out of her mind," Nicole continued. "Steve had sent her the link to this thing, and when she clicked on it, the site accessed her location data before she knew what was happening. She says that now that they have his computer, they also have *her* location data so they know where she is, her exact address. If they killed him, then..."

"I understand," Johnny said, giving Nicole a compassionate squeeze.

"*You* didn't download it, did you?" Tyler asked with a concerned expression.

"*No*, thank God," Nicole replied emphatically. "She never sent me the link, but I *almost* asked her to. But this is not the scariest part in this so-called 'conspiracy theory' story about SIFO."

"What's scarier?" Johnny asked apprehensively.

"The head guy up in SIFO's Equipment and Operations at Bagram was a man named Wallace Gusche. We used to call him 'Wally,' which he hated, but that's neither here nor there. Anyway, Steve told Ash that the documents he downloaded show that Wally was the key SIFO man in this huge smuggling operation over there."

"I don't think you need to worry about *him*," Johnny said, trying to be comforting. "He'd probably living with his ill-gotten gains in Switzerland or someplace."

"*Except for one thing*," Nicole said urgently. "Ten minutes before I phoned you this afternoon, I *saw* Wally Gusche getting into a car here on Main Street."

The two men looked at one another in disbelief.

"Are you absolutely sure?" Tyler asked.

"One hundred and ten percent," Nicole said emphatically. "I'd recognize that face, with its narrow goatee and round tortoise-shell-framed glasses anywhere."

Johnny looked at Tyler, and they both looked at Nicole.

Their jaws dropped as they recalled the man who climbed into his pickup and drove away on that fateful day in Kandahar so long ago.

CHAPTER
FIVE

BROUILLECOURT PARISH, LOUISIANA

JOHNNY ARNAUD and Tyler Roullier met one another at their Bayou Langlois Motors machine shop on Sunday morning for the *stated* purpose of tidying up after a busy week and getting ready for a busy schedule on Monday.

But their *unstated* purpose was a debrief after their conversation with Nicole Kirbye the night before. With phrases like "just a coincidence" and "you needn't worry about that," they'd managed to take the edge off her uncertainties and anxiety, but they had come away unconvinced themselves. The image of the man in the round tortoise-shell glasses, and memories of that day in Kandahar remained vivid, and the two Cajuns were unnerved by the idea that he had been walking the streets of Fredieuville—*yesterday.*

"Are you thinking what I'm thinking?" Johnny asked rhetorically.

"Probably," his partner replied. "I can't shake it. I

woke up at four with all sorts of thoughts slitherin' through my head like water snakes."

"Yeah, people being murdered over a smuggling thing a decade ago...SIFO involved then...and what's SIFO involved in now? Mr. Tortoise Shell then..."

"And Mr. Tortoise Shell *now*, and *your* girlfriend being only two degrees of separation from..."

"We need to figure out how to sort this out," Johnny said. Roullier noticed that Arnaud didn't take exception to the comment characterizing Nicole as his "girlfriend."

"Y'know, if anybody could sort this out..."

"Let's call Tim Tommis," Arnaud said.

After he'd lost the use of his legs on their exfiltration from Afghanistan, the team's tech genius had reinvented himself as the go-to black magician for numerous—the exact number is safe with him—freelance covert operators and old friends still dabbling on the dark side.

Tommis was known only to be based in a "secret undisclosed location" somewhere on the Eastern Seaboard. Almost no one knew it was a nondescript mid-century ranch-style home in Silver Spring, Maryland, and those who knew were prepared to guard that information and the house itself with their lives. Almost nobody in the outside world knew how to contact Tim Tommis—but *all* of the members of Captain Jim Hammer's old team had the magic number.

"Here goes," Johnny Arnaud said, punching the keypad of Bayou Langlois Motors landline.

"May I help you?"

"Tim, it's Johnny Arnaud. I'm here with Tyler Roullier. You're on speaker."

"The two Cajuns...hmmm...It's been a while," Tommis said as his voice recognition magic confirmed Arnaud's identity. "How've you been?"

The ensuing conversation spun off into the usual queries about what had been happening since their last conversation, about what had happened to mutual acquaintances, and about shared memories of things which nobody outside their old team knew, or could understand. When talk drifted that day in the Kandahar mountains to the death of the demon Dadullah, and the tortoise-shell glasses it gave Arnaud the smooth transition he needed to bring the story of those glasses up to date.

"Let me take a look," Tommis said. Arnaud and Roullier could hear the sound of their old friend's wheelchair as he scooted from one computer to another on the hardwood floors of his aerie in the undisclosed location.

"As you've said," Tommis continued after a couple of minutes of rapid keyboard clicking. "SIFO is still alive and well in a nondescript building at Keesler."

"Thought so," Arnaud said. "What do they do there?"

"Like their name says, they are still into infrastructure and funding, but they're more than a purchasing office. They manage shipping and warehousing for Department of the Army installations all across the southeast. They handle all sorts of exciting stuff, from sheetrock to toilets."

"Oh happy, happy, joy, joy," Roullier interjected sarcastically, quoting the idiom from the early nineties cartoon show *Ren and Stimpy*.

"You mentioned our friend in the tortoise-shell glasses, Mr. Wallace Gusche," Tommis said. "Well here he is. He is indeed the man in charge of the place. Gusche has been the director of SIFO since they moved back to the States. Now he's king of a small pond with a small staff of clerks pushing paper. There is virtually no communication with the outside world that does not involve inventories, invoices, bills of lading and that sort of thing. He's buried in a dead-end bureaucracy."

"Where careers go to die," Roullier said.

"Or where careers go to hide in plain sight if you want to run a smuggling gig on the side," Arnaud interjected.

"*Touché*," Roullier said with a grin.

"Gusche has been hiding in plain sight there in Biloxi for years," Tommis said. "Like you say, it's the most boring, dead-end place imaginable...unless you got something on the side. Mmmm, here's something interesting. He does have a DASP detachment down there that answers to him, you know, Department of the Army Security Police. Superficially, they're there as security guards to keep all the sheetrock and toilets safe, but..."

"But if one were to be cynically conspiratorial, you could say he has his own private army with federal badges," Arnaud said.

"Funny you should mention DASP," Roullier said. "Last week, some friends of ours ran into a couple of suits with DASP badges over on Bayou Gadreau. They were looking around the place. Said they were lookin' to do some fishing, which seemed bogus as hell."

"What was SIFO mixed up in over in Afghanistan?" Arnaud asked rhetorically. "Smuggling. Where's the best place to do smuggling between here and Biloxi?"

"The bayous," Roullier answered.

"I can see where you're going with this, guys," Tommis said, laughing. "You're getting a little bit conspiratorial, here. I like it."

"Meanwhile, Gusche works with shipping companies and trucking companies and anybody who moves toilet paper and sheetrock across the docks and up the interstates down on the Gulf Coast," Arnaud said. "I'm sure he also knows or deals with all the shady operators who haunt the waterfront in Biloxi and Gulfport. Time was that they were among the crookedest ports on the Gulf Coast. Have you ever heard of the Dixie Mafia?"

"That rings a bell," Tommis said, flummoxed by not being able to recall more off the top of his head.

"Oh yeah," Roullier interjected. "At one time when we were kids or before, they had a grip on the ports down here almost the same way those famous East Coast crime families ran the ports around New York and Jersey and Philly. Biloxi was the center of it. It was mostly gambling and prostitution, but smuggling was in the mix."

"Now you're being *really* conspiratorial," Tommis said, laughing again. "Let me do some more poking around on this angle, and I'll get back to you."

———

FEHRY COUNTY, ARKANSAS

Rahim Faizullah and his sister Hila thought that they'd never make it out of Afghanistan. They owed their lives to Jim Hammer's special ops team, *but* the team would not have made it without the two gutsy Afghans. They knew the lay of the land, and they knew the right thing to say when they reached the Pakistan border.

The two Afghans probably never imagined that they would wind up in a small town on the northern fringe of the suburbs of Little Rock, Arkansas, but when Brian Herste of the team had offered to "bring them home," he meant it.

However, the road to Fehryville had been a nightmare.

They had been ambushed by the Taliban in the Hindu Kush, and it was here that Tim Tommis, took a 7.62mm round in the base of his spine. This left him permanently unable to walk, but every member of the team, including Rahim Faizullah, pitched in to take turns carrying him across the Hindu Kush to relative safety.

However, when the team was finally ready to be flown out, the US State Department suits at Badaber Air Base near Peshawar in Pakistan stopped Rahim and Hila from climbing aboard the C-130 with their friends.

Did they have Special Immigrant Visas? Well, no.

Did they have Priority 2 Refugee Status? No.

"What they *do* have is this team," Hammer said as they stood on the ramp leading into the transport aircraft. "They are members of this team. We stick together. If they do not board this aircraft now, *we* will not board this aircraft. We have a seriously injured member of the United States armed forces who needs specialized hospital attention ASAP. If he does not get that, whatever happens to him is on *you two*."

At six foot two, and with the shoulders of an Olympic bodybuilder, Captain Jim Hammer was a commanding presence.

The suits flipped through the papers that they had for the team members, realized who Hammer was, looked at one another, made a call, and backed off.

When they at last reached the States, Tommis landed in the Walter Read Med Center, and the Faizullahs got their immigration status.

After that, the team disbanded. Several men mustered out but Hammer himself stayed in and was deployed on another covert op in Southeast Asia. Brian Herste went back to Fehry County and brought his friends home with him.

It was a bit adjustment for sure, but the community was favorably disposed to Afghans who had helped Americans, and there were already a couple of Afghan families in town. Hila and Rahim were fluent in English and both had Kabul University degrees, so they had gotten jobs fairly quickly. Now, a half dozen years later, Hila had her credentials and was teaching math at Fehry County High School, and Rahim was the manager at the Herste family's hardware store, the largest independent in a county where people like to shop local.

They had shaken off the nightmares, and things had been going well—until that day last week when Rahim thought he had seen a face he recognized. It was the hard face and intimidating presence of Abed Qalandar. Rahim and Hila remembered him as a shady Afghan government functionary, not far removed from his past within Afghanistan's warring tribes. He was one of those men who moved furtively through this ministry or that, currying favor and taking bribes.

What is he doing in Fehryville?

Rahim had written it off to mistaken identity until a week later. As they usually did on Sunday evenings, he and his sister had gotten together for a meal at the Helmand Kitchen, the town's only Afghan restaurant. They were sharing a large plate of *qabelee*—rice baked with lamb, raisins, and glazed carrots—when he saw the man again. This time, there was no doubt.

"Hila," he whispered, "I meant to tell you that I thought I saw Abed Qalandar the other day."

"*Abed Qalandar*? Are you sure? What would he be doing *here*? You're probably mistaken."

"That's what I thought, and that's why I didn't mention it, but I think I was right. I think he's *here*."

"*Here*?"

"Here in this room, sitting across there in that corner. Slowly turn and take a look and tell me if you agree it is him."

Hila slowly and casually turned her head, looked, and slowly turned back.

"It's *him*," she hissed. "*That evil man*. How much did he steal? How many are dead because of the information he sold to the Taliban? Who gave him a visa?"

"We probably know those answers," Rahim said. "He cultivated many friends in the American organization over there. But I am more curious about your earlier question, a question I asked myself when I thought I saw him. What is he doing here in Fehryville?"

"And who are those people with him?" Hila asked rhetorically. "One of them is Afghan. I have seen him around, but I do not know his name. I have never seen the three Westerners before, have you?"

"No," Rahim said, glancing at the table. "Whoever they are, they do not seem to be having an agreeable time. Since I have been watching, none of them has smiled."

"Maybe the Westerners do not like Afghan cuisine," Hila suggested cynically.

"I don't think any of them is paying attention to their food," Rahim said. "They are having a very serious discussion. The woman is doing most of the talking, she seems to be the one leading the discussion. She is a very strong presence."

"That wouldn't have happened at home," Hila said with a touch of irony. "At least not *now*. No woman would be *in* a conversation with three men, much less *leading* it."

"Wait," Rahim said, resuming his play-by-play. "They seem to have decided something. They're all nodding. Still no smiles, but they appear to have reached some kind of agreement on something. The waiter has brought the bill. The woman is paying the bill. She is definitely the leader among the Westerners."

Moments later, the people rose and headed for the front door, with the tall, rigid woman striding purposefully and leading the way. Rahim tried to avoid eye contact as they came toward him, but he saw a flicker of recognition on Qalandar's hard, cunning face. Rahim could see that the man was trying to place him out of context.

While Qalandar still had a beard, albeit one trimmed considerably from what Rahim remembered, Rahim and Hila could easily have been Westerners. Rahim, who wore a beard when he lived in Afghanistan, was clean-shaven, while Hila wore her hair long and nicely styled, and her shoulders were uncovered, something that was uncommon in the old country even in the most liberal of times.

"I could see that he *thought* he recognized me," Rahim said.

"He didn't look back," said Hila, who had a view of the four men as they followed the woman out the front door. "Did you know him well? I only knew him by reputation. Did he know what you did for the Americans?"

"Yes, he did."

CHAPTER
SIX

BROUILLECOURT PARISH, LOUISIANA

"OH SURE YOU DO." Tyler Roullier laughed when Johnny Arnaud said he needed to go into Fredieuville to pick up some things at the hardware store. "You talked to her for an hour yesterday. You were still talking when I went home."

Yes, Arnaud *did* want to check up on Nicole face-to-face. There were a million reasons why that wasn't *necessary*, and one reason why it was. That reason trumped the others.

"Oh hi, Johnny," she said as he walked into her office. Nicole was seated at her desk in her inner office, buried in paperwork with her glasses perched atop her head, when she saw him come in. She rose to greet him.

"I was in town running some errands and thought I'd drop by," he said.

"I'm glad you did," she replied, giving him a friendly hug. He could sense she really *was* glad to see him.

"How'd you sleep?"

"Better last night than Saturday night, for sure," she

said. "You know, maybe I was overreacting, being too paranoid. Ash is probably *not* going to be tracked by hired killers, is she?"

"Well, probably not. I sure *hope* not," Johnny said, trying not to sound unconvinced.

"It's hard to be optimistic, you know," she said. "As I said on the phone yesterday, I had started to try to convince myself that when I saw that guy on Saturday, the one with tortoise-shell glasses, it was only my mind tricking me and making me *think* I was seeing Wally Gusche."

He nodded. He knew what happened next.

"Then, when you told me that your friend found out that Gusche is alive and well and running SIFO in Biloxi…well it was like I got hit by a *truck*!"

He put his arm around her shoulders.

"It's probably all just a big coincidence," she said, taking her turn at trying not to sound unconvinced. "Even if I did see Gusche, I can't imagine that he's out to get me. Maybe it wasn't even him? At least, he doesn't know that *I saw him*."

"You're being a logical, rational…" Arnaud started to say.

"A logical, rational *accountant*?" Nicole said, finishing his sentence.

"Yeah, I guess."

"I know," she said. "We just have to find a way to move past this. It's all really just a coincidence, *right*?"

"Neither you nor your friend Ash have been threatened directly…"

"Should we add a 'yet' to that?" Nicole interrupted.

"Keep your eyes open," he said. "Let me know if you see or hear anything. In the meantime, my friend Tim says that he'll be digging and trying to figure all this out. Everything's gonna be fine."

"Okay." she said reluctantly. "I guess I'd better get back to work. I do have a pile back there."

"Are you free for lunch later this week?" Johnny asked on his way out. asked.

"Sure," she said, hoping not to sound as eager as she knew she was. "How about Wednesday?"

"It's a plan, see you then," he confirmed, as she stepped over to give him another hug.

As she was watching his pickup drive away, the land-line in her office began ringing.

"Nicole Kirbye, how may I help you?" she answered.

"Nic, this is Ash. I hate to bother you. I know you're working."

"Never a bother to talk to you, Ash."

"I'm really worried."

"I know that stuff about Steve getting murdered hit you hard, but surely they're not going to bother you way out in Oklahoma."

"This morning when I was dropping the kids at school, this old, ugly lime-green car came by," Ashley blurted out. "Two men inside. They were driving real slow and staring at me."

"I know it's creepy, but we all know that guys like to look at pretty girls," Nicole said. "Most of these creeps are just creeps. It's broad daylight in a public place, right."

"*No.* This was different," she insisted with a quaver in her voice. "*I could feel it.*"

"What did they look like?"

"Other than creepy, they were middle or late thirties, I guess. I couldn't see the driver too well, but the other one had his window rolled down and I could see a tattoo on his neck that looked like a really sloppy drawing of a worm."

"That's *creepy.*"

"I don't know what to do."

"You're still planning to come visit me...right?" Nicole said.

"Yes, I've asked for time off work, and I told the kids' teachers. We're going to get an early start on Thursday."

"Um...well," Nicole said. "I think it might be a good idea to come sooner. Maybe you should plan your early start for Tuesday instead."

———

Johnny Arnaud was on his way back to Bayou Langlois when his phone rang. He was going to let it go to voice-mail until he was back at the shop but glanced at it anyway. It was Tim Tommis.

"Tim, how are you?"

"I tried phoning your office landline but got your answering machine. Who still uses those?"

"Tyler is probably using the grinder down at the dock and didn't hear it, and our part-timer doesn't start until noon on Mondays. I'm almost back there. We'll call you back in five minutes. Did you find out anything else?"

"*Ooooooh* yeah. Talk soon."

Arnaud and Roullier gathered around their office phone, punched in Tommis's number, and put him on speaker.

"About that girlfriend of Johnny's, I have good news and bad news," he led off provocatively. "Which do you want first?"

The two Cajuns gave one another a bewildered glance as wheels of imagination spun uncontrollably.

"Umm, *good*...I guess?" Arnaud said hesitantly.

"The good news is she is *not* a frantic paranoid. The bad news is all those things that you and her are afraid of...well, they're mostly *true*."

"I'm afraid to ask," Tyler Roullier said. Arnaud was speechless.

"Well you don't have to," Tommis said, obviously energized by the excitement of unraveling a conspiracy, and probably also by at least a quart of black coffee. "Because I'm going to tell you anyway."

"Okay…"

"I'll start with those DOD documents that their friend Steve Ambel was quoting. I got 'em…don't ask how… and I looked them over. I've seen some of the appendices elsewhere. I'd say they're ninety-eight percent legit. This compilation of docs that was posted online originated on an obscure website run out of a basement in Colorado by a guy who operated under the name 'DEEPSTATE-WATCH.' Don't bother looking for it. It was taken down last week, and not by its administrator. But I was able to access it."

"Of course you were." Roullier laughed. Tommis had a reputation for this sort of thing.

"I found the report that linked VHE to the Taliban, and SIFO to VHE. I had seen a lot of this info before and corroborated it all pretty fast. You should read the part…I'll send it to you…about the 'massacre' where old Dadullah got his. *Very* dramatic. His killing is blamed on a 'heretofore unknown' rival Taliban faction."

"I never imagined that I'd ever hear *our team* called that," Arnaud said with a chuckle.

"Sadly, here's where it gets unfunny," Tommis continued. "One reason why DEEPSTATEWATCH is no longer online is that the house in Colorado was swallowed up in a sudden four-alarm fireball and it collapsed into the basement. They found what was left of the guy, but it wasn't much. The police suspect arson because it burned so hot."

"And then there was poor Steve in Terre Haute," Arnaud said. "Do you suppose it was the same people?"

"Yup. I'd put my money on no other alternate theory," Tommis confirmed. "Somebody is cleaning house. They're tracking down people who downloaded this stuff from Colorado man's site. The website had this doc up for less than a week so it had not gotten a lot of traction yet. There aren't many people who accessed it. If I've managed to track them all, I'm sure that they have too."

"Who are they?" Roullier asked.

"Curiously, there are three people who are doing serious time in state prisons in various places. They aren't going anywhere. Then there's Steve...and finally, Ashley Grahen."

"*Oh no*," Arnaud said. "They're both..."

"On the hit list," Tommis confirmed.

"Who's um...ordering the hits?" Arnaud asked.

"I started by asking the question, who has something to lose by this information seeping into the mainstream media. Specifically, who was at that meeting in Kandahar? The Taliban don't give a damn. VHE no longer exists and the people who ran it are long gone and into some other mischief somewhere else. That leaves SIFO."

"And Wally Gusche," Arnaud pointed out dourly.

"So it does," Tommis said. "He has his little empire over there in Biloxi, and he's got his contingent of DASP agents with federal badges. Meanwhile, with all of the sheetrock to toilets that SIFO is shipping all over the southeast, Gusche has access to all sorts of shady waterfront goons who work the loading docks and seaports."

"Like an old-time gangster movie," Roullier observed.

"Exactly," Tommis agreed. "And in those old-time movies, there are always thugs to be hired and sent out to break necks and incinerate people who talk too much."

"What do we do?" Arnaud asked uneasily.

"Well, I think that the first thing to do is to tell your friend Nicole to tell her friend in Oklahoma to watch her back," Tommis said urgently.

"I wish I knew what we could do to take this whole damned thing down!" Roullier said angrily. "I sure do wish we had the team back together. Where is Jim Hammer now that we *need him*?"

"Good question," Arnaud said. "What did happen to Hammer? I know he stayed in the Army after we got out. I heard they sent him to South America or Southeast Asia or somewhere."

"I have no idea either," Roullier said. "When you live a covert life, doing covert stuff, the whole point is to *not* leave any trail, right? Tim, do you have any idea where anybody could *find* Hammer?"

"As a matter of fact..." Tommis began.

CHAPTER
SEVEN

INTERSTATE 49, DESOTO PARISH, LOUISIANA

ASHLEY GRAHEN BREATHED MORE EASILY. Both the kids were asleep in the back seat of her little orange Honda, and she had cleared the Shreveport traffic. They were finally on the interstate. Most of her first five hours out of McAlester, Oklahoma, on this Tuesday morning had been on US 270 and US 71, where the speed limit was pretty tight, but on this stretch, she could open it up to better than seventy and make much better time.

Ashley still had more than three hundred miles to go but being on the road did give her a sense of proactively taking charge of the situation.

She had made the decision to go visit Niccole Kirbye in Fredieuville and had gotten time off work. She told Liam's first grade teacher and the people at Ava's preschool that she was going to take the kids out of class starting Tuesday. At the time, Ashley was planning to get an early, but leisurely, start on Thursday. This was before Nicole called to tell her it would be a *very* good idea not to wait.

Nobody in McAlester knew where she'd gone. She'd even mentioned Texas in passing to her neighbors. She hated to lie like that, but after all, she *was* still freaked out by the murder.

When he'd told Nicole about the conversation with Tim Tommis on Monday morning, Johnny Arnaud had conveyed urgency, while leaving out a lot of the graphic details. He knew that Ashley was still freaked out by Steve being murdered and seeing the creeps in the green car who might have been following her. Arnaud was just insistent that she start her trip sooner than later, and Nicole had relayed this necessity. She was glad to be on her way and had even started to relax.

However, her sense of calm was broken by a squeal from the back seat.

She looked in the mirror. Six-year-old Liam was awake and staring out the window, ignoring his four-year-old sister Ava, who had woken up cranky.

An eight-hour road trip with two kids under seven, Ashley thought. *Am I a madwoman or what?*

Her realization that they were overdue for a bathroom break was rewarded by a blue sign promising a rest area in just two miles. Prayers answered.

"Hold on, baby. Just two miles."

She knew that Ava had no concept of the meaning of "two miles," but she hoped the unruffled reassurance of her voice would help put across the idea.

At last, there it was. Ashley flicked the turn signal and moments later, they were inside the not-as-grimy-as-it-could-have-been restroom. No problems. Prayers answered.

Ava clung to Ashley's pant leg as she bought some snacks out of a vending machine, but Liam took an interest in a squirrel. The playful rodent proceeded to run a short distance, stop to look at the approaching boy, then scamper away only to stop again and repeat the whole process. This happened several times as Ashley was battling the vending machine.

As a result, Liam was around a hundred feet away and into a wooded area by the time that Ashley finished kicking her snacks out of the uncooperative contraption.

"Liam, come back here this minute," she shouted, and as she did, she saw something that made her heart stop.

Time stood still.

She was engulfed with a horrific sense of danger mixed with a feeling of utter helplessness.

Down past the end of the parking area, where Liam had been chasing his squirrel through the underbrush and ignoring his mother, were two men. They were walking toward the boy.

The one with the tattoo on his neck that looked like a really sloppy drawing of a worm turned his head, looked at Ashley and smiled. It was a crafty, devious sneer.

"Liam!"

Ashley screamed a blood-curdling shriek.

She glanced around. There was no one nearby to help. The handful of other people were either inside the restrooms, or way down at the opposite end of the parking lot.

Why had she parked here?

She hadn't been thinking.

Dropping her snacks and scooping Ava into her arms, she ran as fast as she could toward her son.

The two men had stopped next to Liam, and one of the men was reaching for him.

"Don't touch my baby!"

She had meant her voice to be stern, but the words came out hysterical.

Moments later, she was a dozen feet from Liam, but

the men were closer. Close enough to reach down and touch his mop of straw-colored hair.

"*Please!*"

"I'm afraid we gotta interrupt your sweet little car trip," the older man with the sunburned complexion said. They were both smirking. These bullies held all the cards, and they were enjoying the game. They were relishing the terror they saw in Ashley's eyes as the tears rolled down her cheeks.

"Actually, we gotta put an *end* to your little car trip," the man with the tattoo said with an ironic chortle. "Your kiddie did a real good job of leading us all into this nice cozy little patch of trees where nobody can see us."

Liam stared at his mother with a confused expression.

"I sure hate to do this, but you've got a big mouth," the man with the tattoo said as he pulled a large knife out of a sheath on his belt. "And we gotta shut you up... *eternally.*"

Terrible thoughts of fear and desperation whirled through Ashley's mind. She was squeezing her little daughter so tightly that Ava began to sob.

"I don't believe I can let you do that," came a voice from nearby.

Everyone jerked their heads toward the sound of a person who had not been part of the conversation a moment ago.

It was another man, noticeably taller that either of those from the lime-green car. He wore faded jeans and a faded gray T-shirt with a picture of a grizzly bear on it. Beneath his gray ball cap he had a rough face that was covered with unkempt whiskers, too short to be called a beard, but too long to be called fashionable. Except for his erect, ramrod-straight stance, one might have taken him for a hobo.

The two men standing next to Liam diverted their

attention to this man, who had made his way through the underbrush without anyone seeing or hearing his approach.

After a moment of sizing up this stranger, the two men went on the offensive. Two against one is usually good odds.

The man with the knife lunged at the stranger, who grabbed his wrist.

Ashley saw the motion of the thrusting arm suddenly stop as though frozen in time and space. She saw the stranger twist the man's wrist ever so slightly.

What followed was a *crack* that sounded like a limb breaking from a tree in a storm. It was so loud she nearly jumped out of her skin.

The second man then fiercely attacked the stranger with the skill of one of those mixed-martial-arts fighters that you see on television sometimes when you're changing stations.

He deftly slipped his leg behind the stranger's to trip him, but the stranger simply stepped aside and struck the man with a single direct blow to his face.

Instead of simply impacting the bones of the nose and eye socket, the fist seemed to penetrate into the man's ruddy face by an inch or two.

Ashley kneeled as Liam ran toward her and as she squeezed him tight to her bosom.

Ava was hiding her eyes, but Ashley and Liam were staring at the stranger in disbelief.

What just happened? Ashley thought to herself. She realized that a terrible nightmare had come to an end in the space of a few seconds, but she did not know what to expect next.

"Who *are* you?" Ashley stammered.

"My name's Hammer, Jim Hammer."

"Where…"

"Your friend Nicole sent me," he said as calmly as if nothing had happened. "No, actually it was Nicole's friend, Johnny Arnaud, who sent me. We go way back. Johnny and I were in the Army together."

"You just saved our lives," Ashley told the man. "Thank you."

"I'm sorry about the mess. Sorry your kids had to see this."

"What's your name, buddy?" Hammer said, looking at Liam, and crouching down to minimize his height and put himself closer to Liam's eye level.

"Liam, sir."

"My name's Jim, but most people just call me Hammer."

"Where did you come from. How did you get here?" Ashley asked.

"I was hoping to catch up to you before you left McAlester, but you were already on the road.. I caught up to you before you got to US 71."

"How did you…?"

"You weren't hard to spot, ma'am," he said with a grin. "There really aren't that many orange Hondas on the road, especially with two car seats in the back. I did try to phone you, but the number I had went to voice-mail. I was going to try to pull up alongside and wave to you but I figured that might freak you out. Then I saw that the green sedan was tailing you, so I figured I'd tail *them*."

"*Oh my god*, I'm so glad you did," Ashley said, dabbing at the tears rolling down her cheeks. "I had my phone off because Nicole said that people can track cell phones, and I did not want us to be tracked."

"She gave you some good advice," Hammer said, looking at the two immobile bodies.

"Thank you so much," she said. "I don't know what to say..."

"Well, *I'd* say let's get rolling," he said with a smile. "We got three hundred miles to go and I've been promised a plate of crawfish for supper. You get the kids loaded while I tidy up a little bit and we'll get on the road. I'll be the blue pickup with the camper shell following you at a respectful distance."

Ashley didn't bother to ask what "tidying up" meant to Hammer in this context. She just scrambled off to buckle her kids into their car seats.

For Hammer, tidying up meant making sure that neither of the two attackers would ever again threaten women, children, or conspiracy theorists, and that their remains were left in a believable debris field. The latter was not hard. This spot, out of sight of both the comfort station and parking lot, was strewn with the empty beer cans, abandoned underwear, and other random detritus that spoke to its being a favorite site for partying and other monkey business.

Hammer pocketed their wallets and cell phones in order to advance the narrative of theft-as-motive and took their car keys back to the green Ford in the rest stop parking lot. He rolled the driver's side window down partway and left the keys in the ignition. Within two hours, the car would be gone. By sundown it would probably be across at least one state line and heading farther and farther from its recent occupants.

As Hammer walked back to his own vehicle, he gave Ashley and her kids a friendly wave.

"Who is that man, Momma?" Liam asked as he waved back to Hammer.

"I think he's our guardian angel," she replied.

"He doesn't look like an angel.

"Oh yes he does."

CHAPTER
EIGHT

FEHRY COUNTY, ARKANSAS

IT WAS EARLY WEDNESDAY MORNING, and Abed Qalandar was just finishing an email to Khairullah Ghani, his collaborator in Doha, Qatar when the phone rang.

"Abed, this is Alexis Mondtrom," she said tersely.

Qalandar was an uncompromising, one-time mujahidin who had reinvented himself as a shrewd and highly successful hustler years ago in Afghanistan.

With his dark, deep-set eyes and his black beard, he had the kind of hard, cruel, lightly scarred face that could be intimidating when a fearsome scowl suited his purpose. He was also a pragmatist who had made a career out of adapting to his circumstances whenever there was money to be made.

He didn't like Alexis Mondtrom, but he respected her. From her closely trimmed blond hair to her severe and confident manner, everything about her was strict and uncompromising. She had built a clandestine operation within the American government itself, controlling it profitably with an iron hand.

Her official title was Special Director for Security in the Field Operations Directorate of the Department of Homeland Security, which was an obscure entity deep inside the mysterious bureaucracy of DHS that almost no one knew about. She operated autonomously, and those few in the chain of command who knew about her and her directorate, also knew not to ask questions.

Qalandar's association with her had already made him some money, and if things worked out as planned, he would soon be very rich.

"Yes, Alexis, how are you this morning?"

"I'm not so well, Abed. I've been thinking about our dinner Sunday night."

"Did you not like the *qabelee*?"

"Oh, that thing with the lamb and raisins? Yeah… no…that was all very nice…very ethnic, very quaint. No, it was that man you introduced me to, what was his name?"

"Khaleq…Abdel Khaleq."

"He was very disappointing. It was obvious that his heart was not into our enterprise. He was more than merely disinterested. I don't trust him. I do *not* want him involved."

"Yes, Alexis."

"Are you sure he is even trustworthy?" Alexis asked pointedly. "I smell a double cross. Could he be working for the cops, or worse?"

"I don't think so."

"*Whatever*. You need to *get rid of him,* for *your sake* as well as mine. Please pull in someone *else* from your organization. I don't want to know anything more about your organization, or your lack of an organization, I just want you to promise me that you'll replace this guy with someone solid before me or anyone else has any contact with you. Understood?"

"Understood."

"Abed, I like you. I like your ideas and your clever ways of sourcing merchandise. I really do. So far you have delivered, *but* I feel like I've been working with just one man. It's like you're just a lone freelancer. I thought that you had a sizable organization behind you. If we are going to continue, if I'm going to continue buying from you, I need to know that I'm dealing with something more substantial."

"Of course."

"I am also concerned about the people who are handling the actual importation of the merchandise. I understand these are Americans who worked for the Security Infrastructure Finance Organization in Afghanistan?"

"Yes, they are, they *still* are," Qalandar said, trying to be reassuring. "SIFO still exists. They operate out of the Keesler air base in Biloxi. These men are very familiar with Gulf Coast ports."

"Can I meet with them?"

"Of course. I will arrange it."

"We'll be in New Orleans tomorrow; that's not far from Biloxi," Alexis said firmly. "Can you tell them that I'd like to buy them lunch?"

"Yes, I will," Qalandar said deferentially.

"As for the rest of it. If we are going to continue to do business with you, I need to have full confidence. When the delivery is made, everyone needs to see that they are dealing with an *organization*, not just a lone, former mujahidin with a satellite phone. Do you understand?"

"Of course."

Abed Qalandar set his phone down on the table.

Just a lone, former mujahidin with a satellite phone.

He found her derisive statement almost amusing. This was exactly what he was, but so far, he had made it work to operate mainly on his own, and he would continue to make it work.

He was on his own, but he had always made it work. He was a crafty operator from the mountains of Afghanistan who had built a lucrative career by adapting to his situation. He joined his cousins in a tribal band when he was ten years old. By the time he was twelve, he had realized he had a gift for languages. He could easily mimic Pashto dialects from any corner of Afghanistan. He could convince people unrelated to him that he was their cousin. By his early teens, he could speak Hazaragi and Dari without an accent.

His skill was in being a *manipulator* of people. He could infiltrate rival mujahidin groups with ease, and at one time he was a member of four such bands, while simultaneously holding an Afghan government side job. He even infiltrated the Taliban. When the Americans came, he learned English, and he learned to manipulate them as well.

One of first things he learned from the Americans was that they paid well if you had something to sell. He started out selling Taliban secrets to his DOD, NSA and CIA contacts. They liked him because he spoke English so well. They came to think of him as one of them, but at the same time, he also sold American secrets to the Taliban.

When the DOD brought him to America, one of first things he learned was what the money they paid him could buy. Americans like to own things, and Qalandar learned to love this. He settled easily into the Afghan community in Fehryville, bought a modest, but comfortable condo and eventually shiny black BMW 7-Series. It was a "pre-owned" car, but new enough to suit his self-image.

Over time, his old connections grew stale, and he was of lesser and lesser use to the Americans. In a moment of revelation, he decided to do as he had so often done in the past. He switched sides, making contact with some old Taliban acquaintances in Qatar.

Though the Taliban have a reputation for almost medieval austerity in Afghanistan, they actually live a lavish lifestyle, especially when those who base themselves in Qatar. Those who he contacted knew the value of money. These men, specifically Khairullah Ghani, were all ears when Qalandar suggested that there were riches to be made in the export market.

For most of Qalandar's adult life, he had worked alone, but the scale of the import-export caper required him to have an organization. For the sake of the exporters like Ghani, and the other Taliban chiefs in their Doha penthouses, creating such an illusion was as simple as a Zoom call with a proper backdrop.

When it came to the people to whom he was trying to see merchandise, people with whom he dealt face-to-face, it was more complicated. The Afghans in Qatar knew Qalandar by reputation, but buyers like Alexis Mondtrom did not—and she did not get where she was by putting her full faith and trust in people like him.

For more than a year Qalandar had been doing small jobs with her, all the while establishing credibility and courting her to become the importer of his Taliban exports. He had sealed the deal by convincing her that he was the leader of a band of accomplices, when he was actually working solo. He had created an import-export front business and used Afghan rugs as a cover story.

He hired Abdel Khaleq to be the smokescreen for the large band that Alexis assumed were behind him. He had deliberately told Khaleq very little but paid him well for the few times that he was required to show up as window dressing. This worked well until the window dressing lost interest in a project about which he was told nothing.

Abdel Khaleq had become a weak link. When the customer complains so loudly about customer service, it was time for action.

Qalandar parked his car about a block from the unremarkable six-unit apartment building that Abdel Khaleq called home. Qalandar knew he would be here because he had a job working from home for a call center in Virginia. Qalandar had been here once, a long time ago, but he remembered it was on the ground floor. It was mid-morning and most people were at work, so there was no one to notice an average-looking man in a heavy coat walking down the sidewalk. It was a cold morning, so his coat and gloves were not out of place.

"Abed," Khaleq said, proceeding to greet him with the Pashto phrase expressing surprise at the visit.

"Abdel, may I come in?" Qalandar said, replying in English. "We need to talk."

"Of course," he said, inviting his guest into his modest living room.

There were a couple of upholstered chairs, mismatched as though they'd come from separate garage sales. A large table against one wall held computer equipment that was the nerve center of Khaleq's call center job. He was wearing a dirty gray T-shirt and a pair of jeans. He obviously did not expect visitors.

"Are you busy?" Qalandar asked.

"No, if I don't answer, somebody else takes the call. It's very mindless and monotonous. I'm lucky that I can speak English so well. I need the job, but I am still trying to become more adjusted to this culture and the call center job, while dealing with infidel fools! This is why I am happy to work with you."

"That's the point I want to discuss, Abdel. You don't seem so 'happy' working with me. Our customers are displeased."

"They're Americans, they are being suspicious," Khaleq said. He sat back down on his office chair, but Qalandar remained standing. "This is not my fault."

"You are paid well from our work with these suspicious infidels. I know you like to call them *infidels*. But I have been generous in sharing this money that came from them, have I not?"

"Yes, you have been generous," Khaleq admitted.

"All I have asked of you is to show up and act interested and in harmony with me," Qalandar insisted. "Instead, you pout and act bored."

"It *is* boring," Khaleq replied. "There is nothing to do but smile, and I grow weary of smiling at the Americans."

"You have a bad attitude, Khaleq, and it grows worse. You're embarrassing. You made our customers believe that you cannot be trusted."

"That's ridiculous."

"It's time for us to end our association," Qalandar said, walking across the room.

"*You can't,*" Khaleq said, acting surprised. "I *need* the money."

Qalandar was now standing behind Khaleq, who was staring at the flickering messages on his computer screen and did not turn toward him.

Qalandar flexed his fingers and thought about how easy it would be to grab Khaleq's head and give his neck a savage twist. There would be a loud *snap*. Khaleq would make a gurgling sound and fall to the floor. Qalandar had done this before. He has done it dozens, maybe hundreds, of times in the mountains and cities of Afghanistan.

He actually enjoyed doing this. There was something powerful and enriching about using his own strength to take away that which another holds most precious—his life.

Since he'd been living in the West, Qalandar had come to learn that in Western minds, this made him a sadist, so he had shelved his more primal instincts and he had adapted. He had, of course, built a career on adaptation. Nevertheless, he had come here planning to kill Abdel Khaleq. That's why he was wearing gloves.

Instead, Qalandar calmly walked past the man.

"I can, and I must *sever* our relationship," Qalandar said, giving Khaleq a sinister glance as he emphasized the word "sever."

Qalandar watched Khaleq squirm fearfully. Sure, he had killed hundreds of men with his bare hands, or with knives and other sharp objects, but he had watched the Westerners kill thousands with their *machines*. Ironically, it was from the Westerners that he had learned subtlety, the art of frightening your adversary into submission.

"Abdel Khaleq, I have paid you generously," Qalandar said unsympathetically. "Have I not?"

"Yes."

"You have never had to wait for payment. I have even paid you ahead, for tasks you have not yet performed. You have been paid…correct?"

"Yes…ummm…"

"If our connection were to end today, could I ask you to repay me? I paid you for work you did not do. Am I entitled to demand that you pay me back?

"Yes…but…"

"Abdel Khaleq, our association *will* end today…it has *already* ended…but I will give you a parting gift. I will *not* ask for repayment."

Qalandar paused to let his words hand in the air.

Khaleq was terrified of saying the wrong thing, so he remained silent.

"Do not tell anyone...*ever*...about the work we have done," Qalandar insisted. "Do I have to spell out the consequences?"

"No."

"*Alhamdulillah*...we will *never* meet again."

CHAPTER
NINE

BROUILLECOURT PARISH, LOUISIANA

JOHNNY ARNAUD WAS UP EARLY on Wednesday morning. He was always up early. He tried to be quiet so he wouldn't wake Hammer, but Hammer was already sitting in Johnny's kitchen drinking coffee and studying one of Johnny's detailed topo maps of the area.

Hammer had crashed at Arnaud's house Tuesday night after he shadowed Ashley Grahen and her two kids to Nicole Kirbye's house in Fredieuville. Arnaud and Roullier had both been there to greet them, and as promised, there had been plenty of crawfish to go along with the joyous reunion of the two women who had not seen one another since they flew out of Bagram Air Base in a C-17 all those years ago.

There were also memories shared among the three men. The two Cajuns had not seen their former CO in years, but unlike Ashley and Nicole, they had not stayed in touch with Hammer. There was a lot to talk about. There was the special operations stuff that was discussed out of earshot of the rest of the party, and a lot of "what ever happened to" questions about former members of the team. Everybody, it seemed, had been in touch with Tim Tommis recently, but after all, he was the team's communications guy.

There were the "how's your life going" questions. Naturally, Tyler Roullier teased Arnaud's in a good-natured way about his budding romance-or-whatever with Nicole Kirbye. Hammer chuckled that he'd picked that up in the body language as soon as he saw them together.

Other lines of catching up were directed at Hammer, who said that since he'd gotten out a few months back, he'd reconnected with old friends in Montana who he'd not seen in two decades. When he mentioned that one of them was "a girl he'd known in high school," there were winks, nods and expressions that urged Hammer to elaborate. He didn't. They remembered him as one guy who spoke little about his private life, and he hadn't changed.

Beyond that, he was exhausted and felt himself fading. He had driven all the way from Montana in a couple of days and was at that point where he saw centerlines racing past whenever he closed his eyes.

White line fever.

———

"You're up early," Arnaud said, stating the obvious. "How'd you sleep?"

"Only an hour difference between Mountain and Central Time," Hammer said. "I feel like a million bucks. How are *you* doing.?"

"I'm sure glad that Ashley and the kids got down here, and got here safe," Arnaud said, pouring himself a cup. "That's thanks to *you*...as she tells the story."

"I was happy to be in the right place at the right time.

They were all set to get sadistic with that young family. I just disabused them of the idea."

"I'm glad that both Nic and Ash remember the small arms training they took back when they were at Bagram," Arnaud said. "I was able to leave 'em with a bit of hardware."

"You and Tyler were sure stepping all over yourselves to equip those girls with an arsenal to protect themselves. How many Berettas did you give them?"

"A couple and some extra mags. They should be safe with those."

"They'll be safe from those two that I met, at least," Hammer said. "And it'll take a while for whoever they work for to start to figure out that something happened to them. I sent their driver's license info to Tim Tommis this morning, so I expect we'll know about their owners sooner than the cops even know where they ended up."

"I guess that's a fitting epitaph for those clowns."

"Depending on buzzard activity, somebody might find the bodies today, or maybe tomorrow, but with no ID on them. I doubt that the state patrol is going to be in a big rush to run DNA and fingerprints on a couple of vagrants found in that rubbish heap. The missing wallets and cell phones will flag it as a robbery. Their car's probably out of state by now. Texas is only thirty miles away. It started out with Mississippi plates, so it will take time to run that down if whoever takes it doesn't change the plates. Even if it *is* found, I don't think it will be on any police department's front burner. Unreported stolen cars sink to the bottom of the pile."

"Did you get anything from their phones?" Arnaud asked, nodding toward the two cellphones that Hammer had collected at the rest stop.

"The phones are burner phones so there isn't a lot on them except numbers and some cryptic caller IDs. No voicemails. Somebody with a 228-area code called them a couple of times last night," Hammer said, holding up one of the phones. "I texted back this morning to say that we're still following 'the Honda.' I said it's over in East Texas now, and headed west."

"Hope they have a nice trip," Arnaud said sarcastically. "As you probably know, the 228-area code is Biloxi. That might tie them back to SIFO or to their off-the-books side business."

"Maybe," Hammer nodded, "but we haven't actually confirmed that there is a side business...yet. What we do know is Gusche was here in Brouillecourt Parish on Saturday and that DASP agents, who are in Gusche's civilian chain of command, were poking around Bayou Gadreau on Friday."

"When I mentioned the Army cops to Nic, she said it might have something to do with the Corps of Engineers because they have flood control stuff going on all over the Delta, but she said that *before* she saw Gusche."

"That's definitely worth looking into," Hammer said thoughtfully. "I've been looking at your maps this morning. I believe I'll take a little drive out to Bayou Gadreau myself this morning. Would you have a fishing rod I could borrow?"

———

Rhetorically speaking, one might ask about the best place to inquire about the goings and comings in a specific neck of the bayou country, and if one did ask, the answer might well be the local bait shop. Since bait shops also sell fishing licenses, this provides a good opening for conversation if one happens to be fishing for anecdotal information as well as for crappie or catfish.

Jim Hammer spotted the sign before he even saw the

turnoff to the side road to Bayou Gadreau. Hand painted by someone who wasted no time with wordiness, the sign read simply BAIT in large red letters. It was the only sign at the intersection. A stubby arrow directed potential customers about fifty yards down the road that runs along Bayou Gadreau to an open-air establishment under the shade of a huge cypress tree. It was more of a shack than a building, but with the look of a place with almost as much longevity as the cypress itself. He could see racks of lures for sale behind the counter.

He nosed into the gravel parking lot next to a pickup slightly newer than his own, and headed toward the counter, where he was greeted by an old, white-haired man with a beard more unkempt than the brambles around the banks of the bayou.

"How's your mornin' so far, sir," the man said, scrutinizing the stranger with bright, sharp eyes.

"Doing just fine," Hammer replied, returning his greeting. "How's your own."

"Things are generally slow down this way a touch after the mornin' rush. What can I help y'all with today?"

"I came down to visit some old friends of mine over on Bayou Langlois, and they sort of had to go to work today. This left me on my own, so I thought I'd try to hook a couple catfish, or maybe even some bass for supper. What sort of bait are folks catching 'em with these days?"

"Well, y'know, for bass, folks use crickets or grasshoppers, but live shrimp are real popular for a lot of kinds of fish."

"How do you rig your line?

"People use chuggers and poppers, y'know poppin' and stoppin' in your cast. The old timers use spooks. They call it walkin' the dog. You flick yer wrist to walk the bait across the top of the water with fast lil' crisscross moves. Just jog the bait so the fish can see it. Do you do much bass fishing?"

"Some, but I'm from out west. We mainly go after trout...rainbows...browns. I've never gone after catfish."

"Well, catfish aren't too particular with what they eat. Depends on their mood. We use everything from craw-dads to worms or chicken livers."

"How do you rig your line?"

"Make up your rig as plain as doable. Those cats run on smell and taste, not the look of the rig. They don't seem to care. In slow-movin' water just a hook and a hunk of stinkbait will do ya."

The conversation paused as the packed up an assort-ment of stinkbait and night crawlers for Hammer and sold him a three-day out-of-state fishing license.

"I guess the next question is where's a good spot down on Bayou Gadreau?" Hammer asked when he'd paid cash for his purchases. "My friends...they run a machine shop called Bayou Langlois Motors...they said Gadreau doesn't get a lot of traffic but it might be worth a try."

"Oh yeah, I know them boys...Johnny and Tyler... they're a hard-workin' pair."

"Yeah, I know," Hammer said with a smile. "I served in the Army with 'em...Afghanistan."

"Thank you for your service, sir."

"Thank you."

"My name's Cecil, by the way, but ev'body calls me Dave," the man said.

"Jim Hammer," Hammer replied, extending his hand, and not asking how Cecil had become known as Dave. "Folks call me Hammer."

"Well, them boys know their way around," Dave said. "They're right about Gadreau. Most folks tend to fish the Langlois and some of those places out that way. If I wasn't laid up with this bum leg, I'd be out on the Gadreau more myself."

"Sounds like I'm in the right place."

"Yes sir. Folks would be inclined to skip the Gadreau because the road ain't in that gooda shape, and there ain't no place to put in with a boat. It's mostly state land and nothin' much out there. The only folks out there is a couple guys with an ocean fishing business...not a tourist charter...they catch fish for restaurants. They sell to people with big trucks full of ice who haul it to restaurant trade down in Baton Rouge or New Orleans."

"I guess Gadreau is pretty close to the Gulf, then?" Hammer suggested.

"Pretty much, yes, sir. It flows into a nice wide place on the Atchafalaya, and it's an easy run to the Gu'f from there."

"Probably a good place some someone like me, without a boat."

"You betcha. You gotta find the right spot. The banks are steep because of all the dredging done by the oil companies years and years ago. Makes it hard to find the ideal spot. If you're fishin' from shore, though, you can throw your hook into the bayou most anywhere along this road, wherever there's a turnout, all the way down to where Gadreau runs into the Atchafalaya. But you don't have to go that far."

"Sounds good."

"But do watch out for gators."

"Oh yeah..."

"I'd say find your spot and go ahead and fish it but do keep your head on a swivel. Don't surprise 'em. Let 'em know you're there, and don't start nothin' with one."

"Thanks, that's good advice," Hammer said. "We don't see them out west."

"You betcha."

"Somebody was sayin' that the Corp of Engineers has something goin' on down there," Hammer said in a making conversation sort of way, changing subjects as he was packing up his purchases.

"I don't know where they got that idea," Dave said. "There's nothing for 'em to do in the way of flood control out here that ain't been done, and Gadreau is deep enough without need for them to be doin' any more dredging. The oil companies done it fifty-sixty years ago."

"I musta misheard," Hammer said with a shrug.

"Wait a minute," Dave said, a spark coming to his eye. "I did see a coupla strangers in nice car driving through late last week. Friday, I think it was?"

"*Nice* car?"

"Clean," Dave clarified. "A nice *clean* car. You don't see clean cars that much down this way. It didn't look like Corps of Engineers, but it was kind of official looking, if you know what I mean. There wasn't no stickers on the doors or anything. It had Mississippi plates, but that don't mean anything. Ev'ry fourth car down this way has got Mississippi plates, y'know. I took 'em for property developers or somebody like that who got lost. They drove in and drove back out a couple hours later."

"From the sounds of it, Bayou Gadreau not the place to develop resort condominiums," Hammer said, laughing.

"No siree." Dave chortled.

––––––

Being in no particular hurry, Jim Hammer drove all the way to the place where Bayou Gadreau empties into the Atchafalaya River.

He parked next to the Fortier Brothers commercial

fishing operation, which had been mentioned by both Johnny Arnaud and Dave from the bait shop. They were the ones who'd had a verbal exchange with the DASP agents down here on this bayou.

The Fortier buildings were locked up behind a chain-link fence and the brothers' boat was conspicuously absent from their dock. They were apparently out in the Gulf hauling in redfish for dinner tables across south Louisiana. An old dog that was napping in the yard got to his feet and came over to sniff Hammer's hand through the fence.

Hammer walked back to his truck, retrieved the rod that Arnaud had lent him, and the baggies of bait that Dave had sold him, and picked a spot. He didn't want to come back empty-handed, and if the fishing was as good as Dave advertised, he figured he ought to at least get at least a couple of catfish.

He cast his line, flicked his wrist, walked his bait across the top of the water, jogging as he went. On his third cast, he felt a jerk.

He reeled in his second fish ten minutes later and kept going. As he cast and jogged, he was thinking about the bayou and correlating the steep embankments with the smuggling theory developed by his Louisiana friends. The theory was still just a theory. There were still a lot of dots to connect, and he always liked to caution himself from jumping to conclusions, but he could picture what they had pictured.

NEW ORLEANS, LOUISIANA

Wallace Gusche and Brent Lynse made the trip to the Crescent City from Biloxi in about an hour and a half and found street parking on Decatur about a block from Michel Carambat's. Gusche always used this restaurant for meetings. He liked it because it was on the edge of the French Quarter so the food was good, but Decatur is a main thoroughfare, and you can get back on Interstate 10 pretty easily from here. Those streets up in the middle of the Quarter are impossible. An old lady can walk through there faster than you can drive.

Gusche and Lynse took their time and were skimming their menus when Abed Qalandar's customers arrived and introduced themselves. Whereas Gusche and Lynse wore Aloha shirts and ball caps to blend in with the tourists, this trio wore business casual.

One of the men wore a blue blazer but no tie, while the other wore seersucker. They did not introduce themselves, but the woman with them introduced herself as Alexis Anderson. Tall and erect, with a short, all-business hairstyle, she wore a sea green pantsuit over a starched white shirt and was obviously the one in charge. When she ordered a club soda, the others followed suit. Lynse ordered iced tea, but Gusche always had coffee.

"What's good here?" the boss lady asked.

"As it says on their website," Lynse explained, "they're known for their gumbo."

"Is that what you're having?"

"Why not?" Gusche replied with a smile, closing his menu.

The two men followed Lynse's lead, but the woman ordered a Caesar salad—*with* the anchovies.

"We met with our supplier over the weekend," she said, getting down to business. She disdained small talk, a quality that Gusche liked in people with whom he did business. "As you probably know, our goods are on the water. They left the Persian Gulf four weeks ago and are due into a port on this Gulf soon. Is that your under-standing?"

Gusche nodded.

"This is the first of many, and we are obviously concerned that all goes smoothly," she said. "He gave us a summary of your work in Afghanistan and told us that you're still associated with the federal government."

"That's our day job, and it gives us access to all the services and subcontractors that we need for what we'll be doing for you," Gusche said confidently. "We handle a huge volume of ocean-going cargo from all over. We bring it in, we offload it, we consolidate it, and we get it shipped. I understand that you're anxious but let me assure you that your goods can be in no better hands."

"Thank you," Alexis said. "We don't normally meet with our suppliers' suppliers, but in this case, our supplier agreed that we should simply speak with you directly."

"I understand," Gusche replied. "You need to be secure in knowing that we can land your cargo profes-sionally, and with a minimum of red tape."

"Or no red tape."

"Or no red tape," Gusche agreed. "How many ocean shipments do we handle every week, Brent?"

"At least a half dozen on a slow week," Lynse replied. "Sometimes twice that."

"Which means we're working through these issues all the time," Gusche summarized. "We know who to call and who not to call when it comes to loading, unloading and paperwork. We know them and they know us, if you know what I mean."

"Among all of this ocean traffic, do you have experi-ence with international shipments?" the man with the blue blazer asked.

"Of course," Gusche replied with a smile. "The DOD

gets its flash drives and staplers from Malaysia and Korea just like Walmart does. It all comes across the same docks that we and our people are working every day."

"I understand you have a long history with our suppliers," the man in the seersucker suit interjected. "Their man here in the States, the man we met with over the weekend, told us that you facilitated a lot of shipments for them over there in years past."

"He probably told you all the details," Gusche said. "It was rewarding, for all parties involved."

The conversation was interrupted by the arrival of their lunches, but when everyone had taken a few bites, the woman in charge resumed her querying.

"There's another thing I need to talk to you about," she said, looking at the two SIFO bureaucrats. "We've been hearing rumors that some DOD documents have gotten into circulation recently. Documents concerning the last days of your moving product out of the war zone overseas. These documents mention *your* government agency and *your* participation in those operations. I understand that you are aware of this?"

"We are aware of this," Gusche said defensively. "This was a preliminary report that was never issued officially. You should know that the Pentagon's planned official audit of our activities over there never happened because the drawdown, and then the pullout. It never happened. If the DOD would have had any problem whatsoever with what our organization was doing over there, we would never have made it through the post-pullout cuts, which we did. As you can see, we're alive and well, and working hard for the Pentagon today."

"All the same, it could be embarrassing for you if these documents get around, and if we're working with you, it could be embarrassing for *us*. In our business, we cannot afford to be to be embarrassed."

"Understood," Gusche said self-assuredly.

"I've heard that there's a pretty graphic description of the aftermath of Akhtar Dadullah's last stand," she said. "Blood and bone and brains splattered all over. More than a few people from that Geneva-based NGO you were working with people were strewn around too. What were they called?"

"Vision for Humanitarian Empowerment," Lynse interjected. "Pretty contradictory choice of names. But they're long gone now."

"It was a *massacre*," she continued. "That's the kind of thing that would have legs if it hit the media. I heard that some wacko blogger already got a hold of it and started sharing it."

"He did," Gusche confirmed. "It was on a very dense and complicated website that had since been taken down. One of the things that this person built into his site was a feature which identifies the location data of everyone who downloaded it. I don't understand how this works, but we were able to us it against him."

"How so?"

"We were able to physically locate *everybody* who saw the documents in question. They have been dealt with appropriately."

"You were able to nip this problem in the bud, then?"

"I think the phrase 'terminated with extreme prejudice' is more to the point," Gusche said with a confident smile. Indeed, he was so confident he almost winked. He was now at that point in the process where he assumed that all his ducks were in a row. At least this is how he conveyed it to Alexis Anderson. She seemed convinced by his self-assured body language.

What could possibly go wrong now?

"You've been awfully busy on that phone of yours," Gusche said as they cruised eastward past the Bay Saint Louis exit on their way back to Biloxi.

"I didn't want to say anything, but I thought I recognized that woman," Lynse replied, still staring at his small screen

"The woman from lunch, Alexis Anderson?"

"Yeah."

"*Did you* recognize her?"

"She's not Alexis Anderson," Lynse said. "There are hundreds of people with that name, but she's not one of them."

"Who is she?"

"She's Alexis Mondtrom. She's high placed in the Homeland Security Department."

"*What*? Are we being stung?"

"No, I actually don't think so. She was mixed up in a corruption thing about ten years ago, but it suddenly went away. It was one of those 'friends-in-high-places' situations. It looks like she knew too much and they didn't want to touch her. She's been mixed up in some shady things through the years, but it looks like she's wrapped in Teflon."

"That could be good for us," Gusche said. "Good to be working with somebody with that kind of impunity."

"It looks like she's done this before," Lynse said. "But it looks like she's breaking new ground, working with the Taliban. Who would have guessed? Homeland Security importing 'merchandise' from the Taliban?"

"Nobody," Gusche said. "That's who would have guessed, and that's probably why somebody like Alexis Mondtrom decided to do it."

"She's definitely one of those who has no fear," Lynse said. "And by the sound of it, she's taking no chances."

CHAPTER
TEN

SIFO HEADQUARTERS, KEESLER AFB, MISSISSIPPI

"MIRANDA, do you have those bills of landing that we talked about yesterday?" Wallace Gusche asked over the intercom.

"Yes, Mr. Gusche, I can bring them right in."

"Thank you."

"By the way, Mr. Lynse called while you were on the phone with the detergent package people. He said he would call you back in a little bit. He had to make another call."

"Okay," Gusche said. *Such was his life, he mused.* If it was *only* about servicing hundreds of coin operated laundromats at Army installations, that would be one thing, but this only his *day* job.

"What's keeping you so busy today?" Lynse asked when he phoned back.

"Exactly six hundred and forty-eight cartons of laundry detergent packets, if you must know. What's keeping *you* busy?"

"I've been dealing with a bit of a problem," Lynse admitted.

"What problem?"

"If you're there for a half hour, I'll come in. Think we oughta talk in person."

"Okay," Gusche said hesitantly.

Problem? Talk in person? Oh shit! Gusche said to himself.

————

"I was just talking with the Coome boys?" Lynse said as he came into Gusche's office, slightly out of breath, and closed the door.

"Yeah, of course," Gusche replied.

Coome Hauling was one of many small subcontracting companies that were part of the tangled web of activities on the waterfronts of the Gulf Coast ports. The legitimate tip of the Coome iceberg was in freight loading and freight hauling services, but they were always happy with the idea of an all-cash side job. They were the contractors with the heavy-duty forklift and the trucks whom Gusche had hired to unload the shipment that was inbound from the Persian Gulf.

They were not big operators, but they were just the right size. It was Randy Coome and his cousin Eddie, with Randy's ex-wife running the office, and casual labor hired by the job off the docks from Bay St. Louis to Pascagoula. The fewer people, the better. Gusche had used the Coome boys before, and he picked them for this one in a poetic moment because they reminded him of moonrakers.

"What's the problem?" Gusche asked. "We have a shipment to unload on *Sunday*. That's in *three days*! Don't tell me that there's going to be a problem after we just got through bragging at lunch yesterday that we're *experts* at this."

"No, there's no problem at all with Sunday," Lynse insisted. "None at all. They're ready to roll, ready to complete the mission as briefed."

"What's the problem then?"

"It's that *other* thing that Randy Coome was supposed to handle. You know, the problem with who saw that DOD document we were discussing at lunch in New Orleans yesterday?"

"Oh *that*," Gusche said in an exasperated tone. "I agreed to outsource that to Randy exactly so I could *forget* that the problem existed…and so I could forget about *how* it was being handled. Don't tell me that they screwed *that* up. What happened?"

"Randy hired some 'fixers' who 'took care' of that blogger in Colorado who started circulating it on that website," Lynse said. "In the meantime, I got Kenny in IT to take the site down as fast as he could and get me all the location data for everybody who accessed it."

"And did Kenny do that? I thought he did, didn't he?"

"Kenny did that and I gave the names to Randy to give his fixers."

"Were there a lot of names of people who saw it?" Gusche asked.

"Weirdly, there were a few jailbirds with too much time on their hands. They won't be a problem. They're not going anywhere. There were actually only two on the outside. There was a guy in Terre Haute and some woman in Oklahoma."

"But Kenny fixed it so that nobody *else* sees this, right?" Gusche said nervously.

"Right."

"You're sure? You gotta be sure because *my name* was in those docs."

"Kenny's sure."

"Is Kenny going to talk?" Gusche whispered cautiously.

"No, he's a nerd's nerd," Lynse said reassuringly. "He lives in a total fantasy world inside his computers. He lives in dark rooms and cyberspace...all that dungeons, dragons, and anime superhero crap, but he can find anything on any computer anywhere. He's one of those. He deleted everything online related to this predicament."

"I don't know whether to worry about him or be glad he's working for *us*," Gusche said. "So what's the problem?"

"Well, the fixers took care of the Colorado blogger and a guy in Terre Haute, but the woman in Oklahoma is still a work in progress," Lynse explained. "She apparently is on a road trip with her kids. The good news is that Randy called to say he got a text message from his fixers. They were on her trail and were following her into East Texas."

"Good news, okay," Gusche said. "I guess you're gonna tell me that there's bad news. Hit me with it."

"The bad news is that the fixers' car was found abandoned this morning about ten miles south of Muscle Shoals, Alabama. Randy keeps track of the VIN numbers of all of the cars he has, even the ones with phony registrations. This one will go to impound while they try to find the owner, which they won't. That's *pretty good* news."

"So what happened to the fixers?" Gusche snarled. "They're supposed to be running down Miss Oklahoma over in Texas!"

"Obviously, Alabama is three states in the opposite direction from Texas," Lynse said. "There was no sign of them in Alabama, and Randy hasn't heard from them since yesterday."

"Tell me this isn't happening," Gusche said, cradling his head in his hands.

"Wish I could. At least they took care of the blogger. If this woman is on a road trip with the kids, it means she's not likely to be spending her time scattering conspiracy theories on the internet. If she does, Kenny's on it."

"Call Randy and tell him to find somebody to find her and, you know, get this wrapped up."

"Already did. They're on it."

————

FEHRY COUNTY, ARKANSAS

At that moment on Thursday afternoon, Rahim Faizullah was on the floor at Herste Hardware, four hundred miles to the north, explaining the installation of a trap on a bathroom sink to a customer with no functional knowledge of plumbing. Thanks to him, and everything he had learned since he left Afghanistan, she had just suddenly grasped the concept of a ninety-degree fitting on the outlet side of a U-bend. Like a light went on.

Herste's customers were mainly tradesmen, but occasionally the store got the do-it-yourselfers. Rahim, they called him "Ray" now, always enjoyed these moments when he could turn on a light for someone. Of course, he never forgot the irony of his having come so far from a culture where do-it-yourself indoor plumbing was as rare as a sports bar.

He had just finished ringing up his customer when he glanced at the end cap with the fire extinguishers. There, pretending to look at merchandise, but staring directly at him, was the bearded face of Abed Qalandar, the corrupt

Afghan government bureaucrat and Taliban sympathizer who he had seen in Fehryville twice in the past couple of weeks.

This time for sure, and maybe the other times, Qalandar saw and recognized Rahim.

Their eyes remained locked as Qalandar walked toward the counter.

"Rahim Faizullah, it has been many years," he said without smiling. "I see that you have made an American life for yourself. Very good."

"It *is* good."

"I see that you now use an *American* name," Qalandar said, smiling and nodding that the name patch on Rahim's denim work shirt, which identified him as "Ray."

"I'm putting the old ways behind. I have a new life here. I see that you too have come to America, Abed Qalandar. How long have *you* been here?"

"Like you, I came in the years when our American friends were generous with immigrant visas for their 'essential' Afghan friends. Like you, I was a friend to the Americans. I was an adviser to their Security Infrastructure Finance Organization. We did very important work."

"I recall that you were also an interpreter for NGOs. I seem to remember Vision for Humanitarian Empowerment?"

"As *you* were an interpreter of the American Special Forces," Qalandar said, as though it was a traitorous occupation. "And *now* you are serving in the family business of...um...an American special operator."

"So I am," Rahim said unashamedly. "What work are you doing in the States?"

"Working with some of my old contacts."

"Americans?" Rahim asked.

"American business people," Qalandar confirmed. "They have money. They like to buy things. They always did. In America, you *must* be paid. Their religion is their dollars, and they pay me in dollars. I am pleased to be part of the American economy."

"What sort of things are you selling to your American friends?"

"Imports."

"From Afghanistan?"

"Of course."

"Carpets and rugs, I suppose?"

"Of course," Qalandar replied with a smile. They both knew that Afghanistan's largest export was never rugs, but the "fruit" of the poppy.

"Does the 'rug business' pay well?"

"Are you interested?"

"I beg your pardon."

"Are you interested in working with us...with me? There are opportunities. You could keep this job and do special projects on the side with your old Afghan friend. Supplement your income, as the Americans say. They have money."

"That's an idea worth considering," Rahim said uneasily. He had been taken off guard and could do nothing but call Qalandar's bluff or play along.

"As the Americans would say, think about it," Qalandar said as he turned to leave. "*Alhamdulillah,* my friend."

"*Alhamdulillah,*" Rahim replied, repeating the Pashto greeting.

He was stunned.

A job offer from Abed Qalandar!

A name, a face, and a memory that had not entered his mind for years.

A job offer?

This was mind-boggling. Until he said that, Rahim had feared that Qalandar would harm him as a collaborator with infidels, although on second thought, Qalandar had collaborated with infidels himself. Apparently, he still was.

Imports from Afghanistan?

As the Americans say, follow the money.

———

It was nearly closing time when Brian Herste walked into the hardware store that bore his family's name, planning to pick up some materials he would need first thing Thursday morning. When he had gotten out of the service, he worked briefly in the family business, but he had branched out as a construction contractor, mainly doing remodels. He had an account at the store and he gave his business to his father and sister who still owned the place.

Rahim was standing at the register running the day-end reports when he came in.

"Hey Brian, how's it going?"

"Real good, Ray. I just need to pick up a couple of things for that Faulkner Avenue job ahead of tomorrow. What's new here?"

"Well, what *is* new? A strange thing happened today," Rahim said warily.

"What's that?"

"Abed Qalandar was in here today."

Herste squinted thoughtfully, trying to place the name. At last, an expression of recognition came, but it was chased from his face by a deep frown.

"That shifty slimeball! I had completely forgotten about him."

"He *did* work both sides," Rahim said grimly. "He

was one of those who had a tongue like honey when he spoke to the Americans, but who used the word 'infidel' for Americans when they weren't listening."

"What's he doing in Fehryville?"

"He said he is importing Afghan rugs to sell to Americans," Rahim explained.

"How long has this been going on?"

"I don't know, but this was *not* the first time I saw him. I thought I saw him on the street two weeks ago, but I wasn't sure. Last Sunday, I saw him again at the Helmand Kitchen. He was with a group of people. It was like they were having a meeting. Not just friends getting together. I didn't think he saw me, but he definitely knew I was here when he came in today."

"That's disturbing."

"When I knew him over there, he knew I had worked with you, and that you were in Special Forces. He also knows all about me working for your family over here. This makes me nervous."

"I can understand."

"And one more thing...he asked me if I wanted to work for *him*."

"*What?*"

"He said I should stay here and 'supplement my income' by doing things for him."

"Like selling rugs? What did you say?"

"I didn't know what to say. When I first looked into those eyes of his, I was afraid he had come to kill me. I was scared. I didn't say yes, I didn't say no. What do you think he'll do if I don't say yes?"

"I don't know," Herste said hesitantly.

"I can't stop thinking...if he knows about me...what might he do to Hila?" Rahim said despondently. "I should call her right away."

CHAPTER ELEVEN

BROUILLECOURT PARISH, LOUISIANA

"LOOKS like you brung the whole family today, Hammer," Dave at the bait shop said with a laugh as Hammer stepped out of the passenger side door of Tyler Roullier's Ford F150 dual cab. "Guess you was pleased with your luck on Wednesday. Didn't I tell you that ol' Bayou Gadreau had some possibilities?"

"That you did, Dave," and we did have us a nice fish fry Wednesday night on account of your recommendations. Dave, this is my old friend, Tyler Roullier from over on Bayou Langlois, and our friend Ash, who's visiting…"

"*Bonjou ma'am*," Dave said cordially, using the Cajun French greeting and stepping out from behind his counter to offer his hand to Ashley.

"And who have we here?" Dave said as young Liam approached him cautiously.

"That's Liam," Ashley said.

"*Bonjou*, young fella," Dave said. "My name is Cecil, but folks call me Dave."

Being especially precocious for six, Liam smiled and took Dave's hand, while two-year-younger Ava held back, clinging to her mother.

"The kids have been anxious to do some fishing, so I figured I'd bring 'em down here," Hammer said.

"Well, as you proved on Wednesday, there ain't no better place," Dave said, crouching to speak directly to the kids at their eye level. "Y'all ready to hook some catfish this morning?"

Ashley smiled. She was pleased that the two men had taken an interest in entertaining her kids, and happy with Hammer's choice of the grizzled, but charming gentleman as a purveyor of night crawlers and grasshoppers. She was also warming up, albeit still gradually, to Roullier's taking an interest in her.

The bait shopping and catfish casting tutorial were more or less a repeat of what Dave had told Hammer two days earlier, but this time addressed to the kids, especially Liam, and Ashley who giggled at the description of poppin' and stoppin' and walkin' the dog with a fishing line.

The kids did not notice when a large chocolate-brown pickup drove by, heading out the Bayou Gadreau road toward the Atchafalaya. It was pulling a trailer with an especially large forklift. Hammer and Roullier exchanged glances, thinking of earlier conversations of a potential smuggling operation down on Bayou Gadreau.

"Do your friends with the commercial fishing operation use heavy equipment like that?" Hammer asked Roullier, knowing that the Fortier brothers had the only business of any size out on the bayou.

"Only one way to find out."

Since Hammer had previously caught his catfish near Dex and Beau Fortier's place, he decided he would take his fishing party out there. This way, taking a look at their compound served a double purpose.

However, they had driven for only a mile when they passed the brown pickup heading the other way without its trailer. Again, the two men glanced at one another. Hammer entertained an urge to suggest a U-turn to follow the other vehicle, but he was now more interested in knowing where, along the narrow road, they had dropped the forklift—and they *had* promised the kids a fishing trip.

He did not have long to wait. Around the next bend, they saw it, parked unobtrusively in a turnoff on the side of the road opposite a place where the slowly meandering bayou ran straight.

"I haven't seen a boat dock or a boat ramp anywhere along this road," Roullier said. "I can't see how anybody could bring anything in here and unload it without a lot of trouble. The banks are too steep."

"Dave told me that the oil companies dredged this years ago," Hammer said. "That seems to have screwed up the banks. He tells me that's why nobody much comes out here to go fishing. That's how I ended up out at your friends' place at the end of the road, almost to where the bayou hits the Atchafalaya. Finally found a good spot."

When they did reach the end of the road, the Fortier Brothers compound was a good deal livelier than it had been two days before. Their fishing boat was in, and the fish hold was being unloaded into a medium-sized freezer truck.

"There she is," Roullier said with a smile. "Eighty-five feet of steel trawler with H-frame rigging, McElroy 504 winches, and a six-hundred-twenty-four-horsepower Caterpillar 3412 V-12 diesel."

"I bet you've had your hands on that engine," Hammer observed.

"That we have. We keep her purring."

"You're off the water early," Roullier shouted when the seafood transfer was completed.

"It was a better than expected morning," came the reply. "Whatcha doin' out here, Tyler?"

"Fishing," he replied, holding up a rod. The difference in scale between this and a commercial operation where results are measured in tons was apparent.

The newcomers were invited into the yard as the fish truck departed, and there were introductions all around. Liam, who showed an interest, was invited to take a closer look at the fishing boat as it was being hosed down by Dex and Beau's two deckhands.

Finally, the conversation reached a point where Roullier slipped in a query about the forklift.

"I don't know anything about a forklift," Dex said. "I didn't notice it when we drove in this morning, did you, Beau?"

"Nope. I can't imagine what it's for. There's always talk of developing some of those parcels up there between here and the highway, but nothing ever comes of it. Most of the folks you see on that road are lost. They're looking for someplace else, and they end up on Bayou Gadreau. Who knows?"

"Unloading from a boat in the bayou?" Hammer asked.

"Not many places where you can land a boat on Gadreau," Dex replied. "They wrecked the banks when they dredged all of that. We were lucky down here. There was a fishing operation here going way back before they brought the dredges in. We had to rebuild the dock, but at least there had already been one, so it was a lot easier here than anyplace else."

Ashley found a shady place to watch as the two men took an intense interest in showing her kids how to fish.

Liam took to it as a six-year-old does, but Ava contented herself with throwing pebbles in the water and watching the turtles.

Hammer did not see any alligators, nor did he frighten the kids with a warning, but both he and Roullier "kept their heads on swivels," looking for signs.

Liam still regarded Hammer with a sense of awe, remembering what his mother said about the man being their guardian angel, but he had taken to Tyler Roullier almost as a big brother.

Ashley was pleased and calmed by the serenity of the warm spring day, which made the incident at the interstate rest stop seem like a distant nightmare. Surrounded my Nicole's "extended family," especially three Special Forces vets, she felt more secure than she had since she had first heard from Steve Ambel with what seemed at the time like impossible conspiracy theories. She was finally starting to unwind.

Relaxing in the shade, she even allowed her mind to wander to Nic's offhand suggestion that she consider relocating to Brouillecourt Parish.

As time went on here in Louisiana, and as Ashley began to realize she was starting to "like" Tyler Roullier, the idea of staying became less and less far-fetched. After her mother had passed away, there was little more for Ash in McAlester, Oklahoma than an ex who would never dream of taking his kids fishing.

But everything Ashley saw as she watched Nicole's "extended family" reminded her that the nightmare was not over.

She had only to think about the conversations she and Nic had been having with the men, conversations about smuggling and Wally Gusche's drug deals with the Taliban—and how Wally Gusche had been seen *here* in Brouillecourt Parish, and about the comments Hammer and Tyler had made about the seemingly innocent forklift, and its possible role in the smuggling.

She knew that the men who probably killed Steve, and who would probably have killed her and her precious babies were gone, but the ambiguous evil *something* that had sent them, was still alive.

As secure as she was, she felt trapped. She could leave any time, but the moment she pulled the tarp off her car, now unobtrusively parked in Nicole Kirbye's garage,

she'd be on the road in a bright orange Honda, which the mysterious "they" knew was *her* car.

Could "they" be lurking behind a harmless forklift just a few miles from where she was sitting?

———

Early in the afternoon, as the "extended family" was sharing some sandwiches and fruit that Ashley had bagged up that morning, the Fortiers were locking up to go home. There was another round of shaking of hands, and the commercial fishermen left the hobbyists to their own devices.

An hour later, when the youthful attention spans had waned, and the five-gallon bucket had a respectable catch in it, they called it a day.

Dave was in the process of closing up when they pulled in for a bag of ice.

"How'd ya do?" he queried as Hammer rolled off a few bills for a bag of ice.

"We got enough for a good dinner for this bunch and the rest of the family. How was your day?"

"Pretty slow. A few cars drove by after you left, and then the fish truck from Fortier's. Only a couple guys stopped and they only wanted fishing licenses. Sold 'em a few lures though."

"Do you get many trucks or trucks with trailers out here, aside from the fish truck?" Hammer asked, recalling that Dave had been distracted when the pickup with the forklift trailer had passed.

"Nope. Pickups maybe, but nothing like that. As you've seen, there's nothing out there on Gadreau to cause a truck to wanna go out there. Unless the driver's lost."

———

FEHRY COUNTY, ARKANSAS

Friday was winding down at Herste Hardware and Rahim, known to all in his present life as Ray, was ringing up a customer with a few pressure-treated two-by-sixes and a box of self-tapping deck screws.

"Porch repair," she said with a resigned smile. "That's going to be my Saturday fun."

"Think how glad you'll be to have it checked off your to-do list," he said cheerfully.

She smiled broadly. He had a way with customers that kept them coming back, and the Herste family appreciated this man whom Brian had smuggled out of Afghanistan, and who has reinvented himself as an archetype of good, knowledgeable customer service.

Seeing no more customers, he nodded to the high school kid who worked part time at the store to grab the push broom. With only a couple of minutes to closing time, he had just started running the end-of-day report in preparation for closing out the till when Abed Qalandar walked in.

"*Alhamdulillah*, Rahim," Qalandar said with a smile.

"Hello Abed," he replied, deciding to stick to English. "What can I do for you?"

"You can tell me that you have thought about my suggestion that you come and help out your old brother from Afghanistan."

"I have thought about it, but I never thought of us as brothers."

"I'm sorry that you feel that way, but I am happy that you have thought about my offer."

"I thought about it, but I decided that I'm not interested. I have my hands full with the job I have."

"It seems to me that your job gives you weekends off," Qalandar said, ignoring what Rahim had told him. "Strange American idea, these weekends. Don't you agree?"

"You've been watching me."

"Like a brother watches a brother."

"Like I said, I'm *not* your brother."

"You have the next two days off, am I wrong?"

"No, you are not wrong. I am not working here at the store for the next two days. Okay?"

"Good. You can come with me to help with a rug delivery. I need another Afghan face to make a good showing when I pick up a delivery of rugs for my customers. You need do nothing more than accompany me."

"Could you find *no one* else in the Fehry County Afghan community to be your minion?" Rahim said bitterly.

"I know many Afghans in Fehryville," Qalandar said confidently. "But nobody who I also knew in Afghanistan. I know you to be a diligent man who will be useful."

"I said no."

"I am not asking you to do this for free."

With this, he took a roll of banknotes from his pocket. Rahim could see that most were lightly circulated hundred-dollar bills. He peeled off a generous number of these and laid them on the counter.

"I'll have more work for you in the future," Qalandar said.

By now, the high school boy had finished sweeping and was looking at Rahim for what to do next.

"That's great, Jason. It looks good. You can go ahead and clock out. I'm almost finished here. I'll lock up. Have a good weekend. See you Monday."

Qalandar smiled at the kid and he smiled at both of the men before going to put the broom away. and gather up his jacket and the paper bag which had earlier contained his lunch. Rahim was sure he had not seen the currency on the counter. He hoped not.

"Strange American idea, these weekends," Qalandar repeated, still smiling as Jason went out the front door.

"I don't want to do this," Rahim insisted.

"How is your *sister*?"

"Leave Hila out of this."

Rahim was starting to get nervous.

"I see she has abandoned Afghan customs entirely," Qalandar said, continuing to ignore what Rahim was saying. "No headscarf, immodest clothing, teaching *male* students in a high school."

"She teaches math. Is math subversive to Islamic law?"

"I'm not the *Qur'anic* police," Qalandar said with a smile. "I'm just making conversation. She can do as she wishes. This is America, where everybody does as they wish. It's the land of opportunity. Maybe I will give *Hila* the opportunity that you want to reject?"

"Leave Hila out of this," Rahim repeated.

"Maybe I should have made this offer to her in the first place? I want to see her continue to prosper. I'll keep an eye on her to make sure. I would hate for her to have any trouble in her new immodest American life."

"Okay, what do you want me to do?" Rahim asked in desperation. "Just leave her alone."

Whatever happened to him, Rahim wanted Hila as far from Qalandar as possible, and he was willing to capitulate rather than risk her being hurt by this man.

"That's the best news I've heard all day," Qalandar said, chuckling. "Pack an overnight bag. I'll pick you up at your apartment complex at five o'clock tomorrow morning. We have a long drive."

"Where are we going?"

"You'll see tomorrow. Sleep well. It will be a long drive and we will be busy," Qalandar said, adding two more bills to what he's earlier placed on the counter and pushing the pile toward Rahim.

CHAPTER
TWELVE

PLAQUEMINES PARISH, LOUISIANA

RAHIM FAIZULLAH HAD NEVER BEEN to New Orleans before. He had always been a little curious, but only because everyone who had been there seemed to have stories about the place.

Seeing the highway signs along Interstate 55 as he headed south in Abed Qalandar's black BMW 7-Series, came as a revelation for someone who had started the day with no idea which direction of the compass they would be following. Qalandar remained tight-lipped about their destination. Rahim was in the dark until he started seeing names he recognized on the highway signs. Qalandar had said almost nothing for the first four hours of their strange road trip. He just chain-smoked Marlboros and stared irritably at the road.

Rahim had agreed to this trip only because Qalandar had mentioned Hila, and he wanted to keep this man away from his sister. He had discussed the trip with her and had given her the nine hundred dollars. She begged him not to go, but he explained why, and she told him not to let Qalandar make him do anything illegal, and to watch his back.

As it was, Qalandar did not take his cell phone, but insisted he turn it off and put it in the glove compartment. It was not one of those with a "find my device" function that worked while it was turned off.

"You didn't tell me that we were going to New Orleans," he said sarcastically as the signs and billboards were now cropping up everywhere, and intending the irony becaue Qalandar had said almost nothing all day.

Qalandar had picked him up early Saturday morning as promised. Rahim glimpsed that he was armed, with a pistol that looked like a SIG P224 in a shoulder holster under his jacket, but Rahim figured if Qalandar wanted him dead, he would have killed him already, and he wouldn't have given him all that cash.

"We're not going to New Orleans," the middle-aged Afghan replied after a long pause, as they turned onto Interstate 10 and were greeted with signs listing the New Orleans exits.

"Okay…" Rahim said.

Rahim had a lot of unanswered questions beyond where they were going. These started with how a man with a shady past and no apparent real job could afford a BMW and was casually throwing around hundred-dollar bills.

The big question that had hung over the whole drive, though, was not so much where they were going but "what in the world are we going to do when we get there?" All Qalandar had told him was that he was supposed to be an "Afghan face." He had one of those, and so did Qalandar. What he couldn't figure out was why Qalandar needed *two* of them.

For around fifteen minutes, they picked their way through the snarl of highways that pass through the Big

Easy. About an hour later, where they were fifty miles south, pulling off Route 23 into the parking lot of an unremarkable diner called "Evonne's" in Port Sulphur, Louisiana, a town with more past than future. Once important in the sulfur industry, it lay on the main ship channel of the Mississippi River as it rolled its last couple dozen miles down toward the Gulf.

"Lunch," Qalandar said.

Rahim glanced at the clock on the car's digital display. It was nearly one thirty.

As he stepped out of the BMW, he tossed his sunglasses on the dashboard and looked around. It was warm and humid but overcast.

The town, and indeed all of the towns they had passed through since they got on the Route 23, had a feel of impermanence and uncertainty. Many homes and businesses, including the diner, were housed in aging double-wide mobile homes, the residual result of the devastation wrought all those years ago by Hurricane Katrina and the shuttering of the old Freeport Sulphur Company. The transitory had become permanent by default.

The phrase "Afghan faces" came into his mind as Rahim's eyes followed the two men in the big bar mirror behind the counter. Arguably, they could just as easily have been taken for crewmen of any of many ethnicities from aboard any of the line of ships that were plying the busy river across the highway from the diner.

Nothing about their appearance really *screamed* "Afghan." There were no turbans, no kaftans. Qalandar wore a white shirt and dark trousers that made him look more like a Bible salesman than a mujahidin, while Rahim dressed like an off-duty hardware store clerk. Qalandar wore a beard but it was trimmed, while Rahim, who had not shaved that morning looked no more "Afghan" than half the men in the diner.

"What's next?" Rahim asked after they had taken a table near the corner of the room and the waitress had served their iced tea. "It's not hard to figure out where we are now, and to know that this road is going to end soon."

"We're meeting some people," Qalandar said impatiently, looking at his wristwatch. It was a flashy knockoff of a name-brand watch, the kind that a small-time hustler might wear to show off his importance. Rahim had long since figured this to be part of Qalandar's American persona.

"People...rug buyers...or rug sellers?" Rahim asked. Though he was five hundred miles from home and literally at the mercy of a man he did not really trust, he was feeling assertive.

"The people who will land the cargo from the ship."

"Middlemen, then."

Qalandar just glowered.

They were most of the way through their sandwiches and the waitress was refilling their tea when a silver, late-model Chevy Malibu pulled up outside.

As Rahim glanced at the two men getting out of the car, he recognized the one with the narrow goatee and the round tortoise-shell-framed glasses.

Despite the damp, warm humidity of the Mississippi River Delta country, he felt the chill of that mountain in Kandahar Province so long ago, when he watched this man, this two-faced American bureaucrat, as he emerged from his meeting with Akhtar Mohammad Dadullah. In Rahim's mind, this man was the personification of corruption.

———

As Wallace Gusche closed the door of the Malibu, he smiled at Brent Lynse, asking simply, "Brent, are you ready to meet the Taliban?"

Alexis had not explicitly used that word, but it was not hard for Gusche and Lynse to deduce who her "suppliers" were.

"Let's do this," Lynse replied confidently as they made their way toward the ramp leading into the diner.

"Mr. Qalandar, it's good to see you found your way to Evonne's okay," Gusche said as he and Brent Lynse walked over to the corner table, correctly picking the "Afghans" in the room. "Who's your friend?"

"This is Rahim Faizullah, an old friend who lives now in Fehryville."

Rahim bristled at being called Qalandar's "friend," but was glad he had not persisted in calling him a "brother."

"Hello, Mr. Faizullah," the man with the goatee said, rising to shake Rahim's hand. "I'm Wallace Gusche, and this is my colleague, Brent Lynse."

Rahim didn't mention having seen Gusche before—on that mountain in Kandahar.

The introductions completed, the newcomers joined the Afghans at the table, and Lynse ordered a sweet tea. Gusche always ordered coffee.

"We met your customers on Wednesday," he told Qalandar. "We don't normally meet with customers of customers, but you requested it, and we want to be transparent. They're a nervous bunch, but I think we assured them."

"Of course. It is the first shipment, but there will be more. The second shipment is only two weeks out, and there will be more later."

"I understand," Gusche said. "We are ready to help. As we did in Afghanistan when the Talib...er...when *your people* needed someone to facilitate transfer without American or coalition interference."

"Yes," Qalandar said thoughtfully. "You did provide good service back then, and I'm sure you will now."

"Thank you for your vote of confidence," Gusche said, knowing by Qalandar's tone of voice that there was an "or else" implied, but Gusche wasn't concerned.

Qalandar nodded. They understood one another. Sensing this understanding, Rahim was on edge, though he maintained an impassive expression. *What had he gotten himself into?*

"But we do need to have the ship's name and an exact time of transit through Arbeville," Gusche said, changing the subject and referring to another town farther downstream toward the Gulf.

"The ship is *Shuaybah Star*, Kuwaiti-flagged and sailing from Hamad Port south of Doha," Qalandar said with precision and detail that surprised Rahim. "Their final destination is the Port of New Orleans. For obvious security reasons, I could not give you this information except face-to-face. I do not trust emails and cell phones which may not be properly encrypted."

"Of course," Gusche replied.

"I spoke with the captain by satellite phone yesterday. He plans to enter the Mississippi by way of Southwest Pass, the main shipping channel, at dawn tomorrow and will be ready to change river pilots at Arbeville. I have the sat-phone in the car and will speak to him again this afternoon. I will be in contact with him, and then you, as he enters South Pass, thirty kilometers from Arbeville. You'll have your exact time."

"Very good," Gusche said, pleased with Qalandar's apparent control of the situation. He remembered him in Afghanistan. Like most Taliban fighters, he had a mean, even savage, streak, but he also had a measure of self-control and a cool efficiency that made it possible for him to infiltrate the American bureaucracy.

His competence in handling complicated transactions had made a lot of money for the crooked NGO that ran opium out of Afghanistan, and for Wallace Gusche, and for himself. He was now operating on an even higher level.

"As I recall, this shipment will be just two twenty-foot containers?" Gusche said.

"Yes," Qalandar said. "We are packing everything into smaller twenty-foot containers for ease of shipment from the source. I assume that works for you to unload?"

"Perfect," Gusche agreed. "Sundays are also perfect for us...for avoiding the red tape. All of the small ports are on skeleton staffing on Sundays. US Customs never has the sharpest tacks in their drawer on the job on Sundays, especially in places like Arbeville, which isn't even really a seaport."

"That's also why we asked for you to get your containers loaded last," Lynse interjected. "Last on, first off. In and out in less than fifteen minutes. Customs only gets involved if the cargo actually comes *ashore*."

———

Rahim Faizullah felt in over his head in a strange world he had never imagined. Just twenty-four hours ago, he had been Ray. He had been in Arkansas selling lumber and deck screws and living a solid, normal American life. Today, he was in the Mississippi River Delta surrounded by people talking about eluding US Customs with containers loaded in the Persian Gulf.

The good news, if you could call it that, was Abed Qalandar had neither harmed him, nor lied to him. He had been asked on this weird expedition simply to be an

"Afghan face," and so far, that is all that had been asked of him. The conversation had been calm and transactional —just three men discussing a shipment of merchandise, with a fourth who contributed only his presence.

The bad news was not that which was transpiring, but the uncertainty about what would take place *next*. The fact that the man named Gusche was involved meant that whatever was happening next was certainly illegal. Nobody had mentioned the type of merchandise. Nobody had used the word "rugs."

"This seems like a lot of trouble to import *rugs*," he said as he and Qalandar drove south, following the silver Malibu toward Arbeville. He knew that Gusche had been involved in the opium trade, so he used the word "rugs" sarcastically.

"Importing goods into this country is always compli-cated," Qalandar muttered. "Do you think that all those cheap nails and screws that you sell at your hardware store reach this country with no red tape? No, they don't. That's another strange American saying. Have you ever seen such tape? Is it really red? Why do they say this?"

"It's just a strange American saying," Rahim said with resignation, thinking how peculiar it was to be having an almost normal conversation with Abed Qalandar.

Indeed, there was nothing sinister about their drive. That morning, as they left Arkansas driving south, Qalandar had said "nobody can know where we are," but he had made no attempt to hide their location from Rahim. Ever since they passed through New Orleans, it was obvious that they were following the Mississippi River on a broad, open highway. They could look up at the tankers, large container ships, and even occasional cruise ships that were less than a city block away, slowly making their way up and down the river.

Rahim had just seen a green sign announcing their

arrival in Arbeville when Gusche's Malibu pulled off the road into a broad, nearly empty, gravel parking lot. Qalandar followed.

"This is where the two of you need to be tomorrow when the *Shuaybah Star* is in the channel right here," Gusche told the two Afghans. "The guy at the other end of that satellite phone needs to see your faces and your friendly waves and be able to see you with his binoculars while you talk to him. You can wait up across the road out of sight and watch him approach. He'll be coming slow."

"Okay," Qalandar said thoughtfully.

"See that ship?" Gusche said, pointing to a large container ship that was stopping in the river channel. "It is where the *Shuaybah Star* will be tomorrow at whatever time they tell you."

"Now, see that small boat," Lynse interjected. "The white one with the red letters on the side that say 'Pilot'?"

The white boat came alongside the huge ship and a man grabbed a rope ladder connected to a gangway on the side of the ship. He scrambled up the ladder and onto the gangway like a circus acrobat. Then a second man descended by the same route and stepped into the white pilot boat, which was three hundred feet from the ship and headed for shore almost instantly.

"One pilot brings the ship in from the sea buoy outside the channel, across the bar from the Gulf," Gusche explained. "Another takes the controls to run the ship upriver to New Orleans through the constantly changing sandbars and who-knows-what-else that make river navigation tricky. These guys know the river like the backs of their hands...they damned well better."

"How long did that take before the big ship was underway again?" Lynse asked when the larger vessel had resumed its northerly movement.

"Five minutes or so," Rahim said, fascinated with the whole process.

"That's why your containers had to be loaded last," Gusche said. "Seconds count."

"I didn't see any containers being moved," Rahim said.

"There's two sides to every ship." Gusche chuckled. "That's part of the reason you hired us."

"Neither did they," Lynse said, pointing to a small building at the edge of the parking lot with a US Customs logo on the sign out front. "If you don't expect it, you don't see it."

"How…?" Rahim started to say.

"It's like a conjurer's sleight of hand," Gusche said. "You never ask how. You just enjoy the results."

CHAPTER
THIRTEEN

BROUILLECOURT PARISH, LOUISIANA

"*SALUT, M'CHER AMI-OH*," Brouillecourt Parish Sheriff Russ Therriot shouted in a jovial tone as he rolled down the window of his big white Chevy Explorer.

"Hello Russell," Nicole Kirbye replied cheerfully. "How's everything?"

It was Saturday afternoon and she was just leaving her office after catching up on a few things. With Ashley and the kids as house guests, and with the big fish fry yesterday afternoon, Nicole had fallen behind on a few things.

"I just wanted to thank you again for findin' me those deductions on my taxes," the sheriff said. "Not that I want to slight the gov'ment what it's due, but I just rather have that eleven hundred bucks in my own checking account."

"That's what I do," she said. "It's always my pleasure to have my clients get happy surprises. What you up to?"

"Oh, just followin' up on a thing out at Bayou Gadreau. Some busybody reported a lotta trucks comin' and goin' out there. Somebody parked a big trailer that's almost blockin' the road."

"Best look into it, then," Nicole smiled.

Before the big vehicle with "Sheriff" written on the side had rounded the bend on Main Street, she was hitting the button on her phone that was marked "Johnny from Langlois."

Earlier in what had evolved into one of those situations which used to be called a "courtship," Johnny Arnaud had once identified himself on the phone as "Johnny from Langlois Motors." She found this to be endearingly "cute," and it had therefore become her pet name for him.

"Hey Nic," he said. "Am I still gonna see you later?"

They had planned to get together that evening, just the two of them. With all the out-of-towners, from Ashley to Hammer, in their social circle, the past four days had been like a nonstop party, and they decided to grab some alone time.

"Absolutely," she said. "I was just leaving work… going home to change…when Sheriff Therriot rolled by."

"What's up?"

"He said he got a report about a lot of activity out on Bayou Gadreau. Somebody reported a big trailer 'almost' blocking the road. After Hammer and Tyler saw that forklift out there yesterday, this could mean that something's happening with 'you know what.'"

He knew she meant the smuggling theory that their circle of friends had been batting around for the past week.

"I dunno," he said. "I'm at work right now and Hammer's here. I'll pass it along."

"I hate to jump to conclusions, but you know," she said hesitantly.

"I know," he said reassuringly. "Before you ask,

Ashley and the kids are out here. I've been trying to work, while Tyler is to teaching Liam how to balance a propeller. That boy is really into mechanical stuff."

"I sure hope Ash doesn't feel abandoned," Nicole said, laughing. "He is sure taken with those kids!"

———

"So what do you think *now*?" Johnny Arnaud asked Jim Hammer. "I know you've been pushing against jumping to conclusions, and taking it slow, but the evidence is piling up here. The forklift? Now somebody is parking trailers out there? What more do we need?"

"Need to do what?" Hammer asked. "I'm not inclined to get into a firefight with a drug cartel, and certainly not with the sheriff involved. Even if we won a shootout, and we probably *could*, then what? The cops would get involved, even after we did them and the people of Louisiana a solid favor. I think we all agree that if this is what we've been speculating, it's a lot bigger than a forklift and a couple of trailers on a bayou."

"I know you always say that taking out foot soldiers never leads to the root of any problem and you've got to work your way to the top," Arnaud conceded.

"It worked in Afghanistan and a lot of other places since, although in retrospect I wish we'd clipped Gusche on the same day we did Dadullah and those VHE punks."

"If we'd known then, what we know now…"

"You ask me what I think," Hammer said deliberately after a long pause in the conversation. "I'm thinking it's time for us to move off passive recon and start figuring out what we need to do to *start* working our way to the top."

———

Dave's curiosity had been roused.

For Dave at the bait shop on Bayou Gadreau, it was not so much that inquisitive friend of the Tyler Roullier's from out west. Hammer was an authentic guy who liked to talk fishing. It was not trucks with trailers. Trucks came and went from time to time. It was not even seeing Sheriff Russ Therriot drive by, although it was a rare day when he patrolled the road out toward the Atchafalaya. The lawman didn't seem in much of a rush, so Dave didn't even think twice.

The thing that really made Dave sit up and take notice was those strangers in their nice *clean* car with Mississippi plates who had passed through about a week ago. Seeing them once was one thing, but why would they be coming back through?

Those two men in the "nice *clean* car," the DASP agents from Keesler, had no idea that they had become subjects of Dave's scrutiny. Nor did Len Ivermin and Jorge Sentyl have any particular urgency in their drive out the Bayou Gadreau road today. Saturdays and Sundays were their day-job days off, and they were doing a side job for their day-job boss.

Today's side job involved a long drive, but it was simple and straightforward, and as usual, it paid in cash.

Their government jobs were solid and secure but being around the shipping industry on the Gulf Coast was like living in a *Godfather* movie. There were just so many opportunities for well-paying, low-impact side work—and money talks with an engaging accent. All they had to do was show up, flash their badges, and play the part of the government agents they already were.

Ivermin and Sentyl were both young, adventurous, and frankly a bit bored with their government jobs—and they had no qualms about stepping outside the lines for the right price. All of this attracted the eye of Wallace Gusche, who saw them as ideal foot soldiers in his far-reaching enterprise, the full scale of which they would never really know.

———

Sheriff Russ Therriot drove the same road that afternoon, also with the same absence of urgency. A trailer "almost" blocking a road was not high on his list of concerns, but it was a box that needed to be checked. If he had to work a Saturday when his deputy called in sick, it was a nice drive. It sure beat nabbing red-light runners out by the truck stop. He figured he'd look it over, write a ticket, and radio it in to dispatch.

As he came around the corner and as the thing came into view, Therriot realized that this was not as simple as he had imagined. It's not something that would be parked by some weekend pleasure-boater. It was a heavy-duty, forty-foot trailer with steel-chain tie-downs and an industrial winch.

He lit up his light bar, pulled in behind it, and got out of the car to look it over. It was encroaching on the road, but a car or light truck could get by without difficulty if it slowed down. He knew that a fish truck serviced the Fortier Brothers compound out at the end of the road, but the trailer was parked in a wide place in such a way that even that could get by. Whoever parked it had done so thoughtfully. This was not just some idiot who picked up a cheap trailer at some rent-me-for-the-day place.

The sheriff was in the midst of trying to figure out what traffic code number to put on the ticket he was going to write when a car approached. It was a black, late-model Ford Expedition with enough aerials to make it look official, though it was unmarked and had Mississippi civilian plates. The two well-dressed men in aviator shades who climbed out had "official" written all over them.

"Afternoon, Sheriff," one of them said with a smile as he slipped off his sunglasses. Both of the men were wearing nice shirts and sport coats, but not neckties.

"Nice day for a drive in the country," Therriot replied. "You fella know anything about this trailer?"

"As a matter of fact..."

"I got a complaint earlier about it partially impacting travel on this stretch of road."

"I apologize for that, sheriff," the man said. "Although as I look at it, I'd say that either of our vehicles, which are admittedly larger than most, would have no trouble passing, and the trailer *is* parked mostly in a turnout."

"Mostly."

"Yes, mostly."

"I take it that you or someone you know parked this trailer," the sheriff said. He really wasn't in the mood to get into an argument, and the guy *was* trying to avoid being confrontational.

"Yes."

"Would you mind showing me some ID?" Therriot asked, glancing at each of the men in turn.

"Not at all," Len Ivermin said, carefully reaching into his inside jacket pocket.

Both men produced wallets with identification and badges showing them to be agents of the Department of the Army Special Police.

"Hmmm," Therriot said, stepping in for a closer look. "What interest does DASP have here on Bayou Gadreau?"

"I'm afraid that as much as I'd like to, I cannot tell you that."

"National security?" Therriot asked, hoping to find himself as part of something larger and more important than his usual routine duties.

"Hmmm..." Ivermin said with a look on his face that made the sheriff guess that he had guessed right.

"Your secret's safe with me," Therriot said, indicating that his lips were sealed.

"Let me promise you that we will have all of this cleared out of here in forty-eight hours," Ivermin added. "You have my promise."

"Okay. I'll take you at your word, but if this is still here same time Monday, I'm going to have to write you up."

The last thing he wanted at the midpoint of the weekend was a jurisdictional pissing match with the feds over a trailer "almost" blocking a road. Certainly not when national security might be involved.

———

Hammer waved goodbye to Tyler Roullier as he pulled out of the gravel lot at Bayou Langlois Motors to take Ashley Grahen and the kids back to Nicole Kirbye's house in Fredieuville.

Johnny Arnaud was off on his date night with Nicole and this left Hammer all alone. He thought about driving back over to Arnaud's place, where he had been crashing, but he liked the sunsets from the Bayou Langlois boat dock, so he popped the cap on a beer and sat down in an aluminum lawn chair to enjoy it.

He phoned Lauren Stahling, his old high school best friend, who was now the County Assessor of Logan County,

Montana, and brought her up to speed on what was going on. In the year since the two of them had gotten back together again after twenty years, they had resumed their friendship and had taken their relationship a step further.

In that year, they'd been through a lot together. They had conspired to dramatically take down an international human trafficking operation and had formed that unique bond of each having killed someone to save the life of the other.

Lauren told Hammer that if he'd promise to take her out for a nice dinner in New Orleans, she *might* take time off from her job as the county assessor and come down to see him as soon as he finished the "project" he had now taken on. She was only *half* kidding—or less.

Then she told him to stop "fussing" about the details of his present project—only *she* spoke to him so directly— and to phone Tim Tommis before it got too late on the East Coast.

————

"What's up, man?" Hammer asked.

"Well, I just got off the phone with Brian Herste, remember him? From our team in Afghanistan?" Tim Tommis replied.

"Yeah, I remember him. I haven't seen him in way too long...I've done a terrible job of staying in touch with people. Arnaud and Roullier have each reminded me of that about ten times since I've been down here. How is Herste?"

"He's doing real good. Has a building contracting business in Arkansas. Mostly remodels, but he's got some commercial work that pays top dollar, so he's good. His family still owns that hardware store there in Fehryville. His sister is the big boss there now."

"I remember her, too," Hammer said.

"I *know* you do," Tommis said with a laugh. "But guess who's their top sales clerk...remember Rahim Faizullah?"

"Oh yeah, our translator," Roullier said. "I remember that Brian took him, and his sister, under his wing when we all got back from Afghanistan."

"Also remember that those two never would have made it here without you frightening that state department clown at the air base in Pakistan."

"I was in no mood for a self-important bureaucrat."

"He got the message, and the Faizullahs got on the plane. All's well that ends well, and that ended well for those two."

"So how is she doing...what was her name?"

"Her name is Hila, and she's teaching math at the high school there in Fehryville."

"That's great, but what was it that you wanted to tell me about your call from Herste?"

"I'll keep it short," Tommis said. "Brian phoned me. Abed Qalandar...you may remember him...walked into Herste Hardware the other day and went up to Rahim."

"Oh, that asshole!" Hammer said after a pause. "Remember that time in Uruzgan Province?"

"Yup. Everybody outside the wire thought he was doing deals with the Taliban, but everybody at Bagram thought he was golden."

"I thought he *was* Taliban," Hammer said.

"You were probably right. He had more faces than a Rubik's Cube."

"I also remember he had a reputation as real smooth operator," Hammer continued. "Spoke English very well. I heard the CIA had him in some kind of school, but I never heard that rumor confirmed. What's he doing in Arkansas of all places?"

"He told Rahim that he's working for Americans who're importing rugs from Afghanistan."

"Oh yeah, *right*," Hammer said.

"Whatever he *is* doing, Rahim told Brian that Qalandar offered him a job...actually a 'supplement your income' job...those were Qalandar's words."

"*What*?"

"Brian said he was dumbfounded. He ais he didn't know what to say. Rahim was afraid Qalandar was going to hurt him, or kill him if he refused."

"After all of what he went through over there, and now this crap over here after all these years," Hammer said furiously. "What happened? What did he do?"

"Hila called Brian this morning in a panic. Rahim came over to her place last night and gave her nine hundred bucks in cash that Qalandar gave him as an advance on a trip they were going to take over this week-end, starting this morning. Rahim was afraid something might happen to Hila if he didn't go along with it."

"Where is he now?"

"Off the grid. She's been trying to phone him all day. So has Brian. Finally, Brian called me to see if I could figure out how to track his phone, but it's one of those old ones that can't be tracked if it's turned off, or lying at the bottom of an irrigation ditch."

"*Oh shit*," Hammer snarled. "What can we do?"

"Hope and pray...and mostly wait. As I told Brian, if Qalandar took him, it was because he needed him for something. As long as he stays useful, he'll stay safe. He's a clever guy. I think he knows what to do."

"What about that other thing you were tracking for me?"

"Not much to report. The two bodies in the DeSoto Parish morgue are still listed as John Doe and John Doe. Without a missing person report, running fingerprints on them goes to the end of the line. The car was found in Colbert County, Alabama, but again, there was no stolen car complaint on file in Mississippi, where the plates are from, so it's sitting in impound with nobody to claim it."

"That's all good to know," Hammer said, looking at a cell phone he had been carrying since the rest stop. "John Doe or his brother John to drop a little text message to their handlers with the 228 area code number in Biloxi to tell them that they're still chasing the orange Honda."

"Pretty persistent for dead guys." Tommis laughed. "That 228 number is a burner phone, but I have a feeling that Gusche is involved somehow."

"What have you heard about Wally Gusche lately?" Hammer asked.

"I've been keeping an eye on SIFO," Tommis said. "There's nothing that I've seen to show that he's smuggling opium into Brouillecourt Parish. There was a huge buy the other day of detergent for laundromats, but it's going direct from the legit manufacturer to Army bases. It bypasses the Keesler warehouse system, so it's unlikely that Gusche isn't stepping on it. Do you have anything new on your end?"

"A forklift and a large trailer have been seen parked out on Gadreau Bayou this week, which feeds into the theory about smuggling, but the only boat dock out there is behind a fence and owned by friends of Arnaud and Roullier, but I've been keeping an eye on it."

"Can you get plate numbers on these?"

"No plates on the forklift or its trailer, and I only just found out about the other trailer. I'm going to go take a look, but in the meantime, the sheriff got a complaint about it blocking the road and he's out there now. I'd rather not trip over him."

"Understood. Wonder what he found. Do you know anybody who knows the sheriff?"

"Nicole does," Hammer said. "He told her about the trailer, and I found out from her."

"That's a real small-town vibe you've got goin' for yourself down there in Cajun country," Tommis said with a laugh.

"*Laissez les bon temps rouler*," Hammer replied. "I hope they're rolling that way for Rahim. Fingers crossed, I guess."

BROUILLECOURT PARISH, LOUISIANA

DATE NIGHT at the Quarter Moon Bar & Grill in downtown, small town, Fredieuville was intended as two people on the cusp of something more real than just casually getting away from the *other* matters of the week.

However, their rendezvous had been crashed by a third party, the elephant in the room. They had avoided it during the pizza, but from the moment that Nicole Kirbye had slipped and said, "I know I shouldn't, but I can't stop worrying." The elephant was in control of the narrative. An evening that had once promised, or at least *suggested*, lips meeting in the moonlight, was now off the table.

The elephant was not the only party-crasher at the Quarter Moon. Sherriff Russ Therriot's abrupt arrival in the room pleased only the wily elephant.

"Good evening, Russell," Nicole said when Therriot tipped his Stetson at her.

"*Salut*, Miss Kirbye...Mr. Arnaud," he replied with a smile.

"Two beer limit," Johnny Arnaud said, tapping his glass and smiling.

"Don't you worry, son, I'm off duty," he replied affably.

"How did things go with your trailer, Sheriff?" Nicole asked.

"Well, we *did* have words," he replied. "I gave 'em forty-eight hours to get theirselves gone from out there."

"So you actually talked to the people with the trailer, then?" Nicole asked.

The sheriff took this as meaning that they were now having a conversation, rather than merely exchanging niceties, so he pulled up a chair and sat down.

"Between you and me, and this is not to leave *this* table," Therriot said, glancing around the room and seeing no one the least bit interested in eavesdropping. "Between you and me, it's the feds."

"*Feds*?" Arnaud asked. "What feds?"

"Army."

"*Army*?"

"Actually, it was civilian cops. Department of the Army civilian cops. Or so said their IDs. Ever heard of an outfit called DASP?"

"Of course," Nicole said. "I was a civilian employee of the Army. Johnny was *in* the Army."

She did not mention that Dex and Beau Fortier had run into the DASP on Bayou Gadreau a week ago Friday, but this fact was not lost on Arnaud.

"What are they doing out there?" he asked.

"It's all very hush-hush," Therriot said in a whisper. "They didn't want to talk about it. I woulda played the 'cop-to-cop' professional courtesy card, but I figured they'd say they'd have to kill me if they told me."

He had meant it as a joke and was startled when neither of them smiled. He let it pass.

"You put your foot down and gave them forty-eight hours, though," Nicole said.

"Well, we can't have part of the road blocked for too long, but I cut 'em some slack. They *are* protecting our country."

––––––––

Jim Hammer got an early start Sunday morning, despite being up late trading conspiracy theories with Johnny Arnaud. When he got home Saturday night, he had told Hammer about what the sheriff said about DASP, and Hammer had briefed him on what Tim Tommis had heard about Rahim Faizullah and Abed Qalandar.

The conversation had gone round and round about whether the two situations were connected, because nobody knew where Faizullah had gone with Qalandar. As for DASP, Hammer and Arnaud did not know *what* they were doing, but they did *where* they were doing it.

Hammer took his borrowed fishing rod, planning to cover his Bayou Gadreau recon patrol in the guise of gathering the raw materials for a Sunday afternoon fish fry. He fully expected to see his friend Dave manning the bait stand. After all, he always seemed to be there. Instead, as he saw as he pulled up in his blue Chevy pickup, he saw it was staffed by an attractive, early twenties black girl in a vermillion tank top with her hair pulled back into a bun. She was talking with three young men who seemed to be customers.

It wasn't until he got within earshot that Hammer realized that their conversation was not cordial. The young woman was being accused of having said or done something untoward to an acquaintance of the trio, and their choice of words was exceptionally earthy.

She was insisting it had been a misunderstanding,

and her own choice of words was also drawn from a rude vocabulary.

Not wanting to insert himself in an argument that was none of his concern, Hammer chose to divert his attention to a bass boat that was up on blocks with a "for sale" sign attached. Buying a boat was far from his roster of interests, but looking it over gave him something to do until the heated conversation cooled, and the threesome got back in their truck to move on.

However, the heated conversation did not cool, and when one of the men grabbed at the girl in a threatening manner, causing her to jump back with an expression of alarm, Hammer started walking toward the counter. When the guy grabbed her tank top, causing her to scream, Hammer hastened his step.

He said nothing as he approached. A man of his overall stature made a statement by his mere presence, and he knew it. His expression conveyed his unmistakable displeasure at seeing a petite woman being harassed by three much larger men. One of them spoke first.

"This ain't none of your business!"

"Shouting is one thing," Hammer said. "And I was hearing that without interrupting, but when somebody starts grabbing at somebody smaller, that kinda gets my attention."

"Like he said," interjected the larger of the three men. "This is between us and her and it's none of your affair."

"Maybe you could sort it out with words," Hammer said. "No offense but seeing somebody small being grabbed by a bigger person kind of rubs me the wrong way."

"Well, maybe you had better get back in that truck of yours and move along if you're so offended. As you may have noticed, there's three of us and one of you. I'd hate

to have to grab you and have to teach you the hard way
to mind your own business."

"I'd hate to see that too," Hammer said, sensing what
the big guy was about to do.

He threw a right jab directly at Hammer's chin,
assuming that Hammer, whose hands were down, would
not have time to raise them to block the punch.

Having grossly miscalculated the reaction time of his
chosen opponent, the man was unprepared for Hammer
to not only stop the punch, but to seize the wrist of the
fist delivering it.

It is axiomatic that when you're outnumbered in a fist-
fight, you should concentrate on the largest of your
adversaries, betting on the odds that the others will
hesitate.

In this case, the largest of the three had already done
the choosing.

Hammer struck the man, not as hard as he could
have, but hard enough to send him sprawling. The other
two held back, befuddled expressions on their faces.

When they moved in to help their fallen comrade to
his feet, he swatted them away with a torrent of expletives. All could see by the way he carried his right wrist
that he was experiencing considerable pain.

Without any further dialogue, they climbed back into
their pickup. The big guy, who apparently owned the
vehicle, gestured for one of the others to take the wheel.

When they had disappeared at high speed around the
first turn in the road back up toward the main highway,
Hammer turned to the young woman behind the counter.

"I'll be needing some night crawlers," he said calmly.
"That's what Dave recommends for catfish in these
waters, and they seem to work."

"You might try some grasshoppers," she suggested. "I
caught some fresh this morning."

"Some of them too," Hammer said. "Guess Dave's off today."

"It's Sunday. Uncle Dave's at church. I don't much care for it, even though I was raised to it, but Uncle Dave says if finds him peace."

"You weren't getting much peace from those guys who were just here."

"Theys a bunch of idiots...that's what they are...no better."

"I hope they leave you alone."

"You rattled 'em. They're not used to bein' rattled. They're spineless."

"Good."

"Thank you, by the way. You didn't have to do that."

"No problem. My name's Hammer," he said, extending his hand.

"Chantelle," she said with a smile.

"Hope they don't bother you anymore."

"Like I said, they're chickenshit."

As Hammer took his purchases and proceeded to drive up the road, it was not hard to miss the DASP cops. They were parked near the forty-foot and looking bored, like cops on a stakeout anywhere.

He decided to allow himself to be seen, and to establish his blue pickup as a non-threatening presence on the bayou. The sheriff had reported that the trailer would have completed its purpose within forty-eight hours. Hammer really did not expect any action in the first twelve or so of these, but he intended to keep checking back, and he wanted to be a familiar presence, seen but not noticed.

He parked at considerable distance from them, near enough to be seen, but not so close that he would be expected to wave in greeting. He purposely ignored them as he took out the fishing rod, baited the hook and proceeded to cast. The steep embankment was not ideal for the purpose, but he went through the motions.

Much to his surprise, he felt a tug on his fifth cast and found himself landing a respectable fish of at least twenty-four inches. He was sure that the cops saw him, possibly with some measure of jealousy, but he deliberately did not look.

As he fished, he thought about the trailer. He thought about the supposed smuggling, the difficulty in landing a boat here, and about the amount of opium that would require a forty-foot trailer.

He also thought about Rahim Faizullah and felt it as his responsibility to rescue him. He cursed his helplessness in not even knowing where to start, and he cursed the fact he was already up to his elbows in another operation six hundred miles from Arkansas, where Rahim had gone missing.

A part of him hoped that Abed Qalandar's devious scheme might somehow be tied into that of Wally Gusche, so that two birds—or in this case, two repulsive malefactors—might be brought down with a single stone, but that was too much to hope for. Wasn't it?

After nearly an hour, Hammer had managed to put a half dozen pretty-good-size cats into his white plastic five-gallon bucket, and he decided to call it a day. He loaded his gear back into the camper shell on his pickup. He slowly turned the vehicle around and disappeared from the sight of the DASP men.

He noticed a pair of fishermen working the bayou on the way back and decided to stop at the bait shop to say hello to get some ice and to say hello to Chantelle.

"Uncle Dave said to tell you thanks from him," she said. "He likes that you was takin' care of me."

"Least I could do," Hammer said. "How's your day. I saw a couple of folks on the bayou already. Watched one of 'em hook one as I drove by. Fishin' is pretty good. Got a few myself."

"Looks like it'll be a good day."

"You ever go out yourself?"

"Nah. Not since I was a kid."

"Well you take care, Chantelle," he said as he climbed into his truck.

"You too, Mister Hammer."

ARBEVILLE, LOUISIANA

Rahim Faizullah woke with a start with Abed Qalandar's cigarette smoke in his nostrils and he realized where he was. He had just spent a less-than-comfortable night sprawled on a sofa in a single-wide in Arbeville, Louisiana. Seated at a table and staring out the window was a man he had now decided was a drug smuggler only half a step, if that, from the Taliban fighters and warlords who were the once and present rulers of the Afghanistan opium industry.

Sunrise was still at least an hour away when they reached the vast gravel parking lot near the Mississippi River to await the arrival of the *Shuaybah Star*, sailing from Hamad Port, south of Doha, to New Orleans.

Brent Lynse and Wallace Gusche were at their silver Chevy Malibu, about eighty feet away. Gusche was talking to someone on his cell phone and making gestures as he stared at the river. Rahim couldn't hear what was being said, but it seemed important.

It was growing light as they first saw the ship inching its way up the Mississippi from the south. There was minimal traffic on the river. A single fishing boat headed south and there were motor barges moving about on the far side of the river.

Qalandar just stood and stared at the approaching ship, occasionally talking to someone aboard through his satellite phone.

Rahim heard him quote the line from the *Quran* that said, "We will show them our signs in the horizons and within themselves until it becomes clear to them it is the truth."

Rahim didn't hear the reply, but he saw that Qalandar was pleased.

"Now, come with me," Qalandar said suddenly, grabbing Rahim by the sleeve. "Stand here and look up at that place on the bridge at the place where there you can see the blue light."

Rahim did as he was told, and Qalandar took up a place about eight feet away. By "bridge," Rahim figured that Qalandar meant the part of the ship that looked like a flat-topped building. He had heard the term before, but that part of the ship did not look like a "bridge." Whatever.

Is this it? Rahim asked himself. *Is this the part where I am paid nine hundred dollars to stand here and look like an "Afghan." What does an "Afghan" look like. I guess it's me without shaving for two days.*

Rahim could see a man near the blue light looking at them with binoculars as Qalandar spoke on the satellite phone in Pashto.

"*Alhamdulillah,*" he said as he insisted that the man look at them and see them.

Out of the corner of his eye, Rahim could see Gusche and Lynse moving around in an animated manner, practically jumping up and down. He had no idea what was going on, but guessed it was something to do with the pilot boat approaching the huge vessel.

Suddenly, there was a great grinding sound, the ship slowed to a stop and the pilot went through the same trapeze act as Rahim had seen on Saturday. One man up, one man down, the pilot boat moving quickly away and the ship slowly starting to move again. The man with the binoculars, who had not taken his eyes off the two "Afghans," finally looked away and disappeared to the inner reaches of this thing they called a "bridge," that looked more like an office building.

With one last "*Alhamdulillah*," Qalandar lowered his binoculars and the satellite phone. He had a satisfied look on his face as he lit a cigarette. Across the parking lot, Gusche and Lynse had calmed down. They all watched in silence as the *Shuaybah Star* chugged upriver toward New Orleans, now under the control of the river pilot.

As the ship moved out of the way, Rahim saw a motor barge puttering downstream toward the Gulf. It was so far from seeming out of place he paid it no attention. Aside from that, all was quiet.

CHAPTER
FIFTEEN

BROUILLECOURT PARISH, LOUISIANA

THE SUNDAY FISH fry in Nicole Kirbye's back yard in Fredieuville might have been cause for fun and laughter, but only Liam and Ava were having fun and laughing. The mood hung heavy with the reappearance of the DASP and their assumed connection to Wally Gusche. The two women had known him before, and had considered him a shifty character then, but the recent revelations about SIFO's role in smuggling then, and the probability of a similar role now, painted him as a serious villain.

The three men had yet to share their brief encounter with him on that snowy hill in Kandahar.

Meanwhile, the two women had never known Rahim Faizullah, but they'd been in Afghanistan and knew what happened to people like him who crossed the Taliban or their sympathizers. They felt the anger and frustration of these three men who could do nothing to aid their friend.

It was around four o'clock, and the sun was still high in the sky when Hammer could stand it no longer.

"I think it's time for me to take a little spin out to my favorite fishing hole," he announced as he stood up from the camp chair in which he had been sulking.

"I can't let you have all that fun to yourself," Johnny Arnaud announced. "I think I'll ride along."

"Me too," Nicole said impulsively. She'd been sitting in a lawn chair next to Arnaud, loosely holding his hand, which she now gripped tighter, refusing to let it go. She was not a woman who was going to let two men go out and satisfy their curiosity and leave her wondering. She decided she wanted to be part of it. "I'm not going to *wait around* to hear what's happening."

"The sheriff said they've got forty-eight hours," Arnaud cautioned. "It's only been about half that amount of time. There might not be much to see."

"That's okay. I could use a drive on the bayou."

Tyler Roullier glanced at the two kids, climbing in a small apple tree, and at Ashley Grahen's startled expression. He smiled at her.

"I reckon I'll hang around here and keep the coals going," he said. "Ash, you ready for another iced tea?"

"I think I'm ready for a *beer*," she said, trying to appear calm.

———

For Hammer and Arnaud, and impulsively for Nicole, it seemed that taking action, any action, lifted a weight from their shoulders, and from the general mood.

The three of them crowded onto the bench seat in the cab of Hammer's old Chevy pickup, with Nicole in the middle, almost on Johnny Arnaud's lap. Neither complained about the crowding.

They passed the bait shop, which Chantelle had closed up for the day, and drove out to the fishing spot that Hammer had used that morning. The DASP men and their Ford Expedition were still there, but they had company. The chocolate-brown pickup that Hammer had passed on the day that the forklift appeared, was back, and an operator was driving the heavy equipment off its small trailer.

As Hammer and Arnaud went through the motions of getting their lines ready to cast, Nicole studied the unfolding activities up the road through Hammer's binoculars.

"Just a bunch of guys unloading a forklift in the middle of nowhere with nothing to lift," she reported sarcastically.

"At least there's *some* activity," Hammer said. "Those poor cops were looking awfully bored this morning."

With plenty to occupy them where they were, they paid no attention to the people fishing a quarter mile away.

It was nearly an hour later when a large, dual-tired pickup rolled in. Its driver went through the usual noisy jerking back and forth that is required to turn a big vehicle end-to-end on a narrow road. He then lined up to attach his truck to the forty-foot trailer.

"Looks like they're in waiting mode again," Nicole reported as Arnaud landed a catfish. He made a show of it, holding the rod up with the squirming fish so that anyone watching from up around the forklift would know that they were definitely fishing, not snooping.

"They don't seem to care about your fish, Johnny," she said. "They're just pacing and looking at their watches."

"While you're at it, see if you can get the plate numbers on the two trucks," Hammer said. "We'll get Tommis to run those later. That'll help in the long run. I already got the one on the expedition."

A short time later, the chugging sound of a large

marine engine could be heard in the distance. The noise grew louder and louder, and finally something could be seen through the trees, coming upstream on the bayou.

"It looks like a boat," Nicole suggested as she squinted through the binoculars.

"It's not a boat," Arnaud said at last. "It's a *barge*."

They watched as it came into view, a huge monster of a thing with two huge metal containers perched on it. The din of its engine quieted as it was throttled back and the barge snuggled against the shore.

"We wondered how they could dock a boat here in this bayou with those steep, dredged banks," Hammer said.

"That would've been hard," Arnaud agreed. "But this is perfect for a barge. The load rides high enough in the water for the forklift to grab it real easy."

Suddenly, the men who had been pacing with monotony were dashing about, hauling lines and anchoring the barge to large cypress trees at either end. The forklift operator was already in motion, nudging up to the barge and preparing to lift the first container.

"Two twenty-foot containers..." Hammer said.

"One forty-foot trailer," Arnaud said, finishing his sentence. "Well planned operation. Fits like a glove. They know what they're doing."

"Prepositioned forklift," Hammer said. "Good planning all around."

"You boys are enjoying this too much," Nicole said mockingly.

"Boys love trucks," Arnaud said with a smile.

"Let's get out of here," Hammer said, reeling in his line. "They're moving fast, and I don't want them seeing us seeing them as they drive out of here."

———

"What happens next?" Nicole asked, glancing over her shoulder as they drove. "Aren't you going to stop them? Can you imagine how much drugs just got imported back there?"

"Doing that would have been satisfying for sure," Hammer said. "But there's a lot of reasons not to."

"Starting with federal cops being mixed up in this," Arnaud said.

"And mainly because we just watched something that asked a whole lot more questions than it answered," Hammer said. "The fact that federal cops *were* there means a lot, but these guys were just moving product. There were no buyers and no suppliers there, just grunts doing a specified job."

"We gotta remember Hammer's proverb," Arnaud said. "Taking out foot soldiers is a tactical solution to a strategic problem. We gotta give up on immediate satisfaction and work our way up the ladder...step by step."

"To where?" Nicole asked.

"We're about to find out," Hammer said as he turned off the road and parked behind the bait shop. "I hope you're ready for a drive. Dave's outhouse is unlocked in case you need it."

"I'll phone Ash and tell her I'm not coming home tonight," Nicole said with resignation.

It was starting to get dark as the two large pickups emerged from the Bayou Gadreau road and turned onto the highway. Hammer pulled out to follow, keeping an eye on the SUV with the DASP men, who had followed the trucks from Bayou Gadreau.

About a half hour later, the two agents, Ivermin and Sentyl, peeled off and turned east on Interstate 10 toward Biloxi. They assumed their job was done.

Hammer moved up, maintaining a respectable distance from the truck pulling the trailer with the containers. Tailing another vehicle is easier at night because all they can see of you is anonymous headlights, but with a trailer, taillights usually have a distinctive configuration so they're easy to distinguish, and easy to follow.

————

FEHRY COUNTY, ARKANSAS

It was late Sunday night when Abed Qalandar stopped in front of the apartment complex where Rahim Faizullah lived. The men had spoken very little on the long drive back from the Mississippi River Delta, but Qalandar now turned to Rahim with some parting words.

"You did very good today," he said, opening the glove compartment so that Rahim could retrieve his cell phone. "I saw that you were scared when we started. I think you feared that I would kidnap you or something. Am I right?"

Rahim shrugged.

"Yet here we are. I am delivering you to your home… alive and unharmed…and doing this with my gratitude. You did very good today."

"I still do not know what it was that I did," he said. "I just sat at a table in a diner and then stood in a parking lot and stared at a man on a 'bridge' for a few minutes. I spent twelve or fourteen hours in a car in order to do nothing for a total of just ten minutes."

"You did what I asked," Qalandar replied. "And that is good. Our associates now know that I am not alone, and that I have trusted Afghan men at my team. In the future, there will be more for you to do. As you have seen, I have not asked you to do this for free."

As he reached to get his cellphone, Qalandar handed

him another wad of money. He held on to it as Rahim touched it and looked at the younger man with his cold dark eyes.

"Remember," he said. "There is a reason why your phone was in there. No one can know where we were or what we did. No one. You are now part of this which you have witnessed. We will be doing this again in two weeks, and more times again in the future. There will be more money, and there will be your *continued silence*. This is important. Tell nobody…not your sister…*nobody*."

He paused as though to let his words sink in.

"You are tempted to call your sister and tell her everything, but you will *not*," Qalandar said calmly. "To burden her with this information is to place her in danger and you *do not* want to do that. I'm sure that you understand what I mean."

CHAPTER
SIXTEEN

RAPIDES PARISH, LOUISIANA

THE TWO HEAVY-DUTY pickups lugging trailers pulled into a sprawling truck stop off Interstate 49 near Alexandria, Louisiana. They were powerful brutes—especially the dually diesel with the heavy-duty frame that was hauling the forty-foot trailer with two twenty-foot shipping containers—but they were also renowned as fuel hogs.

"Sure glad you had enough gas," Nicole Kirbye said, waking up from a hard nap. It was nearly midnight, and she had dozed off with her head nestled into Johnny Arnaud's shoulder.

"I always keep the tank filled," Jim Hammer said as he pulled up to a pump some distance away from the two vehicles that he'd been shadowing for the past three hours. "Besides that, there's no way that I'll run out before they do."

"I'll go get coffee," Nicole said, running her fingers through her mussed-up hair as Arnaud leaped out to begin filling the tank of Hammer's blue Chevy.

They were a couple hundred miles north of Bayou Gadreau, and about a hundred miles south of where Hammer had rescued Ashley Grahen and her kids, but he did not mention this.

In her cutoffs, and with a mustard stain on her Kentucky Wildcats T-shirt, Nicole was not out of place among the clientele of the huge truck stop convenience store, but the other young women patrons were buying Red Bull and cheap wine, not coffee. Nicole added a box of donuts.

"I wonder how much longer," Nicole said as she returned with the purchases. The question was rhetorical. There was no way of knowing this, nor their final destination, until they reached it.

The bigger vehicles had finally finished fueling, and the occupants were taking turns going to the truck stop bathroom. Arnaud suggested that he'd try to eavesdrop and returned with the information that the truckers hoped to be back in Gulfport, Mississippi by Monday night.

"That's all good to know," Hammer said. "It means we aren't going to have to drive all the way to Chicago or Kansas City tonight."

"But that also confirms what you said earlier, that these people are *not* the end customers of whatever is in those boxes," Nicole added.

FEHRY COUNTY, ARKANSAS

Rahim Faizullah was back to work early Monday morning at Herste Hardware, stifling yawns and feeling exhausted. The normalcy of his familiar workplace, after a weekend that could best be described as bizarre, should have been comforting, but it was not.

His sister had been beside herself with worry on Friday when he told her he was going on a trip with Abed Qalandar, but when he had phoned Hila last night to tell her that all was well, she exploded.

Where had he been?

Why didn't he answer his phone when she tried "a thousand times" to reach him?

What did he think he was doing?

Why was he now saying he could answer none of these questions?

Then she cut him off mid-sentence.

A customer wanting to discuss exterior door weather-stripping options provided a welcome diversion. In this case at least, Rahim knew exactly what to say and do. The customer seemed pleased. There were smiles all around.

He had barely finished with this when Brian Herste came into the store.

"Ray, buddy, you're in deep shit with your sister," he said, addressing Rahim by his American name.

"I know," he replied. "She has made this very clear."

"She's only worried about you, man. You ran off with this Qalandar character and she figured that she'd never see you again. She phoned me a dozen times to talk to me about it."

"I'm sorry…"

Seeing that Rahim was tired and jittery, Herste suggested that they take a walk. Asking a coworker to cover for him for a bit, Rahim headed for the stockroom with his friend. When they left by the rear entrance of the hardware store, Rahim stepped cautiously, expecting to see Qalandar's BMW lurking somewhere.

"I didn't know what to do. I was in touch with some of the old team…some of *your* friends. There was even talk of a rescue mission, but nobody knew where the hell you were."

Rahim Faizullah explained his feelings of desperate vulnerability. He feared telling the whole story of Abed Qalandar and the Mississippi Delta drive to his sister, arguing with Herste she was safer if she knew as little as possible.

"I don't know what to say," Rahim said.

"Well a good place to start might be to tell your friends, *and* your sister, what's going on. By the way, where were you?"

"I can't..."

"Yes, you can," Herste said firmly.

―――――

NATCHITOCHES PARISH, LOUISIANA

As he scrutinized every other car in the parking lot behind Herste Hardware, expecting to see Qalandar henchman, Rahim did not know that the author of his fears was a hundred miles away and feeling his own form of pressure, the strain of being stretched too thin.

Rahim did not realize that the crafty mastermind's criminal apparatus was a band of one, and there were no subordinates on the streets of Fehryville to follow or harm Rahim or Hila Faizullah.

Last night, while Rahim was staring at his phone, awash in anguish after Hila had hung up on him, Qalandar was headed south again after a brief, hard nap.

The BMW left the interstate north of Natchitoches, mainly to allow Qalandar to cruise south on the state highway to assess the remote possibility of his being followed. Deciding he was not being tailed, he decided to drive down the main street of this picturesque little town best known for such infidel distractions as its annual Christmas Festival of Lights, and for being the place where they filmed *Steel Magnolias* back in the eighties—neither of which would have interested Qalandar in the least.

A few miles south of town, he made a left on an unmarked gravel road and took it east to the place where there was a large barn backed up against an offshoot of the Cane River. He had picked this place carefully. It was nearly a mile from the nearest house, yet not so remote that comings and goings would attract undue attention. Meanwhile, from the head of the gravel road, it was only about four miles to Interstate 49. Alexis had stipulated this. She wanted easy access for moving her merchandise.

He parked his car discreetly, nose out, on the far side of the barn and opened the big doors. Inside was a forty-foot, tandem-dual interlink flatbed semi trailer of the type used for long-haul trucking.

It was after midnight when Qalandar saw the head-lights of two large vehicles turning off the state highway and coming toward him.

The two unmarked Coome Hauling pickups and their trailers pulled into the large open gravel area in front of the open barn doors and stopped. A heavyset man in a trucker cap climbed out of the cab of the one pulling the containers and walked over to where Qalandar was standing. The men in the other truck were already unloading the huge forklift. It was obvious that they had done this before and knew how to get it done quickly.

"We'll be out of your way inside of a half hour," the man said. "We'll stack 'em with the openings on the ends so your customers can do their inspections. Sound like a plan?"

"Just right," Qalandar said, trying not to appear as eager as he felt.

"Good," the man said with a smile. "While we're waitin' for the forklift, you and I need to do a little paperwork."

With that, he produced a laptop, lit it up and started tapping.

"This here's your invoice for the balance due to us on the unloading, barging and trucking," he said professionally. "Whatever else you owe to Biloxi is between you and them. You can wire your funds to this number that shows right there, and as soon as that goes through, the containers come off our trailer."

CHAPTER
SEVENTEEN

NATCHITOCHES PARISH, LOUISIANA

JIM HAMMER FELT his phone vibrate. If it had been almost anybody other that Tim Tommis, he would have let it go unanswered.

"Hammer, am I catching you at a good time?"

"It's Monday morning here outside Natchitoches, Louisiana, and we're still on an all-night stakeout."

While Nicole Kirbye stretched out and fell asleep in the front seat of Hammer's pickup, Hammer and Johnny Arnaud had been watching the shipping containers in shifts all night.

They had followed the trucks off Interstate 49 and had taken a dirt road parallel to the gravel road taken by the trucks. The trucks had been in and out of there in around twenty minutes, leaving the containers in the barn and a lone figure to close the doors.

"Natchitoches is mid-state, right?" Tommis asked.

"Yeah, between Alexandria and Shreveport. They offloaded two twenty-foot containers from a barge on the bayou yesterday and put 'em on that trailer I told you about. They trucked 'em up here last night. We followed. Johnny's with me. We're waiting to see what happens next. All quiet since the truck left last night. What's happening on your end?"

"Brian let me know that Rahim Faizullah showed up. He's safe."

"Hallelujah," Hammer said. "What happened?"

"A lot, but Brian Herste had to twist it out of him. He's scared to death that Abed Qalandar is going to hurt his sister. Meanwhile, she's mad at him for going off the grid all weekend."

"Sometimes you can't win. So what happened?"

"He agreed to take a drive with Qalandar over the weekend. They went down the river south of New Orleans to Arbeville, the place where the bar pilots trade off to river pilots. Some motor barges were in the area. An ocean freighter slows down. Pilots swap out. Ship continues. Motor barge heads downriver."

"Bound for the Gulf and then to Bayou Gadreau with two twenty-foot containers," Hammer said, filling in the blanks. "Sounds like unbelievably slick ship unloading, though."

"That's the beauty of small containers," Tommis said. "You can't do that with those huge forty-foot containers, but ships have small cranes for loading housekeeping cargo."

"Still a pretty good trick to do it that fast."

"You have to hand it to Coome Hauling."

"Who?"

"The plate numbers you gave me. Come back to a company called Coome Hauling out of Gulfport. They've got a legit front, but they're said to be in all sorts of questionable stuff. This is the Gulf Coast. Ever hear of the Dixie Mafia?"

"As a matter of fact..."

"According to what Rahim learned, this is about to become big business for the Coomes," Tommis continued. "He says that this is just the first of many. They've got more containers coming in two weeks, and more after that."

"Where from?"

"Hamad Port...south of Doha."

"Who's the shipper?"

"I don't know," Tommis admitted, "but Qalandar claims that he's importing rugs from Afghanistan. So, for the sake of argument, let's say that Afghanistan is the country of origin. What's Afghanistan's largest export?"

"As we both know, it's not rugs." Hammer laughed. "But what are they going to do with tons of unrefined opium? It needs to be processed. Two here and more containers on the way? That's a lot to handle...just getting it off the ship and up here."

"Coome Hauling does have made themselves a name in the cargo business for doing things with freight loading that verges on sleight of hand. They've got a good reputation for that."

"Keeps customers happy, I guess," Hammer said.

"Speaking of customers, guess who Rahim ran into down on the Mississippi while waiting for the cargo ship? Tommis teased."

"Enlighten me."

"Our old friend Wally Gusche."

Nicole, who had awakened at the sound of voices, and who was now eavesdropping on the call, used an expletive that summarized the feeling of the three of the people crouching in the brush near Hammer's concealed pickup.

———

"It's the next road to the left," Shane Blessins said as he steered the big gray Cadillac Escalade south from Natchitoches.

"Good, I'm tired of all this driving," Alexis Mondtrom complained from the back seat. They'd driven all the way from Houston that morning.

"We'll see whether our mujahidin acquaintance will be able to deliver," David Anchry said.

"I can't wait," Alexis said.

Blessins and Anchry were both agents of the Federal Security Office, an organization within the Department of Homeland Security that was as obscure as the DHS Field Operations Directorate for which Mondtrom was officially a Special Director. They carried FSO badges, something which proved useful in their work with and for Mondtrom and her various and nefarious activities.

She had handpicked them about a decade ago and had them detailed to her officially as special assistants. They answered to her, and no one else. Their role was a cross between that of a factotum and a bodyguard, but essentially, they were there to do anything and everything she asked, which they found preferable to a job pushing paper in a federal building. If what she asked happened to be outside the lines of their government job descriptions, or outside the law, as it frequently did, she made sure that they received appropriate "outside compensation." They did as she asked, and they knew better than to ask questions themselves.

Standing impatiently by the open barn doors, Qalandar watched the Escalade kicking up dust as Blessins powered down the gravel road.

"You're ready for us, I see," Alexis said, climbing out of the car and brushing potato chip crumbs off her merlot-colored pantsuit. "Where's your new factotum? Gusche said he met your new man...said he seemed to be on the ball. That other guy you had was an airhead. Did you get rid of him like I suggested?"

Qalandar nodded, not going into the details.

"Let's see what we got here," Alexis said impatiently.

———

A quarter mile away, three people lying against an embankment were passing around Hammer's powerful Oberwerk 10x42 HD II binoculars, watching the four people with such clarity it was like they were standing among them.

"Do you recognize any of them?" Nicole asked.

"If we string together what we know and what we've learned this morning from Tim Tommis, then that guy we saw taking delivery of the containers that night must be Abed Qalandar," Hammer said. "I don't recognize the others. Must be the buyers."

"Really well dressed for dope dealers," Arnaud observed.

"We aren't looking at street-corner pushers," Hammer said. "This is a volume wholesale business."

"I don't see Gusche anywhere," Nicole added.

"I think he's the middleman," Hammer interjected. "I think his job is the facilitate moving the stuff across borders or off ships and onto trucks. He's doing now exactly what he had SIFO doing in their off-the-books scams over in Afghanistan. Neither buying nor selling. Just making sure it got moved from point A to points B, C and D."

"Right," Arnaud said. "Over there, the Taliban supplied the drugs, while Vision for Humanitarian Empowerment did the distro to dealers all over Europe. Gusche and his SIFO gang just facilitated transportation on NGO 'humanitarian' flights out of Kabul and Kandahar. They even had their product on some DOD flights."

"And to think that I...people like me and Ash...were part of SIFO back then," Nicole said disgustedly. "If we had known that we were this close to this stuff and totally clueless. It's infuriating!"

"SIFO then, SIFO now," Hammer said. "Anything's possible behind an innocent and believable front. Don't beat yourself up. Lots of people, including a whole DOD chain of command, were clueless."

"They're opening a container now," Arnaud said, squinting through the binoculars once more before handing them off to Nicole.

Climbing up onto a loading dock next to the big flatbed semi trailer, Qalandar lifted the right door handle of the container upward, pulled it forward, rotating the lock rods out of their brackets. With the handles in a vertical position, perpendicular to the door, he jerked the vertical lock bar, and the door swung open.

"He's done this before, obviously," Arnaud said.

He then repeated the process on the left door of the first container, and as the others watched, he quickly opened the second container, swinging all the doors open wide.

The woman in the purplish pantsuit joined Qalandar on the loading dock to examine the cargo—wooden crates stacked floor to ceiling inside the big metal container. She waved her arms, ordering the two men she was with to come up and pull one of the boxes from the container.

"I recognize those," Nicole said. "Those are DOD-issue boxes like we had coming and going all the time back then. See the way the numbers are blocked into rectangles on the upper and lower corners?"

"What's in them?" Arnaud asked.

"I can't read what it says except some of the bigger numbers, but I recognize the way the text rectangles are placed on the boxes," Nicole said. "It sure looks very, very DOD."

As they were discussing text positioning, Qalandar produced a crowbar and handed it off to the two men, who set to work opening the first box.

As they flung the wooden lid aside, the three people lying against an embankment grew wide-eyed.

"What the...?" Arnaud started to say.

"That's definitely *not* opium, guys," Nicole said, staring.

"No, it's not," Hammer said as one of the men opening the box held up a pair of M16A4 assault rifles. "There must be a couple dozen of those in that one box."

He handed the rifle to the woman, who took it and sighted it expertly at an imaginary target before handing it back.

Another box was opened, revealing a large number of neatly packed smaller boxes, which Hammer and Arnaud recognized as tactical radios of the type that they had used in Afghanistan.

"It looks like gear that was brand new back in those days," Arnaud said. "Looks like it was all packed up and never opened. It's like it's just been sitting in those boxes for years."

The two men pulled off their jackets, wiped the sweat off their foreheads, and went deeper into the container to drag out more and more boxes to be sampled.

Finally, they walked up the loading dock to open the second container. Because of the way it was situated, Hammer and his companions could not see into the second container, but they saw the crates as they were unloaded. There were a variety of types of gear, including night vision goggles, Beretta M9 pistols, a great deal more

M16A4 rifles, as well as ammo magazines for all the weapons.

As this strange show unfolded, Nicole was providing a running commentary of her recollection of what these items had cost when they were merely line items on her computer screen at Bagram.

Finally, a box was opened at which Arnaud said simply "saw."

"Saw?" Nicole asked.

"M249 Squad Automatic Weapon, acronym is 'SAW,'" he said.

"Oh yeah," Nicole recalled. "An S.A.W., the five-point-five-six-millimeter light machine gun."

Arnaud looked at her approvingly for knowing the details of a piece of hardware with which few civilians are familiar.

"They sell for eight-to-ten-grand new these days," Hammer said calmly.

"How would you know *that*?" Nicole queried with a wry smirk.

"Don't ask," Arnaud said with a smile.

She just grinned and shook her head.

After the opening of seven randomly selected containers, the men began the laborious process of resealing them and pushing them back into the containers.

As this was going on, the woman retrieved a large Halliburton aluminum suitcase from the SUV and handed it to Qalandar. He opened it to reveal a densely packed load of cash which brought a smile to the bearded face.

The old mujahidin and his overseas collaborators weren't averse to electronic banking; it was just that Qalandar had long ago developed a fondness for the tactile feel of banknote paper made with that of a special blend of cotton and linen fibers.

When it was all done and the SUV had driven away, Nicole took a deep breath and asked, "What just happened?"

"We were wrong," Hammer said. "It was *not* a drug deal. It was the biggest arms sale that you have seen since you worked for the DOD."

"Just to clarify, this is what the rumor said that Wally Gusche was doing in Afghanistan? Arranging deals for the Taliban, right?" Nicole asked. "All that stuff on that website that got Steve Ambel killed...and Ash almost killed? It was true?"

Hammer nodded.

"So it *wasn't* a rumor? He was *really* doing it. He was passing contraband from the Taliban to the pushers in Europe?"

"Yes, and he's really *still* doing it," Hammer said.

"From the *Taliban*?" Nicole asked. "I wouldn't have imagined..."

"Yup," Hammer said. "The Taliban found themselves with mountains of this stuff when the coalition made its fast pullout from Afghanistan. Like you said yourself, it's still packed in DOD packaging. Normally, I wouldn't jump so fast to conclusions, but I'd say that the point of origin for this stuff is the Taliban themselves...and Abed Qalandar is their man in America."

CHAPTER
EIGHTEEN

SIFO HEADQUARTERS, KEESLER AFB, MISSISSIPPI

WALLACE GUSCHE STARED HAPPILY at his laptop screen, still admiring the number of zeros that had just flooded into his offshore account. This meant that the goods had reached Natchitoches, and that Abed Qalandar had taken payment from his customer. Gusche didn't care whether his customer's name was Alexis Anderson or Alexis Mondtrom. All he cared was that the transaction, the first of many, had been a total success!

When his burner phone rang, he recognized the number for Randy Coome.

"I see you got my text last night," Coome said. "I personally watched the two containers get delivered and we got your wire payment. That old Afghan took his in cash."

"He's like that," Gusche said.

"Don't blame him," Coome said. "I hope you got paid too."

"Yes, we did," Gusche said. "I was just looking at my

account. The cunning old bandit takes his own payments in cash, but he routes his payments to us through his own overseas bank. Whatever. Get ready for the next one in two weeks."

"We are. It was a late one last night, but we'll be rested and ready when the time comes."

"Good," Gusche continued. "I'm glad you called because I want to talk to you about that other thing. You know what I mean."

What he meant was the elimination of the individuals who had downloaded and read the posting on the since-deleted DEEPSTATEWATCH website that named Gusche and aired SIFO's dirty Afghan laundry.

"The originator and his biggest fan were removed a week and a half ago," Coome said. "I know you said you did not want to know the details, but if you want to break your own rules, you can read about the Colorado bomb blast and the Terre Haute home invasion in the online editions of the local newspapers. I have and it's there. Nothing about the website, of course. Meanwhile, I think your tech people erased everything that had been posted online, right?"

"Yes, that's right," Gusche said. "But I think we're missing one detail, right?"

"Orange car," Coome muttered.

"You said that your fixers were chasing it across Texas," Gusche reminded him. "But then on Thursday, you told me that their own car turned up abandoned three states away from where they were last seen following the orange car. Have there been any new developments?"

"No sign of them."

"Then I guess you lost them, *and* the orange car?"

"For the time being."

"We need to talk face-to-face," Gusche said. "Meet me at the usual place at two."

When he'd hung up his burner phone, Gusche picked up his desk phone and dialed the receptionist.

"Miranda, could you get me Mr. Lynse."

Brent Lynse was tracked down doing his day job of government business at one of the nearby SIFO warehouses. He was in Gusche's office fifteen minutes later.

"We have a meeting with Randy Coome at the usual place in twenty minutes to talk about our success yesterday," Gusche said as Lynse took a seat. "I just talked to him."

"He ought to be happy with that," Lynse said.

"He wasn't happy when I prodded him on the orange car thing."

"What did he say?" Lynse asked. "I thought you were going for plausible deniability. Remember, you said the less we know, the better. You left it in Randy's hands, and he left it in the hands of his fixers. You said you didn't even want to know the names of people the fixers were supposed to fix."

"Well, I've changed my mind," Gusche said firmly. "Screw the deniability. We need to wrap this up. When I prodded Randy, he all but gave me two of the names, including the one who passed it to the orange car woman."

"How did he 'all but' do that?"

"He pointed out that this guy was terminated in Terre Haute, Indiana. As Randy said, this was a home invasion incident that made the local newspapers, so I looked it up."

"Just like that?"

"Just *exactly* like that," Gusche replied. "His name was Steven Ambel, and we know he worked for SIFO at Bagram.

I even vaguely remember the name. But anyway, we'll have him in our files. We have *all* the SIFO personnel files. It shouldn't take long to find him, and we can easily figure out where in SIFO he was situated. Then we find the people he worked with, cross-reference with current Pentagon personnel files and narrow down the list. The orange-car woman is probably somebody he worked with over there."

"Good idea."

"We need to go about this a different way," Gusche said.

"How do you suggest we do that?"

"We can put DASP, meaning Ivermin and Sentyl, on it. They're in the investigating business. Let 'em investigate. Then we can start sending them out on house calls."

———

Gusche and Lynse met Randy Coome at the Shrimp Bowl on Beach Boulevard at the appointed time. The "Bowl" as locals called it, was their usual spot because it was sufficiently down-market not to attract tourists, and because it was several blocks from the nearest casino. Gusche picked two o'clock because the lunch crowds would have thinned out.

"Successful show yesterday on both ends of the state," Gusche said, beginning the meeting amiably with a congratulatory handshake. "You pulled it off like a hot knife through butter."

"That's what we do," Randy said proudly. "We aim to please."

"I'm pleased," Gusche said.

"But you're *not* pleased about the other deal," Randy said, referencing their earlier conversation.

"I know they weren't *your* in-house guys out there. I know you outsourced the job to somebody…"

"We're not in the business of doing that sort of work," Randy said. "So, I got a recommendation and was hoping for the best. We'll do what we can to make it right, but we'll have to see."

"I think I want to start working this from another angle," Gusche said. "I'm going to put Ivermin and Sentyl, my DASP people, on the job."

Coome swallowed hard. Nobody likes to have a job pulled out from under them, but in this case the awkwardness was lessened by a sense of relief. He had not really wanted to become a broker of hit men. He had enough on his plate with shuffling containers for Gusche —not to mention his regular business.

"We have the personnel files for this Steven Ambel," Gusche began. "We have personnel files for everybody who was with SIFO at Bagram. We'll figure out who he worked with. Whoever he told is probably one of them."

"It's a place to start," Coome agreed.

"You told me how to find Ambel. Do you have any tricks for finding the woman that you're not telling me?"

"When we started this, you said you did not want to know..."

"Yeah," Gusche said with a wave of his hand. "Plausible deniability and all that, but this is getting critical. We have to wrap it up. If your fixers are nowhere to be found, we gotta fix it another way."

"Okay," Coome said. "I figured it might come to this, so I'll give you what I have...what you said you *didn't* want to know."

Randy reached into his shirt pocket, took out a wad of papers and slipped on his reading glasses.

"Here it is," he said. "Now you know. This is all the information that the two fixers managed to find as they were tracking these people. I got her address in

McAlester, Oklahoma, but she's not there, obviously. Okay, here's the name. Her name is Ashley Grahen."

"Grahen? Did you say Grahen?"

"Yeah. Is that a problem?" Coome asked, taken aback by Gusche's sudden alarmed expression.

Gusche set down his coffee cup. This was one of those rare moments when he found himself speechless.

Ashley Grahen.

This was not just a random person following a conspiracy blog. This was not merely a random former SIFO employee. She was somebody whom he *knew*.

Gusche could picture her, and the way her ponytail bounced as she went up and down the stairs. He could picture her bubbly personality that endeared her to some, but which grated on Gusche like fingernails on a chalkboard. She was one of that small number of women who persisted in calling him "Wally," which infuriated him even more.

Ashley Grahen was someone whom he knew, but worst of all, someone who knew *him*.

If she had read the DOD report, digging into all of its hundreds of pages and dozens of appendices, and if she connected the Wallace Gusche of back then to the Wallace Gusche of *now*, she could be a very serious problem—for him *personally*.

———

BROUILLECOURT PARISH, LOUISIANA

Jim Hammer's pickup had just crossed the line into Brouillecourt Parish when the call came in from Tim Tommis.

"I've got an ID for you on your people at the containers in Natchitoches Parish," he said.

Hammer put the phone on "speaker" and set it into its nest on the dashboard so that Nicole Kirbye and Johnny Arnaud could hear what Tommis had to say.

"That woman is Alexis Mondtrom," he said. "She's been part of the Homeland Security bureaucracy for years."

"Which part?" Hammer asked. "There's gotta be more than a dozen agencies inside DHS, from the Secret Service to TSA to FEMA. The Coast Guard is even in there somewhere."

"Actually, there's more than *two* dozen," Tommis clarified. "A real jumble. Some pieces are more autonomous than others, and DHS has its own bureaucracy in DC on top of everything else inside those two dozen autonomous Lego bricks. Mondtrom's title is Special Director for Security in the Field Operations Directorate, which is just a fabricated department. She's technically a cog in the DC part of DHS, but she's not actually *based* in Washington. Since the Field Operations Directorate is just a pretense, she's not actually 'based' anywhere."

"Working from 'home,' I suppose," Nicole interjected.

"Exactly," Tommis said. "Actually, she works from 'field locations.' Answers to basically nobody."

"And the other guys at the barn?"

"The other two in her entourage are Shane Blessins and David Anchry. They work for Mondtrom and both get their paychecks from DHS, and before you ask, they both 'work from home' too. Technically, they carry badges with the Federal Security Office, which is inside DHS the same way the DASP is part of the Army. FSO agents are mainly facilities security people, but they all carry badges. Federal badges. Blessins and Anchry work *only* for Mondtrom."

"Sounds like bodyguards with badges that keep them

and Mondtrom safe from any interference from local law enforcement," Arnaud said.

"Like when the sheriff went out to check on them," Nicole interjected. "They just flashed their federal badges and made him back off."

"What about the guy with the beard?" Hammer asked.

"You were right, he's Abed Qalandar," Tommis confirmed. "I matched the picture you took to the one on his special immigrant visa paperwork from when he was brought into this country years ago.

"My first question after hearing all this is to ask if Mondtrom could be running a sting on Qalandar," Hammer replied.

"Anything's possible, but if you dig down deep enough, Mondtrom's got a dubious past. Some years ago, she was mixed up in a serious corruption probe that went nowhere. It sounds like she had something on some congressman or somebody, and the investigation vanished in a wisp of smoke."

"What's she up to then?"

"There's talk she has had some contact with the Gonzalves Cartel," Tommis said.

"The gunrunners?" Arnaud suggested.

"Yeah, gunrunners and enforcers," Tommis added. "They're notorious out west for running guns to gangs. Local law enforcement is skittish about getting into a fight with them."

"Especially with Mondtrom running interference," Hammer said cynically.

"I guess this ties into what we saw them doing this morning," Arnaud said. "It looked like the Taliban is selling guns back into this country, which is where they came from."

"It's a disturbing thought all around," Nicole said.

"That arsenal had to go somewhere," Tommis said. "It was a *tremendous* windfall. Enough to equip a substantial army or two. The Taliban could use only so much of it themselves. Turning it into hard cash, while undermining the internal security of the United States. That certainly matches their playbook."

"How much material exactly did we leave behind?" Nicole asked. "I saw the numbers as they were when I was there. Is there a way of knowing how much got left after the pullout??

"Well, as a matter of fact there is," Tommis said. "I happen to have a doc right here with the figures calculated by the General Accounting Office and SIGAR, the DOD's own Special Inspector General for Afghanistan Reconstruction. According to *their* own numbers, and you can look this up, we left 385,530 assault rifles, 126,295 automatic pistols, and 64,363 light machine guns behind in Afghanistan. This is not to mention 16,035 sets of night vision goggles and 162,043 tactical radios, like the ones you saw."

"Is that all?"

"Not in the least." Tommis laughed. "The GAO lists over sixty thousand vehicles, from Humvees to pickups to SUVs. There are NATO armies that don't have nearly as much and they got after the pullout!"

"*Wow*," Nicole said bitterly. "I used to know the exact numbers of what that cost. It's staggering."

"And the SIGAR data adds around sixty single-engine airplanes, thirty-three Blackhawk helicopters, and a few C-130 four-engine airlift aircraft."

"Looks like the Taliban is selling to somebody who's declaring war on somebody," Arnaud said.

"Sure does," Hammer replied.

"We got to stop this," Nicole said.

"What are we going to do?" Hammer asked. "Call the

cops. Like we were just saying, both Gusche and Mondtrom are backed up with people wearing federal badges. As we know, federal badges always trump *any* local jurisdiction."

"We have to do *something*," Nicole said firmly. "We can't just let this happen, can we?"

"Maybe we just need to take care of this *ourselves*," Arnaud suggested.

KEESLER AFB, BILOXI, MISSISSIPPI

Deciding to take care of a problem yourself, rather that leaving it in the hands of someone who has not performed, can lead one to liberating self assurance.

Such had been the case for Wallace Gusche when he decided to take Randy Coome off the job of finding the woman in the orange car, and to turn it over to professional cops—his own DASP professionals.

Now that he knew she was Ashley Grahen, someone whom he had known, and who knew him personally, the urgency had become magnified. He needed all the liberating self assurance he could get.

He sent Ivermin and Sentyl into the boxes of personnel files that had been shipped back from Afghanistan, and which had remained untouched in a Keesler warehouse since SIFO had found a home here.

The plan was to find Grahen's file, find the people with whom she worked closely, and build a picture of her circle of friends, the people with whom she would have stayed in touch. This was how Gusche had originally planned to find *her*, before Randy Coome handed over her name.

Now that he knew *who* she was, he could use this

method to build a list of people whom they could start to question about *where* she was. She was on the run. If she was looking for refuge, it stood to reason that she'd find her safe haven with someone who understood *why* she was on the run.

Gusche was not prepared for what came about an hour after the two DASP men rolled up their sleeves in the warehouse.

"Boss, you're not going to believe this," Ivermin said when Miranda escorted him into Gusche's inner sanctum.

"What am I not going to believe?" Gusche asked apprehensively as the DASP agent quietly closed the door. "You've only just started on this."

"We started prioritizing the files by the length of time people were with in Grahen's department at SIFO in that building at Bagram Air Base, and how their time overlapped the time that Grahen was there."

"I remember that building well," Gusche said. "I spent a year and a half on the third floor of that place in Equipment and Operations."

"Well, Grahen was down on the second floor in Sustainment and Infrastructure," Ivermin said, opening a folder. "They had a lot of interaction with Request Oversight Auditing, which was on the third floor where you were."

"So...?"

"We've found a couple of interesting anomalies already. First, one of the people who overlaps Grahen's time was a man in Request Oversight Auditing called Steven Ambel. He was *murdered* in Terre Haute, Indiana about a week ago."

Gusche swallowed hard. The hit was, of course, "need-to-know," and Gusche had previously decided that Ivermin did *not* need to know.

"What's your other anomaly?" Gusche asked.

"In looking through the people with whom Grahen worked on the second floor, one name jumped out. Her name in Nicole Kirbye."

Wallace Gusche gritted his teeth. He remembered Kirbye. She was another of those, like Grahen, who teased him repeatedly by calling him "Wally." He hated that name when he was called that in the first grade and he had hated it ever since. He hated these women—young, attractive, and self-confident young women—because they teased him. They had the audacity to humiliate him with his own name.

"Why does Kirbye jump out in your searching?"

"Here, boss," Ivermin said. "Look at her current address. She lives in Fredieuville, Louisiana, in Brouille-court Parish, *just fifteen or so miles from where the containers came in!*"

Gusche felt himself turning pale. He could see her face, and that damned smile that everyone liked, that is, unless your name was Wallace and she persisted in calling you "Wally."

"Do you be believe in coincidences?"

Gusche heard Ivermin ask the question, but his mind was elsewhere, its wheels spinning.

"I don't know what to believe. I'd like you to drive over to Fredieuville and talk to Kirbye. Go alone. I'd like you not to mention this to Sentyl just yet."

"Okay…"

"This will be 'need-to-know,'" Gusche said with a conspiratorial nod, just short of a wink. "We'll just keep it between you and me for now. Go over there and find out if she's been in touch with Grahen. If they're in contact, they constitute a serious threat to this operation."

FEHRY COUNTY, ARKANSAS

"This is a *nightmare*," Hila Faizullah said angrily, looking at Brian Herste while ignoring her brother. She was infuriated with him for endangering himself and she refused to make eye contact.

"Suddenly, I'm back in Kabul with those misogynists bullying people on the streets and groping women in the alleys," she continued angrily. "And here's my own brother swooping off on a road trip to New Orleans...of all *places*...with Abed Qalandar, of all *people*!"

The three of them were standing in Hila's classroom at Fehryville High. Classes had ended for the day, and Rahim had come here, at Herste's prodding, to tell her everything. Based on her tirade, part of him wished he had kept his mouth shut, but the other part of him told him it was probably best to have it all out in the open.

And out in the open it was.

The Taliban were an open fear for every Afghan, especially every Afghan *woman*, who had escaped their merciless rule. Years had passed since Hila had lived her daily life with this constant abuse, but now her own brother had brought the memories crashing back by consorting with evil!

"Hila, please understand that he did what he did to distract attention *away* from you...to keep you *safe*."

"Why don't I feel *safe*? Should I run home and exchange my sundress for a burqa, so that I won't offend my brother's new 'friend?'"

"Hila, " Rahim said as she hugged him tightly, soaking his shirt with tears.

"Brian," she said, looking at him. "Can this be fixed? What can be done to undo this nightmare, to make it so that my brother doesn't think he has to join the Taliban in order to protect us?"

CHAPTER
NINETEEN

BROUILLECOURT PARISH, LOUISIANA

JIM HAMMER HAD SPENT Tuesday morning at
Bayou Langlois Motors, helping Johnny Arnaud and
Tyler Roullier pull a Mercury 350 HP ECT 6.2-liter V-8
engine from a charter fishing boat. Three pairs of hands
were better than one, which is all that Roullier had on
Monday when he'd been working alone while Arnaud
was driving around the state with Hammer eavesdropping on the Taliban, and while the guys who worked part
time were off.

As they had been working, they had talked about
little else. Arnaud had summarized the thoughts of
everyone sitting around Nicole Kirbye's fire pit the night
before when he said, "Maybe we need to take care of this
ourselves."

Last night, there had been a clinking of glasses and
enthusiastic agreement when he said this. This morning,
the cold light of day found them all starting to grapple
with the question: *If so, what comes next?*

The obvious first suggestion involved bullets and

dynamite, as well as the *who* and *what* they'd seen at the Natchitoches Parish barn.

"That might take care of part of the problem, but it leaves the middleman standing," Hammer said thoughtfully. "What about Wally Gusche and his operation? We also don't know anything about Abed Qalandar and the size and shape of his operation, or how he interfaces with the Taliban overseas. We need to do some recon before we go after this problem with our knives out."

At that moment, they heard a chirping sound across the room and Hammer walked over to retrieve his phone from his jacket pocket.

"Eight-seventy area code," he said as he looked at it.

"Arkansas," Roullier said.

"Hello," Hammer said tersely.

"Captain Hammer?"

"Who's asking?"

"This is Brian Herste, up in Fehryville, Arkansas. Herste, from your team in…"

"Yeah, I recognize your voice, now. Good to hear it, and by the way, I'm not a captain anymore."

"Tim Tommis gave me your number, am I…is this a bad time?"

"No," Hammer said, putting his phone on speaker and laying it on the table where the others could hear. "Actually, it's a pretty good time. I'm sitting here around a V-8 marine engine in Brouillecourt Parish, Louisiana with Johnny Arnaud and Tyler Roullier."

"*Bonne matin*," Brian Arnaud said.

"Howdy from Cajun country," Tyler chipped in.

"Good to hear your voices," Herste said. "I'm sorry I haven't stayed in touch with all you guys."

"No worries. I'm the worst. I have a Christmas card list of zero," Hammer said, eager to get the small talk behind them. "So what's up?"

"As I guess Tommis told you, Rahim Faizullah, our old interpreter, is up here in Fehryville. His sister Hila, you remember her, she's here too. Teaches math at the high school."

"Yeah, he filled me in on all of that," Hammer said. "He told me that Rahim took a ride down to the Delta with Abed Qalandar. He told me that they watched some containers get unloaded and they met up with Wally Gusche, our Mr. Tortoise Shell Glasses from Afghanistan."

"And Tommis told me that you also had your eyes on those same containers," Herste said.

"They brought them ashore right here in Brouillecourt Parish, less than twenty miles from where we're sitting," Hammer said. "Small world."

"*That's for sure*," Herste said. "Rahim said that Qalandar claims to be importing rugs from over in Afghanistan, but with all that cloak and dagger with unloading the containers at a river pilot stop, we figure it's probably opium or drugs of some kind. What's Afghanistan's biggest export, after all, right?"

"Actually, it's *not* opium," Hammer said.

"*What*? What else could it be, and how do you know?"

"We followed them up to Natchitoches, yesterday," Hammer said. "Me and Johnny and our friend Nicole. We watched Qalandar open them up."

"So, what *was* in those containers?" Herste asked. "What else could Afghanistan possibly have that's worth exporting."

"Millions of bucks worth of warfighting hardware courtesy of Uncle Sam," Arnaud said.

"Oh *no*," Herste said. "You mean all that stuff…"

"That got left behind," Hammer said, finishing his sentence.

"I forgot all about that stuff."

"Tommis gave us some numbers," Hammer said. "A third of a million assault rifles and tens of thousands of machine guns, and that's just the start of it."

"Don't forget a few dozen Blackhawks," Arnaud chipped in.

"We didn't see any Blackhawks yesterday," Hammer continued, "but we *did* have eyes on several crates of M16A4s, a bunch of SAWs, and a lot of ammo., and there was Qalandar, right in the middle of it."

"What was he doing?" Herste asked.

"Basically, acting like a rug salesman and getting handed a metal suitcase full of cash."

"*Ooooh mama,*" Herste said. "Who was handing him the cash?"

"Tommis gave us an ID on their pictures," Hammer replied. "They're renegade operators freelancing from inside the Homeland Security Department. The mastermind is a woman named Alexis Mondtrom, a real hard case. She's a Special Director in a phony field directorate. Her security detail are Federal Security Office cops. She had a couple of 'em with her."

"Describe her," Herste asked.

"She stands out," Hammer said. "Tall...short hair, very assertive and very self-assured. Purple pantsuit. Definitely the alpha dog in the pack."

"Rahim told me that he saw a woman like that with Qalandar here in Fehryville about a week ago," Herste said. "No doubt it was her. No doubt with *that* description, though I don't remember the color of the pantsuit."

"The pieces are coming together," Hammer said, sounding pleased. "Where did he see them?"

"In a restaurant. There's an Afghan place here in town. He was with his sister...remember Hila...she saw 'em too. They were with a couple of suits who sound like what you described, and another Afghan guy."

"Any idea who?"

"Rahim didn't know him but he was a cousin of a friend of Hila's."

"How does Hila feel about all this?" Arnaud asked. "I remember her as barely out of her teens...now she's a high school teacher...time flies. How's she taking this?"

"If I was a little freaked by what happened this weekend, she's *seething*. She won't even look Rahim in the eye. To her, Qalandar is the poster child for everything evil she left behind in Afghanistan. To see her brother hanging out with him is unspeakable. It's a lot to process and Afghan women feel especially vulnerable."

"I understand," Hammer said. "We all saw what these idiots liked to do to women over there."

"She's the reason I called you this morning," Herste said.

"Oh yeah?"

"Yesterday, we were in the midst of talking...*shouting* actually...about this and she looked at me and asked what can be done to unwrap this and get Rahim out from under this intimidation. I figured that if anybody could figure out what to do, it would be you."

"Thanks for the vote of confidence," Hammer said after a long pause. "Seriously, I appreciate that."

"I'm not just saying that, man. You got us out of a lot of pretty impossible situations over there. Hila brought that up when we were, um, having our discussion. I was just thinking that *you* might have some idea..."

"I'm thinking of taking a little drive up north," Hammer said after a longer, more thoughtful pause. "Maybe I'll drop in and see you."

"That would be awesome, man. You know you're always welcome."

"You have a sofa I can crash on?"

"Yup."

"Well, just as I was saying we didn't know much about Qalandar's operation, " Hammer said with a smile as he set the phone down. He had that look that Arnaud and Roullier recognized, that look of wheels spinning in his head.

"I've been thinking..." he repeated at last.

"We can see that," Arnaud said with a laugh. "We've always been able to *see* you thinking. You know that... *right*?"

"I notice that you've got a CCTV camera up there on the outside of your shop door."

"Oh, the 'coon cam' you mean," Roullier said with a grin. "We installed it a couple years ago. We have a lot of stuff we don't want ripped off, but we've never got much on the camera except raccoons and other varmints. It's camo-colored, but that isn't much concealment against the side of a metal building."

"The two-legged intruders are put off by the sign out there about 'these premises are protected by Smith & Wesson.'" Roullier continued.

"This is the bayou country," Arnaud. "Smart burglars tend to know that their would-be marks are armed."

"Is it live or recorded?" Hammer asked.

"Both," Roullier replied. "We get a feed that goes to a hard drive here and at my place, but we can look at the feed live at either place, and it also goes to our phones, like one of those doorbells that lots of people have."

"What's the range?"

"It's all Wi-Fi enabled, and all that, so we can look at the live feed from anywhere. It's waterproof and solar powered so it can be anyplace."

"I was thinking about that camera on the drive back from Natchitoches yesterday," Hammer said. "I think that

I'd like to install one up there so we can keep an eye on that barn. Part of figuring how we're going to unwind this little scheme of theirs. Where can I get one?"

"Hardware store in town," Arnaud said. "I can show you how to set it up."

"Great. Let's go. Let's get it hooked up to your computers and my phone. I'm going to leave now and head up to Fehryville to talk to those guys. I'll set it up in Natchitoches on my way north."

"Wait," Roullier said abruptly. "I got a better idea. Why don't you take *ours*. We already have it hooked up to all our devices. That would save a step. It would be easier for us to just add your phone than to go through hooking a new one up to everything."

"Yeah," Arnaud said, walking across the shop toward an extension ladder. "That would be faster, too. I can go in and get a new one for us. While I'm getting that one hooked up, you can be on the move...on your recon patrol."

"All right," Hammer said. "Let's roll."

CHAPTER
TWENTY

BROUILLECOURT PARISH, LOUISIANA

NICOLE KIRBYE SMILED as she said goodbye to her Tuesday morning appointment, which was actually a Monday afternoon appointment that she'd had to reschedule. Fortunately, her client did not seem to mind. It was a gift shop owner whose accounts were always in good shape. Mainly, she just wanted to bend Nicole's ear on the pros and cons of taking on a new greeting card line out of Idaho.

As with the guys at Langlois Motors, Tuesday morning found Nicole Kirbye playing catch-up after missing a workday on account of the unplanned field trip to Natchitoches. She had a pile of work to plow through, and two appointments she had to push off. Luckily, she was able to reschedule the one for this morning, but the other had to wait for Thursday.

In the back of her mind was the conversation that she'd had this morning with Ashley. It had been nearly a week since she and her kids had been Nicole's house-guests, and she was starting to feel underfoot. For the first few days, it had been like a vacation for the kids, what with the fishing trips and handing out at Langlois Motors, but Liam and Ava were starting to ask when they were going to go home again and go back to school.

She knew that the men who had tried to harm them at the rest area were no longer an issue, and with everything that was going on with trailers and smugglers, Ash was starting to feel that the danger in Brouillecourt Parish was greater than it would be at home.

Maybe it was time to pull the tarp off the orange Honda hidden in Nicole's garage and head north?

Still yawning from lack of quality sleep, Nicole had just made another pot of coffee in her office when someone stepped through the front door of her outer office. She had her desk oriented so she could see people as they came in. She continued to resist the temptation to hire a receptionist, but she was almost to the point where she could afford it.

She stood and walked out to meet a man, well-dressed in dark slacks and a blazer. He even wore a necktie. Nicole was also looking presentable, having traded yesterday's T-shirt and cutoffs for a nicely pressed blouse and a businesslike pencil skirt.

"Nicole Kirbye?"

"Yes sir," she said, smiling and nodding to her name on a wall sign. He would also have seen her name on the glass door though which he had just walked. "What can I do for you?"

"My name's Ivermin. I'm with DASP," he said, showing her his ID with his badge clipped into it. "Department of Army police."

"I see," she said, looking closely at his ID. "How can I help you, Mr. Ivermin?"

"We're looking for a person whom you might know."

"Who is this person?"

"Her name is Ashley Grahen," the man said.

If there had ever been a time in Nicole's entire life when betraying emotion was a seriously *bad* idea, this was it. She smiled, earnestly trying to appear calm.

"She may have worked with you when you worked for the Department of the Army at the Security Infrastructure Finance Organization in Afghanistan."

"I was with SIFO, but that was a long time ago," Nicole said, still smiling. "Yes, that name does ring a bell."

She decided she would not deny knowing Ash. She had read once, maybe in a crime novel, that police always ask questions where they already know the answers, so to deny this would be a red flag. She had also read that cops could usually tell when a nervous person was lying.

"How well did you know Ms. Grahen?"

"Like I said, that was a long time ago."

"When did you last see Ms. Grahen?"

"Well, that's a good question," Nicole said, looking away and thoughtfully tapping her pencil on her chin. "Let me think…"

Nicole's mind was spinning. *What to say? What to say?*

She quickly decided that this was a question for which this man did not have an answer. They were looking for Ash, but if they knew where she was, they'd go get her, not waste time asking questions of Nicole, so they did not know where she was.

"There *was* this reunion about a year after we came back," Nicole said. She was not lying. There *had been* a reunion, and Ash had been there. Thinking on her feet, she decided to tell Agent Ivermin about that reunion, and to do so in great detail, and with great enthusiasm. Bury him in irrelevant details while pretending to be helpful.

"I think that's all I need," Ivermin said at last. "If you

hear from her, would you please phone me at this number."

He handed her his card. She smiled warmly as he left.

She never stopped smiling until he had driven away.

Nicole exhaled loudly and staggered back to her desk. She sat down, kicked off her shoes, and closed her eyes for a moment.

When she opened them again, the familiar surroundings made it all seem like a dream—but there on her desk where she had thrown it down, was the card. She picked it up with a quavering hand and noted the address at Keesler AFB, Mississippi.

She felt the way she had felt the day she had seen Wally Gusche in Fredieuville, only ten times worse. No, a *thousand* times worse. Today, she knew what Gusche and his people were doing, and they knew where she worked.

"Johnny," she said when she heard his voice answer the phone.

"*What's wrong?*" Johnny Arnaud asked when he heard the trembling voice on the other end of the line.

"Somebody just came to see me…"

———

Nicole had closed the door between her office and her reception area most of the way and was trying to relax, so when she heard the front door suddenly burst open, she could not see who it was.

She froze in terror, wishing she hadn't left the Beretta that Johnny Arnaud had given her last week at home. Last week, there had been something about the familiar surroundings of the office that made her feel safe.

What a foolish mistake!

When she had reached him a few minutes ago, and he

had said he would be "right there," she had no idea that this meant inside of five minutes.

"Nic, are you here?"

"Johnny, I'm in here," feeling the tension unwind like a clock spring at the sound of a friendly voice. "How did you get here so fast, did you fly?"

There, she said to herself, *I can joke.*

"I was just coming out of Fredieuville Hardware with a new CCTV camera," he said. "I got here as fast as I could. Think I mighta hit fifty-five on Main Street."

"I'm glad you're here," she said, grabbing him as reached her.

"You're shaking. What happened?"

"What's wrong with your old camera?" Nicole said, changing the subject and trying unsuccessfully to appear nonchalant.

"Hammer borrowed it, but never mind that, what happened here? Who came to see you?"

"Where's Ash and the kids?" Nicole asked, visibly worried, a furrow creasing her forehead. "She said she was taking 'em out to Langlois Motors. Did she get there okay?"

"Yeah, they showed up around the time I left."

"Good, let's sit down...okay?"

"Okay..." he said hesitantly.

"Could you hand me a water bottle out of my fridge?"

She took a long drink and set the bottle down on her desk. She thought about asking for something stronger.

"I'm sorry to be so discombobulated," she said apologetically. "I got blindsided here about...oh, I dunno... seems like an hour ago, but it was just before I called you."

"Who blindsided you?"

"Okay, Johnny, we have a problem. I got a visit from a DASP cop named Ivermin."

"*DASP? Here?*"

"Here. He asked for me by name, as though my name printed on the door was not enough. He knew I worked at SIFO and he knew that Ash worked at SIFO too. He asked when I last saw her."

"What did you say?"

"I told him about a long-ago reunion. He seemed satisfied with that and gave me his card. Said to call him if I see her, *blah, blah, blah.*"

She handed him the card.

"Keesler," he said, noting the address. "That means Gusche is involved."

"I'm really freaking out here…" she started to say.

"Oh," he said sarcastically. "I wouldn't have noticed."

"Real funny," she continued. "I'm really freaking out here…because Wally Gusche tracked me down…and he remembers that I knew Ash…and he's got his monkeys out trying to use me to find her."

"Okay, I'm going to stay here with you," Arnaud said. "I'll phone Tyler and tell him to keep Ash and the kids safe."

"Thank you," she said. "But like an idiot, I've been leaving that Beretta you gave me at home."

"That's okay, I've got hardware in the car."

"Of course you do," she said with a laugh.

"I'll phone Hammer and let him know."

"Where is he?" Nicole asked.

"He's on his way to Arkansas. We got a call from Brian Herste this morning."

"Is everything all right up there with your Afghan friend?"

"Yes and no," Arnaud said. "He's okay, but his sister is freaking out about him joyriding down to New Orleans with Abed Qalandar. She specifically asked Brian to call Hammer because Hammer got her and her brother out of jams before, and she thinks he might have some ideas."

"Does he?"

"You've met him. The wheels are always going round and round. We were talking this morning about how we need to get more info about Qalandar's crime machine before we do anything, so this gives him a chance to look into that. That's why Hammer is going up there. Recon. On the way, he's going to stop off at the Natchitoches barn and set up our old CCTV camera. It all goes according to plan. I'll be looking at the barn on my phone in a couple of hours."

————

In fact, Hammer had reached the dirt road parallel to the gravel road where the barn was located at about the same time that Nicole had phoned Johnny Arnaud. The speed limit on that hundred-and-fifty-mile stretch of Interstate 49 is seventy-five, the highest in Louisiana, and Hammer took advantage of every mile.

He looked things over with his binoculars. The scene was quieter than the last time he'd glassed the place. The barn doors were closed, but he saw Qalandar's BMW parked unobtrusively behind the barn.

As Hammer watched, he saw the bearded figure of Abed Qalandar exit a small side door and walk about a hundred feet into the nearby woods to a place he was apparently using as a latrine. He then ambled back to the barn, lit a Marlboro, and went inside. There was no urgency to his step.

Hammer set up the camo-colored camera in an obscure place among some willow saplings and turned it on. Moments later, images of the barn appeared in the app that Arnaud had installed on his phone. It was high-res, not nearly as good as Hammer's binoculars, but when it was zoomed in to the barn, the resolution was pretty good.

Hammer could see through a window next to the door. It appeared that Qalandar was staying here. He had a table and chair, and his coat was hanging on a hook.

This raised a question. If Qalandar was here minding the stash, who did he have running things in Fehryville? It also meant that if Qalandar was here looking after things, Mondtrom's people had not yet picked up *all* of the arms. He also took satisfaction in knowing that anything coming or going from the barn from now on would do so in full view of big screens and little screens from Bayou Langlois Motors to Hammer's own jacket pocket.

He was headed north on US 167, with about four hours left to go, when Johnny Arnaud called from Nicole Kirbye's office in Fredieuville.

When he hung up, he turned off the road and dug into his glove compartment for a cell phone that he'd picked it up at a DeSoto Parish rest stop exactly one week ago. It was time for the persona of a man who lay unidentified in the DeSoto Parish morgue to check in with his handlers.

CHAPTER
TWENTY-ONE

GULFPORT, MISSISSIPPI

LIKE NICOLE KIRBYE, Randy Coome was in his office Tuesday morning trying to make up for an unsettled night with black coffee. Like Nicole, he'd spent Sunday night into Monday on the road to Natchitoches. His side-job bank account was considerably fatter than it had be when that six-hundred-mile run had begun, but as with Nicole, his desk was overflowing with paperwork piled on by his day job.

His ex-wife, who ran scheduling for Coome Hauling called on the intercom from the outer office to tell him that the load of prehung doors had arrived in port a day early. The customer was clamoring for Coome to get a truck down to the waterfront to take them up to Birmingham.

Randy was in the process of calling the loading dock to see what trucks were available when he heard a buzzing in the drawer where he kept his side job burner phones. He put down his office phone in mid-dial, yanked open the drawer and picked up a burner phone.

What the…?

It was a text message from the missing fixers! He stared at the screen with mixed emotions, one measure of disbelief, another of relief.

Job finished. Location remote. Coming to get paid.

He picked up another burner phone to call Wallace Gusche with the good news.

———

FEHRY COUNTY, ARKANSAS

It was evening when Hammer arrived at the nice-looking home on the outskirts of Fehryville. Brian Herste directed him to pull the blue Chevy pickup into an unused carport. There was a cordial handshake and brief, but heartfelt "long time, no see" banter, but the mood of their reunion was somber, with the dark cloud of Abed Qalandar hanging over it.

They stepped into the kitchen, which smelled of fresh coffee. Brian introduced his wife, Kelly, who greeted Hammer with a wary smile.

"So you're the famous Captain Hammer who he talks about," she said directly, but with a smile. "I've heard a lot about you and I know there's a lot more that Brian has *not* said about what you gentlemen did when you…um… worked together."

"Pleasure to meet you, ma'am," Hammer said, shaking her hand. "There's a lot of water under that bridge, but I'm glad it's downstream."

"I hear that you've got some Afghanistan waters *upstream* now, too," Kelly said, nodding to a doorway across the room. "I've been having some interesting conversations with Ray and Hila."

Hammer turned as the Faizullah siblings entered the kitchen.

They looked older than Hammer remembered, as they would, of course. It had been a long time. With Hila, the terrified teenager of their exit from Afghanistan had been superseded by a self-assured young woman who now looked the part of a middle-America schoolteacher. Rahim, wearing a work shirt with a name patch identifying him as "Ray," looked as Americanized as the name he now used.

Both looked genuinely happy to see him. Indeed, both regarded Hammer as a father figure with a reputation for solving tactical dilemmas. Without hesitation, Hila came forward to give Hammer a more than perfunctory hug.

"I'm so glad to see you," she said emotionally. "It's been a nightmare here this week."

"Let's go talk in the living room," Kelly said. "Brian, could you bring the coffee?"

"I guess that Brian brought told you all about my brother's off-the-grid joyride over the weekend," Hila said, assertively taking charge of the conversation in unaccented English. "As you probably know, he drove all the way to New Orleans and back with Abed Qalandar... who apparently has made threats against *me*. I didn't know this man was even in America until we saw him in the Helmand Kitchen restaurant a week and a half ago. My brother said he didn't know either, but..."

"I *didn't*," Rahim said brusquely.

"Tell us about Abed Qalandar," Kelly asked. "Bring us all up to speed."

"He was a shady character who had connections inside the Afghan government. He was always doing deals with government officials," Hila explained. "He also did deals with the Americans, and NGOs, and the rumor was that he also was connected with the Taliban...

all of this at the *same time*. We saw him at the Helmand Kitchen with a bunch of Westerners, and a local Afghan man who I later figured out was Abdel Khaleq, who is the cousin of a woman I know from pilates."

"Tell Mr. Hammer what Qalandar says he is doing here?" Kelly asked.

"My brother says that he says he's importing rugs," Hila said icily. "But from where I'm looking at it, it looks like the two of them are off on joyrides."

"*Hila…*" Rahim started to say.

"Am I wrong? Why don't *you* tell us what happened, then?" Hila said, nodding to Rahim.

"A couple of days after we saw him, he came into the hardware store," Rahim began. "He knew who I was, and he knew that I knew who *he* was from Afghanistan. I never had anything to do with him over there. He is an intimidating man. He has an angry, evil face. I was afraid. It was afraid he might hurt me…or Hila."

"You told me that he offered you a side job," Herste interjected. "Something about him importing rugs."

"Yeah. He said that. At first, I didn't know what to do. Then he came back and handed me nine hundred dollars and said he wanted me to go with him for two days over the weekend. He didn't say where."

"So you *just went!*" Hila said tersely.

"I told him I didn't want to do this," Rahim insisted. "Then he started talking about Hila. He said, 'How's your sister?' He said she'd abandoned Afghan customs; no headscarf, teaching *male* students in school."

"Is he some kind of Sharia law enforcer?" Hila asked sarcastically.

Hammer could tell they'd had this conversation before and the subject still touched a nerve.

"He said he's not the *Qur'anic* police, but when he said that maybe he should have made this same job offer *to Hila,* I freaked out. All I could think was that she was going to be kidnapped. I wanted him as far from her as possible. *That's why I went!*"

"Weren't you afraid he was going to hurt *you*?" Hila asked. For the first time in the conversation, the others could see a softening in her tone.

"I figured I would deal with that as it came," Rahim said. "And in the back of my mind, I didn't think he'd give away nine hundred dollars and then kill me."

"What happened to the money?" Kelly asked.

"Rahim gave it to me Friday night," Hila said. "When I begged him not to go."

"What actually happened on this road trip?" Hammer asked. "What was the 'job' that you did?"

"That was the strangest thing," Rahim said. "My 'job' was to 'look like an Afghan,' first in a café, and then in a parking lot in a place called Arbeville on the Mississippi River south of New Orleans."

"*Look like an Afghan*?" Hammer repeated. "That *is* strange; the oddest bit of ethnic stereotyping I've heard of in a long while."

"I got the impression he wanted me to appear as though I was part of his gang," Rahim said. "I should tell you that the first people who I 'looked like an Afghan' for were two Americans who handle shipments of goods," Rahim continued. "I recognized one of them from the mountains of Kandahar, from that day long ago when Akhtar Mohammad Dadullah died. Hammer? Brian? Do you remember? You were *there*. He was the man with the round tortoise-shell glasses and the narrow goatee. He said his name was Gusche."

Hammer and Herste glanced at one another. How could anyone who was there forget that day?

"On Sunday morning, Qalandar had me stand in a parking lot and 'look like an Afghan' while a man on an ocean freighter looked at Qalandar and me through binoculars."

"What happened with the ship?" Hammer asked. "Was anything unloaded?"

"The ship slowed down to let two men get off and on."

"Sounds like river pilots," Hammer said. "They handle ocean traffic in confined waterways like the Mississippi because they know the river and the shoals and hazards to navigation."

"Yes," Rahim said. "I remember them using that word, 'pilot.' I think that while this was going on, they unloaded something from the other side of the ship so that customs people wouldn't see it. After the ship moved on, I saw a barge going the other way with containers on it...*down* the river."

"What was on the barge?" Hila asked, showing an interest in accepting Rahim's story. "Was it full of rugs?"

"I don't know," Rahim said. "I never saw the barge up close. But they said there will be another shipment coming in two weeks. It's already at sea."

"I'll bet it was *drugs*," Kelly said. "They grow opium poppies in Afghanistan."

"Any idea where the ship was from?" Hammer asked.

"It had a Kuwaiti flag, but they said it came from Doha."

"Does any of this make sense to you, Mr. Hammer?" Kelly asked.

"Yes, it all makes perfect sense. I can tell you for sure that the man with the round glasses, the one called Gusche, is part of a much bigger picture."

"Please tell us more," Kelly said.

"It's a long story."

"I made plenty of coffee."

Hila nodded, eager to hear more.

"Apparently all of what Rahim described ties into something two friends of ours came across a couple of weeks ago. They're friends of mine and Brian's who are down in Brouillecourt Parish, Louisiana now. These guys were in our team in Afghanistan. Johnny Arnaud and Tyler Roullier. We called them the 'two Cajuns.' They have a boat motor maintenance shop down on Bayou Langlois. They have an accountant in Fredieuville. Her name is Nicole Kirbye. She also served in Afghanistan as a civilian employee of a DOD agency called the Security Infrastructure Finance Organization. I hope I'm not getting too much in the weeds here, but all of this is part of the story."

"Go on," Hila said. "We're following the story. We've heard of SIFO."

"Our team never had anything to do with SIFO," Brian said. "We heard of them, but they were inside the wire at Bagram, while we were outside the wire in boonies getting shot at."

Hammer watched as Kelly winced.

"Wallace Gusche, they called him 'Wally' behind his back, was a manager at SIFO back then. Nicole worked under him over there. He was a pompous SOB. There were rumors that he was one of the ones, and there were more than a few over there, who was mixed up in all sorts of corruption. There was a crooked NGO that was sourcing opium from the Taliban. They were smuggling it to Europe. Gusche and his cronies were helping out."

Hammer watched Kelly shake her head in disgust. All the others just nodded. Such activities were news to no one else.

"Nobody thought much about this after we got back," Hammer said. "That was then and there. This is years later and eight thousand miles away. Until a couple of weeks ago, when our Cajun friends heard from a couple of their friends that some Department of the Army cops had been seen poking around a remote bayou down in the Delta. Not much of a red flag until they learned in pretty short order, that SIFO still exists, it's headquartered in Biloxi, Wally Gusche is now in charge, and he has those Army cops in his chain of command."

Hammer could see he had their interest. Who does not love a good mystery story with a cast of serious villains?

"Of course, the conspiracy theory wheels started spinning, and all the Cajuns and Nicole could think of was that Gusche was up to his old tricks and somebody was going to start smuggling something into the bayous. Next, Nicole spotted Gusche on the street in Fredieuville."

"It's all pretty circumstantial, though, don't you think?" Kelly asked.

"Absolutely," Hammer agreed. "Which is exactly what I thought when they first called me about it. But then things started to get suspicious."

Hammer paused to take a drink of his coffee, realizing as he did, he had lost no one's attention.

"There was a long ago and long-buried DOD report about Gusche, the NGO, and the Taliban. It was forgotten for years until a couple of weeks ago, when it cropped up on one of those conspiracy theory websites. You know, there's always a germ of truth in conspiracy theories, but this one was almost entirely true. One of the biggest fans of the website was a friend of Nicole's from Bagram, who lived in Terre Haute. He passed it along to along to another friend of Nicole's. She lives in Oklahoma."

Hammer could see that Kelly was growing skeptical.

"I know what you're thinking, but it certainly got real when the website guy's house went up in a fireball with him in it. Next, the guy in Terre Haute got murdered in his living room, and his laptop gone missing."

"What about the woman in Oklahoma?" Hila asked.

"Nicole invited her to make a quick visit to the bayou country, and bring her two young kids, and *hurry*. They made it as far as a rest stop in middle Louisiana before the bad guys drove down from Terre Haute and overtook them."

"Oh no, *no, no*," Kelly said.

"It ended well," Hammer said. "A good Samaritan intervened. Ashley and the kids are fine."

"And you know this how?" Brian asked with a smile. He knew.

"Let's just say I'm *sure* that those two will not be threatening anyone again...*ever*," Hammer said.

He watched Kelly's jaw drop. She had not thought for years about nature of the "work" that her husband and Hammer had done when the team was together all those years ago.

"Tell them how the barge that Ray saw figures in to your story," Brian urged.

"You saw a barge with a couple of containers early on Sunday morning," Hammer said. "Right?"

Rahim nodded.

"Well, Johnny, Nicole, and I watched a couple of containers come off a motor barge on Bayou Gadreau late on Sunday afternoon. We watched them go onto trailers. These are the same trailers that the sheriff of Brouille-court Parish told Nicole the night before were under the protection of Army cops."

"*Good Lord!*" Kelly exclaimed. "What happened to the containers?"

"Fortunately, I had a full tank of gas in my truck," Hammer said. "The three of us followed them. They got to a barn on a gravel road in Natchitoches Parish around midnight. You want to guess who was waiting for them?"

After a long pause, Rahim said, "Abed Qalandar."

When they asked Hammer what was actually in those shipping containers, he told of crate after crate of automatic weapons from the Taliban'a accidental armory. When he went on to unroll the narrative of rogue federal officials mixed up with the Gonzalves Cartel, eyebrows were raised in surprise, and heads shaken in disgust.

When Hammer was finished, Kelly Herste announced she was ready to declare war, and Hila loudly voiced her own agreement, adding some choice language.

It was Brian Herste who said succinctly, "I think Hammer already has declared war."

Hammer didn't say anything to that. He didn't have to.

When the inevitable question of "what next?" was posed, talk turned to Abed Qalandar.

To the amazement of all, it was Hila who suggested that she would take it upon herself to learn what she could about Khaleq, and about his connection with Qalandar. She would talk to his cousin, her acquaintance, Nurani Yusef.

"My sister, the spy," Rahim laughed. "But seriously, the same news about the gangs and the weapons, and knowing what I know about corrupt bureaucrats from Gusche to the people Hammer saw in Natchitoches, have made me a warrior again myself. You will remember how furious I was about Akhtar Dadullah long ago when you came to extricate us from Afghanistan?"

"Furious and *determined*," Herste recalled. "I remember that you refused to leave Afghanistan until we had lopped the head off that snake."

"Today, the snake has many heads," Rahim said angrily. "Many heads to lop."

"No more monstrous head than Qalandar's," Hila interjected.

"I have told Qalandar for so long that I do not want to do not want to work with him, that I think he believes me," Rahim said. "I will use that to my advantage, to *our* advantage, in this war that's been declared by everybody. You Americans have that saying about keeping your friends close and your enemies closer. If he asks me to go 'joyriding' again, I'll resist and then accept. If Hila can spy on those in his circle of acquaintances, I can spy on the monster himself."

"There are a lot of questions that come to mind about him wanting you as a passive collaborator in the first place," Hammer said, looking at Rahim. "It's curious to see him using you to construct a false front, an illusion of his being backed by a larger gang. It almost seems like he thinks he *needs* you. You said that Qalandar wanted you to 'look like an Afghan,' which is weird and borderline racist in itself, and you guessed he wanted you to look like part of his gang."

"Why didn't he just bring someone from his actual crew?" Kelly asked.

"I don't know," Rahim said.

"*Exactly*," Hammer said thoughtfully. "To answer Kelly's question, either he doesn't want anybody seeing his actual crew...or he doesn't *have one*."

CHAPTER
TWENTY-TWO

NATCHITOCHES PARISH, LOUISIANA

ABED QALANDAR AWOKE Wednesday morning to the angry buzzing of one of his burner phones and grabbed it as quick as he could.

"This is Blessins, did I wake you?"

"Of course not," Qalandar lied. "Where are you?"

"We'll be there this morning with the truck to pick up the load.

"I expected you yesterday."

"I thought that Ms. Mondtrom told you there might be some delays in getting our pipeline set up," Shane Blessins said. "Where are you? Are you still on-site?"

"Of course."

"Oh…that's very good of you to do that. She'll appreciate you staying to look after things *personally*…you could have had one of your people do it."

"When will I see you?" Qalandar asked, ignoring the question.

"Half an hour or so. I have a couple of our people with me to help load. When we're done, they can take over and you can get back to Fehryville. Thank you again for staying."

"Don't mention it," Qalandar said, ending the call and placing the phone on the low table next to his SIG P224.

He lit a cigarette and went to the window. It was getting light, but the morning sun had not yet crested the low hill on the far side of the river. He thought of that verse from the *Quran* that speaks of showing signs on the horizons until the truth becomes clear.

Two nights sleeping on a musty sofa were not what he was used to of late, but years of spending his nights on the hard ground of the Hindu Kush and waking up with ice in his beard had hardened him to minor discomfort.

You could have had one of your people do it.

Qalandar smiled. Even after the hiccup with Abdel Khaleq, Alexis Mondtrom and *her* people still believed that Qalandar had "people." He had recruited Rahim Faizullah to replace Khaleq as a façade for his organization, and Rahim had certainly done his part down on the Delta. He had met Lynse and Gusche. He had said nothing other than "hello" and "goodbye," but he had behaved like a hardware store clerk, making eye contact and being personable.

Qalandar knew it was Khairullah Ghani's people on the bridge with the binoculars, and that this man saw not just Qalandar, but that Qalandar and one of his people.

Admittedly, Rahim Faizullah made a better choice for one of his "people" than Abdel Khaleq. Except for his connections to the American Special Forces, Faizullah would have been a better choice in the first place. Qalandar decided he needed to use him more often. He might have brought him to Natchitoches, but that had gone well with Qalandar operating solo. Alexis was too fixated on the contents of the containers to concern herself with Qalandar's staffing issues.

As Qalandar lit another Marlboro and stepped out of the barn for his morning visit to the "latrine," he had those staffing issues on his mind. He made the decision to use Rahim Faizullah much more. He would give the young clerk a choice that would be hard to turn down. After his payday from Alexis, money was not an object.

And of course, if Faizullah balked, Qalandar could always mention his sister again. His big brotherly concern for Hila was *his* weak point.

FEHRY COUNTY, ARKANSAS

"Nurani, it's good to see you," Hila Faizullah said, greeting her friend, Nurani Yusef on Wednesday morning at Kaylene's Koffee Korral on First Street in Fehryville.

"Good to see you as well…outside pilates," Nurani said, smiling. "I would have thought you'd be in your high school classroom this morning."

"They canceled morning classes today…it was a big plumbing thing that was supposed to be finished over the weekend, but it wasn't. The district decided that rather than waiting until next weekend, they'd just schedule the plumbers now and get the construction site buttoned up for good."

"I guess," Nurani said with a smile. "I suppose that's a good idea. Less disruption in the long run."

"A decision above my pay grade." Hila laughed. "I just hope my teenagers will still remember Inverse Trigonometric Functions until Thursday."

"I *know* that I wouldn't," Nurani admitted.

Tuesday afternoon, Hila Faizullah had gone to Brian and Kelly's house petrified of the dark and mysterious dangers represented by Abed Qalandar and enraged at her brother for his idiotic disregard for his own safety in becoming a confidant to this monster.

She awoke Wednesday morning having become an enthusiastic co-conspirator with her brother and his former Special Forces friends. Hila admitted to herself that she felt "kind of creepy" about using a friendship this way and insisted that she'd try to make it appear casual.

It was more than half an hour into the Koffee Korral meeting on Wednesday morning before Hila casually asked, "How's your cousin Abdel?"

"Oh, he's got a job working from home for a call center back east," Nurani said. "They pay him pretty well and all he does is sit around his apartment in his T-shirt transferring calls between banks and credit card companies and stuff like that."

"I was on hold for almost an hour with one of those last week," Hila said. "Drives you crazy."

"That's what he does." Nurani laughed. "He sits around and drives people crazy. He puts people on hold for a living."

"Does he like it?" Hila asked. "That sounds dreadfully dull. Does he get out much?"

"He has never really acclimated to American culture like we did. For a while, he was spending time with Abed Qalandar. Do you know him?"

"I've heard the name," Hila said. "He worked for the government back in Kabul, didn't he?"

"I just remember him always scheming or scamming," Nurani said. "He always had something going with this NGO or that. He also worked for the Americans. They got him out and brought him here. What he did for them must have been worth it to them."

"What's he doing now?"

"Abdel said he was going to try to import Afghan rugs."

Hila just nodded and changed the subject. She felt self-conscious about steering the conversation too much toward Qalandar. She decided she would make a bad spy.

"Does Abdel get out much?"

"Not really," Nurani replied. "Why? Are you interested. He's kind of cute...for a cousin. Should I...?"

"Nah, I was just..."

"I've got an idea," Nurani said. "I've got some *khichdi quroot* that my mother made for him that I promised to drop off this afternoon. I could do that now...and *you* could come!"

Hila's first instinct was to beg off what she feared was becoming a matchmaking plot, but as she started to say "no," she realized what had happened. She had set out to get some secondhand information about Qalandar from Khaleq by way of Nurani, and now she was being handed an opportunity to talk to Khaleq directly.

Hila had decided she would make a poor spy, but here she was already congratulating herself on becoming a successful covert operative!

It was only about twenty minutes later when the two women arrived at Khaleq's nondescript apartment house, the same one to which Abed Qalandar had come exactly one week earlier planning to murder Nurani's cousin.

"Abdel, this is my friend Hila," she said in introduction.

"Pleased to meet you, Abdel," she said, shaking his hand in the American way.

"Hello," he said, using the American greeting. His enunciation was still much thicker than that of Nurani, whose accent was barely detectable. Hila sensed the slightest indication of a smile in his otherwise dour expression. He was dressed in jeans and a dark red Arkansas Razorbacks sweatshirt.

"Nurani tells me that you work in the financial industry," she said, making conversation.

"I shift calls and activate credit cards," he said, gesturing toward some computers piled on a table that was pushed against one wall of his living room.

"She told me that you also put people on hold," Hila said with a grin.

"That's half the job," he said, actually smiling. "Some days more than half. Would you like to sit down?"

"We don't want to interrupt," Nurani said.

"No problem. If I don't get a call, the next agent in the automatic queue takes it. Nobody knows. Other agents don't see me. Callers don't see me. I don't see them. Nobody sees anybody."

"That's an interesting way to work," Hila said as she sat down in one of his mismatched upholstered chairs. "I'm in full view of thirty people all day long. Sometimes, I wish I could just pick my tooth without being stared at by unforgiving teenagers...not that I ever have their undivided attention."

"I get very tired and annoyed with this sometimes. Actually, most of the time."

"Are you still working on that imported carpet deal with Qalandar?" Nurani asked.

"Not at the moment. His customers didn't like the way I didn't show the right amount of enthusiasm for them. I'm not very good with American customs. I'm not like you, Nurani. You became very Americanized."

"It's almost lunchtime," Nurani said, changing the subject. "Shall I heat up the *khichdi quroot*?"

"Would you like to stay for lunch?" Khaleq asked Hila.

"Sure," she said.

"What sort of work did you do in the rug business?" Hila asked when Nurani had gone into the kitchen. She was starting to feel more relaxed.

"Nothing...I mean, very little. He told me very little, but I heard him use the line from the *Quran* that goes 'we will show them our signs in the horizons and within themselves until it becomes clear to them it is the truth.' He told me that I was there because he liked to have an extra pair of hands in meetings, and because he wants another 'Afghan face' he called it. I only said what he had told me to say. The meetings were all talking, and I didn't do very much talking."

"That's interesting," Hila said, genuinely interested that his experience paralleled that of Rahim.

"I'll tell you what is more interesting," he said. "I was with him for six months and I *never* saw a rug, except for two or three that he was using at his condo over on Davis Court. He said he was importing rugs from Afghanistan, but I never saw any arrive in Fehryville from Afghanistan. The customers I met in the meetings never asked to see one. That made this work as dull as the call center work. "

"He must have a large organization, though?" Hila asked.

"I never saw anyone else," Khaleq said. "On the telephone and in the meetings, he talked like he had a big business, but it was just him. Him, with me to make it look like he had lots of people."

"Maybe he had other staff over in Kabul?" Hila asked.

"They didn't work for him. He was like their agent in America. They kept promising to send rugs, but all they sent was expense money. That was fine with me. They sent money and he paid me in cash."

"Lunchtime," Nurani announced from the kitchen as the microwave pinged.

Using potholders, she delivered the casserole dish to a low table near where Khaleq and Hila were sitting. She next brought plates and flatware and started serving the sticky rice dish made with sheep's milk butter, mung beans, and meatballs. It smelled good.

"One thing I should have said earlier," Khaleq said as he was about to take his first bite.

"What's that?" Hila asked.

"Please don't tell anybody what I just told you. If Qalandar finds out, he'll *kill me.*"

CHAPTER
TWENTY-THREE

SIFO HEADQUARTERS, KEESLER AFB, MISSISSIPPI

WALLACE GUSCHE OPENED his desk drawer when he heard the barely audible chirp of a burner phone. It was the phone that linked him to Len Ivermin. The lead agent in the DASP contingent whom Gusche employed in his side job was returning his call.

"Feel like a cup of coffee, Len?"

"See you in ten."

When he had sent Ivermin to talk to Nicole Kirbye, Gusche had not yet heard from Randy Coome that his fixers had called in to tell him that Ashley Grahen had been terminated. That might have closed the matter, but Gusche could not get Nicole out of his mind. There she was, an old SIFO hand, a friend of the Grahen woman, and living right there in Brouillecourt Parish—the same place where Gusche's moonrakers were landing.

There had to be more to this!

Gusche and Ivermin usually met in the coffee shop of the bowling alley on the base at Keesler.

Even at ten o'clock on a Wednesday morning, there was sufficient background noise to frustrate eavesdropping.

"Tell me more about your meeting with the Kirbye woman yesterday," Gusche said. "I know that you said she didn't know anything useful, but she was one of Ashley Grahen's close pals at Bagram."

"Why is Grahen of so much interest to you?"

"Grahen had access to an old DOD report about an investigation into some of things that we did in Afghanistan that involved using SIFO as a front for helping smugglers over there. It was long buried, but it popped up recently. Grahen could connect what we did over there to what we are doing now, because she knew *me* over there and could make that connection. What's bad for me is bad for you."

"I understand."

"If Grahen discussed the DOD report about SIFO with any old SIFO friends, it would have been with Kirbye. I need to know."

"You think she was lying?" Ivermin asked. "I question people for a living, and I'd say she was eighty percent honest."

"What about the other twenty percent?"

"That's the part where you can't be sure whether they're just nervous about talking to a cop, or they actually have something to hide," Ivermin said. "She *may* have fudged a bit when she said she hadn't heard from Grahen since this reunion years ago, but I don't think they're that close anymore."

"You asked me before whether I believed in coincidences. What about you? Do you think it's a coincidence that this woman is living in the same county...*er parish*... as where our operations are taking place?"

"I checked her out," Ivermin insisted. "She's had an

established business in Brouillecourt Parish for years, certainly since long before we picked Bayou Gadreau."

"Okay, *okay,*" Gusche said. "Tell me I'm being paranoid, but I want you guys to keep an eye on her just in case. When you go down there to monitor things in the lead-up to the next shipment, keep her in your sights."

"Roger that," Ivermin replied.

———

Gusche lingered after Ivermin left the coffee shop, using the clatter and clunk of the bowling lanes to mask his phone call to Randy Coome.

"Can you talk?"

"Yeah," Coome replied. "I'm in my truck."

"I hate to keep coming back to this, but have you heard from your two fixers since that text message yesterday?" Gusche asked.

"No," Coome said with a trace of impatience. "They texted to say that they'd finished the job and were coming back to get paid. Didn't say when. These are the kind of people that you pay with used bills, not wire transfers."

"When you *do* see them, how hard would it be for you to get rid of *them* permanently?"

"Hit the hitmen?"

"Yeah. Anything's doable," Coome said. "At a price."

"Whatever it takes," Gusche said, indicating that he'd meet the price.

As he watched the light go out when Gusche ended the call, all that Randy Coome had on his mind was how much he hated having agreed to take on the job of hiring contract killers to keep Gusche happy in the first place.

———

FEHRY COUNTY, ARKANSAS

"Abdel Khaleq said he worked for Qalandar for six months and never saw a single Afghan rug except for a couple he had on the floor of his condo," Hila Faizullah said. She had been telling Hammer about her conversation with Nurani Yusef, and her introduction to Abdel Khaleq. "He also said that in all that time, he never saw anyone else who worked for Qalandar, so your instincts about him working alone are probably right."

"Speaking of Qalandar's condo, it would be useful if Rahim could get close enough to Qalandar to get a look inside there," Hammer said in a thinking-out-loud sort of way.

"That sounds dangerous," Hila said.

"Yeah, it *could* be," Hammer admitted. "But he invited Khaleq in, and Khaleq is no worse for wear because of it."

"Wouldn't it be safer to do it when we know that Qalandar is not home?" Hila asked. "Like right *now*?"

"*Now*?" Hammer asked. "Rahim's at work."

"You don't need to send Rahim," Hila said. "*I'll do it*. I'll get into his apartment and take pictures of everything. I'll get a picture of anything you want to see. You're better off with someone who reads Pashto like a native."

"You?" Hammer said. "I thought you were skeptical about..."

"I thought it was settled," Hila said firmly. "Kelly and I said we wanted to *declare war*, and Brian said you *already had*. So here we are. We'll all do our part until we bring this thing down."

Hammer could see she was grinning when she followed up with "no offense, but you and Rahim creeping around a condo complex in the middle of the day? No way. You'd look *exactly* like burglars. It's far better to have a woman do it. It would raise fewer questions for anyone who might see me poking around."

"Point made." Hammer laughed. "Let me call Tim Tommis and have him send some software that you can install on Qalandar's computer so he can snoop later."

———

Deciding it would be more anonymous than Hammer's pickup, they took Hila's Subaru. Hammer drove, dropping her off a block away before parking in a spot where he could watch the entrance to Qalandar's condo on Davis Court from the car.

Wearing jeans and a plain light sweater, she fit in perfectly with the other people walking on the uncrowded sidewalks of the neighborhood. She also wore unobtrusive running shoes.

As Hammer knew, this was not her first rodeo. When she was a child, she had done exactly this kind of work to aid her brother and his friends in their clandestine efforts against the Taliban. Good shoes were as useful to a burglar as were the latex gloves she had in her pocket. Back then, being able to make a fast getaway could make the difference between life and the unspeakable.

Hila ascended the front exterior staircase with the assured air of someone who belonged. Qalandar's front door was on the second level of the building and set back slightly from the balcony railing, and she made quick work of the lock using the pick-set that Hammer lent her. It was not her first rodeo.

In a matter of seconds, she was in.

The shades were pulled, but it was such a bright sunny day that the place was not really dark. It smelled of tobacco and sweat and decaying leftovers, the apartment of a man who received few visitors.

Thankfully, it was dead quiet, for just after closing the door, Hila heard a low continuous tone whistling sound.

Alarm!

Why had she not thought of that?

She knew she had only thirty seconds, or maybe just twenty, to neutralize the alarm before all hell broke loose.

Looking around frantically, she spotted the alarm panel and its blinking red LED.

She lunged toward it, pausing as she stared at the keypad.

With a short prayer, she held her breath and stabbed in 4-1-5-3.

Suddenly the whistling stopped and the winking red light was replaced by one of solid green.

Exhaling in a sigh of relief, Hila looked around the room. It was several steps upscale from the bachelor apartment of Abdel Khaleq. Qalandar *did* have money, but it was just as messy.

She had time, but it was not unlimited. Qalandar was still many miles from Fehryville, but they knew from the surveillance camera that Hammer had left Natchitoches and was on his way.

Hila walked across the large Afghan carpet in the living room and stepped into the bedroom. It took no detective work to ascertain that Qalandar made minimal use of the laundry facilities.

Looking into a second room, she found the wily old schemer's computer setup. Among the papers strewn around, she located the piles that seemed to represent what Qalandar had been working on recently. As she leafed through them, she saw the name Ghani again and again. Then she saw several with the name Abbas. She recognized these as men who were members of the Taliban government of Afghanistan, and well-placed in the hierarchy of the Taliban operations in Doha, Qatar.

As she skimmed the documents, all in Pashto, of course, she found several which discussed imports, exports, and related matters. Having systematically photographed these, she decided to tackle the computers.

Slipping on her gloves, she powered up both of Qalandar's tower computers and his laptop. Amazingly, only the laptop demanded a password. Again, she typed in 4-1-5-3 and was rewarded.

She got into Qalandar's email account, installed the software from Tim Tommis, and spent the next fifteen minutes scrambling to download as much as possible from the computer hard drives onto the two sixty-four-gig thumb drives she had brought.

Hila powered down each computer, carefully put everything back where it had been, and took another turn through the rest of the apartment. She looked through random drawers and found some of Qalandar's guns. They were black and they looked like the pistols she'd seen long ago, and recently on television crime shows. She thought about stealing them but did not.

When she had done all that she thought she could accomplish, Hila reset the alarm and quietly opened the door. She was just pulling it shut when she heard footsteps on the staircase coming down from the third-floor unit.

It was too late to run.

Instead, Hila thought quickly, and knocked loudly on the door through which she had just come. It was too late to run, and too late to sneak back inside, so she decided that knocking would establish the false impression she had *never* been inside.

"Good morning," the freckled, red-haired woman said cautiously. "May I help you?"

"Hi, I'm Amira," Hila lied impulsively. "I'm a fiend of Abed's."

She didn't know why she lied. She just didn't want her name associated with the man she perceived as foul.

"Oh a *friend*, are you?" The older woman laughed. "I'm Brenda from upstairs. Don't recognize you. I didn't think Mr. Qalandar had any friends. He's been here four, or maybe five, years and I've never seen him with anyone. He's not very talkative, that one. Keeps to himself. Hardly ever see him around. But that's none of my business."

"I see," Hila said. If Qalandar was "not very talkative" around Brenda, then she more than made up for it.

"Are you in the rug business?" Brenda asked. "He told me one time that he imports rugs from someplace overseas. I've never seen him with any rugs, but that's none of my business."

"Yeah, sort of," Hila said unconvincingly.

"Listen, hon, it's none of my business who comes and goes," Brenda said with a wink. "I won't even mention that I saw you. Good luck when you do find him."

With that, she was gone, lumbering down the stairs to the ground level.

As Hila started down, she saw Hammer on the sidewalk about a hundred feet away. He had started toward her when he saw her run-in with Brenda but was now walking casually back toward the car.

"How'd it go?" he asked when she caught up to him.

"I installed your bug, downloaded a lot of files and rummaged through the paperwork. It was a lot like my typical school days...except for the alarm system."

"Oh yeah?"

"Yeah."

"You seem to have handled it pretty well. How did you get through the alarm?"

"I just typed in 4-1-5-3. That's the number of the *Quran* verse that Abdel said Khaleq heard Qalandar quoting. It reads 'we will show them our signs in the horizons and within themselves until it becomes clear to them it's the truth.'"

"Good move," Hammer said. "Fast thinking on your part."

"The 'truth' is I'm a product of a moment in time when Afghan girls got *educated*," Hila said. "That's why the Taliban kicked us all out of school. They don't want to have *girls* running around knowing too much!"

CHAPTER
TWENTY-FOUR

UPTON COUNTY, TEXAS

"WE MUST BE GETTING CLOSE," Alexis Mondtrom complained from the passenger's seat of the big gray Cadillac Escalade. "Please tell me we're getting close. I'm getting sick of hours and hours of endless emptiness and these wispy little towns with their water towers and forlorn gas stations."

"My device says four miles," Shane Blessins said from behind the wheel in the front seat. It was after ten o'clock on Thursday night as they sliced through the monotonous West Texas darkness on US Route 67. Ahead of them were the taillights of the tractor-trailer rig driven by David Anchry that carried the containers from the Natchitoches, Louisiana barn. This was the middle of nowhere, but agents of the Department of Homeland Security couldn't easily just drop off millions of dollars worth of contraband military hardware to a criminal gang in the middle of *somewhere*.

It was blessed relief for all when they finally saw the

big rig signaling for a right turn. Blessins followed the truck onto a barely marked side road for about a mile and a half until they spotted two dual-cab, dual-tire pickups parked about a hundred feet off the road.

In the glow of the headlights, Alexis recognized Raoul "Buster" Bustamante, one of the principal bosses for the Gonzalves Cartel in North America. Their stock in trade was providing to weapons and muscle for the drug gangs which were systematically taking over cities and towns across the West.

"*Buenas noches*, Buster," Alexis said, greeting the big man. "We come bearing treasures."

"Good to see you too, Alexis," he replied in flawless English. Born in Sinaloa, he was a graduate of UCLA who had done post-graduate work at the Harvard Business School before joining the family business. "Let's see what you have."

One of two pickups was backed up behind the flatbed semi-trailer, and two of Bustamante's men opened the door of the first container. In a repeat of Alexis's own inspection of the merchandise at the Natchitoches barn, six cartel men, and two women, systematically sampled the contents. Bustamante asked for one of the M16A4 assault rifles to be handed down to him, and he tucked it under his arm. This one would be going home with him personally.

The cartel men were especially pleased with the M249 SAWs and were admiring these when a vehicle appeared on the road.

Everyone stopped what they were doing and squinted into the approaching headlights trying to figure out who was interrupting them out here in the middle of nowhere. As the pickup slowed to a stop, they could see that the driver was a man with a cowboy hat, and he was alone in the cab.

When he put the truck in reverse and started to back away, Alexis Mondtrom approached, flanked by Shane Blessins, with her federal ID held high, and gestured for him to stop and get out.

"My name is Alexis Mondtrom," she said as the man in the cowboy hat complied. Her voice was steady and firm. "I'm with the Department of Homeland Security. These men are agents with the Federal Security Office."

Blessins nodded.

Alexis walked over and allowed the man to have a closer look at her ID. She nodded to Blessins who presented his own FSO ID, with his glittering gold badge attached. As he took these out of his jacket pocket, he made sure that the stranger was intimidated by the sight of his shoulder holster.

"Yes, ma'am," the stranger said. "I don't mean no harm."

"Now that you've seen ours, I hope you won't mind showing us yours," Alexis said. She could tell that he was frightened, not only by the unexpected encounter with federal law enforcement, but by the sight of a truckload of automatic weapons.

"Here it is, ma'am," said the stranger. "I'm sorry to have bothered you. I'll be on my way now."

The only thing on his mind was to get away from this place as fast and as far as he possibly could, but Alexis relished the sense of power that came with making this goal as difficult as possible to achieve.

"What are you doing out on this road at this time of night, sir?"

"On my way home. Saw the lights from the highway. Thought I'd give it a look and see. Nobody *ever* uses this road."

"Well, apparently they *do*," Alexis said derisively. "I'm

going to ask that you tell no one about this top-secret federal operation. Can you promise me that, sir?"

"Yes, ma'am."

It was probably Buster Bustamante who fired first, but that doesn't matter. The first shot blended into a cacophony within seconds.

The stranger was dead before his Stetson hit the ground.

———

PEARL ISLAND, DOHA, QATAR

As that unlucky man in West Texas breathed his last, Khairullah Ghani was eight thousand miles due east, enjoying his Friday morning coffee and his view of the sun rising over the deep blue waters of the Persian Gulf. In his luxury apartment high on the fourteenth floor of the Viva Bahriya Tower, the two young women with whom Ghani had shared his king-sized bed last night were scurrying about. One had served his coffee and was preparing his breakfast while the other showered.

Like Abed Qalandar, Ghani had spent years roughing it in the Hindu Kush, but the middle-aged Taliban chief now enjoyed a civilized life far from Afghanistan and would be loath to ever go back. He liked the look of women who spurned the blue burqa, and he had developed a taste for decades-aged Scotch whisky.

He also enjoyed the perks of the diplomatic immunity accorded to him because of his role in the foreign service of the Taliban government of Afghanistan, the very regime whose ideals of morality he shunned with his women and his affection for booze.

Ghani pushed his cup aside on the glass-topped table and flipped open his laptop. As much as he enjoyed the view, both of the sunrise and the nude and nubile late teenage bodies of his young companions, he knew that duty called.

Among the emails that flooded into his refreshed inbox were several from his colleagues and bosses at the headquarters of the Islamic National Army in Kabul, congratulating him on the first successful arms sale to Abed Qalandar clients. "Very soon, abandoned American weapons would be wreaking havoc on American streets," they gloated. They added that the money wired by Qalandar was already in the Taliban accounts in Zurich.

Khairullah Ghani smiled.

Could he please advise them of the progress of the subsequent shipments, they asked. Ghani stopped reveling in success and tapped out a message to Abbas, his man at Hamad Port, south of Doha.

At that moment, his young friend delivered a plate of scrambled eggs with smoked salmon and a second plate with *khubz*, a light flatbread. She smiled at his caress. For her and her sister, life in the Viva Bahriya Tower was like a fairy tale come true. Many of the young women whom they knew were treated coarsely by their Taliban masters, but Ghani was kind to them, paid them well, and bought them nice clothes. He liked to touch, but his touches were usually kind and affectionate.

Ghani was dipping a slice of *khubz* into a dish of *labneh*, yogurt with herbs and olive oil, when Abbas replied to his earlier message.

He proudly reported good news. The Kuwaiti-flagged *Ashuwaykh Star*, sister ship of the *Shuaybah Star*, which had delivered their first shipment was ahead of schedule. Favorable seas had allowed it to accelerate its arrival by six days. It would reach the Mississippi Delta on Monday morning, and the Port of New Orleans that same afternoon. The third shipment had already exited Hamad Port.

Feeling pleased about being a key part of a plan that was coming together nicely, Ghani composed a message to his bosses in Kabul conveying the good news. He smiled at the young woman refilling his coffee cup and stroked her long, luxurious hair.

As he took a sip, he realized he had best let Abed Qalandar in on the good news. He flipped open his laptop and tapped out a message.

―――――

FEHRY COUNTY, ARKANSAS

For Abed Qalandar, the news was not necessarily all that good. However, any message that arrives at midnight after an abbreviated and fitful hour of sleep is an aggravation, but that which aggrieved him most was what the news did to his schedule. Qalandar had been planning on a repeat of *last* weekend, but he had expected to make his second visit to the Delta *next* weekend, not this one.

He had Rahim Faizullah primed for next weekend's drive, and now he had to prime him for going nearly a week early, and for the complication of taking a day or two off from work. In past years in Afghanistan, intimidation was enough, but in the West, intimidation went only so far. Qalandar had been compelled to practice finesse.

Using his younger sister as leverage, he knew he could cajole and browbeat Faizullah into doing his bidding, but it would have been easier if the schedule had remained. But he knew he *could* do it, and he *would* do it. Qalandar had, of course, built a livelihood on his flexibility, and he would intimidate Faizullah into adapting to the changing schedule.

The thought of threatening Hila Faizullah often did flicker through the sadistic side of Qalandar's mind. She had grown into a young woman who checked a lot of boxes for Qalandar's animal desires. He had to caution himself that this was the West, this was where he felt compelled to practice finesse.

Of course, as he lay there in his bed, looking at the small numbers of his digital clock, little did he realize that a day and a half earlier, *she* of his cruel fantasies had been standing in this very room, pondering the foul odor, and thinking about Qalandar himself, a man whom she considered even more foul.

Having dozed off again, Qalandar awoke suddenly several hours later realizing it was Friday, and he owed a call to another woman in his life—the woman whom he hated because she was one of the few people, and the *only* woman, he'd ever met whom he could not intimi-date—someone with whom the lines of intimidation ran the *other* way.

If the shipment was arriving early, Alexis Mondtrom needed to know ASAP.

"Ms. Mondtrom, this is Abed Qalandar," he said when she answered on the seventh ring. "I have impor-tant news."

"This is not a good time, Abed," she said in a prickly tone. He did not know about last night's shootout last in West Texas, nor that she had been up all night, helping to clean up the mess created by the trigger-happy gang of Buster Bustamante.

Alexis was one of those people who never smiled nor used a kind word when a stern word would suffice. Qalandar could relate. He was one of those himself, so he was not put off by her acerbic tone.

"But as long you're on the line," she said impatiently, "what's the news?"

"It's about the next shipment," he said.

"*What the hell*," she scolded. "Don't tell me it's going to be *late*!"

"No. Just the opposite. It will be *early*. It will be in the Mississippi River on Monday."

"*Monday*!" Alexis exclaimed, clearly taken by surprise. "What happened?"

"My colleague in Qatar tells me it is 'favorable' seas."

"Okay," Alexis said after a long pause. "That could work. We'll make it work."

"What's wrong?" Qalandar asked.

"What do you mean?" Alexis asked defensively.

"You sounded upset. Are you ready?"

"Everything is fine. I have a lot of balls in the air right now. Nothing that can't be sorted. I do have to go. Thanks for the call. Talk soon."

But she did sound upset, he told himself. The unflappable Alexis Mondtrom had eyes that drill through you like lasers and she had an answer for everything. What was it? *What if she can't afford to pay for the next shipment?*

He considered this as he lit a cigarette and watched the smoke curl about his head.

What if I have to find another buyer?

He had done it once; he could do it again. He was used to uncompromising gangsters. After all, what was the Taliban, if not the world's most unrelenting and most successful criminal organization?

———

Qalandar's next call was to Wallace Gusche in Biloxi, the man who made things happen.

"Gusche, this is Qalandar," he said. "I have news about our next shipment."

"What about it?" Gusche asked as calmly as he could. As with Alexis Mondtrom, he immediately interpreted talk of a shipment nine days before it was due as indicative of something amiss. "What's wrong?"

"It's good news," the old mujahidin said. "It will be early."

"How early?"

"It's coming on Monday morning...*this* Monday."

"Okay," Gusche said thoughtfully. "As you know, we've been asking for Sunday arrivals because of the slipshod nature of Sunday staffing at the customs office out there. Adjustments will have to be made."

"Can you delay it?"

"Not for six days," Qalandar insisted. "Remember, we have only two small containers on a ship with more than a hundred containers. We are like a flea that takes a ride from a dog. We are unimportant to the shipping company. We can ask only so much. We do not want to draw attention to our containers."

"Okay, I understand," Gusche said. "I'll see you, *and your people*, on Monday."

There it was, Qalandar thought, a validation that Gusche, like Mondtrom, assumed he was backed by an organization. Gusche took for granted that Qalandar had *people*.

———

As he rang up a couple of customers on the register at Herste Hardware on Friday morning, Rahim Faizullah could hardly imagine that only a week had passed since Abed Qalandar had walked in here and told him that they were about to spend the weekend on the road. A week ago, Rahim had been nearly paralyzed with fear of this man. Now, he knew his weaknesses, the biggest of which was that he seemed to *need* Rahim.

This week, for both Rahim and his sister Hila, the fear had dissipated, mostly. It was now more like one of those computer programs that are always "running in the background."

Last week, a big part of the apprehension was fear of the unknown. Now, that part had changed. Thanks to Rahim having been to Arbeville, and to the snooping and wire-tapping that Hila had done on Wednesday, they knew what to expect. Tim Tommis had intercepted and shared the email exchanges between Ghani and Qalandar, and between Qalandar and Alexis Mondtrom.

Last week, Rahim and Hila had been at odds, with Hila mad at him. This week, they were on the same page in the declaration of war on the many headed snake, and in pursuing the strategic plan of operations that was coming together in Jim Hammer's head.

Yet, despite this, all of his confidence was abruptly challenged when Rahim looked up and suddenly found himself staring into Qalandar's hard, cruel face across the counter at Herste Hardware.

Those dark, diabolical eyes and the sinister sneer combined to make Rahim more than merely ill at ease. The dread was no longer running only in the background.

"What can I do for you?" was all that Rahim could think of to say.

"We must leave for Arbeville in the morning," he replied. "And tell your bosses that you must take Monday off."

"You told me that your next...um...rug shipment was not due until the end of *next* week," Rahim said nervously. He dared not let on that he already knew about this change of schedule. The part about leaving for Arbeville on Saturday, however, did take him off guard.

"It's arriving early," Qalandar said. "It will be coming on Monday."

"Why leave *tomorrow* if it's not coming until Monday?"

"I'm not paying you to ask questions," Qalandar said as he handed over a roll of hundred-dollar bills.

CHAPTER
TWENTY-FIVE

GULFPORT, MISSISSIPPI

"*MOONRAKERS!*"

Who the hell was Gusche kidding with this kind of blather?

This job is not some romantic flight of the imagination! This is heavy lifting, precisely timed heavy lifting. This is coordinating the right equipment with the right people—people who have been paid not to talk.

Randy Coome set down the phone. Everything rested on his shoulders, and now this curveball! He had been operating under the assumption that he had more than a week to prepare for the second shipment. Now, he had to pull *everything* back together over a weekend. What if he couldn't pull that crew back together on short notice? Even the Coome cousins did not have a bottomless pool of people who could be paid not to talk.

"*Moonrakers!*"

These are truck drivers, forklift operators, and barge men, all of whom operate day in and day out in the *real* world, not in the swashbuckling world of Wallace Gusche's daydream!

Just as he was starting to dial his forklift man, Coome heard a rattle in his drawer. He knew what it was, and *who* it was. The fixers were texting, the lowlifes who had finally killed that woman in the orange Honda. When they'd texted on Tuesday, they said they'd be coming to get paid. That was three days ago. A three-day drive must mean that they got rid of her a long way from the Gulf Coast. That was good.

Let's meet. Bring money.

At least they were being succinct.

Tonight at 7. Bay St Louis. Warehouses off Harney Road. Txt you which one when I see you get there. Come alone.

Okay, there it is, Coome thought. It was twenty miles away toward New Orleans. Less familiar territory for Coome. Probably more familiar for *them.* He didn't mind. He knew Bay St. Louis as well as most people. The only problem was the "come alone" part. Of course they'd say that. It was almost *pro forma.*

Of course Coome was *not* coming alone.

He picked up another burner phone and called Brawley Eligarde. Coome had him on speed dial ever since he'd gotten the word from Gusche that the fixers had to be eliminated. Eligarde was a good shot at any distance. He should have been a sniper, but a serious felony conviction at eighteen kept him out of the Army. They thought a light sentence would turn his life around. They were wrong. When he got out, he never looked back.

Coome decided that Eligarde should leave for Bay St. Louis as soon as possible, park well away from the warehouse complex, and find a place from which he could cover Coome wherever he went.

Coome took a deep breath. He had the money. It was

in a cheap briefcase in his safe. He would take it to Bay St. Louis. He would use it to tease the fixers, and then he'd bring it back. He also had a Glock 19 that he could easily conceal—to eliminate the fixers as they had eliminated the woman in the orange car, and the others before her.

As he left his office in Gulfport, Coome could smell an electrical storm coming in from the Gulf, and there were distant rumbles of thunder as he crossed the Bay St. Louis Bridge and continued west on US 90.

———

BAY ST. LOUIS, MISSISSIPPI

As he turned off at Harney Road, Brawley Eligarde could see a group of four warehouses squatting about a quarter mile away and looking forlorn. They were part of the detritus of Hurricane Katrina all those years ago, abandoned as economically unsalvageable. Over the years a succession of now-bankrupt holding companies had bickered about and forgotten about them, even as copper pirates stripped them of their electrical wiring and everything else of value.

There was nobody around as Eligarde parked his car in a hidden place behind an old shack about fifty yards from the rusting perimeter fence. As he got out and sniffed the ozone in the air, he could see the line of dark clouds gathering off to the south. He grabbed his slicker out of the back seat, made sure that his car could not be seen, and opened his trunk.

Inside, in its case, was his Remington Model 700 bolt-action rifle with a Leupold scope and its six-round internal magazine filled with .308 Winchester cartridges.

The gate in the perimeter fence was open slightly, so

he pushed it all the way so that Coome would not have to get out of his pickup to open it when he arrived. He found his sniper's perch, a place near one of the canals leading into the bay which offered shelter from the impending storm, and from which he had a clear line of sight into the openings of any of the four buildings.

Eligarde settled in, attached his Harris bipod to the muzzle of his Remington and prepared to wait. He checked his watch. It was barely five o'clock. He had two hours to wait. The fixers would probably arrive before Coome, but whatever they did and whenever they did it, they'd be doing it at the other end of Eligarde's scope.

As he waited, the only sounds were the gathering thunder of the storm, the ominous low hissing of the wind and the splashing of a lone alligator in the nearby canal. He took another slurp of water from his plastic bottle and wished he had brought his flask. He would rather have the taste of bourbon just now.

As he daydreamed about the fire of the whiskey inside his throat, he felt something seize the outside of his throat. He gagged and tried to move he was pinned. Eligarde's first thought was it was the gator, but then someone above him spoke.

"Are you here to kill me?"

"*Ahhh...*" was the only answer that Eligarde could muster with the hand on his throat.

Then, suddenly, as there was a huge clap of close-by thunder, whoever it was released his grip, and Eligarde rolled over.

A large man in a gray ball cap crouched over him, pinning him now with a resolute glare, rather than with his huge hands. Eligarde had his chance now and he took it. He swept the muzzle of the Remington around, intending to jab it into this man and fire it point-blank.

At the last possible moment, just as he was about to

squeeze the trigger, he felt the man's left hand on his own left hand, squeezing, crushing, and stopping the muzzle. He felt the Remington being jerked away and saw a Ka-Bar knife in the man's hand.

A few minutes later, Brawley Eligarde's lifeless body was rolling down the embankment toward the nearby canal.

The alligator submerged as the Remington 700 with the Leupold scope splashed into the murky, muddy waters about three feet away and sank forever into the silt and muck below.

Thunder boomed again as Jim Hammer walked across the gravel open area toward on the warehouse he had preselected for his meeting with Randy Coome.

Ninety minutes later, thunder was relentlessly rattling the corrugated steel of the warehouses as Coome pulled through the open gate. He did not see Eligarde's car, nor the man himself, and hoped he was where he could finish this exercise quickly.

He stopped and looked at the three warehouses and then at his phone. He'd been told that a text message would reveal which warehouse contained his fixers, who were eager for the cash in the cheap briefcase.

It did not take long.

Left one.

As with the earlier messages, it was terse and to the point, and Coome appreciated this.

Coome drove to the open door of the warehouse on the left, stopped, grabbed the briefcase, and got out of his pickup.

With thunder booming ever more loudly and lightning crackling, he walked to the entrance and stared inside. He could see very little, but an abrupt flash of lightning illuminated the interior for a split second. In that illumination, he saw a man standing deep inside.

Only one? Aren't there two fixers? What's going on here?

He entered the cavernous, empty place, buoyed by a confidence in the Glock 19 in the waistband of his jeans.

The man inside made no effort to walk toward him but simply stood and stared.

Though dwarfed by the scale of the vast room, he was a tall man, broad in the shoulders. He wore a short, light rain jacket and a gray ball cap. He was unshaven, with whiskers too long to be fashionable, but too short to be called a beard.

"You're not who I expected," Coome said in a tone that conveyed his irritation. "Who are you?"

"They couldn't come," Jim Hammer replied. "The two jokers you sent to kill the people in the orange Honda can't be here, so you've got me instead to pick up the money. Is that my money in there in that bag?"

"How can I be sure that you...?"

As thunder shook the place and heavy rain started falling outside, Hammer held up a picture, printed by an inkjet printer that showed an orange car that seemed to be on its side.

"Is that the money that pays for two men dead in Colorado and Terre Haute? Is that money that pays for the people in that car? I know that Wally Gusche ordered you to order the hit, but being the middleman is no excuse?"

"He doesn't like to be called Wally, y'know."

"So I've been told."

"It's all just a case of somebody who knew too much for her owned damned good."

"You know there were two kids in that car, don't you? There was Liam. He was six and liked to watch people overhaul marine engines. Ava, she was only four. She liked swamp turtles. You knew about them, *right*?"

"So I was told," Coome said impatiently as he

wondered where Eligarde was, and hoped he'd take his shot.

"Is that the money?" Hammer demanded. "Is that Wally Gusche's money?"

"*Yes, dammit!*" Coome exploded, tossing the briefcase across the concrete floor. "Come and get it!"

As Hammer took one step forward, Coome lost patience with the situation and reached for the Glock 19 in his waistband. He was making the mistake of drawing his gun on the wrong adversary, but he had no way of knowing this.

Before he had a chance to swing the Glock around to aim, Coome found himself staring into the muzzle of a handgun that seemed twice as large.

Compared to a sleek, black Glock, a Colt M1911 is an artifact of another time, little changed since it won two world wars. The weathered natural metal makes it look like a leftover from Guadalcanal or Normandy. The .45ACP rounds of Hammer's weapon of choice dwarfed the jacketed 9mm ones of the Glock, the gun which Randy Coome never succeeded in getting into firing position.

K'pow! B-b-b-ba-booom!

The thunder of the M1911 was overlapped by thunder from above.

The raw lead struck the man who'd hired to men who'd killed two and tried to kill a mother and her children.

As it impacted the bridge of his nose, the momentum of the slug carried what was left of his bewildered face out through the back of his splintering skull—all of this serenaded by another colossal thunderclap.

———

Having moved Coome's pickup inside to be parked near his mortal remains, Hammer relieved him of a wallet and a couple of cell phones he would never again need.

Hammer then fired one final round at the ceiling of the warehouse, hitting a corner of a loose metal frame where one bullet was all that was needed to bring a massive, rusty, wind-damaged skylight down upon the pickup, thus initiating a deluge of rainwater.

It was Hammer's proverb that strategic solutions were reached by working your way up the ladder, step by step. He had taken a first step in a Louisiana rest stop last Tuesday, and this led him directly and methodically to the second rung, here in Bay St. Louis.

He already had a clear idea of the rungs that lay ahead.

Picking up his two spent shell casings along with Coome's wallet and phone, Hammer closed the big warehouse door on a scene that would go undiscovered for weeks, threw up the hood of his jacket, and walked into the stormy night toward his pickup for the drive back toward Brouillecourt Parish.

CHAPTER
TWENTY-SIX

BILOXI, MISSISSIPPI

"WHERE'S RANDY?" Wallace Gusche asked pointedly. "We've only got two days to get ready for that next shipment."

Gusche and Brent Lynse had met Eddie Coome at the Shrimp Bowl on Beach Boulevard, their usual down-market, off-the-grid meeting spot to discuss the surprise arrival of their next batch of containers on Monday morning. The Bowl opened at six and the three of them were the first customers, except for an old man with a raincoat who looked like he had been up all night in the storm. Water was still dripping from the eaves outside.

"When I talked to him yesterday, he didn't say nothing about going anyplace," Eddie replied. "I've been calling his cell phone and both of his burner phones all morning. Just goes to voicemail. I even stopped by his place. He wasn't around and his truck was gone. It's early, though, ain't even nine o'clock yet...maybe he met a lady at the casino last night and got lucky."

Gusche wanted to bring up the fixers, but he knew

that Randy had never briefed Eddie about them. It was a 'need to know' deal, and Randy figured that Eddie didn't need to know, so he kept that close to his vest. Randy had told Gusche that they were coming to get paid. Gusche was worried that something went wrong, but at the moment he had bigger fish to fry.

Of course, maybe Eddie was right and Randy *did* get lucky last night. If not, as Gusche had taught himself in Afghanistan, everybody is expendable, except Wallace Gusche.

"Are you guys ready with the unloading and the barges and everything else?" Gusche asked, turning to what really mattered. These were tasks that were very much in Eddie's wheelhouse. In his day job, running Coome Hauling while Randy took care of a lot of things, he was a master of the loading and hauling trade.

"Yessir," Eddie replied. "Randy got everybody lined up yesterday. They're taking to forklift and trailer over to Bayou Gadreau on Sunday afternoon, and the bargemen are coming up to Arbeville on Sunday night. Randy told 'em he didn't want 'em hanging around on Sunday attracting attention."

"That's sensible," Gusche said thoughtfully as three plates of eggs and side meat were delivered to their breakfast table.

"Randy was sure cranky about what you were calling the bargemen," Eddie said between bites after the course of the conversation maneuvered into small talk. "What was it? *Moon* something?"

"Moonrakers?" Gusche said.

"Yeah. Randy thought it sounded like a fairy tale. It was like you weren't taking these guys seriously."

"To the contrary," Gusche said, almost indignantly. "Moonrakers were the guys from a few hundred years ago who smuggled French booze across the beach into

England under full moons and under the noses of revenuers. Moonrakers are a *good* thing to be."

"Yeah, I reckon so. That is, if you ain't got no good use for revenuers."

———

Fifty minutes after his meeting with Eddie Coome, Gusche was at the Keesler AFB bowling alley with Len Ivermin. Gusche had already broken the news he wanted Ivermin to head over to Fredieuville, Louisiana, immediately to surveil Nicole Kirbye until after the arrival of the "moonrakers."

"Could I ask a question?" Ivermin said.

Gusche nodded.

"You told me about that DOD report about the investigation into SIFO, and how the two women could connect you to what happened then and possibly implode what we're doing now. I've been questioning and following Kirbye for almost a week now and I've been watching you getting more and more nervous about what she does and what she knows about the woman in the orange car. I'm already in this pretty deep," Ivermin continued. "I could do jail time if this goes south, so I think I deserve to know the whole story. My question is this...what's the *endgame* with Kirbye?"

At first, Gusche was taken off guard by his directness, but he wasn't surprised by what he'd said. If it had been him, he would have reached this point before Ivermin had.

"I know you've been patient, Len. Sure...okay. You deserve to know. Ashley Grahen may or may not have had a 'fatal accident,' but Nicole Kirbye *will* have one. I'm going to ask you to make sure she does."

"Wow," Ivermin said calmly. "I should be startled, but

in the back of my mind, I saw this coming. You say that Grahen may or may not have had an accident. Did she or didn't she?"

"I asked Randy Coome to hire some guys to take care of her. They said they did, but there were problems."

"What kind of problems?"

"They went on and off the grid, and their car showed up in Alabama when they said they were in Texas, and things like that. Now, I can't get hold of Randy Coome. His brother Eddie is running the show on Monday. I don't trust Eddie like I did Randy to handle the fixers, although he's as competent as Randy for handling containers. At least I hope so."

"It sounds like Randy may have let you down with Grahen."

"I know that *you* won't let me down with Kirbye," Gusche replied.

———

US ROUTE 65, MADISON PARISH, LOUISIANA

Rahim Faizullah was in exactly the same place where he had been a week ago—geographically. Last week, he didn't know where he was going, nor did anyone whom he knew.

This week, as he sat in the passenger seat of the black BMW, watching the windshield wipers slap their way through the heavy rain, and Abed Qalandar chain-smoking Marlboros, he was not alone. This week, two or three car lengths behind him, Brian Herste was shadowing the BMW in his gray GMC Sierra pickup. It was his older, secondary pickup, but he chose it because it was unremarkable and would blend in with other traffic, and because his *other* truck had "Herste Construction" painted on the doors in big letters.

As they had a week earlier, Qalandar and his passenger made a stop outside Vicksburg, but not at the Waffle House. This time, they made only a stop at a truck stop to refuel. Qalandar stepped away from the car to make a call on his satellite phone and to buy some junk food at the convenience store while he let Rahim pump the gas. Qalandar kept the keys.

As they crawled through the New Orleans interchanges and made their way to Louisiana Route 23 and points south, the rain had mostly dissipated, but there were large ponds of standing water along the road from the previous night's storm. This week, as they dodged the mud puddles while pulling into the parking lot at Evonne's in Port Sulphur, Louisiana, Wallace Gusche's silver Malibu was already there.

PORT SULPHUR, LOUISIANA

"I gotta admit that I don't have the same confidence in Eddie Coome's ability to handle things as I did with his cousin," Brent Lynse said, taking a sip of his sweet tea at their table inside Evonne's.

"Randy's the brains behind that operation," Gusche replied. "No doubt. But Eddie's got years of experience in the nuts and bolts of running a thing like this. And remember, their crew did the *exact same thing* a week ago. They ought to be able to do it again, right?"

"Right, but with the ship is coming in on Monday instead of Sunday, I'm worried about who's going to be manning the US Customs office. On Sundays, they're asleep at the wheel. Who knows about Monday?"

"You could send Ivermin or Sentyl down there with their DASP badges out and use the 'classified national security operation' ploy. That ought to work."

"Only as a last resort," Gusche said. "It potentially complicates things, especially when you use federal badges to pull that trick with *other* federal agents. Not to mention that we need Ivermin and Sentyl using the 'national security' ruse down on the bayou with the trucks and forklift at that same time."

Lynse nodded. It was going to be a complicated few days.

"We also got weather to contend with," Gusche observed, watching the raindrops spitting at the window of the diner.

"Reports say the storm is pushing north," Lynse said, looking at the weather app on his phone. "This should clear out by morning."

"There they are," Gusche said, nodding to the BMW that just crawled into Evonne's expansive, but mostly vacant, parking lot.

"Qalandar's got his same guy with him again this week," Lynse said. "What do you make of him?"

"Faizullah? Hard to read him. He didn't talk much. Just kept his eyes on us like he was sizing us up the whole time."

"He seemed pretty sharp," Lynse said. "Not your average flunky like that other guy he had."

"Qalandar never talks much about his people," Gusche remarked. "Guess he knows how to pick 'em."

"What it was like to pick a crew over there in Afghanistan?"

"Same thing only different over there. the gangs were all made up of cousins and half brothers so there was some measure of loyalty baked in."

"Wonder if Faizullah was part of his crew over there," Lynse said.

"Qalandar called him a friend, but maybe he's some kind of cousin. But it doesn't matter to us...so long as the job gets done."

————

They came in the door with Rahim having a better idea of what he was supposed to do. This week, he came in knowing he was playing a role for which he had apparently passed the audition last week—without being aware that it had been an audition. This time he had his own agenda.

Again, he glanced in the big bar mirror. The man staring back was unshaven, but this time on purpose, because the role he was playing in his *own* plan demanded he "look Afghan," and this time he was playing the part he'd written for himself.

Gusche and Brent Lynse were seated at a corner table with the waitress refilling their nearly empty coffee cups when the Afghans walked in. She took their orders and scurried away as the four men exchanged perfunctory greetings.

"Thank you for meeting us here two days ahead of the big day," Gusche said. "Mr. Lynse and myself have some business over in Brouillecourt Parish to take care of before the transfer on Monday."

"Are your people ready for the transfer?" Qalandar asked in the suspicious tone he often used to keep others from becoming complacent.

"We're ready," Gusche said. He did not mention that Randy was missing.

"What about the weather?" Qalandar asked. "There

was a big storm down here yesterday and the sky is still dark."

"These people know how to unload a ship in the rain. They do it all the time. They're prepared. Like last week, all we need is the vessel's name and the exact time it's due into Arbeville."

"The ship is *Ashuwaykh Star*. It is owned by the same shipping firm in Kuwait as the *Shuaybah Star*, which you unloaded last Sunday. They tell me both ships are of the same design, so you should not meet any new challenges. Again, it will be arriving around sunrise, and again I will have the exact time told to me by satellite phone as the ship reaches South Pass, which, as you know, is thirty kilometers from Arbeville."

"That sounds good," Lynse said. "The second of many."

"My people have a huge stockpile which they wish to convert to cash," Qalandar said. "Alexis has the cash, and you have to means of getting it to her. You provided such a service in Afghanistan when the stockpile was opium, and we will rely on you to do so here in Louisiana."

"You can rely on us as you did back then…and as you did *right here* last week," Gusche said, reminding him of the recent success.

"We're satisfied," Qalandar said with a toss of his head indicating that the "we" included the Taliban over-seas as well as himself. "For now."

"I was wondering if you might be working with some of the same men I worked with back then," Gusche said in a making conversation way. "Of course, Akhtar Mohammad Dadullah was very much the man in charge of that entire operation, but he's deceased, as you know. I'm wondering if you ever ran across any of the people I knew who were part of Dadullah's organization. His deputy was a man named Khairullah Ghani who was Dadullah's sort of right-hand man in Kabul, one of those who never got his hands dirty in the field."

"You know that I will never discuss names of Afghans who I may or may not know in this enterprise," Qalandar growled. Gusche had noticed a flicker of recognition at the mention of Khairullah Ghani's name, but then *everyone* had heard of Ghani, at least everyone associated with the opium trade back in the day.

FEHRY COUNTY, ARKANSAS

It was the middle of the day on Saturday, and Kaylene's Koffee Korral was not too busy. Knowing that Brian and Rahim were on the road hundreds of miles to the south, Kelly Herste and Hila Faizullah had decided to get together to share their mutual fretfulness.

A week ago, Hila Faizullah had sat at home in the dreadful grip of a range of terrifying feelings that included a mixture of anger at her brother and a fear for his life, but mainly a dread of the unknown. She had no idea of the where or why of Rahim's self-inflicted circumstances.

This week, they both now knew the when and why, and they knew that Rahim was safe because Qalandar *needed* him as part of his plan, but the trepidation remained. At least Hila's anger was now redirected from her brother toward the Taliban crony in the driver's seat of the BMW, and in the driver's seat of this whole entire elaborate intrigue, at least for now.

A week ago, Kelly had only the vaguest notion of the circumstances into which her husband had now plunged.

That was then, and this was now. When she understood the nature of these toxic circumstances, she plunged in herself. She had been one of the first to call for a declaration of war against this sprawling criminal enterprise with its cocoon of protection rendered by layers of crooked federal cops.

Nevertheless, she woke up this morning with a bit of trepidation as she watched her husband heading out of the house with his rifle like a modern-day vigilante. It was like he and Hammer's team of off-the-books warriors had never left the mountains of Afghanistan. How could she *not* be worried out of her mind? At least, in Hila, she had a collaborator who knew exactly what she was going through.

"Where are they?" Hila asked when they had doctored their coffees and taken a table in the corner.

"Brian texted when they were heading south out of New Orleans. If they go where they did last week, they'll be at that diner down there about now."

"I just hope…" Hila started to say.

"I know what you're thinking," Kelly interjected sympathetically. "I'm feeling what you're feeling…"

Suddenly they were interrupted by a booming voice.

"*Amira*, the rug dealer's friend! Remember me? Brenda from the condo complex over on Davis Court? We ran into each other a couple of days ago when you were looking for Mr. Qalandar. Did you ever get hold of him?"

Kelly was momentarily confused by Brenda calling Hila by another name, but she recognized the Davis Court address as the scene of Hila's "burglary" last week. Of course, she would not have used her real name!

"Yeah," Hila said. "It's all good."

"That's excellent," Brenda said. "You know, this must be a big week for him."

"How do you mean?"

"Well, first you, then those other people this morning."

"Oh yeah?" Hila said in a tone that urged the chatty Brenda to say more.

"It was another woman. She had a couple of dudes with her, but she was in charge. Maybe you know her... tall, with short hair...she was wearing an olive-green pantsuit...white shirt. *Starched* white shirt. Looked awfully official...like a process server or something."

"No, I don't believe I know her," Hila lied. "Did she say who she was serving notices for?"

"She didn't say, and I didn't ask," Brenda said with a shrug. "It's none of my business, but one of the dudes she was with had a badge. He got it out to show me, but she told him to stow it. I didn't see it. She was definitely the big dog in the group."

"Did they say anything else?" Hila asked.

"Nope. Told me not to tell Qalandar they were here and then just left. Not that I ever tell him anything. The bugger never once offered me a deal on a rug. *Not once.* I'll bet he's dealin' *drugs*, not rugs."

"Oh my," Kelly said, feigning distress.

"But that's not *our* business, right, girls?" Barbara said with a laugh.

"No ma'am," Hila said. "Nobody's business but their own."

Her easy, off-the-cuff paraphrase of a long-ago classic by blues legend Bessie Smith was indicative of how completely Hila had embraced American culture.

Kelly's attention was on Qalandar's morning callers.

"Wonder what Alexis Mondtrom and her boys are doing in town," she said. "Maybe she doesn't know that Qalandar is out of town? Or maybe she does and they're here for the same reason that *you* visited Davis Court on Wednesday?"

"I wonder how she'll get past the alarm code," Hila said. "That *Quran* verse was a lucky guess...an educated guess, but nonetheless lucky. I don't picture Mondtrom as a Quranic scholar."

CHAPTER
TWENTY-SEVEN

BROUILLECOURT PARISH, LOUISIANA

THE WEATHER WAS dark and gloomy, and it looked like it could rain as it had on Friday. Fredieuville had seen only a fraction of the storm that hit New Orleans and points east last night, but more heavy weather was predicted all across the Gulf Coast. For Nicole Kirbye, as for the two Cajuns at Langlois Motors, Saturday was a workday. With all of the disruptions over the past week, the necessities of their day jobs had slipped and Saturday became the time to catch up.

The center of gravity in the international intrigue that had been consuming all of them had shifted to Fehryville and to the Mississippi River Delta, so Brouillecourt Parish, from Fredieuville to the bayous, was momentarily out of the operational spotlight. They all knew that this would change when the barges slithered up Bayou Gadreau on Monday, but for now, the only thing with which Nicole had to contend were columns of figures.

It was quiet this morning in the small strip mall just off Fredieuville's Main Street where she had her office.

The insurance broker to the left of her was closed, but she could see through the plate-glass windows that the pediatric dentist next door had a full waiting room. People didn't like to take kids out of school for teeth cleanings, and the doctor obliged.

One of the kids smiled and waved at Nicole, and she waved back. She had the kind of infectious smile that made anyone want to smile back.

Half a mile away at Nicole's home, however, there were no smiles.

She had not noticed DASP Agent Len Ivermin as he rolled past the strip mall, but he had eyes on her. She might have noticed the big black DASP Ford Expedition, but Ivermin had traded his usual vehicle for a small green Subaru that blended easily into the background—seen, perhaps, but unnoticed, definitely.

When he was sure that Nicole was going to work and not merely stopping into the office to pick up something, Ivermin drove to her house. He parked about a block away and strolled the rest of the way through her a quiet, leafy neighborhood on foot. As he had exchanged his SUV for something that blended in, he had traded his dark suit for a pale-yellow polo shirt, khakis and a royal-purple LSU ball cap. *Nobody* looked out of place in south Louisiana in an LSU ball cap.

He circled the block on foot without being seen getting too close to her modest, single-story bungalow until he was sure that the neighbors were not paying attention. He then slipped through the small gate that led to her back door, his movements mostly concealed by the position of her semi-detached garage. Ivermin didn't think of himself as a peeping tom, but peep he did, surreptitiously peering in windows until he was sure no one was at home. If it came to a confrontation, he had a federal badge, but he did not want it to come to that.

A few practiced flicks with his lock pick took him into her kitchen. A quick observation of cereal bowls in the sink, and an open box of Fruit Loops on the table told him that Nicole had house guests. A stroll through the rest of the house confirmed what the Fruit Loops suggested—at least two of her house guests were under the age of ten. Ashley Grahen and her kids? Probably.

There was no computer visible, nor a laptop. He decided that in her business she probably carried the laptop with her.

Remembering what Gusche had said—repeatedly—about an orange Honda, Ivermin poured himself a handful of Fruit Loops, secured the back door and headed a few steps to a door that led into the garage.

It was dark inside, but his eyes quickly adjusted to the light cast from a single, small, dusty window. There was a lone vehicle, but it was covered completely by an old gray canvas tarp. As he flicked back the edge, he was immediately rewarded by the sight of a bright orange fender and a chrome Honda logo on the grille. He took a picture with his cell phone, and then a close-up of the Oklahoma license plate. With his federal laptop in the car, he'd be able to run this plate number within the hour.

Wallace Gusche would be pleased.

———

"Looks like it might rain," Jim Hammer said as he pulled his pickup up next to the bait shop on the Bayou Gadreau road and walked over to the counter where Dave was slowly unrolling himself from a sitting to a standing position.

"Well there, old buddy, that would be a theory that would have the odds in its favor," Dave replied in agreement.

"That was sure a big one last light," Hammer commented.

"We missed most of it," Dave said thoughtfully, staring at the darkening sky through the branches of the big cypress tree above the bait shop. "Heard she dumped a lotta water over on New Orleans and points east."

"That's what I heard too," Hammer said, not mentioning he was on the road between New Orleans and Bay St. Louis during the worst of it.

"You fixin' to get yourself some cats before the deluge moves in?" Dave asked.

"I don't mind fishing in the rain," Hammer said. "I always figure the fish live in water, so they don't care if it rains."

"Nope, they don't," Dave agreed. "Round here, a heavy rain'll muddy the waters, but catfish chase bait with their nose when the visibility goes down and they got a good sense of smell. At the same time, a heavy rain washes a lot of stuff they like to eat off the land and into the water. They're happy."

"Guess I'll give it a try then," Hammer said as Dave put a fistful of night crawlers into a baggie.

"These are on the house," Dave said, handing over the bag of worms.

"Oh yeah? Thank you..."

"Yeah, man. I never had a chance to thank you properly for helpin' out my niece last Sunday when those punks came 'round hasslin' her," Dave said. "She told me that you took on three of them, and they were *not* little fellas."

"I've seen worse odds," Hammer said with a grin. "Besides, I only took on one. The other two just melted away on their own."

"Well it's much appreciated. You didn't have to, but I'm glad you did."

"I have a really low tolerance for that kind of shit," Hammer said. "What makes 'em think they can get away with that?"

"What makes a bully be a bully?" Dave asked rhetorically. "Punks and cowards. That's all they are."

"Sunday was kind of a big day down here last week," Hammer said, changing the subject. "I saw they were unloading containers from barges down there on the bayou."

"I heard about that," Dave said. "But didn't see nothin' on account of it was my day off. That's why Chantelle was here."

"Does that happen very often?"

"Almost never...and that would be generous. I can't remember it happening ever, except when the Fortier boys were building their pier down there. Unless you're bringing in something that's going to be used down there, there's no reason to do it. There are a million better places to unload a barge if you're gonna truck your containers somewhere else."

"Ever get smugglers down here?" Hammer asked.

"You mean like drugs from down in Central America or wherever?

"Yeah."

"I suppose you got drugs comin' in everywhere on the coast from Key West to Brownsville," Dave pondered. "But like I said about containers, it seems to me that there's a million better places to do it than Bayou Gadreau. Of course, just because it don't make no sense to me, it don't mean some idiot ain't gonna try'n do it."

"Well put."

"I've lived around here all my life and I know what these bayous ain't good for and what they are good for."

"Like catfish," Hammer said.

"Like catfish," Dave agreed with a smile.

Eyeing Hammer thoughtfully, Dave's expression grew serious.

"Can I ask you somethin'?"

"Sure."

"Are you some kind of a cop?" Dave said. "It's none of my business, but you're askin' about containers and smuggling, and all of your interest in Bayou Gadreau has got me wonderin'?"

"No sir, I'm *no kind* of cop," Hammer said with a slight smile. "But I guess I've been making myself a little too transparent. Yeah, you nailed it. I *do* have an interest in smuggling on Bayou Gadreau...but I'm not a cop and I'm *sure* not the smuggler."

"None of my business any old which way," Dave said in a conciliatory tone.

"If we can keep it between you, me, and the night crawlers, I'll tell you about it."

"Deal."

Hammer had sized Dave up as a man of his word, and hoped he'd sized right.

"About a million years ago, I led a Special Forces team in Afghanistan," he began. "And there was a lot of other stuff going on over there in those years. With all the layers of NGOs and civilian government bureaucrats stepping all over each other, and all the money being dumped in there, I'm sure it comes as no surprise that there was a lot of corruption."

"*Corruption*? *Bureaucrats*?" Dave said sarcastically. "Tell me it ain't so."

"Well, in one case, a Swiss NGO was buying opium from the Taliban and smuggling it into Europe. The transportation was being made possible by crooked American government types. There was one bureaucrat in particular, a sort of squirrelly character with a narrow goatee and tortoise-shell glasses. He was the kingpin. Don't ask me how I know, but I know."

"Do tell," Dave said, enjoying the intrigue.

This being story time, Dave sought refreshment and handed his pocket flask to Hammer when he paused his storytelling to catch a breath. The taste of the whiskey was most satisfying.

"Like I said, this was a million years ago, and nobody had thought much about Mr. Tortoise Shell for a long time," Hammer continued. "Then one day, some government cops started showing up down here on Bayou Gadreau. You've seen 'em...well-dressed and driving a big black SUV."

"Yeah, I *have* seen 'em, and so's Chantelle. They was around here a week ago when those barges came in."

"Well, that's not even the punchline. Just after they started coming around, Mr. Tortoise Shell was seen here in Brouillecourt Parish. It turns out that he's still in the smuggling business and those bent government cops work for *him*."

"What's your part in all this?" Dave asked. "As if I can't guess."

"I'm going to shut it all down."

"You could just call the cops," Dave suggested.

"The badges of *federal* cops, and there are a lot of them involved, always trump local badges. And I don't know who's been bought off that I don't know about. I learned in Afghanistan that sometimes if you want something done, you gotta do it yourself."

"Better to ask forgiveness than ask permission?" Dave said, paraphrasing the old axiom famously coined many decades ago by the data processing genius Admiral Grace Hopper.

"I'm not really in the habit of asking for either,"

Hammer said with a smile that put a grin across Dave's face.

"Anything I can do to help," Dave said in the form of an offer. He liked Hammer's style.

"Thanks," Hammer said with a spark in his eye. "You just never can tell."

————

As Nicole Kirbye wrestled with her numbers, as young Liam Grahen watched the two Cajuns wrestle with a Hurth ZF 45A 1.2:1 marine engine transmission, and as Dave and Hammer shared another sip under the cypress, Wallace Gusche and Brent Lynse were in the silver Malibu westbound out of New Orleans on US Route 90.

"Every time I see an off ramp for New Orleans, I think about the gumbo at Michel Carambat's," Lynse said.

"You just ate lunch," Gusche said from the passenger's seat. He had let Lynse take the wheel so he could check his emails. "What's wrong with those shrimp po'boys we got at Evonne's?"

"They're not Carambat's gumbo."

This culinary exchange was abruptly interrupted by Gusche's cellphone alerting him to a text message.

"It's Ivermin," Gusche said. "He's in Fredieuville checking up on the Kirbye woman. I gotta call him back."

————

"Hi Len, what have you got to tell me about my old friend, Nicole?"

"She's at work today, so I thought I'd take a look around her house."

"You broke in?"

"Best way to have a look around her house."

"That's breaking and entering," Gusche reminded him.

"I didn't break anything," the DASP agent clarified. "Besides that, I have a badge."

"Don't you need a warrant to go with a badge...oh, never mind...what did you find in the house?"

"It's not so much what I found in the house, but what I found in the *garage*."

"Don't tell me," Gusche said. "An orange Honda?"

"Oklahoma plates and all. I ran the plates and they came back registered to Ashley Grahen of McAlester. Looks like Kirbye lied to me when I asked her about her and the Grahen woman."

"Well, it looks to me like Randy Coome's fixers lied to *him* about finishing off the woman in the orange Honda, or else Coome lied to *me*," Gusche said angrily.

"Or else they killed somebody else in a different orange Honda," Ivermin suggested. "There's no question about who belongs to *this* orange Honda."

"What else did you find? Computer? Laptop?"

"She takes the laptop with her to work. I saw her carrying it. Mainly, though, I found kids' stuff all over the house. Grahen is staying here with the kids."

"But they're obviously not there now," Gusche said. "Any idea where they are?"

"Not far. This place looks lived-in. What do you want me to do?"

"Looks like you have two instead of one, if you know what I mean."

"Roger that."

"Keep an eye on the house for now, and hold tight," Gusche said. "I don't want to do anything about either of the two until we can do it to *both* of them."

"Understood," Ivermin said. Like most people in law enforcement, he'd worked with a gun on his hip for years without ever exercising deadly force, but now he had decided he had no natural aversion to the idea.

"Lynse and I are heading out to the bayou this afternoon and we'll connect with you in a few hours," Gusche said. "Time is on our side. We can take care of the two women tomorrow. We have almost two days before the moonrakers come in."

"Oh yeah, right, the *moonrakers*," Ivermin repeated. As with Lynse and Coome, he found Gusche's use of the term, and his interest in esoteric lore, to be a bit on the quaint side.

CHAPTER
TWENTY-EIGHT

BROUILLECOURT PARISH, LOUISIANA

NICOLE, *what did you do?*

So deeply was her head submerged in the spreadsheets on her two Dell monitors that the sudden sound of the door to the street in her outer office startled Nicole Kirbye like an IED going off in the street.

She looked up suddenly. She usually sat so she could keep an eye on the front door, but she had drifted so close to papers spread across her credenza that it was not visible.

Nicole, what did you do?

She had meant to lock it. Why had she not? Was she growing *that* complacent?

Nicole, what's wrong with you?

The door had opened and someone was in her outer office!

Time stopped.

Her heart stopped.

"Nic...are you here?"

Oh my lord...It's Johnny Arnaud!

"Yeah, Johnny...I'm back here."

She glanced at her wall clock. Was it really that late? It was still daylight outside, but with the dark overcast, she had lost track of time. Sinking into complicated spreadsheets can do that to you.

So glad was she to see him that she gave him an amorous hug and a lingering kiss before she even bothered to ask why he was there.

"*Whoa*...I'm glad you're glad to see me," he said, pleased with the zeal of her unanticipated welcome.

"I'm glad it was you," she said. "I got kinda jumpy when I heard somebody open the door."

"Don't worry, Nic. Nobody has any reason to hurt *you*. Besides, you're in safe hands."

"I like those hands," she said, holding up his right hand and kissing it. "I just can't get that DASP agent out of my mind."

"He can't hurt you. He's two hundred miles away. He doesn't have any jurisdiction down here anyway."

"I know, I know," she said. "But I'm still glad you stopped by."

"I was thinking that maybe you'd want to take a break and step over to the Quarter Moon."

"I'd love nothing more," she said in what was, for her at that moment, an understatement. "Just give me a couple of minutes to mark where I'm at, run a couple of backups, and get all this shut down for the night."

"Sure. Did you get caught up?"

"Yeah, mostly," she said. "It'll be a short day tomorrow and I'll be ahead of the game Monday morning."

"Oh yeah," Johnny said. "Monday."

"Oh...that's right. Those damned containers are coming on Monday. What's Hammer going to do?"

"Nothing that he's saying much about. He's like that."

"How are Ash and the kids?" Nicole asked.

"They're great," Johnny said with a laugh. "They're all out at Bayou Langlois. As usual, Liam's got his eyes on the innards of that Hurth ZF 45A transmission that we rebuilt, Ash has got her eyes on Travis, and Ava's off harassing small reptiles."

"I just hope she doesn't get in trouble with any large reptiles."

"Naw, Tyler's got eyes in the back of his head when it comes to gators."

"I hope so," Nicole said.

———

"Still no sign of the Grahen woman, but Kirbye just left her office with her boyfriend," Len Ivermin told Wallace Gusche. He was calling from the green Subaru, which not two hundred miles away as Johnny Arnaud had guessed, but parked across the street from the strip mall.

"Boyfriend?"

"Yeah, they were holding hands and walking to his truck. He looks to be a local yokel...like a mechanic or some kind of tradesman. Jeans and work boots, but a conspicuously clean shirt, like he was dressing for a Saturday night date."

"Oh, how hopelessly cute," Gusche said acerbically. "Follow 'em and see where they go. If it's a date, they're not going to be anywhere near the Grahen woman, so you can leave 'em be for the night. Lynse and I are almost to Bayou Gadreau. Meet us there as soon as you can."

———

"I hope he knows the way," Lynse said. "Are you sure we're on the right road?"

"This was the right road when we turned off that main road back there about ten minutes," Gusche said, staring at his phone and tapping the screen impatiently. "But I've lost service, so I don't know where we're supposed to turn off again. Have you seen any signs?"

"Yeah, but none that say Bayou Gadreau."

Since leaving US Route 90, the Chevy Malibu had made a series of turns onto progressively narrower and less well-marked roads that twisted their way, snakelike through the swampy terrain of the Bayou country.

The darkness of the thick cypress forests and the ominous skies combined to create a foreboding landscape.

"We have to be close. It said eight miles the last time it showed a distance," Gusche said. "I wish I'd thought to bring Ivermin's paper topo map. There's just a lot more of these little side roads than show on the map on my phone. Can't tell which one."

"I have an idea," Lynse said. "Let's stop and *ask* somebody. See that sign."

In big red letters, the sign tersely read BAIT.

About fifty yards down the road, they saw a ramshackle bait stand beneath a massive cypress tree.

"Pull over here," Gusche ordered.

He stepped out of the Malibu and walked confidently toward the stand. Seated behind the counter, and rising slowly to greet him was an older man with a scruffled white beard and a blue T-shirt that had seen better days.

"How're you doin,' sir?" the man said with a congenial expression.

"I'm fine," Gusche said.

"What can I do for ya, sir? You fixin' to toss your line into these waters this afternoon? Never mind the weather, the catfish *are* bitin.' An old boy I know went out this morning and passed back through an hour ago with four or five in his cooler."

"No," Gusche said. "I'm just looking for directions."

"Well, sir, a lot of folks do get a little turned around down through here with all these wiggly little bayous and cricks runnin' ever which way."

"I'm looking for Bayou Gadreau," Gusche said, holding up his cell phone. "Google said I was getting close, but I lost service. I can't tell which road to take."

"Well, you're not the first to figure out that old Google gets lost down here just as greatly as anyone else," the old man said with a laugh. "Fact is you *found it*. That there piece o'water yonder is Bayou Gadreau. You follow this two-line road that you came in on and in an hour or so it'll take you right to the mouth, the place where this old bayou runs into the Atchafalaya River."

"Thank you," Gusche said. "Your help in appreciated."

"Don't mention it," Dave said, sitting back down. "If you get the itch to toss in your line, you just come see me."

"Thanks. I will."

As the Malibu disappeared around the next bend, Dave reached for his landline and placed a call to the "old boy" he'd talked to earlier in the day and told Jim Hammer he had seen the man with the round tortoise-shell glasses.

About fifteen minutes later, Dave made note of a green Subaru cruising past at just over the limit and heading down the road that followed Bayou Gadreau.

———

Len Ivermin slowed down when he spotted Gusche's silver Malibu pulled at the side of the road.

"Where the hell are we going?" Gusche greeted him as he stopped and rolled down his window. "The country is a maze and I can't get a Wi-Fi connection. How did you find this place?"

"I used a map," Ivermin said, trying not to appear smug. "You wanted a place that was hard to find."

"So I did."

"Follow me," Ivermin directed as he took the lead.

Finally, they reached the place where the dredging of years ago had straightened the course of the bayou for a short distance, and where the road was wider. Ivermin pulled into one of the several turnouts along this stretch and parked.

"This is where the barges came in last week," he said when Gusche and Lynse had gotten out of the Malibu. "You can see where the trailers were parked and where they tied up the barge so that the forklift could go to work."

"Middle of nowhere," Lynse observed.

"Not much traffic on the road down here," Ivermin said. "Just a couple of guys down at the mouth with a commercial fishing boat and the occasional good old boy fishing for catfish."

"Yeah, we stopped to get directions from that old character at the bait shack and he tried to sell us on the idea of doing that," Gusche said. "I said maybe later."

"I just hope that the odd fisherman doesn't get in the way or start asking questions," Lynse interjected.

"That's what Sentyl and I are here for," Ivermin said. "Just a big smile and a 'howdy.' If we have to, we just let 'em think we're making them special by taking them into our confidence about something 'hush-hush' that's going on."

"Well, I wanted to see the place where our moonrakers are coming ashore, and now I've seen it," Gusche told Ivermin. "So tell me about Kirbye and Grahen."

"We're not going to get them both in the same place tonight," Ivermin theorized. "Kirbye's out with her boyfriend, and if she's taking him back to her place, then Grahen won't be coming back with the kids tonight."

"Where are Grahen and the kids?"

"Not far. There's an open box of cereal on the kitchen table and toys all over the place. If not tonight, they'll be back soon."

"Good. This is unfinished business that I look forward to wrapping up. I don't want this shadow hanging over the arrival of our *third* shipment."

ARBEVILLE, LOUISIANA

Abed Qalandar was sitting in an aluminum folding chair outside the single-wide mobile home where he and Rahim were biding their time, waiting for the Monday morning arrival of the Kuwaiti-flagged *Ashuwaykh Star*. He hated the heat and humidity of the Mississippi River Delta. The heat he could stand. There was heat in places like Kandahar and Qatar, but he never acclimated to the humidity.

Out of the blue, a phone call broke the monotony.

"Abed, this is Alexis Mondtrom," she said as he answered. "I assume that all is well with our schedule for Monday morning."

"Yes. I...we...spoke to Wallace Gusche face-to-face four hours ago, and I spoke to our man on the ship by satellite phone two hours ago. We are prepared."

"Good," she said. "I'm calling with a change of plans. I want to meet you earlier that we met with the first shipment. I would like you to come directly to the barn after you unload the merchandise. I want to wait with you, and move the product out immediately on Monday night, instead of waiting until later like I did before."

"Yes, Alexis," Qalandar said. "This will be done."

Qalandar was pleased. Getting the transaction out of the way sooner, rather than later, meant that he would not have to wait at the barn overnight. He would wait to tell Faizullah that they would not be returning to Fehryville right away.

Qalandar hadn't asked why she wanted an earlier rendezvous, nor had Mondtrom told him that after Busta-mante's gang murdered the man in the cowboy hat, she too wanted to streamline the transaction time.

The man's pickup had been disposed of in a remote place across the New Mexico state line by Friday morning and his body would never be found, but Busta-mante's propensity for impulsive violence was a compli-cation she wanted to minimize in her dealings with the cartel underworld in the upcoming transaction.

CHAPTER
TWENTY-NINE

BROUILLECOURT PARISH, LOUISIANA

GUSCHE AND BRENT LYNSE spent much of the blustery Sunday morning watching Eddie Coome supervise the prepositioning of the forklift and trailers on Bayou Gadreau as they had been prepositioned eight days earlier. Eddie had been here a week ago and had been more involved than his cousin Randy in accomplishing the same task, so he knew what to do. Eddie may have been an understudy, but he was appearing to be a quick study.

They spoke of Randy and of attempts made by all of them to reach him. His movements, since Eddie had last seen him in passing on Friday morning, were unknown. Eddie was starting to get worried. Gusche was merely perturbed.

On the way out of Bayou Gadreau, Gusche had glanced over to the bait stand where he had met the grizzled septuagenarian the day before. Today, instead of the whiskered bumpkin, his eyes were treated to the sight of a striking young woman in her early twenties in a turquoise tank top with her braided ebony hair tied up in a bun. She smiled at Gusche in an inviting way that made him decide to stop.

"Good morning, sir," she said. "I see you've just come up from the bayou. By your stopping, it makes me think you might have caught the bug to go after some o' them nice, juicy catfish lurkin' in them murky, mysterious waters down yonder."

"Well..." Gusche said, his voice slowing subconsciously by his attention to her charming drawl. "As I told the older gentleman who was standing here yesterday..."

"That would be my uncle Dave," she said.

"Yes, as I told Dave yesterday, my friend and I are just doin' a little sightseeing. This is awfully pretty country down here."

"If not for all that construction that's goin' on down on Gadreau."

"Construction?"

"You musta seen 'em. Lotsa trucks and equipment goin' down the bayou. Same thing last week. They must be buildin' something out there."

"Oh yeah, right," Gusche said.

"You're not from around here, huh?" she said. "My name's Chantelle. What's yours?"

"Wallace..." he said, hesitating to part with a surname.

"Glad to meet y'all," she replied, extending her hand. "That's an awful formal name. I reckon folks call you 'Wally' sometimes."

"No," he said, bristling. "Nobody *ever* calls me that."

———

ARBEVILLE, LOUISIANA

It was late afternoon on Sunday when Jim Hammer and Brian Herste laid eyes on the man with the goatee and the round tortoise-shell glasses for the first time since that cold day of drifting snowflakes in the Kandahar mountains all those years ago.

Hammer and Herste had picked a vantage point on a rise from which they could see not only the forlorn little trailer park where Qalandar and Rahim were staying in a tawdry single-wide, but beyond that, they had a good view of the big gravel parking lot on the banks of the Mississippi River, and of the ships which passed, one after another, headed north toward New Orleans, or south toward the Gulf.

"I got my thirty-ought-six in my truck," Herste suggested as Hammer handed him his powerful Oberwerk 10x42 HD II binoculars.

The comment, known by both men to be rhetorical, touched a nerve, in the way that the way ones who get away always gnaw at you over time.

They both knew that Wallace Gusche had been spared that day so that the team would not tip their hand before the big fish showed his face. That fish, the infamous Taliban warlord, Akhtar Mohammad Dadullah, *did* show his face that day, and Hammer had turned that face into chopped meat with a .50 caliber round from his Barrett M107 sniper rifle.

However, at that moment, as Dadullah's entourage was about to be slaughtered in a withering fusillade from Hammer and his team, Wallace Gusche was gone. He was ten minutes and a mile away. He wa so close, he heard the shots. Those few minutes had bought him a lot of years, and he did not even know that these years were all borrowed time.

Today, on this hot, muggy day of spattering rain-drops, Wallace Gusche was again given a pass by the same team in the interest of a mission. *If he only knew whose eyes were on him as he greeted that would-be Taliban warlord, Abed Qalandar.*

He stepped back into the silver Malibu where Brent Lynse was waiting and they drove away. As he had on that day long ago, Gusche again became the one who got away, though he did not get far.

Hammer followed them with the binoculars as their car crossed the parking lot and nosed in next to a small building with a flagpole flying the stars and stripes.

———

Gusche and Lynse stepped out of the car and strolled over to the building with the US Customs logo on a shield next to its front door. With this, and with the flag snapping in the brisk wind, the place looked much like a small-town post office in any of a multitude of towns and hamlets across the country—the kind that the Postal Service is always trying to consolidate with the small-town post office in the next town to save money.

"Good afternoon, sir," Gusche said, greeting the man who had been snoozing at a desk behind the counter, and who abruptly stood and walked over to the counter.

"How can I help you?"

"My name is Gusche," he said, producing his federal picture ID as a law enforcement officer might present a badge. "I'm with the Security Infrastructure Finance Organization. We're a Department of Defense unit based over at Keesler that's responsible for stocking and trans-porting Army infrastructure material throughout the southeast."

"My name's Faralaco, Dennis Faralaco," the man said, extending his hand. "How can I help you today?"

"My colleague and I are making informal visits to ports of entry on the Gulf Coast this week to familiarize ourselves with each of them. We do a lot of shipping and it's useful to know the lay of the land and the locations."

"On a Sunday?"

"US Customs operates 365 days a year, does it not?" Gusche said using his "official" voice.

"Yessir, we do, but Arbeville is not all that active. The shipping that passes through here is not coming *here*. Incoming ocean-going traffic that passes through here are bound for New Orleans or points north...Baton Rouge...Memphis...Saint Louis, and all the way up to the Twin Cities. We're here to maintain a presence for that rare exception. We might get one or two ships stopping here for one reason or another, but it doesn't go through customs if it doesn't come ashore."

"How often does that happen?" Gusche asked.

"Less than once a month," Faralaco said. "Nobody stops in Arbeville."

"What about the exchange of bar pilots for river pilots?"

"Except that."

"This must get awfully boring here for you?" Gusche asked.

"I get by," Faralaco said, chuckling. "I'm counting down until retirement."

"How many of you are there here?"

"Just one, but there are several of us in this sector. We rotate. I'm at Port Sulphur on Thursdays and every third weekend I'm here."

"So you're here regularly on Mondays and Tuesdays?" Gusche asked.

"And Wednesdays."

"Are you on duty twenty-four-seven?" Gusche asked.

"Nope," Faralaco said. "Seven to seven. That's why I work four days a week and get overtime for weekends."

"What if there's a need for customs after hours?"

"If they need us, they'll let us know ahead of time. Otherwise the night shift at Port Sulphur takes care of it."

"Great," Gusche said. "Thanks for your time and all this information."

"Always glad to help the Army," he said. "Thank *you* for your service."

Gusche just nodded.

———

With the low overcast and the intermittent drizzle, dawn crept in surreptitiously on that Monday morning. There was no cool silver brightness to backlight the horizon, and there would be no warm sun to illuminate the rich green of the river country landscape. Across the river, two barges waited unobtrusively for containers to be transferred.

"You're in a good mood for such a stormy day," Lynse said as he watched a ship sluggishly making its way up the Mississippi past the broad parking lot at Arbeville. "That's thanks to our conversation with Dennis Faralaco yesterday," Gusche replied. "I knew from my own experience that US Customs didn't put their best foot forward at these small ports on Sundays, but apparently, they don't take these places seriously at all. Qalandar talked to his guy aboard the *Ashuwaykh Star* this morning and he said to expect them by six. Dennis won't even have his teeth brushed by six. Today should go well. That's why I'm in a good mood."

"You can thank Randy Coome for picking Arbeville," Lynse reminded him.

"If I could *find* Randy Coome to thank him," Gusche replied. "Eddie said he's checked with all of Randy's women friends. *Nothing.* As soon as we get everything wrapped up in the next day or two, I'm going to get DASP involved and do a proper search."

"There's your Taliban friends," Lynse said, nodding toward Qalandar's black BMW, which had just arrived and parked about thirty yards away. "I guess we're all set."

They watched Qalandar exit the car and get out his satellite phone.

Gusche looked at his watch and squinted downstream on the river.

Gradually, a small lump on the horizon moved and grew in size. It was a ship. Was it *the* ship?

Gusche and Lynse took it as a good sign that Qalandar was talking on the phone while gesturing. That man, Faizullah was out of the car now.

————

Rahim closed the door of the BMW and turned up his collar. At least there was a pause in the drizzle. The *Ashuwaykh Star* was no longer just a gray silhouette in the mist. Detail was visible. He saw the containers stacked on the deck, and he recognized that part of the ship that looked like a flat-topped building, the part he now knew was called a "bridge." He knew that in there was a man in there who confirm that that it was Abed Qalandar and his "people" who were meeting the ship.

He saw Wallace Gusche's silver Malibu across the lot. He thought about how a man like Gusche could survive and flourish inside the American government bureaucracy for all these years. He thought about the length and breadth of the current smuggling scheme, and he wondered whether it would be possible to pull the whole thing down as Hammer planned to do.

If not, was it in vain that he was standing here again, doing nothing but "looking Afghan?" He had done this last week when he thought Hila was in peril. He was doing it this week to help end this diabolical madness. He hoped that he'd never have to do this again. He hoped that Hammer knew what he was doing. If not, what would Rahim do to Qalandar? He was formulating an idea.

"Look up at the blue light," Qalandar said. Rahim remembered this from before and played his role as though this was theater. In fact, it *was* a role, and this *was* theater. The man near the blue light looking back at them from the bridge, who also "looked Afghan," was communicating in Pashto with Qalandar on his own satellite phone.

Finally, when Rahim heard the word *"Alhamdulillah,"* crackle through on the phone, he knew that his stage career was over for the day. He hoped never to play this role again.

At that moment, there was a great groan as the ship slowed and the pilot boat moved in for the exchange of pilots. Rahim knew that as all attention was riveted on this highwire act, the containers on the opposite side of the ship were being lifted onto the barges. It would all be over in a moment. The pilot would take control and the *Ashuwaykh Star* would be moving upriver toward New Orleans.

Rahim caught something out of the corner of his eye and glanced around as a white pickup with a US Customs insignia on its door drove up and parked next to Wallace Gusche's silver Malibu.

———

By his casual manner on Sunday afternoon, Dennis Faralaco may have conveyed the impression of inattention to his profession, but in fact, he was diligent when it came to looking after this stretch of waterway to which he was assigned. His shift may have run from seven to seven as he told Gusche, but in fact, he had not mentioned he usually arrived early, with his thermos of coffee and a donut or two, to check his official messages and settle in for the day.

"Good morning, Mr. Gusche," he said as Wallace Gusche climbed out of the Malibu. "I didn't expect to see you again this morning. I figured you'd be on your way upriver or back to Biloxi."

Faralaco was cordial, but there was a trace of suspicion in his choice of words.

"We *are* headed back to Biloxi today," Gusche said, thinking on his feet, or rather scrambling in his mind, to come up with a plausible reason for taking so much interest in the Arbeville waterfront, which was so insignificant as to be hardly a waterfront at all. "But we made a quick stop back here. We spent the night up in Port Sulphur, and I was trying to explain the process of swapping the bar pilot to the river pilot to Mr. Lynse. Thought it best to show him."

"Yeah, I'm from western Nebraska," Lynse said. "I was never around anything much bigger than a twenty-foot bass boat. Never even saw the ocean 'til I was nearly thirty. I'm really behind the curve on this nautical stuff. But I'm really impressed with what I've seen here this morning."

"I never get tired of watching this, and I'm from the Gulf Coast myself," Faralaco said, softening a bit. "I'm glad that Mr. Gusche took the time to show you."

As they were talking, Faralaco had his back turned to

Qalandar's car, and it was only after it had pulled out that he noticed the car in motion.

"Whoa, wait a minute," Faralaco said. "Did you see who was driving that Beamer?"

"They were here when we got here," Gusche said. "I didn't really pay attention."

Faralaco looked at Lynse, who just shrugged.

"I'd take that as suspicious," Faralaco said.

"I wouldn't worry about it," Gusche said. "We would have noticed if they'd have touched something. They were probably just out watching the river...like we are."

"I suppose," the customs man said, not fully convinced. "This is not a gated or posted area. Maybe it should be, but that's above my pay grade."

Gusche just smiled understandingly. What Faralaco had said was a well-used mantra across the entire government workforce.

———

Hammer and Herste, who had watched the interaction from their nearby vantage point, parted company. Herste immediately began following BMW, while Hammer waited to follow Gusche.

Because of the tap that Hila had put on Qalandar's communications, they knew that the Qalandar was heading for the barn in Natchitoches, and not back to Fehryville as it had last week. They also knew that Alexis Mondtrom would be there.

While Hammer and Herste knew all this, Rahim did not, and there was no way of letting him know. As they were leaving Arbeville, Brian Herste tried to position his GMC where Rahim could see he was still following. He hoped for the best.

In Hammer's axiom, the solution to a strategic

problem is in working your way to the top. In this case, two of the heads of the multiheaded serpent who lived at the top would soon me coming together in Natchitoches, and in the meantime, Hammer's sights were on Gusche, the one who'd once gotten away.

The plan was coming together, but there were still a lot of unpredictable moving parts that were still in motion.

CHAPTER
THIRTY

BROUILLECOURT PARISH, LOUISIANA

HAMMER FOLLOWED Gusche's silver Malibu up through the Monday morning traffic in New Orleans, and then west on Route 90, staying well back to avoid detection. When they crossed the Atchafalaya River and turned south into the side roads of Bayou country, Gusche slowed down considerably, and Hammer thought he might have been spotted. After a while, though, Hammer figured out that Gusche was just unused to these roads, many of which were unmarked, and he was afraid of getting lost.

As Hammer might have guessed, the Malibu had turned at Dave's big, red-lettered "BAIT" sign and disappeared down the road that followed Bayou Gadreau.

"Figured I might be seein' you down here today," Dave said when Hammer stopped under the big cypress tree and walked over to his stand. "Old Tortoise Shell is down there again today, and Chantelle says he stopped to chat with her yesterday. Didn't say nothing except to say that he didn't want to go fishing."

"Some folks don't like to fish in the rain," Hammer said, nodding at the sky.

"Did I tell you about the green car I saw going down there on Saturday about the same time as Tortoise Shell and his silver Chevy?"

"Yeah, a Subaru, I think you said?"

"Right...anyway, he went down around the same time and the Chevy and came back with him. I figure they must be together."

"Thanks," Hammer replied. "I think I've got an idea of where they might be going,"

"Good luck," Dave said as Hammer walked back toward his truck.

Hammer turned and gave him a thumbs-up.

———

"I thought you'd be going in to work today," Ashley Grahen said as Nicole Kirbye walked into Bayou Langlois Motors. "But you're dressed like you're going to a picnic."

"The sun was out, at least up in Fredieuville, so I felt like wearing a sundress," Nicole said. "You know, to lighten the mood after all those dark days of rain.

"I guess," Ash replied. She was sitting at a table looking at her device while Johnny Arnaud was across the equipment bay working on a motor.

"I did have a meeting first thing this morning with a customer at their place to hand off a file that I was working on over the weekend," Nicole continued. "But when I went back to the office, I couldn't concentrate because of this being the day that is...well, y'know... with that other shipment of containers is coming in. I didn't have any more appointments today, so I thought I'd come out here. I figured I'd stay close to you guys since today is the big day down on Bayou Gadreau."

"Great," Ash said. "The 'big day.' I'm on pins and needles about this too."

"Where are the kids?" Nicole asked.

"Oh, Tyler took them fishing. Same thing. Because of the day that it is. To keep them distracted so they don't see Mom fussing about this thing."

"Have you heard anything?"

"Hammer called Johnny to say that the big ship came in, and now Qalandar is on his way up to Natchitoches with Rahim. Brian Herste has been following them, I guess. Hammer's coming back here to Brouillecourt Parish. I guess he'll be going over to Bayou Gadreau and then up to Natchitoches. There's gonna be trouble. I'm trying not to think about it."

"I know," Nicole said, giving Ash a hug.

At that point, they heard the riffling sound of tires in gravel as two cars pulled into the lot outside.

"Somebody's here," Nicole shouted to Johnny as the two women stepped outside to see who it was.

They saw a green Subaru and a silver Chevrolet, and getting out of the latter was the man with the face that had haunted Nicole since she had seen it on Main Street a little over two weeks ago.

Narrow goatee. Tortoise-shell glasses.

Wallace Gusche.

A mixture of fear and anger came over her, but she pushed it aside.

What could he do to her?

Did he even *remember* these two women from Sustainment and Infrastructure at Bagram from so long ago?

Nicole brought her sunglasses down from the top of her head and folded her arms across her chest to give herself a more imposing stance.

"Wally Gusche," she said sternly, deliberately using the name that so aggrieved him. "I never thought I'd lay eyes on you again."

"I'm flattered that you remember me after all these years, Ms. Kirbye," he replied, using the formality of her surname. "I see Ashley Grahen here too. This is like a Bagram reunion here. Hello, Ms. Grahen, remember me?"

She just nodded as Gusche continued walking casually through the big twenty-by-thirty-foot vehicle access opening in the building.

"Good morning," Johnny Arnaud said, extending his hand and trying to appear cheerful and unsuspecting. "I'm the owner here at Bayou Langlois Motors. How can I help you?"

"I'm Wallace Gusche," he said, showing Arnaud his federal ID and shaking his hand. "As you can see, I'm with the Department of Defense's Security Infrastructure Finance Organization over at Keesler Air Force Base. This is my colleague Brent Lynse, and the gentlemen in the Subaru with the badge is Special Agent Ivermin of the Department of the Army Special Police."

"Well this all sounds very official," Arnaud said, feigning a lack of awareness. He could see that Ivermin, and possibly Lynse, were armed. "Apparently you know my friends already. What brings you gentlemen out here to Brouillecourt Parish?"

"Yes, I had the pleasure of working with these ladies when they were employed by SIFO at Bagram Air Base in Afghanistan some years ago."

"That's real nice," Arnaud said. "What can we do for you here *today*?"

"I've come to have a word with these two young ladies."

"How did you know we were here...*Wally*?" Ashley demanded angrily, using the name he hated.

"You needn't raise your voice with me, Ms. Grahen," Gusche said smugly. "The fact is Agent Ivermin has had you under surveillance for some time."

The two women looked at one another.

"That's really *beyond* creepy," Nicole said. "Surveillance? For *what reason?*"

"It seems that you ladies have been trafficking in classified documents, which is a federal crime," Gusche said pointedly.

"Are you talking about that DOD investigation that linked SIFO with an NGO called Vision for Humanitarian Empowerment that was in bed with the Taliban and smuggling opium into Europe?" Nicole said caustically.

Gusche was momentarily taken aback that she had been able to summarize the whole scenario so succinctly and so vigorously off the top of her head, and she knew the whole story.

"This is a very serious allegation against SIFO, an organization which *you*...both of you...worked for personally," he said, forcefully trying to take control of the conversation.

"Personally?" Nicole retorted. "If we're talking about the same document, I believe that *you* were mentioned in that document *personally*. Wally Gusche was mentioned in it as the one at SIFO who *personally* arranged the flights that took the opium to Europe for VHE."

"You're really grasping at straws here to prop up your fantasy," Ms. Kirbye.

"Hardly a fantasy," Arnaud interjected. "I happened to be there *personally* to watch you walk out of a powwow with Akhtar Mohammad Dadullah. As you damned well know, he was the Taliban dude running that whole operation. The place was crawling with VHE slimeballs that day too."

"When was that?" Gusche asked, looking a very little speck nervous.

"The day that Dadullah died in Kandahar...the day when that asshole got his head blown off. You remember that? I watched you get in your vehicle and drive away five minutes before that happened. I watched you cheat death by five minutes."

Stony silence ensued.

The expression on Gusche's face told that he did remember; that he knew Arnaud did as well. All the details.

The expressions on the faces of Lynse and Ivermin told that neither of them had ever heard that story, but that they now understood Gusche's urgency in disposing of the two women. Now this man would have to go as well.

"Take them into custody," Gusche demanded. "All of them."

"I don't think so," Arnaud said, stepping between the women and Ivermin, who was moving toward Ashley.

"*I do think so,*" Ivermin said emphatically, drawing his Beretta M9 from his shoulder holster.

"*Stop this, you fool!*" Nicole demanded loudly, hoping to distract Ivermin before he harmed Johnny. "Put that stupid thing away right now!"

As Nicole shouted, she took a step backward and Gusche grabbed her and tried to drag her toward him.

Johnny Arnaud saw an opportunity and he took it.

Len Ivermin was tall and fit, but Johnny Arnaud was ex-Special Forces and he lifted five-hundred-pound marine engines for a living. In an earlier life, he used to disarm armed men for a living.

He grabbed Ivermin's wrist and pulled him off balance. Twisting hard, he forced Ivermin to drop the gun, but Ivermin fought back. He'd had some hand-to-hand combat training somewhere along the way, and he would not be a pushover.

He pulled Arnaud down onto the concrete floor and slugged him hard enough to draw blood.

As this was going on, Nicole was screaming obscenities and struggling to get free of Wallace Gusche as he tried to twist her arm.

Finally, she got away, but he grabbed her again. Continuing to step back as he lunged, she hit him in the face as hard as she could with her fist. Blood appeared, dribbling from his nose. As he stood there, momentarily dumbfounded, the blood flowed down his chin and onto his shirt.

There! She had gotten in a good, solid punch!

For a second time, he let go, but he angrily grabbed a large wrench and came after her.

Seeing a small open side door, she decided to run for it. She made it through, but he was hard on her heels. Outside was a narrow walkway that connected to some scaffolding near the boat dock. Again, she turned to run. She moved more quickly. He was wearing office shoes and she was wearing sneakers.Climbing over some stacked aluminum piping connected to the scaffolding slowed her down, allowing him to gain on her for a moment, but as he reached it, he too was slowed down. She made it over the obstacle easily, even in her skirt. He was out of shape, overweight and he was struggling, while she was much more athletic.,

The platform led out over the muddy green waters of the bayou, and it looked like it connected to the dock somewhere up ahead. She couldn't tell because there was so much scaffolding everywhere.

As she ran, Nicole was looking down to watch where she was stepping. The further she went, the more rickety it became, reaching a point where the walkway consisted of a series of two-by-eight planks.

When she did look up, she realized she was trapped.

It was a dead end!

The walkway ended about fifteen feet from where she stood. At this point, it was twenty feet from the dock and around twelve feet above the water. It was too far to jump to the dock. The only other option was to dive into the water and swim.

Then she had an idea.

With Gusche approaching, she had to act quickly.

When she pretended to slip and fall to her knees, she could see a smile on his face as he moved toward her slowly and deliberately.

At last, he was twelve feet away, the length of one of the planks. His shirt was covered in blood from where she had clobbered him, and rage shone in his eyes.

As he raised his foot to step carefully onto the next plank, she slipped the fingers of both her hands under the other end of the same piece of lumber. As he stepped down, she lifted and twisted the wood firmly and suddenly.

Gusche lost his balance and slipped through the spindly aluminum framing. Because he was still clutching the wrench with which he planned to bludgeon her to death, he fumbled his last chance to grab the frame before he fell.

Flailing his arms clumsily, he fell the dozen feet to the water below.

"*Fuck you, bitch!*" Gusche shouted as his head popped to the surface a moment after he submerged completely when he fell.

Gurgling more expletives, he began to swim toward the pier.

As Nicole stood and stared, she saw something in the

water about twenty feet from Gusche that looked like an old piece of waterlogged tree limb—except it was *moving*.

The alligator had been slumbering nearby when it heard the splash of Gusche's fall, and it had smelled his blood.

Nicole paused. She couldn't take her eyes off the unfolding spectacle.

The big reptile, she guessed it to be nine or ten feet, accelerated quickly and effortlessly as it neared Gusche, hitting him hard, just at the waterline.

As Gusche began to shriek, it hit him again below the water.

Soon his head was bobbling frantically at the center of a pinwheel of churning water.

Blood, a lot of blood, was boiling to the surface now.

In a matter of seconds, Gusche's head had disappeared from view, and she heard sounds like and axe hitting a tree trunk, which she took to be the alligator taking large bites.

As white pieces of torn flesh became visible in the pool of blood, Nicole began walking carefully back down the platform in the direction from which she had come.

———

Inside the building, Arnaud and Ivermin grappled with one another on the concrete floor like MMA tryouts, each trying to get the leverage to control the melee. As Ivermin rammed his elbow into Arnaud's throat, the Cajun finally decided to finish the fight.

Mustering all his energy, he let go of Ivermin's arm, grabbed his head and twisted it sharply until a cracking sound announced a broken neck. As the other man went limp, Arnaud pushed him away and reached for the gun. It was not there.

As he looked up, he saw that Lynse now had it. He had been pointing it at Ashley, but he turned it on Johnny Arnaud.

Seeing the SIFO man no longer focused on her, Ashley ducked for cover behind a dumpster.

K'pow! K'pow! Ping!

Arnaud was in the midst of trying to get up as the shots were fired.

He paused for a split second to see if she'd been hit but saw that the two shots had gone wild.

He also found himself staring into the muzzle of the Beretta.

Lynse was too close to miss and too far for Arnaud to reach him if he tried to grab for the gun from his position on the floor.

Lynse aimed carefully, but Arnaud could see him being uncertain whether to fire into his torso or attempt a head shot.

Though this man was obviously unused to shooting at people, he had the advantage. At this range, experience didn't matter. All he had to do was squeeze the trigger. The bullet knew what to do.

Arnaud knew that Lynse was too close to miss, but too far for Arnaud to jump him before he squeezed the trigger.

Watching Ashley out of the corner of his eye, Arnaud saw her look away and heard her start to speak.

Lynse noticed this, moved back a couple of steps and looked that way as well.

Arnaud saw what they saw.

Standing in the doorway was Jim Hammer, his Colt M1911 in his hand.

Lynse swung the Beretta around and raised it to fire at Hammer, but he was too late.

A thunderous explosion of gunpowder, much louder

that the shots that Lynse had squeezed off earlier, reverberated throughout the room.

The .45-caliber round struck Lynse in the chest and flung him four feet across the room like an armload of dirty grease rags.

Already on his feet, Johnny Arnaud did not pause to look at the aftermath.

He lunged toward the side door and ran for it at stunning speed.

"*Gusche has got Nic,*" he shouted, with the last two words reaching Hammer's ears after Arnaud was outside.

As Ashley watched, she saw Hammer holster the Colt and sprint toward the door to follow him.

A few minutes later, Hammer was back, quickly followed by Johnny Arnaud, whose arms were intertwined with those of Nicole Kirbye.

"*Nic, are you okay?*" Ashley gasped, rushing toward her friend.

"I'm great," Nicole said calmly, showing no sign of letting go of the man at her side.

If anything, he looked more freaked out than she did.

"*Where's Gusche?*" Ashley asked as she worked her way into the embrace to give Nicole a hug. "What happened?"

"Gator bait," Arnaud answered succinctly.

"Good idea," Hammer said, reaching down and picking up the lifeless body of Brent Lynse with his right hand. "Let's take the garbage out before the kids get back. They don't have to see this mess."

———

When he drove in and saw the cluster of unfamiliar cars in front of his place of business, Tyler Roullier told the kids to wait in the car as he approached the building cautiously.

"What happened?" Tyler asked as he came into the room. "What are all those cars doing here?"

It was a calm scene of domestic tranquility. Johnny Arnaud was seated in a folding chair with Nicole perched on his knee, while Hammer was pushing a mop. Ashley had just walked inside from the direction of the dock with an empty five-gallon bucket.

"Wally Gusche and his friends came to call and they made a mess of the place," Ashley said. "We've been tidying. It's all good now."

"Where's Gusche?" Tyler asked.

"Well," Ashley said thoughtfully. "As your friend Johnny put it so well..."

"Gator Bait," Johnny repeated with a laugh, jumping into the conversation at the mention of his name.

"Where are my kids?" Ashley asked with a bit of concern.

"Look, Mom," Liam said as he came into the room with his sister trailing behind. "I caught me a catfish."

"I did tell 'em to wait in the car," Tyler said sheepishly.

"Fish fry?" Ashley asked.

"I'm afraid I'm gonna have to take a rain check," Hammer said. "I gotta go meet Brian Herste up at the barn in Natchitoches. We've got to get Rahim out from under Qalandar...and take care of the garbage up there."

"Wait a minute, Hammer," Arnaud said firmly. "I'm comin' with you."

CHAPTER
THIRTY-ONE

INTERSTATE 49, NATCHITOCHES PARISH, LOUISIANA

RAHIM FAIZULLAH WOKE with a start as Abed Qalandar dodged his black BMW out from behind a northbound big rig. Rahim was still groggy from a hard nap when the cigarette smoke hit his nostrils. He wondered where they were, other than shooting along an uninteresting mid-south artery with a wall of eighteen-wheelers in the right lane, and random, anonymous cars and light trucks in the passing lanes.

Rahim wondered whether Brian Herste had managed to follow him this far. He thought he had glimpsed him as they left Arbeville, but his GMC, if it was him, blended into the traffic, and Rahim didn't want to have Qalandar noticing him looking back.

As on his first field trip with Qalandar, this one was plagued by monotony mixed with uncertainty. At least this time he knew that Hila would be safe, no matter what happened to him.

Then he saw exit signs for Alexandria race by.

"This isn't the way to Fehryville," he said. "We're still in Louisiana."

"We will be stopping elsewhere before we return to Fehryville."

"Where?"

"You'll see."

The Alexandria exits raced by, and soon they passed a sign indicating that the BMW was entering Natchitoches Parish. Qalandar took an exit that dropped them onto a secondary highway that meandered through the rolling hills and cattle pastures of farm country.

A series of turns put them on progressively narrower roads, with fewer and fewer cars. Finally, after about five minutes on a gravel road, Qalandar drove into a narrow space between an old barn and a cluster of trees. Rahim mentioned he needed a restroom, and Qalandar pointed into the woods.

When he returned, Qalandar had the doors of the barn opened, revealing a large space with the tracks of numerous vehicles on the floor. Recalling Hammer's description of the barn where the previous containers had been delivered, Rahim knew exactly where he was. He also knew that somewhere within sight of the barn doors there was a CCTV camera providing a live feed. He wondered where it was exactly, and whether anyone was watching.

From Bayou Langlois to the front seat of Hammer's pickup, they were.

———

"I still can't believe that you got Bustamante to go along with these changes to the handoff protocol," Shane Blessins said from behind the wheel of the big gray Cadillac Escalade.

"It's a seller's market," Alexis Mondtrom said from the back seat. "We're the only ones selling what we have for sale. He can pick his stuff up in East Texas as well as he can in West Texas and this will save us that extra twelve-hundred-mile round trip to a handoff point almost to New Mexico."

"He's got to appreciate the quality of the merchandise," Blessins added.

"He does," Mondtrom said. "You could see it in his eyes."

"This isn't just a load of random pre-owned gear," Blessins recounted smugly.

"If he and his gangs are going to rule these cities and towns around the country, he gotta appreciate a proper military-grade arsenal and basically never-used material," Mondtrom said. "Where else is he going to get it except from the US Army...or in this case, the US Army once removed?"

"The Gonzalves Cartel is going to end up better equipped than most of the police departments in these towns and cities," Blessins continued. "Not just guns, but all this other stuff from tactical radios to night vision gear."

"That's the idea," she said. "Bustamante knows that he's got himself a five-star platinum goose with this equipment, and he's not going to screw that up. But he also knows that shooting that cowpoke out there in West Texas could have screwed him in so many ways."

"He opened fire first," Blessins reminded her. "So if it had gone sideways, it was on him."

"Well, it didn't, and I want to keep it that way. Is Anchry still back there?"

"Yes, ma'am."

David Anchry, the other FSO agent in Mondtrom's support detail was following in a heavy-duty, dual-tired

Ram 3500 pickup with a 410-horsepower Hemi V8 that was pulling an empty forty-foot trailer.

"If Gusche and Coome can use a dually pickup to bring the containers two hundred fifty miles from the swamps, we can use one to take 'em the same distance to East Texas. Saves *so much* bother not having to scrounge a big rig."

"When you were talking to Bustamante, I thought you were going to make him drive all the way to the barn in Natchitoches," Blessins said.

"*No way*," Mondtrom said emphatically. "I don't want that SOB anywhere near *my* supply chain!"

"Speaking of which," Blessins said. He was already signaling for the exit.

———

Rahim Faizullah watched the two vehicles, one large, the other larger, as they charged toward the barn, sending frothy clouds of spray into the air as the splashed through all the puddles that had collected in the runs on the road during the recent storms. He stood back to avoid getting wet as they came to a stop. Anchry pulled the Dodge Ram and the trailer into the barn, while Blessins parked the Escalade near where Qalandar was standing.

"Hello Abed," the tall woman with the short hair and the sea-green pantsuit said to Qalandar as she climbed out of the Escalade.

"This must be one of your people," she said, nodding to Rahim. He recognized her from that night in the Helmand Kitchen in Fehryville two weeks ago, but she did not remember him. "I'm glad you brought your team with you today. I hate to see you on your own. It's no fun to be a loner."

It startled Rahim to watch someone teasing Qalandar.

It was incongruous to see someone toy with an individual whom he saw as so intimidating, but she was a rather imposing person herself.

"This is Rahim Faizullah," Qalandar said in introduction.

"How are you, Mr. Faizullah?" she said perfunctorily, shaking his hand before walking into the barn to look around.

Far from being uncomfortable with Mondtrom's banter, Qalandar was pleased with her acknowledgment of his having a team.

"I brought my own this time," she said, gesturing toward the truck and trailer. "I want to streamline this process. I want to have your forklift put the containers directly on this instead of bringing in a trailer later.

"Good," Qalandar said. He was just glad that the transfer would be over and done more quickly than before.

"I've heard from Eddie Coome," Qalandar added. "They've got the containers and are already on their way."

"Excellent," Alexis said. "Do you have any coffee?"

"No," he said, obviously disinterested in American customs of hospitality.

"Okay," she said. "I suppose I'd have been surprised if you did."

———

Eddie Coome was at the wheel of the truck pulling the forklift trailer and had just crossed the Natchitoches Parish line when he saw the blue flashing lights in his side mirror. In a panic, he flicked his eyes to the speedometer. He knew they were on the stretch of Interstate 49 where the speed limit was seventy-five and the needle was barely above it. Ahead of him, the truck pulling the containers was going exactly the same.

They couldn't be busting us for two or three miles over, he thought.

Of course they can, he answered himself. *They're cops. They can do any damned thing they want!*

As the State Police Dodge Charger charged past him, he could see the blue silhouette of the state map on its door.

Ignoring Eddie, the cop raced past the other truck and proceeded to pull him over.

Eddie slowed down and turned into the curb some distance behind the other truck as it was pulling over.

"Damn it, Randy, *where are you*?" Eddie said out loud.

"Randy *always* knows what to do," he explained as the man in the cab with him stared at him like he was nuts.

He set his flashers, grabbed a clipboard with a bunch of paperwork, and climbed out of the cab. He could see the cop in his blue Smokey Bear hat talking to the other driver as he walked up the highway. He turned as Eddie approached.

"Who are you, sir?"

"I own the company that owns this truck. Was he speeding? I looked at my own speedometer and it didn't look like…"

"I see you have paperwork there," the cop interrupted. He had a too-large rain cover on his Smokey Bear hat and it made him appear vaguely comical. "Are you aware that paperwork pertaining to this vehicle must be *in the vehicle*?"

"It is…but if you need anything else it might be in here."

Looking at the driver, then at Eddie, and then back, he

asked, "Do you know why I pulled you over here today?"

"Goin' too fast," the driver said.

"I see that this vehicle is registered in Mississippi," the cop said, ignoring the comment about speed. "Are you gentlemen aware that you are required by the Department Traffic and Development in this state to have an Oversized and Overweight Permit, and a Louisiana PrePass transponder, so that when you go by the weigh-in-motion sensors on the freeway, your transponder gets scanned."

Both men nodded.

"You can see the transponder right there," Eddie said, pointing to the dashboard.

"Are you aware that you also need a Containerized Cargo Class I Permit to move containers on Interstate and non-interstate highways in Louisiana? With that, you're permitted to haul prepackaged containers originating from or destined to an intermodal facility."

"We have Louisiana Class I Permits," Eddie said, hoping that they really did. Randy always took care of things like this. "They *should be* in the glove compartments of both these vehicles."

"What are you hauling in these containers?"

Okay here it is, Eddie thought to himself. *Randy would know what to do. What was he supposed to say? What if he said, "a million dollars worth of military small arms and heavy weapons?" Ha ha.*

"Construction equipment," he said instead, frantically buying time.

He dreaded what would come next.

"You wouldn't mind if I took a look?"

Oh come on, man. Do you not have anything better to do out here today?

As they walked back down the length of the trailer to

the rear of the second container, Eddie tried to think of what to do.

He couldn't.

He was screwed and he knew it.

Time stood still.

Suddenly, there was a horrendous explosion of sound —screeching tires, smashing metal, and breaking glass. The two men nearly lost their balance in the concussion.

A quarter mile back down the highway, in the direction from which they'd come, two big rigs had collided, crushing an SUV between them. One of the rigs was on its side and still slithering up the highway as they looked. Cars were slipping and sliding on the slightly wet pavement and trying to avoid hitting the pileup. At least a half dozen were not so lucky.

"*You're free to go*," the cop yelled at Eddie as he sprinted toward his patrol car. He sounded disappointed to be letting Eddie and his trucks slip out from his control. "Drive safely."

Eddie waved at the driver of the truck with the containers, indicating he should get moving immediately, then jumped into his own truck and fired up the engine.

NATCHITOCHES PARISH, LOUISIANA

THE MOOD in Hammer's blue Chevy pickup was somber. He and Johnny Arnaud knew what was about to happen, and what they were about to do. After their visit to Natchitoches a week ago, it had been Arnaud who said simply that "maybe we just need to take care of it *ourselves.*"

Ever since, they had been working toward doing exactly that.

As they drove, Hammer related the analogy of the snake with many heads that Rahim Faizullah had coined on Tuesday night at the Herste house, the night that the Fehryville people had declared war on that snake.

Hammer and Arnaud talked about these things and about the process of solving a strategic problem by working your way up through the foot soldiers, to the top, and about the multiheaded serpent who lived at the top of this particular strategic problem.

"Between you and Nicole, one of those heads, as well

as a couple of Gusche's foot soldiers aren't in the mix any longer," Hammer said.

"Nicole and her gator," Arnaud said with a smile. "I guess we're one down, and two to go with the heads of the beast. I hope both Qalandar and Mondtrom both show up as planned so we can finish this."

"At least we have a couple of advantages going into this," he added after a long silence. "Neither of the two realizes that anybody has declared war on them...or that Gusche already lost."

"They should have thought of this before they *started* this," Hammer said.

"Greed does funny things to people," Arnaud replied. "Turns them into snakes, I guess you could say."

The rain had moved on and the sun was out by the time Jim Hammer made a right turn off the county road and started up the dirt road that ran parallel to the gravel road where Abed Qalandar's barn was located. The last time he'd driven this road, he had been aware that the dust kicked up by his Chevy pickup could be seen as far away as the barn. Today, with all the rain, this was not an issue.

Hammer had caught up and followed Eddie Coome's two-truck convoy for about an hour, but he had passed them and pressed ahead, planning to arrive ahead of them and get set up. Luckily, they had missed the enormous multi-car, multi-truck pileup. Northbound Interstate 49 would be completely shut down for hours and hours.

They were aware that Qalandar's BMW had already reached the barn, because Arnaud had pulled up the "coon cam" CCTV monitor on his phone. When Mondtrom's gray Escalade arrived, he gave Hammer a play-by-play.

As they drove in, they could barely see a gray pickup nestled into a patch of willows.

"Looks like Brian made it," Hammer said with a sense of relief.

"Looks like he found the spot where we were last week," Arnaud said.

As Herste had done, Hammer turned around and oriented his own truck so it was pointed back down the road for a fast exit.

"Looks like the cavalry has arrived," Herste said, turning around from his position on the embankment where they'd been last week.

"All two of us," Hammer replied. "You've got a good spot."

"I picked this because I've been looking at your CCTV camera angle. I almost didn't see the camera. You hid it pretty good."

Herste had his Winchester Model 70 .30-06 hunting rifle lying on a tarp.

"Hello Johnny, it's been way too long," he said. "Looks like we're getting at least part of the team again."

"Yup," Arnaud said as the two men shook hands. "Just like old times."

"I heard that your girlfriend fed Wally Gusche to the gators this morning."

"Yup, but she was pretty modest about it. She says the gator did most of the work, and he got lunch out of the deal."

"I'd like to meet her sometime," Herste said with a smile.

"When this is over, y'all need to come down for a fish fry."

"Looking forward to it."

"What's the plan?" Arnaud said, turning to Hammer,

who was already unzipping the rifle case that contained his .338-caliber Barrett Mk22 sniper rifle.

"Since we've been monitoring the show down at the barn through the webcam," Hammer began. "That's allowed us to see pretty much everything you've seen down there. Nothing's going to happen until the containers get here. We passed the trucks with them and the forklift on the highway, so it won't be long."

"Can't wait to get this over with," Herste said.

Arnaud nodded.

"We saw what happened last week, so we know the drill," Hammer continued. "When the containers get transferred to that truck that's down there now, we'll wait until the people delivering the containers are gone. Mostly, they're just working stiffs who work for a trucking company. They almost certainly don't know what's in those containers. We don't need to have them wind up as collateral damage. The head guy at that trucking company *was* in on it, but we won't be seeing him."

"Where's he at?" Herste asked.

"He's deceased," Hammer said. "Mr. Randy Coome, who also hired the hit men who killed two guys and tried to murder a young family, has passed away."

Both men nodded. They knew what Hammer meant.

"Brian, you got your rifle out. Johnny, you take the Barrett. I'd like you guys to cover me while I go down there. I'll extract Rahim while they're all distracted with the forklifting," Hammer continued.

The others nodded. Neither repeated the "just like old times" comment, but that's what they were thinking. Just like old times, complete with apprehension building into confidence, and the determination to get it done and do it right.

"If you don't see me needing covering fire, hold your

fire. On my signal, *or* if you lose track of me, count to twenty after the last shot you hear being fired down there and open fire. Brian, take out everybody left standing... and Johnny, put a round into the gas tank of the pickup inside the barn, and a second one into the Escalade tank."

"Incendiaries?" Arnaud asked.

"Yup. I've loaded this magazine with ten API571 armor-piercing incendiary rounds, and here's a backup. You probably don't need armor piercing, but why take a chance?"

"When you get a fire going, that old barn will ignite like it's made of paper," Hammer said. "The roof will collapse fast. Don't wait for me or anything else. Grab the camera, take our two vehicles and get out of here *fast*. I left the keys in my ignition. Turn south when you get to the county road. Somebody in one of these nearby farms will call it in, and there will be fire trucks coming from the north toward town. I'll be in touch."

They sat down to wait, taking turns looking at the scene before them with Hammer's Oberwerk HD II binoculars. As he glanced out to the west, toward the late afternoon sun sinking toward the horizon, Arnaud saw two trucks in the distance pulling onto the dirt road leading to the barn. When he turned back after a moment to hand the binoculars back to Hammer, he was nowhere to be seen. He held his breath and listened. Hammer had completely disappeared.

———

As Eddie Coome made a right turn onto the gravel road that led to the barn, the sun was going down and it was getting dark. His hands had almost stopped shaking from his encounter with the State Police. He wished that Randy was here. He had neither the stomach, nor the nerves, for this kind of thing. Next time, he vowed, he'd let Randy do it all *without* him.

Eddie had taken the lead in the two-truck convoy, so his pickup was in the lead as they reached the area where the other vehicles were parked.

An impromptu meeting was held between the drivers of the three trucks to decide where to position everything for the unloading and reloading, and the trucks all began to shuffle around.

The forklift was unloaded and the containers were gradually shifted from one trailer to the other. Things proceeded smoothly, and at last this part was over. The forklift was reloaded and Coome got his trucks lined up to make their exit.

Rahim Faizullah stood to one side, wondering what would happen next.

As Coome climbed out of his truck and walked back to the trailer where the containers were now, Qalandar and Mondtrom ascended the wooden stairs to a loading dock that was next to the trailer. Everyone watched as Qalandar lifted the right door handle of the first container, pulled it forward and rotated the lock rods. With this, he pulled the lock bar, and the door opened, revealing the crates within.

Coome used a crowbar to open a crate which Mondtrom had picked. For the next fifteen minutes, this process continued. From his point of view on the ground, Rahim could not see what was in the boxes, but he could see satisfied expressions on the faces of Qalandar and Mondtrom.

Though he was standing only about twenty feet away, they ignored Rahim like he was just part of the help—which he then realized was exactly the case!

Mondtrom and her Federal Security Office men

walked back to their SUV, while Coome and Qalandar opened their laptops on a large wooden crate.

The exchange of money, Rahim observed. Here was Qalandar paying the deliveryman. Here was Eddie Coome also collecting on behalf of Wallace Gusche, who had employed Coome Hauling to do the heavy lifting.

It was just a transaction. It was just like Afghanistan, where Gusche chartered the freight-carrying airlines to move opium into Europe.

These were all just transactions, and just like any transactions these days, they were just beeps of sensors.

Almost everything is electronic these days, Rahim thought. Back at the hardware store, more than nine out of ten transactions involved inserting chips or waving cards over sensors. The younger clerks didn't even know how to make change. Of course, neither had Rahim when he first came to this country.

With the electronic banking completed, Eddie Coome was so anxious to get back in his truck he didn't even put his laptop into its case. He just threw both on the seat of his pickup.

Meanwhile, David Anchry was already inside the barn and eager to get underway in the Dodge Ram 3500 pickup that was attached to the forty-foot trailer holding the containers.

While Coome and his trucks were splashing back down the gravel road, Rahim noticed that Alexis Mondtrom was having a heated phone conversation. The usually unflappable woman looked anxious.

He wondered what was going on, but he was beyond caring.

He heard her whisper something urgent to Shane Blessins.

"Bustamante has been killed in a coup."

This meant nothing to Rahim. He did not know who

"Bustamante" was, and he didn't care. His goal was now to kill Qalandar—with his bare hands if possible—just as he was so vehement in his antagonism toward Akhtar Mohammad Dadullah all those years ago.

Regardless of whether Hammer was out there somewhere ready to execute a plan, Rahim had formulated his own plan. As soon as all the transactions were over, it would be *his* turn for a final transaction with the man who, to him, represented Taliban evil in America.

As Rahim watched, Mondtrom walked briskly to where Qalandar stood and handed him a Halliburton aluminum suitcase. It was now the turn of Alexis Mondtrom to pay the Taliban's man in America. It was a transaction that neither Mondtrom nor Qalandar thought of as an act of war. Rahim disagreed.

This time, the transaction was not electronic. While Qalandar was adept at wire transfers, when it came to getting paid *himself*, he preferred cash. Like many in the world, and like so many in the *underworld*, he felt that there was nothing quite like cash.

Qalandar opened the case on the ground just fifteen feet from where Rahim stood.

In the light from the barn, Rahim saw it was completely full of bundles of bills. He had no idea how much was there. He did not know that the volume of a stack of one hundred hundred-dollar bills, or ten thousand dollars, is just under 6.9 cubic inches. He saw only that there were a *lot* of cubic inches within this suitcase!

Rahim saw Qalandar pick up several bundles of bills at random and thumb through them. It looked like it was all hundred-dollar bills. *So this is where he gets those hundreds that he gives me*, Rahim said to himself.

Qalandar nodded his approval. It was just a transaction, but it was a big payday for the diabolical former mujahidin.

Mondtrom was fidgeting, like she was in a hurry. This Bustamante thing had her on edge.

"Put this in the car," Qalandar demanded, handing the case to Rahim, who was surprised by how heavy it was.

As he started toward the BMW on the far side of the barn, Rahim heard an urgent, deep-throated buzzing sound coming from down the road. It was growing louder and closer *fast*!

The people at the barn barely had time to process what was happening when they found themselves surrounded by four roaring, circling Yamaha YZ450F dirt bikes that raced in from the gathering twilight.

Each of the riders had a pistol and was shooting, but because the bikes were in motion, their bullets hit no one.

Shane Blessins, who was in the open area in front of the barn, pulled his gun and fired two shots from close range at the nearest bike as it raced past. One round went wild, but the other hit the rider, and his YZ450F slid out from under him. He was injured, but he had not dropped his own pistol. He fired back, striking Blessins in the left arm. Blessins returned fire and the rider crumpled to the ground.

The wounded Blessins fell as he tried to dodge a second Yamaha that seemed hell-bent on ramming him. Blessins got off a shot, killing the rider just as a motorcycle slammed into him, shattering his body.

———

Alexis Mondtrom pulled her own Glock 19M from her purse and processed what was happening.

Should she try to make it to the Escalade?

No. Too exposed.

Instead, she dashed for a small door that led to a

storeroom on one side of the barn. She recognized this as the room where Qalandar had been staying when they came to pick up the previous week's shipment.

Deep inside the barn, David Anchry had already shifted the Ram 3500 pickup into reverse and was trying to back up with the containers on the trailer. He was apparently hoping to get out and make a run for the open road, but he had to stop because the Escalade was in his way.

At this moment, one of the bikers came along the driver's side window of the stalled Ram. He dismounted and pulled off his helmet. From her vantage point, Mondtrom immediately recognized a familiar face from Bustamante's crew!

She realized that these people must be part of the revolt that had toppled Bustamante, and they were now trying to hijack the containers. The Gonzalves Cartel was in the midst of a civil war, and *this* was part of it.

The man who'd removed his helmet walked up to the Ram 3500 and fired at Anchry from point-blank range. Then, he suddenly turned, his attention captured by the approach of someone else. Mondtrom could not see this other person clearly because of the trailer.

Who is that? Mondtrom wondered.

She didn't linger long to look. She hurried inside the smaller room and took cover. Through a crack in the plywood siding, she saw an armed man she didn't recognize moving behind the trailer inside the barn.

The biker who had just shot Anchry fired twice at this stranger. He missed both times, but he fell to the stranger's first shot.

Who is that? Mondtrom wondered, as the last of the four bikers—she hoped she had counted right—roared to a stop in a spray of gravel inside the barn. He took aim with his pistol, intending to kill the stranger.

The cartel biker died trying. He tumbled from his seat as the bike fell out from under him. Both the engine and the rider were dead before what little dust there was inside this corner of the barn had settled.

Mondtrom watched the stranger emerge from behind the trailer and holster his sidearm and start walking her way.

Always more curious than reserved, and always more aggressive than apprehensive, she stood and cautiously stepped back into the main part of the barn. She had her gun out, but the man had put his away. *Fatal mistake, mister*, she mused.

After those frenetic minutes of thundering Yamahas, it was eerily quiet except for the sputtering of a Yamaha lying on its side near the Escalade.

"*Who the hell are you*?" Mondtrom demanded. "Are you with the Gonzalves gang too? Which one of you killed Bustamante?"

"Since I got out of the Army, I've not been much of a joiner," came a calm reply from the tall man with the gray ball cap and a somewhat matching T-shirt with a grizzly bear on it. "But it sure looks like *you* got yourself double-crossed by the Gonzalves bunch."

"I'll admit that this hasn't been my best day so far this week," she said, as she flicked her eyes toward the Escalade, planning her escape from this untenable situation.

"And here it is only Monday," he continued.

"You're a real smart ass, aren't you?" Mondtrom said, taking a step back into the room at the side of the barn.

She raised her pistol, gripping it with both hands and pointed it at the stranger. Alexis Mondtrom was no stranger to handguns and was comfortable with her Glock. "Reach down and use your thumb and forefinger," she demanded. "Remove your weapon from the holster and drop it on the ground. I *am* a federal agent and I *am* placing you under arrest."

"If you want to talk about federal crimes," the man said as he laid his M1911 pistol on the ground. "What *is* in those containers that you just bought?"

"If you want to talk about federal crimes, shall we talk about what happens when all that hardware hits the streets?" he continued after a long pause. "How about last week's hardware? And next week's...and what about *your* part in all this?"

"Like I said, you're being a real smart ass," she hissed.

"On the subject of federal crimes, you just paid Abed Qalandar a lot of money for what's in those containers," he said. "On the subject of Qalandar, I don't see *him* around here anywhere."

He's right, she thought. *Where is that damned Afghan gunrunner?*

She looked around. She had been so preoccupied that hadn't thought about Qalandar. Had he and that kid with him died in the crossfire? Were they lurking somewhere?

"*Qalandar, where are you?*" Mondtrom shouted. "You can come out now. I've got the situation secured. *Qalandar!* Show yourself."

Silence.

"All that money..." the man said in a taunting voice.

"*Asshole,*" she said firmly with the confidence of someone who would not miss when she took her shot at this brazen asshole from a distance of less than twenty feet. "I've completely run out of patience with you!"

She had complete control of the situation and complete control of the only weapon visible.

The conclusion was foreordained, inevitable.

Or was it?

Alexis Mondtrom was an expert. She spent all her required hours, and more, on the range, but she was unaware that the man she now faced had hundreds of hours in combat, *live* deadly combat. If they still carved notches on pistol grips for successful kills, his pistol grip would have been carved away to nothing long ago.

Tonight had not been the first time that Jim Hammer had seen a plan fall apart, but it was never easy. It was never easy when this happened at the last possible moment—which was usually also the *worst* possible moment.

Tonight, that worst moment came when he was about to grab Rahim Faizullah and haul him from harm's way. Qalandar had ordered Rahim to take the Halliburton case to the BMW, and Hammer was making his way in that direction when the dirt bikes suddenly exploded out of the darkness and changed the equation inexorably.

Immediately, Hammer's way forward was interrupted by the unexpected challenge of the gun battle between two of the bikers and Shane Blessins, which unfolded practically in Hammer's lap.

Next, he had to fight his way through the other two bikers, but this only brought him into a standoff with Alexis Mondtrom.

Hammer was not in the most ideal of situations.

She had disarmed him, and she could not miss him at this range with her Glock.

She did not know that Brian Herste and his Winchester Model 70 .30-06 were within easy range, *but* Hammer knew that when she had stepped back into the side room, Herste no longer had a clear shot.

As they faced one another, and as parsed nanoseconds seemed to last minutes, Alexis Mondtrom assumed she owned the situation. Her finger closed tightly and carefully upon the trigger.

However, she did not know that this man in the grizzly T-shirt had plucked a Beretta from the hand of the second biker whom he had sent across the last horizon, and he had tucked this weapon into his waistband.

The Montana kid who years ago had spent hours and hours practicing his fast draw skills with a gun much heavier than this one, brought the Beretta into firing position in a thin slice of one of these parsed nanoseconds.

The jacketed 9mm round ripped through the fabric of the sea-green pantsuit and into a pumping human heart, causing an eruption of human blood, which created an ever-widening red stain against that polyester cloth.

The only sound that was left after the body hit the floor was that of the ignition of a shiny black BMW 7-Series being started in the darkness outside, behind the barn.

CHAPTER
THIRTY-THREE

NATCHITOCHES PARISH, LOUISIANA

IN THE BMW, Abed Qalandar knew it was time to run.

He and Rahim Faizullah had stepped around the corner of the barn just as the Yamahas had descended, and they had not been seen by the bikers.

They stood frozen for a moment as the gunfire erupted, but Qalandar quickly urged them toward the car. He popped the trunk, and Rahim threw the Halliburton case inside.

Rahim had planned to attack Qalandar as soon as he was unencumbered by that heavy thing. He would then subdue him before he could reach his SIG P224. Rahim had planned it all in his mind.

Sometimes the best laid plans end in success. Sometimes they fail.

For Rahim, it was the latter.

Slightly off balance as he tossed the heavy bag into the trunk, he was toppled completely off balance by Qalandar and shoved inside. The trunk lid came crashing down, and he found himself in darkness.

This was not the first time that Qalandar had thrown someone into a car trunk, and he always modified his trunks for this eventuality. He had long ago disabled the trunk release cable and had cut out the glow-in-the-dark handle near the trunk latch.

In the nearly airless darkness, Rahim had visions of his greatest horror. He was a prisoner in a Taliban dungeon!

Both men thought of escape, but on entirely different planes. For Rahim, it was the impossibility of liberating himself from this terrible prison. For Abed Qalandar, it was to flee the tumult that was ongoing just around the corner.

On a night of plans, when Hammer's plan had stumbled, and when Rahim's had backfired, Qalandar had the satisfaction of knowing he had a carefully planned escape route!

During his long hours of boredom last weekend, he had taken walks in the woods. You can take the mujahidin out of the mountains, but you can't take the mountains, or at least the rolling hills,out of the mujahidin. On these walks, he found an abandoned road that led from the site of the barn to another, more established, gravel road about a mile away.

In the mountains, as in these rolling hills, the mujahidin were always thinking about getaway routes, even when it was not always apparent from which specific threat they might need to escape. It was not that he distrusted Alexis Mondtrom specifically; it was only that he trusted no one.

As he had casually walked this road, he thought about his BMW 7-Series driving here. It was rough in places, but it could be used in an emergency. Now, he had that emergency.

Tonight, he executed his escape plan. The car bumped

and wallowed and splashed through the ruts, the brush, and the puddles, but the 4.4-liter V8 engine pulled it slowly through.

At last, he was on the gravel road, and soon after on a paved county road. He had gotten away!

————

Signaling to Johnny Arnaud to start putting incendiaries into gas tanks, Jim Hammer had run around the corner of the barn to look for Qalandar and Rahim.

As the first incendiary round struck, Hammer had eyes on the BMW just as the scoundrel slammed the trunk on his bellowing captive.

Before Hammer could reach them, the car was moving away steadily, and into the woods.

He had expected Qalandar to come back out to the gravel road to make his escape, but here he was going the opposite direction—*deeper* into the woods. Was he just in a panic and about to get himself stuck in an impasse—or did he know what he was doing?

Either way, Hammer knew he needed to give chase *somehow*. It was never easy when a crumbling plan continued to crumble, but sometimes, you just need to improvise.

As he looked around, he saw two vehicles now aflame, but he saw two that were *not*. A pair of dirt bikes lay on their sides near him in the places where they'd eluded the control of their dying riders. He picked up the first one and looked it over. The front fork was bent. Not bad, but it would be hard, even impossible, to control it at high speed.

The second one passed his hurried inspection in the flickering firelight of the burning vehicles. He climbed on, got it started and quickly familiarized himself with the gears. It was more complicated than his old Norton, now parked in his aunt's garage back in Obsidian, Montana, but he'd ridden motocross bikes a few times. It was like riding a bicycle, you never forget. *Right*?

By now, Qalandar's BMW was just a pair of taillights deep in the trees. He had a good head start, but Hammer had an advantage. Qalandar did not know he was being followed—*yet*.

Hammer had excellent night vision, so he decided not to use the lights. He picked up the road in the firelight and found it was more well-defined the farther he went. Soon he was gaining on the BMW.

Qalandar was moving deliberately and slowly so as not to damage his underbody panels on the rough terrain. Hammer had no such issues with a vehicle which was built specifically for even more challenging topography.

Finally, Qalandar reached the gravel road and made a left turn. The BMW was picking up speed.

They reached the intersection where the gravel road met the paved main county road just as the fire trucks raced by, coming south from Natchitoches city, sirens shrieking and red lights blazing.

Qalandar turned north, in the direction from which the responders had responded.

Hammer could easily match Qalandar's speed, but he held back fifty yards or more to keep the sound of the noisy bike as far away from Qalandar's ears as possible. There were a few cars on the road, so Hammer figured he could turn on his headlight and still blend in as long as he maintained his distance.

The next question on his mind involved where they were headed.

As he was executing his own plan B, he wondered about Qalandar's plan B. What contingency had he worked out in case something went wrong, as things had gone so completely wrong back at the barn? Was he going to start angling toward the interstate? Now that he had his money, was he headed back to Arkansas, or somewhere else?

The biggest question on Hammer's mind was what did this man intend to do with Rahim?

The BMW took a road that bypassed the town of Natchitoches and then continued north rather than cutting back toward Interstate 49. One question answered.

They continued for about fifteen minutes, out of the fringes of Natchitoches and into the country. Hammer was in the midst of deciding when and where to make his move, and what this move would be, when it was Qalandar who made a move.

Up ahead, Hammer saw the right turn signal on the BMW start to flicker, and the car moved off the highway onto a side road.

Hammer slowed down and was preparing to turn when the car stopped. He saw the interior light come on as the driver's side door opened. He saw Qalandar get out, but he was too far away for Hammer to tell what he was doing.

Hammer had just reached to turn off his headlight when suddenly, he glimpsed a man on the edge of the road, just outside the white line. He had not seen him over there in the glare of the headlight.

"I don't mean no harm, sir," the man said, raising his hands in the moonlit darkness as he saw that he'd been seen. He was neither young nor truly old. He was not well dressed, maybe only a cut or two above shabby.

"I don't mean no harm," he repeated, his eyes on Hammer's holstered pistol. "I don't have me nothin' worth takin'. I ask only that you let me be."

"What are you doing out on this road in the dark?"

"I've been tryin' to hitch a ride. Last ride was goin' only so far as the north side of Natchitoches. Been walkin' for a while. Maybe an hour or more? No luck."

"Where are you tryin' to go?"

"Up to Shreveport, sir," he said sadly. "It's my momma. She's taken a turn for the worse, and they reckon this might be the end."

"I'm really sorry to hear that."

"My car broke down south of Alexandria," he continued. "Got a real good ride right away, and then another, but now this. I'm the sorriest mess you'll ever meet, sir."

"I doubt that," Hammer replied. "Don't you think you'd have better luck on an Interstate onramp?"

"Walkin' on interstates scares me, even on the ramps. Have you ever hitched an Interstate at night?"

"Actually, I have," Hammer said. "I hear you."

"Time was that I had me a bike, too," he said, nodding at the Yamaha. "I used to zip all over south *Loo-zee-ana* on my lil' Honda. But that was then, and this is now."

"Say," Hammer said thoughtfully. "I have an idea. Why don't you take this bike up to Shreveport?"

"What you talkin' about?"

"Take this Yamaha to Shreveport to see your momma?"

"I don't understand."

"I got this bike when the previous owner passed away," Hammer explained. "Now, it looks like I too may have reached the end of my need for it. Looks like your need is greater than mine just now."

"You mean...*me*... ride *your* bike to Shreveport?"

"That's my suggestion."

"How would I ever get it back to you?"

"You'd pass it on," Hammer said, thinking on his feet. "You'd give it to the next person you meet whose need is as big as yours is now, at *this* moment...and tell him to do the same."

The old man just stared at Hammer with an expression of disbelief.

———

Abed Qalandar watched the lights on the main road with great suspicion. It was about ten minutes ago, as he cleared the lights of Natchitoches and passed into the countryside, he noticed the single headlight of a motorcycle in his rearview mirror.

Was it paranoia exaggerated by the debacle at the barn, or was it a sixth sense finely honed by all those ambushes and skirmishes in the Hindu Kush? Was he *really* being followed?

He had turned off the highway partly because of this. He could watch for that motorcycle to make a threatening move. He also stopped because of the annoyance from Rahim Faizullah's intermittent pounding and shouting from inside his trunk.

As Qalandar pulled about sixty yards down into what appeared to be some kind of roadside park, he kept his eyes on the main road. The single light had also stopped up there and was sitting still. Qalandar turned out his own lights, retrieved his SIG from its holster and slid out of the car.

As he watched and waited in the darkness, the motorcycle began moving again. It moved, slowly at first, toward the turnoff that Qalandar had taken.

He tensed and held his breath.

Then, instead of turning, the motorcycle accelerated past the turnoff like it wasn't even there, and continued up the highway, gathering speed. He watched its taillight as it raced away into the distance on a long straight stretch. Up there, nearly a mile away, the highway curved, but he continued to be able to see the taillight through the trees.

The sound of the motorcycle diminished into the distance, overshadowed by other sounds of other cars, none of which paid the least attention to the turnoff.

Qalandar took a deep breath, lit a Marlboro, and started processing what had happened to him tonight and over the past few weeks.

All of his years of planning had led him to a commanding presence in what amounted to one of the biggest small arms trafficking operations in history. The Taliban were on the verge of moving mountains of merchandise and earning mountains of hard currency. Alexis Mondtrom's clients were getting what they needed to control the states and cities where they did business. Qalandar was on the threshold of something truly monumental.

Now, suddenly, it had toppled like a stack of glass-ware piled too high.

Qalandar had survived, but now he would need a new customer. It had not been easy finding Mondtrom. Now he'd have to find another like her.

Being unaware of the identity of the bikers and having not heard Mondtrom muttering about the demise of Raoul Bustamante, Qalandar had the idea he could go directly to the Gonzalves machine. This could be his new plan.

In his mind, he figured he could talk to Wallace Gusche and keep the arms flowing. *Yes, that would work.* Perhaps Gusche could arrange warehousing for the shipments that were coming—the ones *already* aboard ships?

Something could be done. Something *would* be done, and he would do it! So long as there were greedy people who wanted to sell arms, and greedy people who needed to have them, there would be a way.

In the cool night air, Abed Qalandar had a smile on his leathery face as he finished his cigarette and lit another. His master plan had hit a bump in the road, but he was formulating a new plan and all was well.

In the near term, however, Qalandar knew he must turn his attention to the noise inside his trunk.

Alas, Rahim Faizullah had outlived his usefulness. He had performed his assigned tasks without problems, but he had now seen too much. After an hour, or however long it he had been in the trunk, they could never again trust one another.

Rahim would have to go.

Of course, so too would others.

He should have killed Abdel Khaleq earlier. That would be done now. And then there was Hila Faizullah, who would ask questions that would be difficult to answer.

Qalandar had long fantasized about the slow and punishing death of this attractive young woman, and about the things he would do to her. It had been a long time since he had enjoyed such pleasures. He looked forward to it.

———

Abed Qalandar was not expecting what would happen when he popped the trunk again. He *should have* known, but amid the visions of disappearing taillights, new customers, and the dream that his wonderful show would go on and on, his mind was elsewhere.

The Halliburton suitcase came first, ejected from the trunk with such force that it knocked him over onto the damp grass of the roadside park.

Rahim Faizullah then boiled out of the cramped and humid space, his hair drenched with sweat and fury in his eyes.

He slugged Qalandar in the face so hard that his nose felt broken.

For a moment, he pummeled Qalandar, shouting phrases such as *"you evil monster and your evil scheme."* Gradually, though, the old warrior got the best of him and flung him to the ground.

"You've been softened by infidels," Qalandar said as he stood. "You cannot remember how to fight. You're of no use to me now."

As Qalandar started to take out his SIG, Rahim kicked the back of his legs so hard he dropped the gun.

"Who's forgotten how to fight?" Rahim growled as they grappled for the weapon, which slid out of reach on the slick grass.

Qalandar lunged, grabbed the gun and aimed it at Rahim's face. They were so far from any houses that no one would hear the shot.

Suddenly, a huge, muddy boot stomped down, crushing Qalandar's wrist.

They both looked up as Jim Hammer kicked Qalandar's head so hard that they could hear his neck snapping.

There was a bit of anticlimactic gurgling, but in a moment, Qalandar's body relaxed and his eyes fixed into a lifeless stare.

"Thank you," Rahim gasped as Hammer reached down to pull him to his feet.

"Sorry I didn't get to you sooner," Hammer said.

"It was so hot in there…" Rahim said, trying to catch his breath. "I doubted that I would ever escape. I passed out and woke up thinking I was in prison in Afghanistan. I wanted to die, but I wanted to kill Qalandar before I died. I wanted to see him dead...like Dadullah and all those other monsters."

Just then, two sets of headlights turned off the main road. Rahim recognized Brian Herste's GMC Sierra pickup, and Hammer recognized his own Chevy.

"We followed you on your cell phone tracker," Herste said as he climbed out of his vehicle. "Are you all right?"

"Rahim could use some water," Hammer said. "Other than that, I think this thing is all over. Gusche is gone. Mondtrom is gone. Now Qalandar's gone. It's all over. They lost a war without realizing that anyone had been fighting back...until it was too late."

CHAPTER
THIRTY-FOUR

NATCHITOCHES PARISH, LOUISIANA

ON THE MORNING AFTER, by the time the investigators showed up to poke the embers in Natchitoches Parish, Rahim Faizullah and Brian Herste were at Kaylene's Koffee Korral in Fehryville with Hila and Kelly and working on their second cups of coffee. They all had awakened early. They couldn't sleep. They just wanted to get together and be together. They just wanted to take the day off and enjoy one another's company as they basked in the realization that the terrible shadow that had descended across their lives was gone.

The investigators swarmed through the site of the burned barn like college kids on spring break. First came the local sheriff and her team, but state people were soon called in, and within an hour or so the feds had also shown up. Some of the bodies carried federal badges—the Federal Security Office—and one of the dead was a Special Director for Security in the Field Operations Directorate at the Department of Homeland Security.

Alexis Mondtrom, or her charred remains, still had clutched her service weapon.

Mondtrom's cell phone was not found. Nobody knew she had actually had *three*, just as they would never know which body of water into which Jim Hammer tossed them after he had downloaded all the data to Tim Tommis.

The bodies identified as those of members of the Gonzalves Cartel would prove invaluable in constructing the narrative of what had "happened." It soon became "obvious" that a shootout between federal agents and the notorious cartel had taken place here just hours after Gonzalves Cartel kingpin Raoul "Buster" Bustamante had been gunned down by rival gang members in West Texas.

At first, the late Alexis Mondtrom emerged as a tragic paragon of heroic law enforcement. It was only after a few weeks, when the feds could find no evidence that she had actually been *investigating* the Gonzalves Cartel, that the luster began to crack. The many crooked dealings of Alexis Mondtrom started to come to light.

As indicated by the dates in her secret bank accounts, these had been going on for a number of years. Her dealings with the Gonzalves machine were by no means the most far-reaching of her carefully concealed misdeeds. So extensive was her corruption, and so embarrassing to the government, that the investigations in which her name appeared were wrapped up and sealed permanently within months. It was a matter of optics. Her bosses did not want to look bad.

When the containers cooled down after the fire, and were finally cracked open, jaws would drop. When the FBI started running serial numbers and discovered what they had found, the Pentagon was alerted to send people to identify the contraband. Because of security concerns, and because of the embarrassment which would flow from this, a curtain of secrecy was brought down within the hour. No more than mere inklings would ever reach the media, and that would soon blow over.

None of the investigators would ever find any trace of Abed Qalandar at the barn, nor at any place in the entire arc of the developing official narrative of what had happened there that night. The Gonzalves gangsters had never known about him, so they never talked. Of course, Mondtrom's phone—or phones—which would have pointed many fingers in his direction, were never found.

It would be like Qalandar had never been there at all. He had vanished into a bayou. As Johnny Arnaud had put it so well, and so simply, "gator bait."

———

BILOXI, MISSISSIPPI

On the morning after, Eddie Coome had awaked just before noon, wondering about his cousin Randy, and not about a vast international conspiracy of which he knew little. When he saw something about the Natchitoches barn fire on the news that morning, he knew what had happened, and started to realize the scale of this machine in which he had been a cog. He expected a knock at the door from the cops, but it never came. He asked himself what Randy would do, and the answer came back to keep his head down, which is exactly what he did. After all, that was what he assumed that Randy, wherever he went, was doing.

Eddie went back to work, running Coome Hauling without Randy, and handling both its legitimate and dubious jobs. Being much more risk averse than his cousin, he would take on fewer and fewer of the latter. He didn't have the stomach for it.

When Randy's decomposed remains were finally discovered many months later, it raised more questions, but these remained unanswered. Eddie would have a number of theories rolling through the back of his mind, but no one with whom to share them without telling tales about himself that he did not want told.

DASP agent Jorge Sentyl would go to work the next day to find everyone wondering what had happened to Len Ivermin. Only Sentyl knew *where* Ivermin had been on Monday, but like Eddie Coome, he knew to keep quiet. Unlike the other people at DASP, Sentyl had some idea of *what* Ivermin had been doing. He just did not know *where* Ivermin had been on Tuesday. Nobody did.

The two young DASP men who had no qualms about stepping outside the lines for the right price to become foot soldiers in the great scheme of Wallace Gusche had been there when it fell apart. Like Eddie Coome, Jorge Sentyl had been just outside the crosshairs when the whole thing collapsed, and he knew this without really knowing the full scale of the "whole thing,"

Like Eddie, Sentyl feared a knock at the door, but for him, when it came, it was a perfunctory query about what he knew of Ivermin's last movements. He told only what he dared to tell, but they were apparently satisfied. They would never ask again. The investigators in Biloxi had bigger fish to fry.

Looking into the disappearance of Wallace Gusche, the director of SIFO, would become a big deal. DASP would barely be involved in this investigation. The Department of the Army would decide to kick it upstairs to the Army Criminal Investigation Division. Like the Navy's parallel and better known NCIS, Army CID is a serious criminal investigative outfit. For a while, they would pull out all the stops looking for Gusche and Brent Lynse.

Poor Miranda, Gusche's hard-working administrative assistant, who had been expected to know everything about her boss, would be grilled repeatedly with the same disappointing results each time. Of course, she knew nothing about Gusche's big scheme. He kept all the details on his laptop, and he kept his laptop in his car.

CID would paw over traffic camera video and watch Gusche's silver Chevy Malibu driving to and from New Orleans over and over, but there are no traffic cams down on the bayous. Nor were there any cameras at the Shrimp Bowl on Beach Boulevard, and no one bothered to check the one camera that existed at the Keesler AFB bowling alley.

When the Malibu could not be found, there were rumors that Gusche and Lynse may have absconded with some money that had gone missing from the SIFO accounts. Nobody really knew whose burner phone might have launched these rumors, or made calls from faraway places, but the narrative of Gusche and Lynse being fugitives would eventually dominate the narrative.

––––––––

BROUILLECOURT PARISH, LOUISIANA

On the morning after the barn fire, Jim Hammer woke up and made coffee. Like he had for most of two weeks, Hammer spent his last night in Brouillecourt Parish at Johnny Arnaud's home. He was the only person in the house that morning. As he enjoyed his coffee, he admired the blue sky which preceded the sunrise. It would be a good day to be on the road.

Nicole Kirbye spent that night in her own bed in her own home, but she was not alone. In the morning, while Johnny Arnaud was in her kitchen waiting for Mr. Coffee to complete the job to which he'd assigned it, he poured himself a handful of Fruit Loops from the box on the table. He had no idea that Len Ivermin had done that same thing with that same box three mornings previously, nor did Nicole know that the DASP agent had violated her home. But this did not matter. Ivermin was never coming back.

Liam and Ava Grahen woke up that morning at Tyler Roullier's house beginning to realize that they had a new home, and a new extended family. In the coming years, they would think occasionally about guardian angels and come to know that they had a lot of them.

Liam and Ava's mom was already planning to sell the orange Honda. Let someone else own this machine that had been a centerpiece of a war even as it rested silently beneath a tarp.

As for the silver Malibu, the green Subaru, and the black BMW, there are a million miles of murky, bottomless waterways throughout the untracked corners of the bayou country, and these have always held secrets that will never be known beyond these dark and anonymous places.

The people who knew the story, or at least most of it—four people from Fehryville, Arkansas and four who were part of this extended family here in Brouillecourt Parish—did get together a few weeks later for a fish fry on the boat ramp at Bayou Langlois Motors to talk about old times and new.

They talked about old friends from another war in another place, and new friends from a new war that would never be discussed beyond their circle, if it were ever discussed at all. Mainly their conversation reached the decision that they'd not let so much time pass without reunions.

They talked about a Halliburton suitcase and what was to be done with what had been inside. They decided on an even split. Hammer had wanted no part of this, but they voted a slice of their pie for Tim Tommis for what he'd done from far away.

They brought out that cheap briefcase that Randy Coome had thrown on the floor next to Jim Hammer, and they unanimously accepted Hammer's recommendation that this money, intended to pay for the *deaths* of Ashley Grahen and her kids, should be used instead to help bankroll the *lives* of Ashley Grahen and her kids. They had, Hammer said, earned it. Everyone agreed.

Tears rolled down Ash's cheeks. Liam asked why his momma was crying, and she mumbled something about a guardian angel.

Dave and Chantelle would never see Hammer again, but he would live on as a good memory. The forklift never came back to Bayou Gadreau. Sheriff Russ Therriot would drive down there occasionally to look, but he would never see anything like what he had seen that one Saturday afternoon. Nor would he ever figure out what "national security" affair had brought it there in the first place.

———

Within the legends and lore of the world within and beyond the bayou country, there would always be moonrakers.

As they had on the on the Wiltshire coast of the West Country of England three hundred years back, when the term was supposedly coined, they would continue to ply dark shorelines, pitch-black dunes, and shadowy littoral inlets of the world, like those of the bayous. Moonrakers would continue to sail under crews of heroes and gangs of villains. They would keep on providing namesakes for seafood cafés and waterfront bars for as long as waterfronts exist.

Moonrakers would continue to rake the delicate skeletal crescent of the new moon for as long as there is a moon to rake.

They would stir the souls of those drawn to the barely perceptible sights and faint sounds that whisper in the background of the crashing surf or the hushed bayous for as long as the as long as there are human imaginations that find inspiration in myths, legends and unresolved mysteries.

EPILOGUE

PEARL ISLAND, DOHA, QATAR

KHAIRULLAH GHANI WAS in his luxury apartment high on the fourteenth floor of the Viva Bahriya Tower, enjoying the sparkle of the Doha city lights, and a tumbler of Glenfiddich Small Batch Eighteen, a pleasure that was expressly denied him at home in Afghanistan, the nation whose government he served.

Scrolling through those emails which had arrived in the previous hour, he was pleased to see one from Abed Qalandar. Ghani was even more delighted to learn that the second of the two arms shipments, the one carried surreptitiously aboard the *Ashuwaykh Star*, had arrived. It had been unloaded and delivered without a problem. Qalandar went on to say that the customers were thrilled and were looking forward to the *third* shipment.

Being pleased himself that Qalandar's customers were so pleased, Ghani pulled up his shipping manifest app on his other computer and tapped out an effusive reply.

They could expect the third delivery in just eight days, while the following two were both already on the water and would reach the Mississippi River at roughly ten-day increments after that.

If not for the Scotch whisky, Ghani might have been more guarded in his reply, but Qalandar was doing such good work he should know the status of the pipeline he had established. Ghani went on to provide Qalandar with the names of these three vessels. He would need to know them soon enough, so he might as well know them now. Ghani even provided the name of a ship that would soon be loading in Qatar's Hamad port.

With a smile on his bearded face, Ghani then composed emails to all of his bosses at the headquarters of the Islamic National Army in Kabul, as well as the central government of the Islamic Emirate of Afghanistan, conveying the good news about the *Ashuwaykh Star* and its cargo. He remembered and reminded them of their earlier comments about the irony of abandoned American weapons "wreaking havoc on American streets."

Ghani smiled. He hated the Americans and looked forward to seeing this havoc and mayhem on the international news channels.

FEHRYVILLE, ARKANSAS

Hila Faizullah tapped out a popular Pashto greeting as a sign-off on the email she was composing and clicked the "send" icon. Next, she translated the list of ships and shipping details that she had blocked and copied from Khairullah Ghani's earlier email and sent it to Jim Hammer and Tim Tommis.

As she looked up from the screen, her eyes moved about the room, this strange and alien place that exuded what the Americans like to call "bad vibes."

Two weeks ago, Hila had loathed Abed Qalandar in the strongest of terms as though he were the devil. Today, she contemplated the irony of her having *become* Abed Qalandar.

Since his death, she had stepped into his home office in the condo on Davis Court and had used her command of conversational Pashto to assume his identity in order to communicate routinely with Ghani.

"All done...for now," Hila announced.

"Good," Kelly Herste replied from her perch near a window she had opened for ventilation. "Let's get out of here. I saw Brenda get in her car and drive away, so the coast is clear."

Hila stretched her arms and wiggled her fingers, stiff from furious typing. She would like to have taken a deep breath at this moment, but the foul stench of a condo occupied by a man with an aversion to laundry and dish-washing was offensive.

Both women were wearing surgical gloves, in part to avoid fingerprints, but also because they were repelled by the idea of touching anything in this place for health and safety reasons.

"Okay, we can roll as soon as I read these instructions that Tim Tommis sent and pull the hard drives from the tower computers. I'll also take the laptops when we go."

Through those laptops and through the hands of Hila Faizullah and Tim Tommis, the ghost of Abed Qalandar would continue to communicate with Khairullah Ghani through the coming weeks.

One after another, the shipments would continue to reach South Pass at the mouth of the Mississippi River, and continue upstream to Arbeville, where Dennis

Faralaco would note the changing of the pilots. But Wallace Gusche would not be there to watch, nor the Coome Hauling crews to unload containers to a motor barge.

One after another, the containers would pile up at the Port of New Orleans. It's a busy port, so it would take a very long time for anyone to get around to checking all these unclaimed containers that came in on different ships. One can imagine the astonishment of those who would lift a door handle, pull it forward rotating the lock rods out of their brackets, and jerk open those doors of the containers.

It would be a very long time before these were connected to the container at the barn, but the nature of the connection would never be fully understood. In the meantime, the curtain of government secrecy had already come down on the matter of containers containing *this* particular stockpile of military hardware. It was a matter of optics. There were many people throughout the bureaucracy who did not want to look bad.

As the weeks went on, the tone of the communication between Qalandar and Ghani would gradually grow less amicable as Ghani complained more and more loudly that he was shipping merchandise and not being paid. Qalandar would promise and would buy time, but eventually Ghani's masters in Kabul began to complain themselves, and to hold Ghani himself accountable.

In the end, Khairullah Ghani would be summoned back to the country where the mood, like life itself, is as greasy and black as the opium that is Afghanistan's leading export; to the land where women are bagged in burqas; to the place where "justice" is defined by horrific sadism; and where Scotch whisky never touches the lips of enemies of the regime.

The two women had gone to Davis Court that

morning to create the illusion in that condo that Abed Qalandar had been in a big hurry when he moved on. Kelly opened drawers to make it look like he had packed and had thrown his toothbrush and multiple personal items into a duffel bag that they would take away. Nobody would notice he was gone until he was a few months late on his mortgage payments. Even then, it would be many more months before anyone actually stepped inside. Brenda would notice, but she'd already made it clear that Qalandar was none of her business.

Hila and Kelly gathered up all that they were taking, left the light on in the bathroom, set the alarm, and slipped out the front door unnoticed.

———

NEW ORLEANS, LOUISIANA

Lauren Stahling stepped out of the shower and dried the long brown hair that tumbled across her shoulders with a towel and wrapped a dry towel around herself.

She checked her dress, which was hanging from a hanger on the latch of the armoire. It was still damp, but it had been sopping wet when she hung it there last night after they'd been caught in the rain while walking home from dinner. It didn't matter. Lauren was not ready to wear clothes just now.

Stepping to the hotel window, she pulled back the curtain and looked out at Dumaine Street. The rain had stopped, but the heavy precipitation overnight was in evidence in puddles of standing water. It was not yet six o'clock, but it was starting to get light. It was still overcast, but she saw a patch of blue.

She looked at the ring on her finger. It was a curious and delicate little silver ring surrounding sparkling sapphires. The interesting, intertwined design had caught her eye, and her attention last night at a little "voodoo jewelry" store in an alley off Royal Street. Sensing more than mere passing interest, he had impulsively bought it for her.

As they left the shop, she held her hand up in the light of a gas lamp, smiled and asked him, "Does this mean we're going steady?"

He replied with a kiss that lasted for some time. This was as romantic as he got, but it was just right for her. His embrace always made her a little weak in the knee, especially under a gas light on a dark street in the Big Easy.

Long ago, at Logan County High School in Montana, he had been her best friend and closest confidant. They never "went steady" back then and there was nothing romantic about their friendship—until that one night, not long before graduation, when passion kicked down the door and crowded into their lives. With great chagrin, they each blamed themselves for something that they each assumed had fatally damaged their friendship. This impasse went unresolved. She went off to college, and he joined the US Army.

Last year, after twenty years, he came home a retired captain, decorated with five Silver Stars and three Distinguished Service Crosses among other things—and she was the County Assessor of Logan County. They both tried, cautiously at first, to explore a rekindling of the friendship—while ignoring what had happened that night on the cusp of high school graduation.

Last year, after twenty years apart, they were brought together, incredibly, by their own independent decisions to go to war with an international human trafficking ring that had moved into Montana.

When this job was done, and he decided to go back

east to eradicate the kingpin of the ring, she surprised him by insisting that she go too. The woman with the routine job discovered an addiction to dangerous adventure, and to this one-time best friend who was now becoming so much more.

In the course of the ensuing adventure, they each killed a man to save the life of the other, and their escapade ended with them making love in the firelight of the kingpin's airplane after Lauren's friend and lover had shot it down.

Last night, they made love in the Crescent City under a crescent moon.

He had come south on another quest, this time to help men with whom he'd served in combat long ago. When he'd finished, he phoned her to say he was coming home, but she told him to stay put. *She was coming to him.* She'd never been to New Orleans, and she had a restaurant list.

She studied his back as he lay in their hotel bed, breathing rhythmically. She admired the broad, tanned shoulders and well-defined muscles. She felt sad about all the vicious white scars, but they seemed not to bother him. Neither he nor she ever talked about them.

Lauren let the towel fall onto the floor and slipped her own well-proportioned body into the bed. She leaned close, inhaling the smell of his body and letting her hair tumble onto his back as she kissed the nape of his neck. She didn't care about the view just now; she was in the mood for a playmate.

As he rolled over and took her into his huge, powerful arms, she wrapped her legs around his body.

A long while later, when they had finished, the pair lay comfortably in a tangle of elbows and knees, which lay at odd, but perfect, angles.

"Is it too early for you to take me out for beignets and

coffee?" Lauren Stahling asked in a whisper after a long while.

"Here in *Nawrlins*," he whispered in reply, using the Cajun phonetic pronunciation for this place, "it's *never* the wrong time for beignets and coffee."

"I was thinking we should go someplace for a couple of weeks," she said after a pause. "Just the two of us...not tell anybody where we are."

"Like the mountains...camping?"

"I was thinking somewhere far, far away. Some place where you can't get yourself into trouble."

"Just say when," Jim Hammer said, betraying more than passing interest in this idea. "I'm retired. My schedule is wide open."

THANK YOU

Thank you for taking the time to read *The Next to Last Moonraker into Brouillecourt Parish*. If you enjoyed it, please consider telling your friends or posting a short review. Word of mouth is an author's best friend and much appreciated.

Thank you.
Bill Yenne

A LOOK AT:

GHOST ARMIES OF THE NAPALI COAST (JIM HAMMER 3)

Paradise was supposed to be a break from the battlefield. But war has followed Jim Hammer to Hawai'i.

After taking down an international human trafficking ring and dismantling a rogue arms-smuggling operation linked to the Taliban, Jim Hammer and Lauren Stahling escape to the remote beauty of Kaua'i. It's meant to be rest, recovery—maybe even redemption. But when their flight is nearly hijacked over Pearl Harbor, vacation turns into a mission.

On the island's untamed North Shore, a forgotten 19th-century journal leads them to ancient ruins hidden deep in the mountains. What begins as a search for lost history spirals into something far darker—a chilling 1940s murder, a hidden electronic warfare facility, and whispers of an impending nuclear deception that could trigger global catastrophe.

As Hammer and Lauren navigate wild cliffs, haunted legends, and military secrets, they find themselves alone against a new enemy—one hidden in the jungles of the Nāpali Coast and the shadows of world power.

And when the ghosts of the past rise alongside the threats of the present, only one question remains: Will they stop the war before it begins? Or vanish into legend like the armies before them?

AVAILABLE FEBRUARY 2026

ABOUT THE AUTHOR

 Bill Yenne is the award-winning author of three dozen books on historical topics especially non-fiction books on military history and hardware. His various works have been translated into six languages. He has contributed to encyclopedias of both world wars, and his work has been selected for the official Chief of Staff of the Air Force Reading List. Yenne has appeared in documentaries airing on the History Channel, the National Geographic Channel, the Smithsonian Channel, ARD German Television, and NHK Japanese Television. His book signings have been covered by C-SPAN.

Among his fiction works are the Raptor Force action-adventure series and the Bladen Cole Western series, both published by Berkley (PenguinRandomHouse).

He is the recipient of the Air Force Association's Gill Robb Wilson Award for the "most outstanding contribution in the field of arts and letters [as an] author whose [many] works have shaped how thousands of Americans understand and appreciate airpower." (Previous Gill Robb Wilson Awardees include Edward R. Murrow, Ted Koppel, Tom Brokaw and Tom Clancy.)

Bill Yenne grew up inside Montana's remote and rugged Glacier National Park, where his father was the supervisor of backcountry trails. He spent his summers on foot or on horseback in the remote mountains, and his winters becoming a voracious reader and history buff.

In the course of gathering material for his books, Yenne has traveled far and wide. He followed the entire 3,000 miles of the Lewis and Clark Trail; he flew in the jump seat of a B-52 bomber on a training flight for a classified Cold War mission; he fired a Thompson submachine gun in an organized shooting competition (and did pretty well); and he has climbed to the top of two dozen Gothic cathedrals across Europe. He is also an amateur silver medalist in the annual Kauai Canoe Club outrigger races.